The search for an
appropriate husba
indeed a noble purs
But why does it kee
leading her back to a most
inappropriate man?
D1015973

"What would you do if I were to take you in my arms and kiss you?"

"I would slap your face, my lord," Cassandra said without hesitation, the firm note in her voice belying the way she seemed to strain ever so slightly toward him and the immediate realization that she very much wanted him to do just that.

"I see." Reginald narrowed his eyes and considered her for a moment. "Well, that's that then." He turned to his study of the book-lined shelves, his hands again clasped behind his back.

"What's what then?" She stared in annoyance and more than a little frustration. "Aren't you going to kiss me?"

"I think not," he said coolly.

"Why not?"

"It would be highly improper."

"I realize that but—"

"Furthermore I have never kissed a friend before. I'm not sure I'm entirely certain how to do that or," he shook his head somberly, "whether I would enjoy it. I should hate to be slapped for something that wasn't especially worth it."

Cassandra straightened her shoulders. "I can assure you, Lord Berkley, it would most certainly be worth it."

Avon Romances by
Victoria Alexander

THE PURSUIT OF MARRIAGE
THE LADY IN QUESTION
LOVE WITH THE PROPER HUSBAND
HER HIGHNESS, MY WIFE
THE PRINCE'S BRIDE
THE MARRIAGE LESSON
THE HUSBAND LIST
THE WEDDING BARGAIN

VICTORIA ALEXANDER

The PURSUIT OF MARRIAGE

AVON BOOKS
An Imprint of HarperCollins*Publishers*

This is a work of fiction. Names, characters, places, and incidents are products of the author's imagination or are used fictitiously and are not to be construed as real. Any resemblance to actual events, locales, organizations, or persons, living or dead, is entirely coincidental.

AVON BOOKS
An Imprint of HarperCollins*Publishers*
10 East 53rd Street
New York, New York 10022-5299

ISBN: 0-06-051762-X
www.avonromance.com

First Avon Books paperback printing: June 2004

Printed in the U.S.A.

10 9 8 7 6 5 4 3 2 1

This book is for Alex,
because you amaze me every day
in a very good way.
You own my heart and I wouldn't
trade you for the world.
You should know that.

Prologue

The power of women to influence king, country and all of mankind cannot be underestimated. It is a power at its greatest when it is exerted subtly, in a clandestine manner and achieves its purpose before its existence is so much as suspected.

T. Higgins

Spring 1821

"I must say, I am deeply disappointed." The Duchess of Roxborough gazed over the ladies assembled in the parlor at Effington House and heaved an overly dramatic sigh. "We are failing in our responsibilities, ladies, and we simply must do better. In the year or so since the formation of The Ladies Society for the Betterment of the Future of Britain, our various members have assisted, as it were, in the forming of a mere three unions."

Marian, Viscountess Berkley, glanced at her very

closest friend, Helena, the Countess of Pennington—or rather, now, thanks to her son's marriage, the dowager countess.

"That of Lord Pennington . . ."

Helena smiled in a most gracious manner that didn't appear the least bit smug unless, of course, someone knew her as well as Marian did. Marian was well aware of how terribly satisfied Helena was by the results of her machinations, which last year had finally brought her son to the altar. Oh certainly, there had been deceit involved on Helena's part, a monumental amount of deceit by some standards, but she firmly believed—and as her dearest friend it was Marian's duty to share that belief—that she had simply steered events in the right direction. Helena claimed what happened after that could well be attributed to fate.

". . . that of Miss Heaton . . ."

Lady Heaton, mother of the aforementioned Miss Heaton, beamed with the pride of accomplishment.

"Thanks to an overly impressive dowry and the threat of a fair amount of scandal," Helena said under her breath to Marian.

"I think scandal is highly underrated as a tool to encourage marriage," Marian whispered. "We should employ it more often."

". . . and Miss Putnam."

Lady Putnam smiled weakly. If anyone was well aware of the role of scandal as an inducement to wedded bliss, it was Lady Putnam, whose daughter Althea had been involved in a rather flagrant misadventure with a young lord, ending in a quick trek to Gretna Green and a hasty wedding.

"I'm not sure if Lady Putnam deserves the credit for that marriage," Marian murmured, "or the blame."

Helena bit back a smile, and Marian grinned to herself. Not that Marian would hesitate for a moment to use the threat of scandal to force her son into marriage with the right young woman. The problem was finding the right young woman.

"Perhaps, ladies, we have forgotten the very reasons for these gatherings." The duchess's brows drew together in a most reproachful manner. "We are here for the express purpose of assisting our marriageable children in the finding of suitable matches, without their knowledge, of course. As we are all well aware, young people today do not appear to be pursuing marriage as actively as they should. Indeed"—the duchess's gaze settled on her sister-in-law Georgina Effington, Lady William—"some seem to be pursuing anything but marriage."

Lady William stood and smiled uneasily at the assembly. "As some of you probably know, my daughter Cassandra has discovered a talent for the refurbishment and redecoration of houses."

"She's really quite wonderful," a lady behind Marian whispered.

"And while I am confident she wishes to marry, I fear this pastime of hers—"

"It's scarcely a pastime given what she charges," another woman murmured. "Still, well worth it to say your designer was an Effington."

"—will keep her too occupied to see potential matches that may present themselves. In short, while I have always encouraged a certain amount of independence in my daughters, I fear for her future. Indeed, I think her actions might well be in opposition to the stars themselves. Therefore," Lady William heaved a heartfelt sigh, "I am more than willing to entertain any proposals or suggestions."

"Excellent, Georgina." Her Grace beamed at her sister-in-law. "Cassandra well deserves a good match, and I daresay there are any number of possibilities represented in this very room."

A wave of enthusiastic murmurs swept around the room.

"Marian." Helena considered her friend thoughtfully. "In spite of this venture of hers, Cassandra Effington would be an outstanding match for any young man."

"Indeed she would," Marian murmured. "And, given her heritage, an excellent viscountess as well."

Certainly, nothing Marian and her friends could possibly do would ensure such a match. There were no guarantees in endeavors of the heart. Given that, was there any real harm in nudging things in the right direction in the hopes that fate would then take a hand?

"Lady William." Resolve brought Marian to her feet. "I have a house sorely in need of refurbishing. And better yet," she flashed the assembly her brightest smile, "I have a son."

One

An independent, stubborn woman is surely God's revenge upon an unsuspecting mankind.

L. Effington

Spring 1821

"Do you see them yet?" Miss Cassandra Effington shielded her eyes against the late morning sun and gazed into the distance.

"No." Anthony, Viscount St. Stephens, shook his head. "Any minute now, I should think. As I understand it, the course is not overly long."

"And did you wager a great deal on the outcome?" his wife, the former Miss Philadelphia Effington—Delia to her closest friends—said coolly.

"Not a great deal." He chuckled and slanted her an amused glance. "Did you?"

"Nothing of significance." Delia grinned. "And only with Cassie, so it scarcely counts."

"It most certainly does count," Cassie said firmly. "I fully expect you to pay promptly when you lose."

St. Stephens laughed. "Dare I ask which of you wagered on your brother and which chose Lord Berkley?"

"I, for one, would never wager against a member of the family." Delia's voice was firm. "Beyond that, Christian is an excellent rider with a fine eye for horseflesh."

"Christian is overly arrogant, although I daresay no more so than Leo or Drew." Cassie rolled her gaze toward the heavens. "It's a common trait among Effington males and among our brothers in particular."

St. Stephens raised a brow. "So you wagered on Berkley then?"

"Most certainly." Cassie nodded. "It will do Christian a world of good to lose at something, anything. Besides, from what I have heard of this Lord Berkley, he is rash and reckless and something of a rake. While those are not qualities I particularly look for, it seems to me, if one is wagering on a contest of this nature, those unsavory attributes would be most beneficial."

"Christian is rash and reckless and something of a rake," Delia murmured.

"Yes, but I am well acquainted with Christian and cannot bear the thought of how much more swaggering his step will be should he win. As I have never met Lord Berkley, I don't give a fig as to the effect of victory on his character."

St. Stephens laughed. "Well said."

Cassie grinned.

Delia's brows drew together. "If you feel that way, Tony, why did you wager on Christian?"

"You're making assumptions now, my love." St. Stephens's grin widened.

"I see. You too are lacking in family loyalty. Very well then." Delia's eyes narrowed. "Perhaps you would care to place another wager on the outcome?"

"I should indeed." A wicked light flashed in his eye. "If I can set the stakes."

Delia gazed up at her husband with a wicked smile of her own and Cassie sighed to herself, discreetly edging away from the couple. Not that they would notice. At these moments Delia and St. Stephens stepped firmly into a world of their own.

It was at once charming and most annoying. Cassie was delighted that her sister had found love, but did she have to be so very much in love? Delia and St. Stephens had been married nearly a year, after all. Indeed, they were here, at least in part, to serve as Cassie's chaperone, and those longing, yearning, *wicked* looks the couple continuously traded were not at all proper, although Cassie admitted her own reaction could well be simple jealousy. After all, of the two sisters, Delia had never especially sought marriage, yet here she was: married, in love, and blissfully happy.

While her twin was four-and-twenty, edging perilously closer to a firm position on the shelf with not a real possibility for a match in sight.

Cassie wandered a few steps farther away, ignoring her sister's peal of laughter and ignoring as well the intriguing thought of precisely what stakes St. Stephens had proposed. As much as Cassie hated to admit it, she was indeed jealous. Oh, she would never wish any of Delia's happiness taken away. Cassie simply wanted it too. Not that there was any chance of that at the moment.

Perhaps it was time to lower her standards.

Cassie idly scanned the crowd gathered on a rise overlooking the road. The assembly chatted with anticipation and excitement and strained for the first glimpse of the riders. It was an interesting gathering of the ton's younger members—in truth, a set considered rather fast. Still, the majority of those present were married couples ostensibly acting as chaperone for those as yet unwed among them. It was all very proper even if there wasn't an elderly, disapproving matron in sight, and therefore a slight, distinct undercurrent of forbidden adventure lingered about it all.

The race and accompanying wager between Christian and Lord Berkley had become quite the topic of interest in the past two weeks. So much so that Lord Warren had arranged both the contest and a festive outing on his estate on the outskirts of London. His lordship had also made a specific point of inviting Cassie to the event, not that she'd had the least intention of missing it.

Her gaze drifted to Lord Warren, chatting with a small group and obviously charming every lady present. She couldn't help but wonder how many of those ladies had also received personal invitations. The man was unquestionably attractive, with an excellent title and a tidy fortune. He was witty and dashing with a reputation for excess in all matters, including women. Not at all to Cassie's taste. Lord Warren might well be interested in her, but she hadn't the least bit of interest in him. Rather a shame, really. He was an excellent catch.

"Perhaps it's time you lowered your standards," the wry voice of her oldest brother, Leo, sounded behind her.

"I was just thinking the same thing, although I daresay you're not the one who should be giving advice in matters of this nature," Cassie said mildly and turned toward her brother. "I don't see you racing headlong toward the altar."

Leopold Effington grinned down at her with the engaging smile that had turned any number of young ladies' heads, none of whom had ever similarly engaged him. "My standards are apparently as high as yours."

"It's rather a pity, isn't it? You should think at this point at least one of us would be wed." Cassie glanced at her sister and St. Stephens. "At least Delia has found happiness."

"I daresay Delia has earned it." Leo offered his arm and Cassie took it. Sister and brother strolled aimlessly for a few moments. "Perhaps we have not suffered enough to earn happiness?"

Cassie glanced up at him, relieved to note the teasing twinkle in his eye. "I should be happy to make you suffer with a well-placed kick to your backside if that's what you wish."

Leo laughed. "I shall pass if you don't mind. Besides, I am barely nine-and-twenty and have plenty of time left to enjoy myself before the need truly arises to settle myself with a wife." He sobered. "You, however—"

"Don't say it, Leo," Cassie said firmly. "Or I shall be forced to deliver that kick and a great deal more."

Leo ignored her. "I'm serious, Cass, it's past time you were wed."

"*You're* not married. Neither is Drew or Christian."

"That's another matter entirely. We're men and we—"

"Not one more word. I've heard it all before and you well know I feel it's entirely unfair. No one thinks it's the least bit odd that you aren't wed, and you are far older than I."

"Indeed, I am ancient," Leo said with a grin.

"Indeed you are." Cassie heaved a resigned sigh. "It's not as though I have no desire to marry, you know. I have always wanted to make a good match."

"You have had ample opportunity."

"Ample opportunity? Apparently you have paid scant attention to the facts of my life, brother dear." She blew a disdainful breath. "For whatever reason, Delia has always attracted men with an eye toward marriage even if they tended to be exceedingly dull, with the exception of St. Stephens, of course. Whereas I have always caught the attention of men of questionable reputations, whose interest in me had nothing to do with marriage. Rakes and the like. Men suspiciously like my brothers."

"I say, Cass, that's not fair." Leo frowned ruefully. "Accurate, perhaps, but not especially fair."

"Nothing is especially fair when it comes to men and women and this whole pursuit of marriage." Cassie glanced at her brother curiously. "Why are you exhibiting this sudden interest in my marital state?"

"It's not sudden. Your future has always been important to me," Leo said in a lofty manner. "And now that Delia is wed and happy—"

"You thought you'd turn your complete attention to

me?" Cassie shook her head. "I don't believe you for a moment. Besides, you and Drew and Christian have always kept a rather annoying watch on me in the mistaken opinion that I was about to plunge into scandal."

"Well, you do have a certain air about you."

"Yet here I am with a relatively spotless reputation—"

Leo raised a brow.

"I said *relatively*, but even you must admit, aside from a tendency to say exactly what I think—"

Leo opened his mouth to speak.

Cassie waved off his unspoken comment. "Which I have no intention of changing, by the way, my behavior has always been quite within the bounds of respectable behavior."

He narrowed his eyes. "Perhaps your chances of marriage would be enhanced if you were to at least give the appearance of being somewhat more biddable—"

"I will not change who I am to lure a match, nor do I particularly want a man who would prefer such a woman in the first place."

"Even so, there are any number of possibilities." Leo nodded in Lord Warren's direction. "What of Warren? I have it on very good authority that he is quite taken with you."

"My dear brother, Lord Warren is exactly what I don't want in a husband. He is the kind of man who would have a mistress installed before our vows were barely out of our mouths. No, if nothing else, I expect fidelity from a spouse, and men like Warren don't have a faithful bone in their bodies."

"Come now, Cass, you could give the man the benefit of the doubt. Why, I myself have a certain reputation, yet I fully intend on being entirely faithful to my wife when the time comes." He grinned. "If the time ever comes."

She ignored him. "Effington men always have been a bit different in that respect. I suspect it's because love usually plays a role. Perhaps when I find a man I can not only trust but also love—"

"Perhaps you should lower your standards."

"You said that, Leo, and you needn't say it again. I have no desire—" She pulled up short and studied her brother carefully. "You haven't answered my question. Why are you so concerned about my prospects?"

"I told you I—"

"Leo?"

His brows pulled together. "Blast it all, Cass, it's this, this, this *pastime* of yours. You should be married. Having children, that sort of thing. Not, well, *employed*."

"I see. I should have known." She bit back a grin. "First of all, dear brother, I'm not employed. I employ myself. It provides me with a sense of independence and competence and I quite enjoy it. And secondly, it's not a pastime, it's a business."

"A business." Leo groaned. "That's even worse."

"Actually, it's quite wonderful." Cassie leaned toward him confidentially. "And I am making a substantial amount of money."

Leo's brow shot up in surprise. "Refurbishing houses? I find that hard to believe."

"Believe it. I have a very exclusive, and very wealthy, clientele who employ me to decide on paint and paper and furnishings and whatever else I deem appropriate for their very opulent homes."

"And they pay you for this?" He stared at her as if he couldn't comprehend why anyone would pay good money for such a thing. It was such a very *male* look that it was all she could do not to laugh aloud.

"Indeed they do. In truth, my fees are exorbitant, and I am well worth it. I have excellent taste and a natural gift for decoration and design." Cassie had discovered said gift last year when she'd helped Delia refurbish the house she'd inherited from her first husband, and she'd honed it further when she'd done the same thing for the house Delia now shared with St. Stephens. "Most of my clients thus far have been women, and quite frankly, one of the reasons they are so eager to acquire my services is because I am an Effington. They adore having the advice of an Effington and are willing to pay outrageously for the privilege. Indeed," she cast him a satisfied smile, "they do not so much hire me as I select them."

"Still and all, you're, well, *in business*."

"You needn't sound so stuffy. My services may be overpriced but there's nothing at all disgraceful about this. I daresay there are far worse things I could be doing."

"You could be doing needlework," he muttered.

She shot him a scathing glance.

He glared in return. "Regardless, Cassandra, do not forget you are an Effington—"

"And you would do well to remember we are but a few generations removed from cutthroats and pirates who made their fortunes in ways much more unsavory than selecting carpets and directing paperhangers."

He stared for a moment, then sighed in surrender. "You're right, of course." Still, the man was not about to give up. "But can't you just do what you do for, well, fun?" His expression brightened. "That's it, Cass, do it for fun, refuse to accept so much as one more penny, and I shan't say another word about it."

"Are you daft? That's the stupidest thing I've ever heard you say." She scoffed. "I have no intention of wasting my time redoing the homes of people for nothing. People who wager and lose more money in an evening than hardworking folk earn in a lifetime. The ton may well look down its collective nose at the legitimate earning of money, but it also measures worth very much in terms of monetary value. If I were to give away my services, they would lose their worth. Part of the appeal of having a room designed by Miss Cassandra Effington is that very few can truly afford it. I, dear brother, am a luxury."

"But you have no need of money."

"One can always use more money," she said loftily. Cassie was not about to admit to her older brother that she fully intended to donate the money she'd made to a worthy cause. She simply hadn't decided what, but was confident the cause would present itself when the time was right. "Besides, it fills my days in a useful manner and—"

"Regardless, I don't approve." He pressed his lips together firmly. "And I don't like it."

"You don't have to, because I do." She favored him with her sweetest smile and was gratified to see his resolve soften, if only just a bit. "Now then, Leo, shall we talk about your life? Your own prospects for marriage? The business nature of your own endeavors?"

"I shouldn't call it business exactly," he said uneasily. "It's really more of a—"

A shout sounded and all eyes turned toward the bend in the road and the sudden appearance of the riders: Christian on his favorite bay, Berkley on a sorrel-colored steed, both fine-looking animals. The rhythmic thud of well-shod hooves beating the ground and the growing cheers of the crowd swelled with their approach. The contestants were neck and neck, the men flattened so hard against their mounts that it was difficult to discern man from beast. The men looked as well matched as the horses.

Christian was on the far side of the road, and even from here, Cassie could see the intensity of his effort in the line of his body and furrow of his brow.

"Good Lord, he's going to lose." A sense of awe rang in Leo's voice. Not at all surprising. To the best of Cassie's recollection, Christian had never lost at anything.

"Why do you say that? They appear even to me."

Leo narrowed his eyes and shook his head. "There is still a hundred yards or so remaining, and Christian is spent. I can see it from here. Whereas Berkley—"

"Berkley does look more at ease, doesn't he?"

"I'm afraid so."

She studied the other man carefully. The difference between Berkley and Christian was apparent only under close scrutiny, but indeed his lordship did look a touch less strained, a tad more relaxed, as if the level of his endurance had yet to be reached whereas Christian's had already been breached. Even as she watched, Berkley inched ahead.

The men thundered across the finish line, Berkley a

good half horse length in front of Christian. The crowd erupted in cheers and good-natured groans. Half the gathering surged down the rise to greet the victor and console the vanquished, and the other half wandered toward the linen-covered tables and the late-morning feast that had been laid out unnoticed.

Cassie and Leo started toward the riders. Christian slipped off his horse, his expression a mix of chagrin, annoyance, and genial acceptance. For a man used to winning, he seemed to innately know how to lose with grace. Cassie pushed aside a touch of guilt at wagering against her brother and turned her attention toward the gentleman who had just helped increase her savings.

Berkley still sat upon the sorrel amidst an air of confidence and congeniality. Someone handed him a tankard, and he downed its contents in one long drink, then laughed with the exhilaration of victory. And perhaps of life itself. It was a surprisingly contagious laugh, and she found herself smiling in response.

"Berkley is unmarried," Leo said idly. "And I understand he is not averse to marriage."

"From what I have heard of Berkley, he is no better than Lord Warren or you." She shook her head firmly. "I have no desire to reform a rake, Leo."

There was no doubt in her mind that the man was indeed a rake. Not merely because of rumor and gossip, but more because of the way in which he carried himself, the assured manner in which he sat his horse, the very look in his eye.

Berkley scanned the crowd, probably looking for one lady or another. He was handsome enough, and it was apparent from his bearing that he well knew it. He was obviously tall, with walnut-colored hair, charmingly disheveled, still too far away to discern the color of his eyes. His gaze skimmed past her, then returned and caught hers. His smile broadened, then deepened, in a disturbingly intimate manner, as if they shared something as yet unrecognized but quite personal nonetheless. It was at once rather intriguing and most disquieting and completely improper. She pointedly shifted her gaze. She had no intention of encouraging a man like Berkley.

Of course, she wasn't entirely certain what kind of man she should like to encourage. She knew she wanted someone respectable but not dull. Exciting but not dangerous. Strong but not overbearing. Loyal and trustworthy but not a lapdog. And this mythical paragon would love her without reservation for the rest of his days. In short, the man of her dreams would be very nearly perfect and probably did not exist.

Leo said something she didn't quite catch, but she smiled and nodded nonetheless. Perhaps he was right about lowering her standards if she did indeed wish to marry. She wanted marriage, but marriage alone was not enough. And if she was true to no one else, she should be true to herself. If that meant never marrying at all, so be it. It was not a pleasant prospect. She did not relish the idea of one day being the aging, eccentric aunt to Delia's children. Perhaps the cause to which she planned on giving her earnings should be her own future? At least if her fate was to become the peculiar, maiden aunt in the family, it would be nice not to have to depend entirely on Effington financial support.

She could say what she wanted to her brother and her sister and anyone else within hearing about her independence, earning her own way, and doing precisely as she wished, but deep down inside she knew she didn't really believe any of it. Or, at least, not all of it.

Cassie would give just about anything to be in her sister's place. To be happy and well wed and in love. But she would rather be alone than trapped for the rest of her days with the wrong man.

Cassie Effington absolutely would not lower her standards. No matter how great the price.

Viscount Berkley, Reginald Berkley—Reggie to those who knew him best—slid off his horse and ignored the pain that shot through his ankle when his foot hit the ground at an odd angle. Not especially difficult to do. His blood surged with the elation of victory, and Reggie suspected he would not feel much of anything save triumph at this moment.

Except, of course, compelling curiosity.

At once he was besieged by jubilant acquaintances and well-wishers, their exuberance in direct proportion to their winnings. At last the crowd thinned, dispersing toward the offered repast or, more likely, to collect wagers owed.

"Well done, old man." Marcus Holcroft, the Earl of Pennington, clapped his closest friend on the back and grinned. "I wasn't entirely certain you could pull it off."

"Did you wager against me then?" Reggie asked absently, scanning the crowd for another glimpse of the intriguing young woman whose direct gaze had briefly met his.

Marcus gasped in mock dismay. "I would never do such a thing." His grin returned. "However, it was rather tempting. Effington is well known for his prowess in the saddle and a reputation for success. Still, you are not without a certain—"

"Who is that?" Reggie spotted the lady and nodded in her direction.

Marcus followed his friend's gaze and chuckled ruefully. "That, my dear Reginald, is the sister of the man you just defeated."

"I thought as much."

Certainly Reggie had seen the twin daughters of Lord William, the brother of the Duke of Roxborough, before. At a ball or a park or an outing or something somewhere. They were of an age where they'd been out in society for probably a half dozen seasons. Indeed, he counted their cousin Thomas, the Marquess of Helmsley, among his closest friends. He might even have been introduced to one or another at some point in years past, although he couldn't for the life of him recall it. And surely he would have remembered. Not simply because this female pretending to pay him no notice was lovely—there were any number of others he could name that were far more lovely—but there had been something quite distinct about her when her gaze had met his. Something intense and compelling. Something that had quite taken his breath away.

"But which one is she?"

Pennington glanced at the lady, then indicated a couple some distance away. "Given Lord St. Stephens over there is escorting a woman who looks precisely like the lady in question, and in a most possessive manner, I suspect that to be his wife and the sister who has attracted your attention to be *Miss* Effington. I believe her name is Cassandra."

"Cassandra," Reggie murmured, liking the way the name sounded on his tongue. The way it rolled off his lips. *Cassandra.*

"Oh no, you don't." Marcus shook his head firmly. "Not again."

"Not again, what?" Reggie directed his question toward his friend, but his gaze stayed firmly fixed on Miss Effington. *Cassandra.* She moved through the crowd in an effortless manner, at ease and full of grace.

Marcus groaned. "I thought you had put this business of losing your heart at the drop of a hat behind you. I distinctly remember you vowing to be more restrained with your emotions."

"Yes, of course," Reggie murmured. If Miss Effington turned in his direction . . . "I wonder what color her eyes are?"

"It doesn't matter. Reggie." Marcus leaned closer and lowered his voice. "That promise was part and parcel of a—what did you call it?"

"A concerted effort to control the vagaries of my life." Blue probably. With her fair hair, blue would be nearly perfect.

"Which included avoiding damsels in distress—"

"She does not look at all distressed." Reggie was exceedingly fond of blue-eyed blondes. "Indeed, she looks quite composed."

"She looks like she is doing an excellent job of completely ignoring you."

"Surely nothing more than a ruse—"

"Reggie." Marcus's voice had the unrelentingly firm tone of a parent. "It was my understanding that the ridiculous scheme that you and I and various other assorted companions have spent the past half year nurturing was for the express purpose of saving you from yourself. I thought you had decided if your reputation was"—he cleared his throat—"*enhanced,* and you were made to appear somewhat, to use your words, *dark and dangerous*"—Marcus rolled his gaze skyward—"ladies would fall at your feet rather than the other way around."

"Come now, Marcus." Reggie dragged his gaze away from Miss Effington and grinned at his friend. "You must admit you've derived a great deal of enjoyment from inventing rumors of my scandalous adventures. My exorbitant wagers—"

"Pity they were mostly with me," Marcus muttered. "And nowhere near exorbitant."

"My now legendary exploits with women—"

Marcus snorted.

"And the duels. Completely your idea, I believe."

"They were a nice touch." Marcus nodded smugly. "Quite brilliant really. Nothing like a duel to give a man an air of illicit allure."

"Indeed they do, although I daresay I've contributed to the cause as well." Reggie grinned.

"In the arrogance of your manner and the swagger of your step perhaps." Marcus considered him curiously. "In truth, I didn't know you had it in you."

Reggie shrugged modestly. "One does what one can."

"Pity this campaign of yours hasn't seemed to have

borne much fruit in terms of hordes of women falling at your feet."

"You've noticed that, have you?" Reggie shook his head in mock despair. "Still, the season has barely begun, and it's far too soon to give up hope. One would think the occasional public triumph, like today's, will help."

"Speaking of which . . ." Marcus's gaze slipped past him, and Reggie turned.

Christian Effington strode toward them. "Excellent showing, my lord." Effington nodded a bow and grinned. "Damned fine job, even if it was at my expense."

"My apologies," Reggie said with a grin of his own and a complete lack of sincerity.

Effington laughed. "Not at all. I must say it has been some time since I have been bested by someone who was not a relation. My older brothers have made it their purpose in life to keep me humble by defeating me in varied and assorted endeavors on a regular basis."

"And does it work?" Marcus raised a curious brow.

"To keep me humble?" Effington grinned. "Not in the least."

Effington's laugh was infectious. Reggie wondered if his sister's was as engaging.

"This is dashed awkward, my lord, but I find myself in the difficult position of having to beg a favor." Effington glanced at Marcus, who murmured a polite excuse and discreetly stepped away. Effington lowered his voice in a confidential manner. "I seemed to have misjudged the current state of my finances, and as such I'm not . . . that is I'm unable . . . what I mean to say is I can't—"

"A bit short of funds, Effington?" Reggie said casually.

"Yes, that's it exactly." Effington blew a sigh of relief. "Damned hard to admit aloud, though. I don't know how I got myself into this mess, but it seems I don't have the money on hand at the moment to make good on our wager. If you could see your way clear—"

"To take your note?" Reggie shrugged graciously. "I don't see why not. The wager was a paltry hundred and fifty pounds, after all." Reggie didn't so much as twinge at the amount, as if the making of such immense wagers was not at all unusual for him. As if this wasn't the first time he had played any game for stakes so high.

"Yes, well, what seemed paltry a few days ago seems rather more significant today." A rueful smile curved Effington's mouth. "However, I am confident I can pay you within a month at the most, possibly even a fortnight. I do appreciate your understanding about this."

"Think nothing of it, Effington."

"If there's ever anything I can do for you . . ."

Reggie hesitated, but the opportunity was too good to let slip by. "You can introduce me to your sister."

"Cassandra? You want to meet Cassandra? How very interesting." Effington studied him carefully. "Why?"

"Why?" Reggie started. "I'm not certain I can answer that." *I want to know the color of her eyes.* "She's lovely, of course."

"Of course. And I suppose that suffices as a sufficient reason. I know I have sought the acquaintance of any number of ladies on the basis of a fetching appearance. Still, this is not another lady but my sister." Effington narrowed his eyes. "Are your intentions honorable?"

"Frankly, Effington, I don't know that I have any intentions at all. I saw your sister in the crowd and I wish to meet her. There's nothing more to it than that." Reggie drew his brows together in annoyance. "At this particular moment, my intentions extend no further than an introduction." Reggie ignored a twinge of conscience, although it wasn't exactly a lie. He really had no idea what his intentions were. Said intentions very much depended on the lady herself.

"My apologies, my lord." Effington blew a long breath. "Do you have sisters?"

Reggie nodded. "One."

"Is she out in society yet?"

"No. She's a bit young."

"Younger than you, eh?" Effington nodded sagely. "Do consider this a warning, then; there is nothing more trying than watching a younger sister navigate the treacherous waters of the world. It is a dangerous place filled with men who are, well," he grinned, "very much like myself.

"Still," Effington's assessing gaze raked over Reggie, "you seem a decent enough sort. A bit of a reputation, but nothing really dire."

"I shall have to do better," Reggie murmured.

"Better?" Effington drew his brows together in confusion, then his expression cleared. "Ah yes, *better*. I see. Reform and all that. Excellent idea. Especially in regards to Cassandra. I never suspected it of her, but of late I have discovered she's a bit stuffy regarding her preferences in men."

"You do realize I am seeking nothing more than an introduction." Reggie's voice was cautious.

"Yes, of course. Again, my apologies." Effington grimaced. "Habit, I suspect. You see, my brothers and I have always thought Cassandra was the sister most in need of keeping a close watch on. She has an air about her that seems to give the impression that she is given to scandal. Probably because she is rather annoyingly independent and prone to speak her mind, and act as well without due consideration to the consequences. In truth, her recent activities could even be termed somewhat eccentric."

"Try not to make her sound too appealing," Reggie said under his breath.

Effington winced. "I seem to be making rather a mess of this, don't I?"

"Rather."

"Apparently my sister isn't the only one who speaks without thinking. Do try to ignore what I said."

"Perhaps it would be best if Lord Berkley actually met Miss Effington," Marcus said smoothly.

Reggie wondered exactly what point in the odd conversation had caught the earl's attention, although knowing Marcus, he had probably listened to every word.

"Yes. Most certainly. I shall fetch her at once." Effington leaned toward Reggie confidentially. "You won't be sorry." He grinned, nodded, and was off.

"You might well be sorry." Marcus's thoughtful gaze followed Effington's progress. "I have the distinct impression that Effington is overly eager to see his sister wed. And furthermore that he thinks you are an excellent match."

"I asked for an introduction, not her hand."

"I'm not certain Effington sees the difference." Marcus studied his friend. "You will be careful, won't you?"

Reggie laughed. "I have no intention of being trapped into a marriage simply to alleviate the responsibility felt by anyone's brothers."

"That's not what I mean." Marcus paused. "What I'm trying to say is that you're already intrigued by this lady. I can see you once again losing your heart. And I can see as well it being crushed. Again."

"No, Marcus, never again. It has taken me far too many years to learn my lesson, but learn it I have. If there is a heart to be lost this time"—Reggie cast his friend a wicked grin—"it shall not be mine."

"We shall see," Marcus said softly without the least bit of conviction.

"Indeed we shall." Reggie's voice rang firm and confident.

Even so, he watched Effington make his way through the crowd toward his sister and knew full well, regardless of his words, that he could indeed easily give his heart to Miss Cassandra Effington. He knew it just from the look of her.

But he'd been down that road far too many times before, and he would not tread it again. He absolutely would not offer his affection to any woman until he was certain it was returned.

It was Marcus's successful marriage and the obvious love he shared with his wife that had forced Reggie to reassess his own life. What he'd seen was a man who'd freely and unadvisedly given his heart over and over again and had inevitably suffered heartbreak in return. Oh, certainly, he'd never known devastation so great that it hadn't been cured by a few days in a drunken stupor. And yes, his wounded heart had typically healed within a fortnight, usually less. And perhaps it had been as much his pride as his heart that had been at stake.

Still and all, it would not happen again.

For once in his life he wanted to be loved before he offered love. He wanted a woman to want him as much as he wanted her. And he absolutely refused to ever again declare himself before he was certain his affection was returned.

No, he would keep his distance from Miss Effington. She was dangerous. Extremely dangerous. And not at all what he'd had in mind when he'd started his campaign to attract the fairer sex.

Besides, she didn't look even remotely likely to fall at his feet.

Two

The men women seem most taken with are those I wouldn't let alone in a room with my sister for so much as the blink of an eye. A crowded room at that.

Reginald, Viscount Berkley

"I should like to congratulate you on your victory, my lord." Cassie gazed coolly into Lord Berkley's intriguing gray eyes and tried to ignore just how intriguing they were.

"And did you win a great deal, Miss Effington?" Lord Berkley raised her hand to his lips. His gaze never left hers, in a manner both disconcerting and altogether too polished. No doubt he'd had a great deal of practice.

"If indeed I wagered at all, why on earth would you think I had wagered on you?" She resisted the urge to pull her hand from his. Doing so would be an admission of sorts that the intimacy of her hand in his was the tiniest bit uncomfortable, and such realization would only add to the smug twinkle in his eye. The man was obviously far and away too arrogant as it was. "After all, your contest was with my brother."

"In truth, Miss Effington, I don't know that you had wagered on me." His gaze trapped hers, and she was gripped by the disturbing idea that he saw far more than other people. As if his gray eyes, his *most intriguing* gray eyes, looked beyond the surface of her words to the privacy of her thoughts. "I can only hope."

"Your words are as practiced as your manner, my lord." She withdrew her hand from his in a most deliberate way. "But I daresay, from what I have heard about the infamous Viscount Berkley, you have had a great deal of experience."

Christian groaned. "Cassandra."

"Infamous?" Berkley raised a brow in what appeared to be surprise, then he laughed. "I don't believe anyone has ever called me infamous before." He flashed a grin at Lord Pennington. "What do you think, Pennington? Am I infamous?"

"Becoming more so every moment, I should think," Pennington said coolly.

Berkley laughed again, and she ignored the nearly irresistible urge to join him. No doubt that contagious laugh was a large part of his charm. Infamous or otherwise.

"May I ask you, Miss Effington, if you find men of an infamous nature interesting?"

"Not in the least. Indeed, I find they should all be avoided." She tried not to cringe at the overly prim tone in her voice. She hadn't meant to sound quite so stuffy.

"All of them?" His eyes widened in surprise.

"Every one."

"But you have not met every one."

"I have met enough."

"You have never met me."

"Nonetheless, I do think—"

"I think you should allow me the opportunity to persuade you that underneath this infamous facade is a delightful and really quite charming—"

"I have no doubt of your charm, my lord," she said firmly. "Nor do I have any doubt you employ it whenever possible."

He shrugged in a manner of feigned humility. "When one has a gift, one finds it necessary to share."

"When one is presented with something unpleasant in the street, one finds it necessary to avoid stepping directly in it," she said pleasantly, gazing at him with an innocence every bit as contrived as his modesty.

Christian groaned again. Pennington snorted.

Berkley stared for a moment, then smiled slowly. A smile that crinkled the corners of his eyes and triggered the oddest sensation deep in the pit of her stomach. "Excellent, Miss Effington. Really very good. I am most impressed."

"I'm pleased you enjoyed it," she murmured and tried to ignore the heat that flushed up her face. Whatever had possessed her? While she was typically forthright, she was never actually rude. Until now.

"I did. Very much so." Berkley chuckled. "Now, would you allow me the privilege of escorting you to the luncheon tables? I know I am famished, and surely the severe nature of your observations has honed your appetite as well as your words."

This time Pennington groaned, and Christian no doubt winced, although she didn't see him. Indeed the rest of the world seemed to fade into the distance.

Berkley's gaze locked with hers and carried a distinct challenge. Cassie lifted her chin and met his gaze without flinching. The moment between them stretched, lengthened like a silent duel of wills. Her heart thudded in her chest, and while she was intensely aware of all things physical, she was more aware of an odd connection with this man, this stranger. A meeting of minds, perhaps. A recognition of a strength not unlike her own. It was at once frightening and the most exciting thing she'd ever experienced.

Whatever else he was, Lord Berkley was no fool. What harm would it do to trade barbs with him? She had no intention of further involvement, but engaging him in a battle of wits would be most amusing.

"Indeed I will, my lord, if you accept my apology." She offered him a contrite smile. "I fear my words might have been somewhat impolite."

"Somewhat," he said and offered his arm.

Cassie glanced at her brother. "Are you coming?"

"In a moment." Christian's voice was excessively cheery. "I wish to speak to Lord Pennington first about a matter of mutual interest, if he doesn't mind. Do go on ahead."

"What matter?" Pennington's brows drew together.

Christian cast him a warning look, then nodded pointedly at his sister and Berkley.

Pennington glanced from Christian to Berkley, and the confusion on his face cleared. "Oh. Yes, of course. A matter of mutual interest. Certainly. I can see where it would be."

Berkley leaned closer to her, his voice low. "They're both quite mad, you know."

She laughed in spite of herself. "I have long suspected it of all my brothers."

She took his arm, trying to ignore the hard muscles beneath the fine fabric of his coat and the unnerving way the heat of his skin could be felt even through the layers of material, and they started toward the tables.

"I must apologize for my brother as well as myself," she said lightly. "He is not overly subtle, is he?"

Berkley laughed. "Not overly, no."

She heaved a long-suffering sigh. "He thinks you're an excellent match, and he and my other brothers want me to marry. They're not especially concerned as to who I wed, only that I do so. They would prefer someone with an acceptable title and income, but I think their only true requirement in a husband for me is his ability to walk upright and speak rather than grunt, although even that is probably open to negotiation."

"How nice to know I meet their minimal standards," Berkley said wryly.

"That is yet to be determined." She laughed and shook her head. "Oh dear, I should probably apologize to you yet again. I have an annoying tendency to speak my mind. To say exactly what I think. It has, on occasion, proven awkward and produced consequences that I did not foresee."

"I can well imagine."

"Nonetheless, it is my nature, and I see no need to change it."

"Nor should you."

"Do you really think so?" She glanced up at him.

"Indeed I do."

"Most men of my acquaintance would advise me to hold my tongue or, at the very least, temper my words."

"Ah, but you have not yet been acquainted with me." Amusement colored his voice. "Although I would advise you to curb voicing your opinions about the behavior of *most men* or even *infamous men*. We are not all alike."

"Still, I am rarely wrong."

He laughed, and she realized how very pompous she sounded. Odd, she couldn't recall ever sounding pompous before.

"I warn you, I am a firm believer in honesty as well." She paused, a rather startling number of past incidents, most in tandem with her sister, parading through her mind. "Under most circumstances."

"Honesty is an excellent quality." He bit back a smile. "Under most circumstances."

"Therefore I feel compelled to be truthful with you. I should not want you to escort me under false pretenses."

"I am merely accompanying you to a meal," he said mildly. "I'd scarce call this a declaration of intentions."

"Of course not." They reached the tables laden with an appetizing array of offerings, including an inciting display of sweets. Cassie barely noticed. "I didn't mean . . . Regardless." She released his arm and turned to meet his gaze. "Lord Berkley, I am trying to explain to you that in spite of my brother's obvious intention of introducing us with an eye toward a future match, I must tell you I am not, well, interested."

"Interested?" He narrowed his eyes in confusion. "What do you mean, *interested?*"

"In you." She caught herself. "Oh, I don't mean you as an individual, I mean you in the broader sense. The type of man you are. I simply have no interest in a man of your reputation."

"Infamous?" he said slowly.

"Exactly." She nodded and cast him a pleasant smile.

He studied her thoughtfully. "Most women of my acquaintance find men of a certain nature, dark and dangerous and the like, to be rather exciting."

"No doubt women of your acquaintance do, which is exactly why they are of your acquaintance." She met his gaze directly. "I, however, do not. A man with a reputation for gaming and drinking and consorting with countless numbers of unsuitable women—"

"Countless?" Surprise sounded in his voice, and he actually appeared pleased.

She pulled her brows together. "Surely that does not surprise you?"

"No. No, of course not." He tried and failed to suppress a delighted grin. "I was there, after all."

She sniffed in disdain. "At any rate, my lord, I am not interested in any man whose life is as fast and loose as yours. I do not find rakes and scoundrels to be the least bit attractive. Furthermore, I have no intention of reforming any man or molding him to my specification. No, I want a man who is already—"

"Perfect." Berkley's eyes narrowed. "That's what you're saying."

"Nonsense, there is no such thing as a perfect man." She thought for a moment. "Although I suppose that is what I'm saying."

"I see." His tone was level and noncommittal.

"I suspected you would. And while you are quite a bit nicer than I had expected," she drew a deep breath, "you and I simply will not suit."

"I see," he said again.

"Is that all you have to say?"

For a moment, she had the oddest hope that he would protest her words. Demand a chance to win her hand. Her heart. It was a ridiculous idea, of course. He was not at all what she wanted in a husband. It was probably nothing more than his infectious laugh or the intriguing nature of his gray eyes that had put such an absurd thought in her head.

"My dear Miss Effington." He chose his words with care. "I fear you and your brother have jumped to a far-fetched conclusion of permanence based on nothing more than a request for an introduction and an innocent walk in the midst of a rather substantial gathering."

"Oh no, I didn't think—"

"Oh, but you did." His voice was cool, as if he were discussing something of no significance whatsoever. "And as you are a proponent of honesty, *under most circumstances*, I feel I should be entirely honest with you."

"Of course," she said weakly. As much as she preferred honesty, she wasn't entirely certain she wanted to hear whatever honesty compelled him to say.

"You are obviously intelligent and confident in your own nature, qualities I quite admire in a woman. In addition, you are forthright and outspoken. While the tendency to speak your mind is perhaps not as preferable as your penchant for honesty, one never has to guess precisely where he stands in your eyes. And that is most beneficial. In that spirit, therefore, I must confess to what you already know."

His gaze was calm and unwavering, his voice level and matter-of-fact. The only evidence at all that indicated otherwise was the gleam in his narrowed eyes, eyes that now looked more silver than gray.

"While you have no desire to marry a man in need of," he cleared his throat, "*reform,* I have no desire for a wife with an unyielding view of the world and those in it. I am not perfect, Miss Effington, nor do I wish to be. Frankly, I cannot imagine anything more frightfully dull than perfect. You are clever and lovely and may well be perfect in many ways. Indeed, I suspect there is a great deal more to you beyond what is readily apparent. I regret that I have neither the fortitude nor the endurance required to know you better.

"Therefore, Miss Effington, I must admit I quite agree with you. We will not suit. However, I do wish you luck in your quest for . . . for . . . *Lord Perfect.*" He nodded a curt bow, turned, and started off.

At once regret swept through her, accompanied by the strangest feeling that perhaps, just this once, she had made a dreadful mistake. Without thinking she called after him.

"Forty pounds, my lord."

He turned back and raised a brow. "Forty pounds?"

She drew a deep breath. "That's how much I won."

He studied her for a moment, and the slightest hint of a smile turned up the corners of his mouth. He nodded again, turned, and strode back down the hill.

She stared after him. He was indeed a fine figure of a man, this infamous Lord Berkley. Tall and handsome with eyes that saw into her soul and a laugh that echoed in her blood.

"Dash it all, Cass, why couldn't you have been the least bit pleasant to him," Christian said from behind her. She hadn't even noted his approach. "Berkley is an excellent catch."

"I was pleasant. I am always pleasant. Unfailingly pleasant."

Lord Pennington joined Lord Berkley, and she would have given a great deal to know exactly what they were saying. What *he* was saying about *her*. Certainly she'd been honest, perhaps even blunt, but she wouldn't have termed her manner unpleasant. A heavy weight settled in the pit of her stomach.

Perhaps she had been a touch unpleasant.

"No doubt." A note of resignation sounded in Christian's voice. He turned to peruse the repast laid out on the tables, and Cassie sent a silent prayer of thanks heavenward that he had turned his attention elsewhere.

"He certainly doesn't have the appearance of a man who has just finished a pleasant conversation," Christian said idly.

She rescinded the prayer, plucked a piece of cheese from a platter, and thrust it at her brother. "This looks good."

"Indeed it does." Christian grinned and took the morsel. "I'd say he has the appearance of a man who has had a narrow escape. Even a man running for his life."

"He simply realized we would not suit." She forced a light note to her voice, as if it did not matter. It didn't, of course. He was not at all what she wanted in a husband.

"He determined that after only a few minutes, did he?" Christian raised a skeptical brow. "Perhaps you should tell me again how pleasant you were."

"Unfailingly pleasant," she muttered.

Christian snorted in disbelief. "Regardless of what you may have heard about him, Berkley is an excellent catch."

"I heard you the first time you said it, and you may say it a hundred more times and I shall continue to disregard it. You know full well I have no wish to marry or reform a rake."

"I have heard you say it a hundred times, and I daresay I will hear you say it a hundred more." Christian smirked. "And I shall continue to disregard it." He popped the cheese into his mouth.

"The way you and Leo and Drew persist in ignoring my opinions and desires about whom I shall wed is becoming altogether tedious." She blew a frustrated breath. "Why is it that you persist in believing that I am too feebleminded to make my own decisions on an issue as important as the rest of my life?"

"On the contrary, dear sister, we think you are far and away too clever for your own good. We think you have too many opinions and some of them entirely wrong.

"For example, Cass, everyone but you accepts that reformed rakes make the best husbands. It's practically gospel. Why, I myself shall make an excellent husband at some point in the future. Some far, far distant point."

He flashed the same irresistible smile all three brothers shared. The smile her mother said was written in the stars. The very smile that made the knees of unsuspecting women weak and was cast by any number of men of questionable reputation.

Cassie was anything but unsuspecting.

"I do not envy whatever foolish woman takes on the task of your reformation," she said firmly but couldn't quite hide an affectionate smile.

She truly liked her brothers, all three of them; they were most amusing, even if she did not always approve of their behavior. When she thought about it, and the subject had preyed on her mind a lot recently, they had a great deal to do with why she had no interest in men with any sort of disreputable qualities. Oh, certainly Leo and Drew and Christian were not bad sorts overall, but Cassie had watched them through the years cut a swath through society and leave a trail of broken hearts in their wake. Even so, she had little pity for those poor creatures left pining over her brothers. Their nature was no secret, and any woman who became involved with them well deserved the consequences.

Only a fool would allow herself to get involved with men like her brothers. Her gaze drifted back to Berkley. Or a man like that. Cassandra Effington was no fool. She knew his type of man as well as she knew herself.

She had long suspected, somewhere in the back of her mind, that her avowed aversion to disreputable men, infamous men, was a ruse. That, in truth, she was very much attracted to men who skated on the edge of scandal. To men who, like her brothers, lived life according to their own rules. Men who were as untrustworthy as they were charming. Men who would break her heart.

Men exactly like Lord Berkley. He was dangerous. Very dangerous, and she would do well to avoid him in the future—not that that would be at all difficult, given how *pleasantly* she'd treated him.

It was for the best. The man she wanted, the perfect man for her, *Lord Perfect,* was waiting somewhere in her future. And she was confident someday they would meet. Why, hadn't her mother said such a meeting was foretold in the stars?

And surely he would wipe away any lingering memories of a knowing, silver gaze and seductive laugh.

"I've been something of a fool, haven't I?" Reggie muttered as he stalked down the rise, Marcus at his side.

"Now and again." Marcus's forehead furrowed curiously. "Did you have a specific incident in mind?"

Reggie slanted him an annoyed glance. "Why didn't you tell me this plan of mine was absurd?"

"I did tell you. Several times, in fact."

Of course Marcus had tried to dissuade him. As much as Reggie hated to admit it now, he distinctly remembered Marcus's arguments. Arguments that seemed rather more valid at the moment than they had six months ago. "You didn't do a good job of it though, did you?"

"I did an excellent job. Beyond listing the more ridiculous aspects of your proposal, I believe I pointed out that while women do not fall at your feet precisely, you are considered extremely eligible and there are now and always have been any number of ladies more than interested in pursuing an acquaintance with you."

"Regardless." Reggie waved away the comment. "Why didn't you stop me?"

"Nothing short of the forces of nature could have stopped you." Marcus shook his head. "I learned in those long past days of our youth, when you were getting into any number of scrapes I had tried to talk you out of, and pulling me in with you, that when you have set your mind on a particular course dissuading you is next to impossible. Indeed, I have always considered your dogged determination to be something of a force of nature in and of itself."

"Even so—"

"Beyond that." Reluctance sounded in Marcus's voice. "As absurd as it sounds, I thought it could be rather amusing and possibly . . . perhaps . . . there was the slight chance . . ." He blew a resigned breath. "It could actually work."

Reggie snorted. "It hasn't thus far."

"I was wrong." Marcus shrugged, then grinned. "Although it has been entertaining."

Reggie ignored him. "I really can't understand what happened. It seemed foolproof. Women love the type of man we have made me out to be. They should be flinging themselves at me in great numbers. Yet I am no better off now than I was before."

Marcus heaved a long-suffering sigh. "Need I mention, again, you were not in dire straits when we began. Women have—"

"Not the right woman." Reggie's jaw clenched. "Never the right woman." The right woman, or at least the woman with the potential for being the right woman, was never the one to show interest in him of an affectionate nature. He had always been the one to fall in love. And he had always been the one left alone.

Marcus's tone was level. "I gather Miss Effington refused to fling herself in your direction."

"Miss Effington is an extremely intriguing lady who knows precisely what she wants and refuses to settle for less. Furthermore she does not hesitate to voice her desires in no uncertain terms."

"That does not sound promising," Marcus murmured.

"No, it doesn't, does it?" Reggie cast his friend a rueful smile. "Especially as she has no interest in men of an infamous nature."

"That is a problem."

"And ironic as well." Reggie paused, gripped by the memory of that one mesmerizing moment when they'd gazed into each other's eyes. "There was something between us when we met—"

"You've said that before," Marcus said quickly. "Any number of times. It's the point at which I realize you are about to plunge headfirst into—"

"This was different, Marcus."

"You've said that before too."

Reggie resisted the urge to argue with his friend. Marcus was right: Reggie had made similar claims before upon meeting a charming lady. But this was indeed entirely different. Reggie wasn't quite sure how exactly, but it was. There had been a spark in Miss Effington's lovely blue eyes when her gaze had met his, a light of connection, an unstated admission perhaps that there could well be something special between them. As if in that moment, her soul had recognized his. He'd lost count of the number of times he'd fallen in love, but never once had he experienced anything remotely like this kind of mutual acknowledgment.

It was a ridiculous idea, of course. Why, she didn't even like him. Or rather, she didn't like what he was pretending to be.

"Well, I'm in for it now, aren't I?"

"I would say so." Marcus grimaced. "There's really no way to reverse what we've done. You know as well as I, gossip of the sort we initiated feeds on itself and grows in the process. This victory of yours today will only enhance what we've set in motion. Congratulations, Reggie." He laughed. "Like it or not, you are indeed the infamous Viscount Berkley."

"I could reform," Reggie said hopefully.

Marcus shook his head. "No one would believe it. Especially not Miss Effington."

"It scarce matters, I suppose. She does not like who she thinks I am and would like me even less, if possible, if she knew the truth." For a moment he considered exactly how to explain to Miss Effington that he wasn't at all infamous but simply wished to be seen so to attract women who would then swoon at his feet, overcome with love. No, she would think it not only absurd but a bit pathetic as well.

"But *you* like *her*."

"No, Marcus. I could like her. Very much. But I shall not allow myself to do so. Even though my method of changing my habits regarding the fairer sex does not appear to have been successful, I am quite serious nonetheless. Allowing myself to fall heels over head again without the least bit of encouragement from the lady in question is nothing more than falling into old ways."

"But Miss Effington—"

"It is pointless to pursue the matter." Reggie ignored a sharp stab of regret. "She shall go her way, and I shall go mine. If in the future our paths cross again, I shall be polite. Nothing more."

Marcus studied him thoughtfully, then nodded. "I must admit I'm impressed."

"Why?"

"Regardless of the dim-witted nature of your original plan, you are obviously indeed determined to change. It's most admirable." Marcus clapped him on the back. "The least I can do is lend my ongoing assistance beyond what I have already accomplished, unless, of course, you'd prefer to continue along this path. Another duel, perhaps?"

"I think not, but I do appreciate the offer."

Marcus grinned modestly. "One does what one can for one's friends."

They could make light of it, but, for as long as Reggie could remember, Marcus had been his closest friend. Indeed, they were as close as brothers. Neither had ever let the other down, and neither ever would.

Yet with Marcus's marriage last year, there had been a subtle change in their relationship. Not that Reggie felt he had lost a friend. No, if anything, he had gained one in Marcus's wife, Gwen. It was another irony that Marcus, who had never especially looked for love, had found it, yet Reggie, who had spent much of his life falling in and, unfortunately, out of love, had yet to find anything that could be called true or lasting or, for that matter, even a woman who would return his affection. *The right woman.*

Perhaps he should lower his standards.

Perhaps he should give up the idea of love in a marriage and simply look for a suitable wife. There were any number of prospects. Marcus was right; Reggie was considered an excellent match. Still, there was something that struck him as vaguely unsavory about the idea of marriage for the sake of marriage alone, without a semblance of affection or, better yet, love. He wanted what he had seen in the happy marriage of his parents. His father had been gone for nearly a dozen years now, yet Reggie could still remember the relationship his parents had shared. The secret smiles, the private glances, the obvious affection, and the devastating sorrow his mother had endured upon his father's death.

He wanted what his friends had. Marcus and his wife had not started out on the best of terms. Indeed, their nuptials had been predicated on the threat of financial disaster, but love had swiftly followed. Or his friend the Marquess of Helmsley, who had had no intention of marrying at all but had originally been trying to find a suitable match elsewhere for the lady who ultimately claimed his heart.

Was happiness in marriage so much to ask for?

Perhaps it was, at least for him. Perhaps he should simply content himself with what was achievable. Certainly he could make a suitable match this very season. He could have his pick of eligible young ladies, and affection, possibly even love, might come with time.

"Forgive me for interrupting your contemplation," Marcus said, "but where precisely are we going?"

"Where?" Reggie pulled up short and looked around. They had reached the road. He hadn't even noticed.

"I grant you it might well take a lengthy, meandering walk across the countryside to resolve the various quandaries of your life, but I suspect it cannot be accomplished in a mere morning." Marcus studied him thoughtfully. "I must admit I find these rare introspective moments of yours most unnerving. It is not in your nature."

"My apologies," Reggie said wryly.

"Think nothing of it." Marcus shrugged in an overly gracious manner, then sobered. "I wish you would see yourself as others see you, old friend. You never have, you know."

Reggie considered the earl for a long moment. Marcus knew him better than anyone but on this he was mistaken. Reggie had a very realistic view of who and what he was. He had a fine title, a nice fortune, and he was not unattractive. But when all was said and done, there was really little out of the ordinary about him. In an opera, he would be a voice in the chorus. On stage, a bit player. In a novel, a minor character. It was the lot he'd drawn in life, his nature as it were.

And his nature was not given to brooding.

He smiled slowly. "You have always been prone to pronouncements of an analytical nature, Marcus, but never this early in the day."

Marcus stared for a moment, as if debating his next words, then smiled. "I don't know what came over me. I shall have to watch myself in the future.

"As for now." Marcus nodded at the gathering they had left behind. The crowd milled around the tables, laughter and the sounds of good cheer drifted on the breeze. "I, for one, am hungry and curious as to the whereabouts of my wife. I suggest we return to the festivities. Besides," he grinned wickedly, "there may well be any number of young ladies waiting to fall at the feet of the victorious Lord Berkley."

"The victorious *infamous* Lord Berkley, if you please." Reggie laughed and Marcus joined him. They started back toward the gathering, side by side, much as they had done everything in their lives.

Why not savor this moment of triumph? Reggie had won the race, after all, and he deserved to take some pleasure in it beyond his winnings. The oddest sensation of satisfaction filled him. He might well be an ordinary sort of man, but he might also be the only one who knew it.

For the moment, at least, he was the infamous Lord Berkley, and he might as well enjoy it.

Three

Mothers are the givers of life, the bearers of heritage and for all of that, should be treasured and revered. They are also, more often than not, a necessary evil.

Marcus, Earl of Pennington

"What on earth took you so long? I thought you'd be home hours ago."

"Did you?" Reggie absently handed his hat and gloves to the butler, Higgins, who had been with Reggie's family, in one position or another, for as long as Reggie could remember. He glanced up at his younger sister.

Lucy swept down the curved stairway that dominated the foyer of Berkley House with the dramatic flair of an accomplished actress or a sixteen-year-old girl tottering far too eagerly on the brink of womanhood.

"You have no idea what I've been going through."

Lucy leaned against the newel post, heaved a theatrical sigh, and placed the back of her hand against her forehead. "It's been dreadful, simply dreadful."

Reggie slanted a questioning glance at Higgins, who rolled his eyes toward the ceiling but held his tongue.

Reggie bit back a grin. "I know I shall regret this, but what dreadful calamity has overset you today? Last week, it was Mother's refusal to allow you to come out this year."

Lucy raised her chin. "I am nearly seventeen."

"You are but sixteen and you behave accordingly. Yesterday, I understand there was some sort of upheaval over a dress that was decidedly inappropriate and far too revealing for a well-bred young woman of your age."

"I am quite mature for my age." She tossed back her dark hair. "Everyone says so."

"I believe that's part of the problem," Reggie said under his breath. "And just last night, you flew into something of a snit because you were forbidden to attend this morning's race."

"It wasn't at all fair and you well know it." Her brow furrowed. "Did you win?"

"Indeed I did."

"Excellent." She flashed a triumphant grin at Higgins.

The corners of the butler's mouth twitched, as if he was trying not to smile.

Reggie lowered his voice and leaned toward the older man. "Has she been wagering with the servants again?"

"I would never permit such a thing, my lord," Higgins said in a lofty manner.

Reggie studied the butler carefully. "You placed a wager for her, didn't you?"

Higgins's eyes widened in feigned innocence.

"Come now, Reggie," Lucy said quickly, stepping to her brother's side. "A lady can always use a bit of extra spending money. Besides, it scarcely matters at the moment. We have much bigger problems." She gave a heartfelt sigh. "It's Mother."

"What's mother?" Reggie narrowed his eyes.

"Lady Berkley has taken to her bed, my lord," Higgins said in his usual noncommittal way.

"Why?" Reggie's gaze skipped from Higgins to Lucy. "She can't possibly be ill. Mother has never been ill a day in her life."

"She's not just ill. She's . . . she's . . ." Lucy's lower lip quivered.

"Lady Berkley says she's dying, my lord," Higgins said.

"Dying?" Reggie shook his head in disbelief. "That's impossible. She was perfectly fine yesterday and completely healthy."

"But today she's on her deathbed." Lucy's eyes filled with tears. "We're going to be orphans."

"Nonsense." Reggie turned to Higgins. "Have you called for a physician?"

Higgins nodded. "Doctor Hopwood has already come and gone."

"And?"

"And he says he can find nothing wrong. The incompetent quack." Lucy sniffed in disdain. "Mother is obviously direly ill. Any fool can see it."

Reggie raised a brow. "Higgins?"

"It is difficult to say for certain, my lord." The butler chose his words with care. "One cannot discount the opinion of a highly regarded physician, and although her ladyship's color appears a shade pale, it is not especially so—"

"Higgins!" Lucy glared.

The butler continued. "Yet Lady Berkley has never, to my knowledge, been ill, nor has she feigned illness. I believe it might well be a grave mistake to disregard her claims now as to the state of her health."

"I see," Reggie said slowly. Higgins's assessment was both sobering and chilling.

The idea of his mother's death was not something Reggie had given much thought to, and it now brought a distinct pang of distress. He had always assumed Marian Berkley would be there forever. Certainly, from a rational point of view, he had known she was getting older and would join his father in the hereafter one day. She'd seen nearly fifty years, after all.

If truth were told, well, he rather liked his mother. Lady Berkley was kind and amusing and carried a delightful air of charming confusion about her. Better yet, for the most part she did not intrude upon his life. She had her friends and her activities and the raising of Lucy, all of which kept her far too busy to interfere with her son. While they all shared the grand house on Portman Square in London and the manor at Berkley Park in the country, they never seemed to be under one another's feet. Indeed, there were days when they scarcely set eyes on each other.

Still, there was something about knowing a parent was around—should you ever have *need* of parental advice or assistance or even affection—that was comforting and provided a pleasant bit of security in an insecure world.

Reggie did not like the idea of losing her, of being an orphan, any more than his sister did.

"I should see her." Reggie started up the stairs.

"She's been asking for you." Lucy followed close at his heels.

"My lord," Higgins called from behind, "before you go up I should mention something else Dr. Hopwood said."

Reggie halted in midstep and turned toward the butler. "What is it, Higgins?"

"Regardless of the true nature of her illness, the doctor said she should be humored, especially concerning any unusual or odd desires or requests. He advised we provide her with whatever she asks for. Such requests could well be the result of some kind of delirium or diminished capacity, and refusal might only worsen her state. Such aggravation is to be avoided at all costs, at least until he can determine precisely what is wrong," Higgins added.

"Very well." Reggie nodded. "She shall have whatever she wants."

He reached the top of the stairs and headed toward the wing of the house shared by his mother and sister. His own quarters were in the opposite wing, another concession to the separate nature of their respective lives.

The door to his mother's suite was closed. He knocked softly and waited.

Nothing.

"Try again." Lucy frowned. "She may be asleep."

Reggie paused, his fist poised to knock again. "Then perhaps we shouldn't—"

"Of course we should," Lucy huffed. "If she's dying, we haven't much time left." She pushed open the door and stepped inside. "Mother?"

Reggie and Higgins traded glances, then followed Lucy.

The drapes were drawn against the early afternoon sun. The room was dim, shadowed, and a chill shivered through Reggie. His mother had a passion for light and always insisted the windows be open to the sunshine. That she did not do so now was a very bad sign.

"Mother?" He stepped toward the bed.

"My boy, is that you?" Lady Berkley's weak voice sounded from the bed.

"What is this, Mother?" He reached the bed and stared down at her. She lay propped up upon a virtual hill of pillows, which only served to dwarf her small frame. He had never thought of his mother as especially diminutive; no doubt the liveliness of her personality enhanced her stature in his eyes. But gazing down at her now, he realized how very petite she really was. "How are you?"

"I'm fine, dear heart, nothing to worry about." Lady Berkley sighed and raised her hand slowly to take his, as though the effort was entirely too much for her. "Nothing at all." Her voice was so low that he could barely hear it.

Her very denial sent fear through his heart. He sat gently on the bed and stared with concern. The light was too poor to see clearly, yet her color did indeed seem pale. He forced a confident note to his voice. "The doctor says he can find nothing wrong."

"And we must trust the doctor." She cast him a brave smile. "I'm sure he knows far more than I."

"Of course. And you shall be fine." Still . . . Reggie pulled his brows together. Doctors had been wrong before. "Is there anything you need?"

"No, nothing." She brought her free hand to her mouth and coughed delicately. "Not a thing."

A sense of complete helplessness washed through him. "Surely there is something I can do to make you feel better?"

"You are a dear, dear boy for asking, but there is nothing I need. Well . . . perhaps . . ." She sighed. "No, I couldn't . . . no."

"What is it, Mother?"

She turned her head away. "No, it is too much to ask."

Reggie glanced at Higgins, who nodded his encouragement. "Ask anything, anything at all."

"If you insist. I should never presume otherwise." Her gaze met his. "Before I go—"

"Mother, you're not going anywhere." Lucy's voice rose in dismay.

"Of course not, dear." She smiled at her daughter, then turned her gaze back to her son. "First, you must promise to look after your sister."

"Of course, Mother." The promise caught in his throat, and he swallowed hard.

"And second, before I go—"

"Mother," Lucy wailed.

Marian raised a hand to quiet her daughter with a surprising show of strength. "I should like to see you settled."

"Settled?" Reggie's brows drew together. "You mean wed?"

"It is my heartfelt wish. My . . ." She pulled her gaze from his and stared off into the distance, her voice barely audible. "My last wish, as it were."

"Certainly, Mother, I can see that, but—"

"A good match. From a good family. But more, someone you could care for." Her voice had a musing quality, as if her mind were wandering. "Is there any-one . . ."

Luminous blue eyes flashed in his mind, and he pushed the thought away. "No, not at the moment."

"Pity." She fell silent for so long that he wondered if she'd drifted off. "Before I go, then, I should at least like you to be prepared."

"I needn't prepare for your death as you are not going to die," he said with far more confidence than he felt.

"That remains to be seen, but what I meant was prepared for a wife." Again she met his gaze with hers. "Dear Reginald, I have given this a considerable amount of thought, and now that the end may be near—"

"Mother!" Lucy moaned.

Her mother ignored her. "I should hate to see you bring a new wife into this house. Everything here is so . . . so . . ."

"Out of fashion, my lady?" Higgins prompted.

She favored the butler with a grateful smile. "That's it exactly."

"The house appears fine to me," Reggie said.

"It's far from fine. The public rooms, at least, need

to be completely refurbished." His mother's voice was weak but determined. "They are positively shabby."

"The furniture does look a bit worn, Reggie," Lucy said thoughtfully. "I can't remember when the walls were last repainted or papered. Why, Mother hasn't replaced anything in years."

"I've been very frugal," his mother said wistfully, as if admitting to a vile crime. Frugality was never a quality he would have attributed to his mother.

"Nonetheless, I see nothing wrong with the furnishings or the walls or anything else," Reggie said firmly. "I can't believe this is your dying wish?"

Higgins cleared his throat and leaned toward Reggie, his voice low and pointed. "Delirium, my lord."

"Of course," Reggie murmured and thought for a moment. He wasn't entirely certain he would want a wife who was influenced by such things, but if buying a few pieces of furniture or painting a room or two would ease his mother's obviously confused mind, make her happy, and, better yet, improve the state of her health, why on earth not? It seemed a rather simple request. "Mother, if this is what you want—"

"You are a saint and I am a lucky mother. Now then." She squeezed his hand. "I want the public rooms completely refurbished. Drapes to carpets. Paint, paper, furniture, everything. We shall make it a fitting setting for your new bride."

"I daresay, I would hope anyone I chose to marry would not care about such things," Reggie said wryly.

"I know I would care about such things," Lucy said under her breath.

"My dear heart, you know so little about women." His mother smiled up at him affectionately.

"Apparently." As ridiculous as his mother's request seemed, it also seemed innocuous. Besides, he wasn't sure, but she did look a shade better. Perhaps the doctor was right about humoring such absurd requests. He got to his feet. "I shall see to it at once, although I must admit I haven't even a vague notion where to begin such an endeavor."

"Darling boy, I would never thrust such decisions upon you." Lady Berkley's eyes widened, as if she could scarce dream of such a thing.

"I know I cannot imagine leaving the selection of furnishings to Reggie, let alone paint or paper." Lucy snorted. "He can barely tell the difference between a chiffonier or a commode, or an emerald green from a sky blue."

"I have no difficulty determining one color from another—I have simply never particularly cared." Reggie cast his sister a quelling glance. "Nor do I care as to the difference between one piece of furniture and another."

"Of course you don't, nor should you. And it will not be necessary." Even his mother's smile seemed stronger. This was obviously a good idea. "The daughter of an old friend of mine has exquisite taste and has guided the refurbishment of the houses of several ladies I know with excellent results. Oh, certainly, it's a bit eccentric of her, as she is from a good family and she charges an exorbitant amount to do so, yet she is well worth it."

Reggie narrowed his eyes. "How exorbitant?"

"Mother said she was well worth the cost." Lucy

frowned and crossed her arms over her chest. "Surely you can't begrudge her this, regardless of the expense? It is, after all, a dying wish."

"Now, now, Lucy." Lady Berkley smiled in the resigned way of a martyr on the road to the coliseum and collapsed back against the pillows like a sail bereft of wind. "If Reggie thinks it's too much—"

"No, not at all," Reggie said quickly. "If this is what you want—"

"Excellent. I have instructed Higgins to send a request for her to call later this afternoon. I leave it all in her hands." She cast him a frail smile. "And yours."

"Of course." Reggie forced a pleasant smile to his face and struggled to keep a note of reluctance from his voice.

The last thing he wanted to do was waste his time listening to an eccentric lady's musings about sofas and fabrics. Still, if it helped improve his mother's health, he could endure an afternoon with some woman who was no doubt past her prime and filling her empty hours by refurbishing other people's houses. He would approve whatever plans she had, but beyond that, he would keep as much distance as possible between himself and this *eccentric*.

"Now then, children, you may run along." Lady Berkley sighed, as if their conversation had quite sapped her strength. "I have a few items I need to discuss with Higgins."

Reggie frowned. "Is that wise? Surely any instructions for Higgins can wait until you have rested?"

"It will take but a moment and will ease my mind. I find it difficult to rest easily knowing the household is not in order." She waved weakly toward the door. "Go on now, and do close the door behind you."

"Very well." Reggie caught Higgins's gaze. "See to it she does not overtax herself."

"I would never permit that, my lord," Higgins said staunchly.

Reggie stepped to the door, paused to allow his sister to exit before him, then pulled the door closed behind him.

"Reggie." Lucy gazed up at him, her gray eyes wide with concern. "What do you think?"

"About Mother's illness?"

Lucy nodded.

"I don't know what to think." Reggie shook his head. "She is not the type of woman to take to her bed without due cause. I cannot recall her ever being indisposed or ever claiming to be. I fear she may well at least believe she is indeed on her deathbed."

"Perhaps she simply wants the house refurbished and is reluctant to spend the necessary funds?" A hopeful note sounded in Lucy's voice.

"Perhaps." Reggie considered the idea aloud. "Although I have never noticed Mother to so much as hesitate when it comes to expenditures. Indeed, she has always rather relished spending money, and the more immense the sums the greater her enjoyment. In addition, she has never used anything as serious as the state of her health to get what she wants. That alone gives her illness a certain level of veracity."

Tears welled up in Lucy's eyes. "Then she's really—"

"Don't be absurd," he said sharply and put a comforting arm around his sister's shoulder. "I am confident

Mother will be with us for many years to come. We simply have to weather this situation and follow the doctor's advice in regards to humoring her requests. I am sure she'll be completely back to normal in no time."

Lucy sniffed. "Do you think so?"

"Most certainly." Reggie's voice held a conviction he did not entirely feel. "Besides, Mother's main purpose in life in recent years has been to see me married." He cast Lucy an encouraging grin. "She would never permit herself to die until she has seen me safely wed."

"I see." Lucy pulled out of his embrace and studied him for a moment. "Thank you, Reggie. I must say you have made me feel much better."

"Have I indeed?" He raised a brow. "Why?"

"Why? Because given your astounding success thus far in finding a wife," Lucy smirked, "Mother may well live forever."

Cassie perched on the edge of a settee in the grand drawing room at Berkley House and cast an assessing eye around the chamber and its decor. The overall impression at the moment was one of an aging lady with her best days behind her, although the room was of good proportions with a great deal of potential and lovely ornamentation, even if some repair was in order. The tingling sense of excitement Cassie had come to expect upon beginning a new project welled within her, even if it was tempered today by a distinct touch of unease. As much as she prided herself on patience when it came to dealing with the ladies she accepted as clients, it was next to impossible to sit here, where the

Berkley butler had deposited her, in a collected manner and wait for whomever it was she waited for.

She surrendered to the restlessness that gripped her, stood and crossed the room, as much to ease her nerves as to better examine a carved marble Adam's fireplace.

It was the height of irony that after her rude behavior toward Lord Berkley she now found herself in his home, soon to be in his employ, at the request of his mother, no less. And odder still, at the insistence of her own.

Her immediate impulse upon receiving Lady Berkley's note when she'd arrived home from the race and Lord Warren's accompanying fete was to turn down the commission. She certainly didn't need the money; she had several other equally stimulating projects currently under consideration, and she did not relish the thought of continual encounters with Lord Berkley. While her mother was not as scandalized by Cassie's work as her brothers were, Lady William had never been overly enthusiastic, either. Nevertheless, her mother had been quite adamant about Cassie accepting this particular project, claiming Lady Berkley had not been feeling at all well of late and a refurbishment of her house might improve the state of her health.

She also said she considered Lady Berkley a dear, dear friend and Cassie should take on this project as a personal favor. That too was a bit odd. Cassie had had no idea her mother had ever even made Lady Berkley's acquaintance. Still, London society was in many ways like a village, where nearly everyone was well aware of nearly everyone else, and it was not at all unexpected that her mother and his would know each other.

"It's you." An amused chuckle sounded from the doorway.

Cassie drew a deep breath and turned, forcing a light note to her voice. "I did not expect to meet you again so soon, my lord."

"And yet here you are in my own home." Lord Berkley strode to her, took her hand, and raised it to his lips. "I must admit I am surprised, but I suppose I shouldn't be."

"You expected me, then?" She gazed into his gray eyes and, for the second time today, resisted the urge to yank her hand from his. And ignored as well the odd desire to keep it enfolded in the warmth of his touch forever. "Your mother must have mentioned our appointment."

A shadow of concern crossed his face, then vanished. "My mother said only the lady she wished to engage was . . . eccentric."

She pulled her hand free and drew her brows together. "And therefore you thought of me?"

He grinned. "You were described to me just this morning as eccentric."

"By my brother, no doubt." She knew she should be annoyed, and she would certainly let Christian know of her displeasure, but Berkley's amusement was irresistible. Besides, she suspected the impression she'd left him with earlier today was not overly favorable, *eccentric* being the least objectionable adjective he could use for her, and she much preferred that he not think of her as a complete shrew. She smiled wryly. "It could have been worse, I suppose. He could have said I was daft."

Appreciation sparked in Berkley's eyes. "Or mad."

"Even insane."

He nodded. "Cracked."

"Addlepated," she shot back.

"Nicked in the nob."

She grinned. "Around the bend."

He raised a brow. "Not all there."

She thought for a moment. "The walls don't go all the way to the roof."

"One brick short of a full load," he said without pause.

"Half-witted."

"Simpleminded."

"Featherhead."

"Noodle brained."

She laughed. "Not the brightest star in the sky."

"Oh, but you are." His voice was cool, but there was a distinct gleam in his eye. "I cannot imagine any celestial being that could possibly outshine you."

"Ah, the infamous and charming Lord Berkley makes his appearance," she said in a lighthearted manner that belied the hammering of her heart. The change in their banter caught her off guard, as did the pleasure she took in his compliment. "You do know how to turn a phrase, and I must say I expected no less, given your reputation. However, I am impressed that you managed to restrain yourself until now."

"Restraint, Miss Effington, is a virtue I have never been especially gifted with, nor have I ever seen its particular value."

"Restraint, my lord, is what separates the civilized from the uncivilized," she said, then tried not to wince at the sanctimonious tone of her voice.

"I have never particularly thought of myself as uncivilized, but then I had never thought of myself as infamous before meeting you, either." He crossed his arms over his chest and leaned against the mantel. "You, Miss Effington, are teaching me all sorts of interesting things about myself."

"I should apologize."

"Why?" He raised a brow. "Did you not mean it?"

"Oh, I meant it. I simply shouldn't have said it."

"Why not?"

"Because it was rude." She sighed and shook her head. "You have been nothing but pleasant to me—"

"And charming?" He wagged his brows wickedly.

She laughed in spite of herself. "Most charming, and I have been nothing but disapproving and impolite. In truth, we have barely met, and I have already judged you."

"And found me lacking."

"Not lacking, exactly." She thought for a moment. "Rather too much as opposed to not enough."

"Too infamous?"

"Something like that," she murmured and tried to ignore the heat that swept up her face. She couldn't remember the last time she had blushed at all, yet this man had managed to get her to do just that—not once but twice in the same day. It was most unsettling.

"We have not started off on the right foot, you and I, have we?"

"It would not seem so."

"Perhaps we can remedy that." He thought for a

moment. "All we need to do is begin again. Start fresh as it were."

She narrowed her eyes. "What do you mean—start fresh?"

"My dear Miss Effington, I don't believe we've met. Please, permit me to introduce myself." He squared his shoulders and adopted a distinct air of formality. "I am Viscount Berkley, Reginald Berkley, Reggie to my closest friends, which I am not overly fond of because it sounds more like the name one would give a hound rather than a gentleman, yet I endure it nonetheless. The aforementioned closest friends, if questioned, would call me of relatively good character, often amusing, an excellent son and thoughtful brother, all in all a decent sort in spite of what anyone may have heard to the contrary. I pay my debts promptly, care deeply for those who are in my employ or under my protection, and am unfailingly pleasant to small children and domesticated animals."

"You failed to mention infamous."

"I failed to mention it because, until this very morning, I had never been called infamous."

She studied him skeptically. "Never?"

He nodded. "Not once. However, I am at your service, Miss Effington." He swept an exaggerated bow. "My charm, my infamy, anything you may wish."

"Anything?"

"Anything at all."

For a long moment she stared at him, and all manner of possibilities came to mind. Most of them highly improper, completely scandalous, and absolutely sinful. She firmly pushed each and every one out of her mind.

"And you are?" he prompted.

"Oh yes, of course." She dropped a polite curtsey. "I am Miss Effington, Cassandra, Cassie to my dearest friends, which I rather like probably because it doesn't sound at all like the name of a hound."

He laughed and she grinned.

"My closest friend is also my twin sister, Lady St. Stephens. I am the daughter of Lord and Lady William, William and Georgina Effington, my uncle is the Duke of Roxborough, which means I have an endless number of Effington relations, including three brothers, all of whom have always believed I should be watched closely."

He raised a brow. "Why?"

"Because they have always felt I would be the sister to tumble headlong into scandal," she said without thinking and at once wished she could take the words back.

His eyes widened with curiosity. "Indeed. Dare I ask why?"

"My outspoken nature, I suspect." It was pointless to avoid the subject now that she had foolishly brought it up. She drew a deep breath. "The attitude of my brothers has always been that a woman who refuses to curb the impulsive nature of her tongue will no doubt fail to curb other impulses as well."

"I see." He paused for a moment. "And are they right?"

"Not thus far. I have never strayed seriously beyond the bounds of proper behavior." She thought for a moment. "Except of course, for this." She gestured at the room. "My brothers view my work as not entirely scandalous but not especially proper, either. Indeed, they think it quite—"

"Eccentric?" He laughed.

"Exactly." She grinned. "Not merely that I enjoy the redecoration of other people's houses, but," she lowered her voice and leaned toward him in a conspiratorial manner, "that I do it for payment, which puts it in the most scandalous category of business."

He gasped and clasped his hand over his heart. "Not that."

"It's quite distressing, I know, but there you have it. Add to that the fact that I am as yet unmarried, and I suspect my brothers see my fate as nothing less than dire." She shook her head in mock dismay. "I shall truly become the eccentric Miss Effington. The unwed aunt to their children who does the oddest things with her days and is talked about by the rest of the family only in whispers. They will nod their heads and say what a shame it all is. If only she'd kept her mouth shut, her life would have been so much different." Cassie heaved a dramatic sigh and fluttered her eyelashes.

"Ah, but then it would not have been your life."

"What do you mean?"

"Only that you are shaping your life so that it suits you rather than others. You are doing precisely what you wish to do. Not many women, or men either, for that matter, can say that." Admiration sounded in his voice. "It takes a great deal of courage."

"Some would call it stupidity rather than courage."

"Perhaps, but I am not among them." His gaze trapped hers. "I cannot see your fate as dire but rather filled with excitement and adventure. I should think the whispers of any nieces and nephews would be along the lines of what a wonderful life she has and I should hope to grow up to be just like her."

"How very remarkable. Do you really think so?"

"Indeed I do, Miss Effington."

"My brothers would not agree."

"You are not living your life for your brothers but for yourself."

"Of course," she murmured. For a long moment she stared into his eyes, deep and gray and almost irresistible and could see reflected there this life that he predicted and wondered as well if that life would be lived alone. She could certainly see why he had the reputation he did. Why, the man wasn't merely charming, he was intelligent and well spoken and even kind. And extremely dangerous. She must not forget that.

"Yes, well, we shall see about the future." She cast him her brightest and most impersonal smile. "At the moment, my lord, I think we should attend to the business at hand." She gestured at the drawing room. "Is this the only room your mother wishes to have refurbished?"

"I'm not sure. I don't think so. I believe she intends all the public rooms in this part of the house to be decorated. Both drawing rooms, the dining room, possibly the ballroom, perhaps even the library, although that is my own personal favorite and I quite like it just as it is." His brows pulled together thoughtfully. "I must confess to you, Miss Effington, this is all rather new to me. It was no more than a scant few hours ago that I had any idea my mother viewed this house as being quite so—"

"Shabby?"

"Do you really think so?" He glanced around the room as if seeing it for the first time. "Perhaps it could do with a bit of . . ." He cast her a look of male helplessness and shrugged. "Something."

"Precisely why I'm here, my lord. I am an expert at," she grinned, "something. Now then." She stepped to the settee, picked up her sketchpad, and took the pencil she kept attached to the book by a ribbon. "I am eager to speak with your mother about her thoughts for the house and what sorts of things she prefers, what styles she likes. Will she be joining us soon?"

"My mother is not feeling well at the moment. She has taken to her bed and . . ." He paused abruptly and stared, as if she were the answer to a puzzle.

She wasn't at all sure she liked that look. "I do hope it is nothing serious."

He considered her for a moment longer. "I should have known."

"You should have known what?"

"Nothing, Miss Effington, nothing at all." A slow grin spread across his face. "I am confident she will regain her health at any moment."

"It might be best if I came back at another time."

"I believe that would be detrimental to my mother's plans." He chuckled.

"Certainly I was under the distinct impression she wanted to proceed with the redecoration at once."

"Ah yes, the plans for the house." He nodded. "That was exactly what I was thinking."

"I should speak to her, though. Do you think she's up to it?"

"Not today." He shook his head thoughtfully. "No, she has left this entirely in my hands."

"Really?" Cassie furrowed her brow. "How unusual. I must confess, my lord, I am more accustomed to working with the lady of the house than the gentleman. Gentlemen, at least from what their wives have told me, as well as my own experience with the male members of my family, tend to be reluctant to make changes in their surroundings, whether because of comfort or cost."

"You will find me not reluctant in the least. Indeed, I am quite eager to hear your thoughts on my home and how it can be improved." He straightened. "Would you care to see the rest of the house now? At least the rooms in question?"

"Yes, of course."

He offered his arm, and she hesitated. This was not a social occasion. She was here to perform a service. Still and all, it would be rude not to take his arm. She drew a deep breath and steeled herself against the disturbing feel of his firm muscles beneath the light touch of her hand.

He bit back a smile as if he were amused at her discomfort and worse, well aware of the odd effect he had on her. Did she have the same effect on him? It would certainly serve him right.

"I should probably tell you something about the house itself. It was constructed about a half century ago, I believe."

He led her through one room, then another and another.

The house would have been most confusing, but in the past year, she had seen several other houses of a comparable age, built along the same general floor plan: one room opening into the next, that room, opening into another and again until, if one continued to proceed in a clockwise direction, one ended up where one began. Altogether, it was somewhat larger than her family's home and smaller than her uncle's. It was indeed in need of refurbishing, but it had excellent lines and proportions—bones, as she thought of them.

They ended their tour in the drawing room in which they had begun.

"There you have it." Lord Berkley pulled his brows together. "In truth I have never given the house or its furnishings much consideration, but today I have seen it through your eyes. I must confess it's not quite up to snuff, is it?"

"If it was, my lord, you would not need me." She cast him her most professional smile.

"And that would be a great shame, Miss Effington." He smiled, and her stomach flipped at the oddly intimate nature of it. "As it is, you have a great deal of work on your hands. My dear Miss Effington, you may well have found a lifelong pursuit here at Berkley House."

"A lifelong pursuit?" Her voice rose. "What do you mean, a lifelong pursuit?"

"I daresay at some point we should probably want every room in the house refurbished. And it's an exceedingly large house." The corners of his mouth quirked upward in a wicked manner. "What did you think I meant?"

"Nothing," she said quickly. "Nothing at all." She forced a brisk note to her voice and started toward the door. "I have seen all that I need to see today. I should like to return as soon as possible with some preliminary drawings. The day after tomorrow I should think, if that is convenient for you?"

"I am at your complete disposal." His voice sounded behind her, and she suspected he was grinning in an annoyingly satisfied manner. A lifelong pursuit indeed.

She whirled to face him. "And perhaps then your mother will be up to meeting with me. It would be most beneficial at this point if I am to decorate it with her in mind."

"About that." He shook his head slowly. "You're not in truth doing this for my mother."

She pulled her brows together in confusion. "I'm not?"

"No indeed." His grin widened. "You're doing it for my wife."

Four

While honesty is indeed the best course, in dealing with the fairer sex, it is, on occasion, beneficial simply not to reveal too much. Omission rather than outright deceit. Although, deceit has its place. . . .

Anthony, Viscount St. Stephens

"Your wife?" Her eyes widened with shock. "You couldn't possibly have a wife."

He raised a brow. "Your surprise is most unflattering, Miss Effington. I know you have already declared we would not suit, but is it inconceivable to you that I could have a wife? That someone would wish to marry me?"

"Not at all, my lord." She stared in obvious disbelief. "But I, and most of the people I know, believe you to be unmarried."

"I never said I was married." He smiled coolly and struggled not to laugh out loud. For a woman who had already declared that she had no interest in him, she was certainly overset to learn he might not be available.

She narrowed her eyes in suspicion. "You said you had a wife."

"Did I?"

"You said I was to decorate this house for your wife. Therefore it's logical to assume there does indeed exist a wife."

"My apologies, Miss Effington. I should have said future wife."

She studied him for a moment, then shook her head. "You're not betrothed, either. I would certainly have heard about such an engagement."

"Would you?"

"Indeed I would." She cast him a smug smile. "I have extensive family and a great number of acquaintances. I would have heard about your betrothal before the proposal was out of your mouth."

He laughed. "I had no idea you were so well informed. I shall have to remember that."

"Yet, as I have heard nothing regarding your intention to marry—"

"What have you heard?"

"What?"

"About me." He studied her curiously. "What have you heard?"

"Come now, my lord, surely you don't—"

"Surely I do. In fact, I'm quite intrigued as to precisely what you have heard."

"The usual kinds of things for a man of your reputation. Inordinate gambling, illegal dueling, illicit liaisons—"

"Illicit liaisons?" He laughed.

She glared. "Why is it, my lord, whenever I confront you with one of your sins you seem both surprised and pleased?"

"I don't know." His grin widened. "Obviously, it's yet another flaw in my character. You have already determined I am not perfect."

She drew her brows together. "And I believe I have already apologized about that observation."

"Have you," he murmured. "I can't recall."

"Well, perhaps not specifically . . ."

"Nonetheless, I make no apologies about my lack of perfection. However, we are not discussing my deficits—"

"Are you betrothed, then?" Her voice was cool, as if the answer didn't matter to her in the least. He wondered if indeed it did. And why.

"No."

She shook her head. "Then I'm afraid I don't understand."

"Nor should you, although I am beginning to understand." The true purpose of his mother's so-called dying wish was becoming all too apparent. "My mother is convinced she is about to take her last breath—"

"Oh dear." Genuine sympathy sounded in Miss Effington's voice. "My mother said she was unwell, but I had no idea."

"It was quite unexpected and has come as something of a shock to me as well."

He resisted the urge to confess the suspicion he'd reached in the past hour that his mother's illness was feigned and nothing more than a ploy to entice an excellent marriage prospect into his presence. Pity his mother had no idea Miss Effington had already decided she had no interest in becoming the next Viscountess Berkley and no interest in him whatsoever, although there had been a moment or two when he'd wondered if she had perhaps changed her mind.

If she had, he'd be a fool to reveal his suspicions. He had no doubt she would not take kindly to the manipulations of his mother or anyone else. While Reggie was not especially pleased by his mother's plot, if indeed it was a plot, Miss Effington was a most intriguing young woman. Regardless of her previous declarations that they would not suit, it might well be worth the time and trouble to become better acquainted with her. After all, she could be wrong.

"My mother has long wished to see me happily wed."

"In that she is no different than most mothers," Miss Effington said wryly.

"She has the oddest notion that, in order to make a suitable match, I should have a suitable home." He shook his head. "Apparently, she has abandoned the idea that I can make such a match on my own and only the lure of a house refurbished in the latest style can attract an appropriate spouse."

Miss Effington snorted. "That's absurd."

"I thought so."

"Why, I'm certain you have any number of excellent qualities that would attract a suitable match."

"Are you?" He raised a brow. "I understood you thought I was most unsuitable."

"For myself you are. But I am rather," she thought for a moment, "discriminating."

"You shall quite turn my head, Miss Effington," he said wryly.

"Come now, my lord, we have been all through this." She rolled her gaze toward the ceiling. "It's your past that I object to. I have no desire for a man of a certain reputation."

"Infamous?"

"Yes." She nodded. "However, there are any number of eminently eligible ladies to whom reforming you would be a challenge they would leap at."

"I have never thought of myself as a challenge to be leapt upon."

"*At,*" she said firmly. "Not *upon.*"

"Pity." He grinned. "Still, I do like the idea of being a challenge."

"I'm not surprised," she murmured.

"What are my excellent qualities, then?"

"I have no doubt you are already well aware of each and every one." Her voice rang in the prim manner of a governess.

"Do humor me, Miss Effington. Besides," he considered her thoughtfully, "you have not been the least bit reticent to point out my faults, stomping on my pride rather thoroughly in the process, I might add."

"Your pride or your arrogance?"

"One and the same, I should think." He heaved an exaggerated sigh. "Regardless, you have quite wounded my pride or my arrogance or whatever you wish to call it, and the least you can do to make amends is tell me what these excellent qualities of mine are."

"That's fair I suppose. Very well. First of all," she ticked the qualities off on her fingers, "you have an honorable title, you are not unattractive, and I understand your fortune is respectable as well."

"You are well informed," he teased.

She ignored him. "You are an excellent rider. From what I saw this morning, at any rate."

"I did make a good show of it." He grinned.

"You have a great deal of charm—"

He nodded firmly. "Indeed I do."

"You can be most amusing."

"I should have gone on the stage." He blew a breath of regret. "I could have been famous."

She stared in disbelief, colored by definite amusement. "However, you are not overly humble."

He shrugged. "What would be the point?"

She cast him a reluctant smile. "You are kind to your mother."

"Don't forget small children and domesticated animals."

She laughed. "I could never forget small children and domesticated animals. All in all, my lord, you could be considered something of a catch."

"But not for you?"

"We have already determined that."

"It's my infamy again, isn't it?"

She nodded in a somber fashion that belied the teasing twinkle in her eye.

"I was afraid of that." He heaved a heartfelt sigh. "Nonetheless, I shall have to carry on."

She raised a brow. "Bravely, no doubt?"

"It's a quality you neglected to mention."

"Do forgive me."

"Of course." He waved away her comment. "However, it does seem a shame to let these excellent qualities of mine go to waste, therefore, Miss Effington."

He stepped closer to her, took her hand before she could protest, and raised it to his lips. His gaze trapped hers. Beneath the cool resolve in her blue eyes he was fairly certain he caught a glimpse of something else. A doubt possibly as to whether she'd been too hasty in dismissing him. A question perhaps as to whether they might indeed suit after all.

"If we cannot be lovers. . . ." he said in a low voice. Surprise flashed in her eyes at the scandalous suggestion, but she did not pull away. How very interesting. ". . . can we be friends?"

She stared at him for a long moment. Indecision warred with interest.

"My companions, even your cousin Helmsley, will tell you I am a very loyal friend. A friend who can be counted on in times of crisis."

"I have any number of friends," she murmured, her gaze still locked to his.

"One can never have too many friends, Miss Effington." He brushed his lips across the back of her hand and felt her shiver beneath his touch. Very good.

She drew a deep breath, pulled her hand from his grasp, and stepped back, as if to put a safe distance between them.

Very good indeed.

"You're right, my lord, and I accept your kind offer of friendship. Besides, we shall be dealing with one another a great deal through the refurbishment of your house. All will go that much more smoothly if we get on well together." She favored him with a too bright smile. A smile that struck him as hiding more than it revealed. "Perhaps, when I return, your mother will—"

"I doubt that." His voice rang a bit too cheerily, and she cast him an odd look. He cleared his throat. "What I mean to say is while I am confident that she will recover, I do not expect her recovery to be quite so quick as to see her out of bed within the next few days."

"Do give her my best." She turned and headed to the foyer, her step brisk, as if she could not wait to depart.

"Of course."

He skirted around her to reach the foyer a step in front of her and signaled to Higgins to call for her carriage. A middle-aged woman sat on a bench near the door and stood at their appearance. A maid, probably, and no doubt Miss Effington's chaperone for her appointment here today.

"I shall see you the day after tomorrow then."

"Good day." Miss Effington smiled pleasantly, nodded at her maid, who fell in step behind her, and sailed out the door Higgins opened in perfect timing to her pace. Reggie stared thoughtfully after her.

Higgins closed the door and glanced at Reggie. "Is there something else, my lord?"

"I'm not entirely sure. And I'm not entirely sure I wish there to be."

Miss Effington was a confusing contradiction in a most compelling package. She was independent and stubborn when it came to doing precisely as she pleased, as evidenced by this so-called business venture of hers. She didn't so much as attempt restraint in what she said. She was opinionated and judgmental.

Yet in spite of all that, she did not seem to take the rules of society lightly. She did not travel unaccompanied, and he noted a distinct tendency to be a bit sanctimonious and even stuffy.

But she was also lovely and amusing, with a sharp wit and an air of intelligence about her. She would be a challenge for any man, and life with her would never be boring. Indeed, Miss Effington would likely be an adventure to well fill the rest of a man's days.

"I'm afraid I don't quite understand, sir."

"Nor do I, Higgins." Reggie shook his head. "Women in general are a curious lot. I daresay—" He stopped and studied the older man. "Do you think my mother is really ill?"

"I have never known Lady Berkley to feign illness before, my lord."

"That's exactly what you said earlier today, and I should have caught it the first time. Because she has never done it before does not mean she is not doing it now." Reggie shook his head. "You can be an evasive devil, Higgins, but I shan't press you on this. Divided loyalties and all that. Let me ask you something else then."

"Yes, sir?"

"Speaking in a strictly hypothetical manner, do you think my mother wishes me to be wed so much that she is willing to pretend to be on her deathbed to put me into close proximity to a lady of good family who would indeed be an excellent match? Is she that devious, do you think?"

"Most certainly, sir, although perhaps devious is too harsh a word." Higgins's brow furrowed slightly. Reggie had rarely seen him so expressive. "I have always thought Lady Berkley is far more clever, and far less frivolous, than most people give her credit for."

Reggie studied him carefully. "Do you know something I should know?"

"I think not, sir." Higgins paused. "That is, nothing you would be better off knowing, therefore it is accurate to say I know nothing you should know."

Reggie raised a brow. "Divided loyalties again, Higgins?"

"I have only your best interests at heart, sir."

"Of course." Reggie thought for a moment. "Do you think my mother has only my best interests at heart as well?"

"Undoubtedly, sir."

"Then I suspect I am in for a great deal of trouble." Reggie blew a resigned breath. "But then I would wager you already knew that."

"Indeed, sir." Higgins's expression was properly neutral, but there was a definite spark in his eyes. "And that too is something you are better off not knowing."

"I was barely aware of his existence before our meeting after the race yesterday morning, yet I am confident I have never met a man who is quite as annoying as he is." Cassie prowled the perimeter of her sister's beautifully appointed parlor. "Or as confusing, which serves to make him all the more annoying."

"I imagine it is something of a new experience for you," Delia said mildly. She sat on a settee perfectly proportioned for the room, a cup of tea in her hand and an amused smile on her lips. "I can't remember any man ever having had the upper hand with you."

"He doesn't have the upper hand," Cassie said sharply. "He has no hand at all. Nor will he. Ever."

"My apologies. I mistakenly assumed he was winning in this game you play with men."

Cassie pulled up short and stared at her sister. "I don't play games with men."

"Of course not. The fact that you have a few well-practiced phrases that you advise can be used in any number of situations would never be considered part of a game. For example . . ." Delia adopted a sultry tone. "I fear, my lord, you have me at a disadvantage." She fluttered her eyelashes and sighed dramatically.

"Oh, that." Cassie shrugged. "That's not . . ." She caught her sister's amused gaze. "Well, perhaps it is. Perhaps it's all one enormous, endless game, this pursuit of women by men and men by women with wedded bliss as the ultimate prize."

"Not always," Delia murmured.

"Always," Cassie said firmly. "Why, look at you."

"I wouldn't if I were you."

"Nonsense." Cassie waved away the objection. "You are the very picture of happiness in marriage. Oh, certainly, it was not especially easy to come by, and this is your second try, but well worth it nonetheless. Therefore if this is indeed a game, you are most definitely a victor. Don't you agree?"

"Yes, I suppose so, but we are not talking about me." Delia set her cup down on the table in front of her in a deliberate manner. "We are talking about you and Lord Berkley and the game you are playing with him."

"I am not playing a game with him. I have no interest in him whatsoever." She pushed aside the vaguest twinge of doubt and continued her aimless trek around the room, following a path along the edge of the Aubusson carpet selected specifically as a counterpoint to the high, embellished ceiling. "And furthermore, I've told him so."

Delia's eyes widened. "You told him what, exactly?"

"I told him we would not suit." Cassie straightened a painting on the wall a mere fraction of an inch. "I told him I had no interest in a man of his infamous reputation."

"Infamous?" Delia laughed. "And how did he respond to that?"

"He seemed rather pleased to be considered infamous, although I can't imagine he hasn't been called that before." Cassie glanced at her twin over her shoulder. "Furthermore, he agreed. That we will not suit, I mean. And for the life of me, I cannot determine why I find his agreement so blasted annoying."

Delia studied her sister carefully. "Why do you think you and he would not suit?"

"Because I have no interest in reforming a rake." Cassie had made the statement so many times that it flowed from her lips without conscious thought.

"Why not?"

"Why not?" Cassie turned toward her sister. "I should think that would be obvious."

"It's not, nor has it ever been. Why not, Cassie? You've made this declaration over and over again since the very first days of our coming out and I've always wondered why you were unyielding on the topic. Indeed, I've long considered it one of the contradictions of nature itself that you are so adamant about this, especially as the men who have typically pursued you have been the very kind you have never expressed interest in."

"Perhaps that's why." The light tone in her voice belied the restlessness that gripped her. "Men have always assumed, our brothers included, that I would be the one of us most prone to scandalous behavior. Of course, events have proved they were mistaken."

"Of course," Delia muttered.

Delia was never especially pleased when references were made to her past indiscretions, indiscretions that had ended in not one but two marriages, although it was a continued source of satisfaction to Cassie that Delia was the twin who had been the center of scandal. On the other hand, Delia's life had turned out beautifully, so perhaps scandal was a small price to pay.

"For the most part, the men who have pursued me have rarely done so with marriage in mind—"

"Not that you have given them the opportunity to prove otherwise."

"I admit that, and I think my course of action has always been both proper and sensible. But," Cassie met her sister's gaze, "what if they were right all along?"

"What if who was right about what?" Delia stared in confusion.

"Everyone. Our brothers, men in general, everyone." Cassie drew a deep breath. "What if they were right about me all along? What if I am the sister most prone to scandal?"

"*Most prone* is no longer accurate. *Equally prone* is perhaps more precise." Delia grinned. "But I shall welcome the company."

"As well you should, as it is entirely your fault."

"My fault?"

Cassie nodded. "Your past actions and difficulties have led me to reexamine my own life."

"I'm glad I could be of help," Delia said under her breath.

"I am completely serious about this. I too have wondered why I am so set against any kind of involvement with men of a questionable reputation. Everyone seems to agree reformed rakes make excellent husbands. Lord knows, I have no lack of confidence, and surely if anyone can reform such a man, it would be me."

Delia choked back a laugh.

Cassie ignored her. "I suspect it's due to the behavior of our brothers. I would certainly pity a woman foolish enough to risk her heart with any one of them. But I think what I really fear isn't so much being hurt as it is"—she caught her sister's gaze—"that in many ways I am just like them."

"Like these women?"

"No." Cassie dropped into a nearby chair that nicely complimented her sister's settee. "That I am just like our brothers."

"I scarcely think—"

"That I am indeed drawn to scandalous behavior." She leaned forward. "That once I turn down that road to impropriety and scandal and ruin and disaster, I shall never turn back."

"Cassie—"

Cassie's voice rose. "I have fought my entire life against this urge to be wild and free in spirit and do precisely what I want and damn the consequences."

"I have not noticed any particular reticence up until now," Delia said dryly.

"Oh, certainly, I have always spoken my mind, and yes, there have been a few incidents through the years," Cassie ignored the skeptical look on her sister's face, "barely worth mentioning, I might add. And indeed I am currently involved in an enterprise of a business nature that many consider unseemly, even improper, but I have in truth held myself in check."

"Thank God," Delia murmured.

"I think, somewhere deep inside, I want to *be* a rake, a rogue or a scoundrel. Maybe that's exactly the sort of person I truly am. And Lord help me, in spite of everything I've always sworn"—she winced at saying the words aloud—"that is precisely the type of man I want, even though I know in my very bones, such a man would lead me down that ghastly road."

"To scandal and impropriety?"

"Don't forget ruin and disaster."

"I could never forget ruin and disaster." Delia shook her head. "I had no idea. You've never said a word to me about this."

"Yes, well, you'd never said a word to me about your desire for adventure and excitement until you'd already run off with your first husband and returned home a widow." Cassie slumped back into the chair. "Apparently there are some secrets we can never share with even those closest to us."

"Apparently." Delia refilled her cup in a slow, deliberate manner, as if she needed the time to choose her next words. "So now that you have had this revelation about yourself, what are you going to do about it?"

"Do?" Cassie shook her head. "Nothing."

Delia raised a brow. "Nothing at all?"

"Nothing at all." Cassie plucked at an errant thread on the arm of the chair. "I shall continue to live my life exactly as I have thus far. In truth, I see no need to change anything."

"You don't?"

"Absolutely not," Cassie said firmly. "Understanding my nature, accepting it through the very act of confession to you, simply makes it easier to control."

"I see."

"Furthermore, I see no need to change my mind about the kind of man I wish to marry."

"The mythical paragon who can't possibly exist save in a romantic novel?"

"You needn't take that—"

"Let me see. What is it you want again? Ah, yes." Delia thought for a moment, and Cassie steeled herself. "You want a man who is respectable but not too respectable. Exciting but not too exciting. A man neither too strong nor too weak. Neither dull nor dangerous."

"It sounds rather silly when you say it." Odd, Cassie had never especially thought of her requirements in a husband as silly before; rather, they'd seemed solid and practical. At this moment, however, her sister's list of Cassie's qualifications sounded quite absurd.

"It's always sounded silly." Delia studied her sister. "But I suppose it's a good sign that you at last recognize it as such." She shook her head. "You're looking for a man who is nothing short of perfect and, dear heart, such a man cannot possibly exist. And if he did, your Mister Perfect—"

"Lord Perfect, if you please," Cassie muttered.

"*Lord Perfect* would bore you to death before your vows were barely said. It's the imperfect nature of men that makes them endearing. If they were perfect, they'd be unbearable." She smiled in a confidential manner. "Of course, we can never let them know how imperfect they really are."

"I think they suspect."

"Certainly, but they don't know that we know." Delia grinned wickedly, and Cassie laughed in spite of herself. "So," Delia began again. "What are you going to do?"

"I'm going to refurbish Berkley House for Lord Berkley's," Cassie tried not to choke on the words, "future wife."

Delia's eyes widened. "I was not aware he was betrothed."

"He isn't, but his mother is ill and she would like to see him wed before she dies." Cassie furrowed her brow thoughtfully. "It's very odd. He appears to care for her, yet he does not seem overly dismayed at the idea of her death."

"Perhaps he's confident of her recovery?"

"Yes, I'm certain that's it." Cassie had had the distinct impression that his certainty had grown with every word that had passed between them at his house, but surely she was mistaken. Even so, it was most perplexing. "At any rate, Lady Berkley has the most peculiar notion that a newly refurbished house will help attract a suitable match."

"How very strange. Although," Delia grinned, "I would not put it past our own mother to do such a thing."

"Indeed, Mother encouraged me to take this commission. For the sake of Lady Berkley's health."

"Really?" Delia stared at her sister thoughtfully. "I thought she was no more delighted by your work than our brothers are. Her encouragement is somewhat hard to believe."

"She claims Lady Berkley is a dear friend and that she would consider it a favor if I were to accept her as a client." Cassie wrinkled her nose. "Except that Lady Berkley is bedridden and I won't be dealing with her but with her son."

"Ah, we are back to Lord Berkley then."

"I suppose you could say that."

Delia considered her twin for a long, assessing moment. "What is it about the man that annoys you so?"

"The way he seems to see right through me," Cassie said without thinking, then at once wished she could take the words back. "Did I say that aloud?"

Delia bit back a smile. "Yes, you did."

"I didn't mean to. What I meant to say was that I find his arrogance annoying. And his confidence. His too polished manner. His wit. His charm. His laugh—"

"You find his laugh annoying?"

"It's contagious." Cassie shook her head. "It makes me want to laugh with him. *He* makes me want to laugh. And his eyes, Delia, he has the most intriguing gray eyes. They are positively endless. You want to fall headfirst into them."

"Do you?"

"Indeed you do. It's most disquieting. And he's quite nice, really. And kind. To"—she thought for a moment—"small children and domesticated animals."

"And you know this because . . ."

"Why, he told me."

"So you believe him to be honest as well?"

"I believe so. Under most circumstances, that is."

"It sounds to me," Delia said, choosing her words with care, "that what you find most annoying about this man is that you like him."

"Oh dear." Realization slammed into Cassie, and she slumped deeper into the chair with the shock of it. "It does sound very much like that, doesn't it?"

"It sounds like you may well more than like him."

"Absolutely not." Cassie sat up straight. "I will not allow anything more than friendship to pass between us. We have already agreed to be friends—"

"Have you?"

"You needn't smirk like that. It's completely insignificant." Cassie waved her sister's comment away. "We will be spending a certain amount of time in one another's company, and it would simply be more pleasant if we were not constantly sniping at each other."

Delia laughed. "You didn't tell me he snipes."

"He doesn't." Cassie grimaced. "I do. But I shall watch my tongue around him from this moment forth."

"Because he's kind to small children?"

"Yes." Cassie's voice rang with a firm note. "And because I have been rather rude to him up to this point."

"When will you see him again?"

"Tomorrow. I will have some preliminary drawings to show him so we can begin to decide what kind of setting we can provide for the future Viscountess Berkley."

Delia shook her head and chuckled in a knowing

manner at least as annoying as anything Lord Berkley had done.

"Delia, regardless of the fact that I apparently harbor a tiny bit of fondness for Lord Berkley, he is not the match for me. We do not suit as anything more than friends. He is not the kind of man I wish to spend the rest of my life with. He is not my Lord Perfect."

Cassie leaned toward her sister. "And he never will be."

"So how is the eccentric Miss Effington?" Marcus handed Reggie a glass of brandy.

"Stubborn, with strong opinions she does not hesitate to express." Reggie sipped Marcus's excellent liquor thoughtfully and settled back in the chair he had long ago claimed as his own in the spacious library at Pennington House.

The two friends had discussed all manner of critical and frivolous subjects in this very room through the years, and, even though Marcus was now married, the Pennington library continued to be their sanctuary. Reggie blessed whatever gods of fortune—as well as the helping hand of Marcus's mother—that had led Gwendolyn Townsend, now Lady Pennington, to Marcus. The earl could well have ended up wed to a woman who would not be as tolerant of the frequent presence of her husband's oldest friend.

"In truth, Marcus, I find myself wanting to either throttle her or," he grinned, "kiss her."

Marcus raised a brow. "Do you indeed? I thought you and the lovely Miss Effington had decided you would not suit?"

"Miss Effington decided we would not suit before we had so much as had a single conversation. Remember, she does not want a man of my," he cleared his throat, "*disreputable nature.* However, I am not entirely sure she feels quite as strongly about that as she once did. Now that we have begun to get to know one another, that is."

"And how do you feel?"

"If you're going to remind me that I swore I would not turn my affections toward Miss Effington, you needn't. I remember exactly what I said."

"As do I. You said you would not fall heels over head again without encouragement from the lady in question." Marcus studied him over the rim of his glass. "Has there been such encouragement?"

"No." Reggie thought for a moment. The mere fact that the woman gazed up at him with the oddest hint of anticipation in her eye and seemed to hold her breath when he so much as took her arm could not really be considered encouragement. "Not that I can see, at any rate. But she has agreed to be friends."

"Friends?" Marcus's brow furrowed. "I take it this is a good sign?"

Reggie chuckled. "I don't know, but it should be very interesting to find out."

Marcus narrowed his eyes. "What are your intentions, Reggie?"

"I don't know that either."

"You're not—"

"No, no, don't be absurd." Reggie waved off his friend's concern. "At the moment, my only intention is to provide Miss Effington with whatever assistance she needs in the refurbishment of my house. I shall be both polite and pleasant and behave toward her much as I would any woman of my acquaintance with whom I am friendly. Much as I behave toward your wife, I should think."

"Oh, that should impress her," Marcus said wryly. "Gwen views you very much as the brother she never had."

"Does she?" A pleasant sense of delight washed through Reggie. He'd liked the new Lady Pennington, Gwen, since the moment he'd first met her, and to know she returned his friendly affection was gratifying. "I must say I'm really quite flattered and pleased."

"I wouldn't be if I were you. Like any good sister when faced with an unwed brother, I suspect she will soon turn her attention to matchmaking."

"Why would you suspect that?"

Marcus shrugged. "Comments she makes that have become more frequent lately. About how happy we are and how alone you appear to be."

"Good God. First my mother, now your wife." Reggie drew a deep swallow of the brandy for fortification against the machinations of the women of his world. All of whom, at the moment, seemed to have but one goal in mind.

"What about your mother?" Concern sounded in Marcus's voice. "She hasn't taken a turn for the worse, has she?"

"No, but I certainly wouldn't put it past her." Reggie shook his head. "I'm not certain, mind you, but I suspect this whole business of I'm-dying-refurbish-my-house-with-the-help-of-Miss-Effington is for the sole purpose of throwing the eligible Miss Effington and myself together."

"Or your mother could really be dying." Marcus sipped his brandy thoughtfully.

"I tell you, Marcus, every instinct I have tells me this is a plot. My mother and your mother are close friends. Your mother maneuvered the circumstances of your marriage, and quite successfully, I might add. With you as a sterling example, why on earth would you think my mother wouldn't do exactly the same thing?"

"Point taken. Still." Marcus raised his glass in a salute. "She could be dying."

Reggie scoffed. "She's never been ill a day in her life. And one rarely goes from perfect health on a Tuesday to one's deathbed on Wednesday without a physician able to find any cause whatsoever. I would wager a great deal she'll recover immediately upon my betrothal."

"To Miss Effington?"

"To anyone. I'm not entirely sure how she hit upon the idea of Miss Effington rather than some other young woman, but Miss Effington did mention her own mother commenting on my mother's health."

"Sounds very much like a conspiracy to me."

"Doesn't it, though," Reggie said darkly. "As much as I would like to marry, I do not intend to allow my mother to select my bride for me."

Marcus cleared his throat.

"It doesn't always work out as well as it did for you." Reggie raised his glass to his friend. "You, old man, are the lucky exception."

Marcus laughed. "I am indeed lucky." He studied his friend for a moment. "So, are you determined then not to be caught in this alleged plot?"

"Absolutely." Reggie swirled the brandy in his glass. "Probably." He shrugged and met his friend's gaze. "I don't know."

"That is a problem."

"No, it's not." Reggie struggled for the right words. "As much as I disagree with Miss Effington in that I think we would suit rather well, I absolutely refuse to lose my heart to a woman who will not return my affection. I meant it when I said I would not tread that path again.

"Miss Effington has told me in no uncertain terms that she is not interested in me. I will not set myself up for disaster yet again." He drew a deep breath. "Besides, there is something about the woman, I can't explain exactly what, some sort of odd feeling deep in the pit of my stomach, that tells me loving and losing this particular woman would be far more devastating than anything I've ever known." He met his friend's gaze. "I would be a fool to pursue anything beyond friendship with Miss Effington."

"I see." Marcus studied him in a noncommittal manner that was most unnerving.

"Aren't you going to say anything?"

Marcus shook his head. "Not one word."

"You want to, though. I can see it in your eyes." Reggie leaned forward. "You can barely contain yourself. Come now, tell me what you're thinking."

"Very well." Marcus reached for the brandy decanter, as always conveniently placed on a side table, and refilled his glass. "You are no fool, Reggie, as you already recognize the danger this woman presents. I too would hate to see you fall back into old habits. However," he reached forward to top off his friend's glass, his voice deceptively casual, "I have always thought that it is almost impossible to truly recognize danger until it is bearing down upon you. Until it is, as it were, too late."

Reggie stared for a long moment, then slowly shook his head. "Not this time, Marcus, I will not permit it." He paused, then blew a resigned breath. "While I am certain that you are mistaken, and I am confident in my ability to be the master of my own fate, there's something else that has occurred to me that will no doubt strengthen your belief in your infallibility."

"I do enjoy it when that happens," Marcus grinned.

Reggie braced himself. "Don't you think this house refurbishing venture of hers—"

"Business is what it is."

"Yes, of course, this *business*, then, is a bit odd for a woman to take on?"

"Odd?" Marcus snorted. "Odd is an understatement and precisely why her brother referred to her as eccentric."

"Setting that aside, do you think she is doing this because she wants to or," he met his friend's gaze directly, "because she has to?"

"Effingtons are notorious for doing precisely what they please, and she would not be the first woman in that family to dabble in enterprises, even businesses, best left to men. I daresay this particular Miss Effington would not do anything she did not wish to do."

"I don't mean that exactly," Reggie said slowly. "I was just wondering . . ."

"Yes?"

"Is it possible her family could be facing financial difficulties?"

"The Effingtons?" Marcus laughed. "They're one of the wealthiest families in the country."

"As an entire family, perhaps, but I'm wondering if her father, Lord William, might not be—"

"That's absurd."

"Her brother did beg off paying me the wager I won."

"Even so." Marcus shook his head. "Reggie, you are jumping to unfounded conclusions."

"They're not in the least bit unfounded," Reggie said staunchly. "Why else would a young woman of good family put herself in a position—"

"Bloody hell, I can't believe it!" Marcus leaned forward and stared at his friend. "You're doing it again!"

"Doing what again?" Reggie forced an innocent note to his voice.

Marcus leapt to his feet and stared at his friend. "Did you think I wouldn't notice?"

Reggie sipped his brandy. "Notice what?"

Marcus groaned. "Don't make me say it."

"I have no idea what you're talking about," Reggie said coolly.

"Hah!" Marcus snorted. "Very well then. Allow me to explain."

"Please do," Reggie murmured, knowing full well what Marcus was about to say. Reggie had already acknowledged the very same thing to himself.

"Miss Effington has no interest in you—"

"I believe we have established that."

"And Miss Effington, or rather her family, might possibly be in financial straits." Marcus crossed his arms over his chest. "Which puts her firmly in the category of a woman in need of assistance. A damsel in distress!" He aimed an accusing finger at his friend. "Exactly the sort of woman you have always lost your heart to and exactly the sort of woman who has always mangled it."

"Not this time, Marcus," Reggie said coolly.

Marcus narrowed his eyes in suspicion. "Why would this time be any different?"

"Because this time, old friend, I am well aware of the situation and well aware of my own weaknesses."

"Aware or not, once again you have found a woman in need of rescuing and you are charging ahead!"

"Not in the least." Reggie shook his head firmly. "Miss Effington and I have agreed to be friends, nothing more. As her friend, the least I can do is aid her in her monetary problems. I shall increase the fee for her services, but it shall go no further than that. Indeed, I would do no less for you."

"You almost deserve each other, you know." Marcus snorted in disgust and dropped back into his chair. "The infamous Lord Berkley and the eccentric Miss Effington."

Reggie laughed. "That does sound like a match made in heaven."

"Or somewhere considerably lower," Marcus said under his breath. He fell silent for a moment, then met his friend's gaze, a distinct gleam in his eye. "I believe I shall rescind my order to Gwen that she abandon any notion of finding a match for you."

Reggie raised a brow. "You issued an order to your wife? And you have lived to tell about it?"

"We have developed a unique system of dealing with one another. I issue orders. She ignores them. I feel better for having put my foot down and she does exactly as she pleases." Marcus smiled wryly. "It would be most annoying if we did not care for one another."

Reggie laughed and pushed aside the twinge of jealousy that struck him at his old friend's happiness.

"However the topic at hand is not my life but yours. And now that I know all the details, I am convinced your Miss Effington is right." Sympathy shone in Marcus's eyes, but his voice was firm. "You and she will not suit."

"You could be wrong," Reggie said idly. "She could be wrong."

"Do you wish her to be?"

"I don't know. There would be a certain amount of satisfaction to it, but I don't really seem to know much of anything when it comes to Miss Effington. It is most annoying." He blew a long breath. "Nonetheless, you and she are probably right: There is no possibility of a future between the two of us.

"She is not my Miss Effington, Marcus." The oddest feeling of regret passed through him. "And she never will be."

Five

Women are charming, delightful creatures who should be savored and enjoyed. But under no circumstances should a rational gentleman attempt to understand one.

C. Effington

"These are good," Lord Berkley murmured, his attention focused on the sketches spread out before him on the long table in the Berkley House library. "Quite good."

Cassie brushed aside the unexpected rush of pleasure at the compliment. "They're very rough. Nothing more than initial thoughts on paper, really."

"No need to be modest, Miss Effington, these are brilliant." He straightened and studied her with an appreciative eye. "You have a great deal of talent."

"You're kind to say so, my lord, but you should know I'm not the least bit modest," she said firmly, returning her gaze to the sketches. "I am well aware of my own abilities."

He laughed. "I would be surprised if you weren't. I daresay any woman doing work such as this for payment as opposed to her own personal satisfaction would have to have a certain amount of confidence if only to survive."

She glanced at him. "Would you feel similarly if I were a man?"

He hesitated, as if realizing he treaded on dangerous ground. "Yes."

She raised a brow.

"Well, perhaps not entirely. Surely you do understand, Miss Effington, for a young woman of excellent family, in truth, for any young woman, to do what you do is highly unusual."

"Of course I understand that." She shrugged. "The decoration of houses, at least for payment, has long been the domain of men, of architects and the like."

"And it doesn't bother you to intrude upon that domain?"

"Not in the least. What bothers me is that women of talent in this world have few acceptable ways to use whatever gifts God has seen fit to grant us outside of our own homes. Yet that is the way of it and I doubt it shall ever change."

"I see. You are accepting but not content."

"They are two entirely different things, aren't they?" She furrowed her brow and considered the idea. "I should be quite content, really. Up till now, I have never known strife or tragedy or need. Indeed, my life to this point has been one of privilege."

"Still, in spite of that, you have turned your skills to your benefit in what I understand is a quite profitable business."

"But don't forget, my lord, I am not like most women. I," she cast him a rueful smile, "am eccentric."

"It seems to me eccentric is used to describe anyone or anything who does not meekly fit into the role the world finds acceptable. In your case, Miss Effington, I am beginning to think eccentric is a high compliment."

"Do feel free to pass on your sentiments to my brothers, although I would wager that they will not agree with you."

"I should take that bet and allow you to make a tidy profit from it." Lord Berkley grinned, and again she noted what a pleasant smile he had. Genuine was the word for it. As if he was truly delighted by the world and all he saw in it. It was an intriguing thought. Far too intriguing.

Cassie turned her attention back to her drawings. "As I said, these are quite preliminary. There is still more planning to be done and endless decisions to be made before we can bring in painters and paper-hangers."

"Preliminary or not, I like your ideas."

"Do you?" Her gaze scanned the papers lying on the desk.

While she was pleased with her efforts thus far, she was not at all used to dealing with a gentleman rather than a lady. She wasn't nearly as familiar with male sensibilities regarding such things as furniture and fabric, and in spite of her avowed confidence in her own abilities, she'd been concerned as to whether he would approve of her designs. Beyond that, the ladies she'd worked with previously were as enamored of her name and family as they were of her taste. She was fairly certain Lord Berkley was not similarly inclined.

"I do indeed. Although I admit I might be less approving were you to include this particular room in your plans."

"As per your instructions, I was to leave your library alone. If you have changed your mind—"

"Absolutely not," he said quickly and turned to study the library. "I don't see a single thing in this room I would wish to change. I like the way it looks, and more, I like the way it, well, feels."

His gaze moved slowly around the room as if to take in every detail, well known and cherished. Richly paneled walls were hung with ancient family portraits and far more contemporary paintings she recognized as the works of Mr. Turner and Mr. Constable. At either end, floor-to-ceiling shelves filled to overflowing with finely bound books with the appearance of age and use. It was a masculine room that fairly shouted of the affairs and concerns and business of men and men alone. She would have been surprised if Lord Berkley, or indeed any man, would want such a bastion of masculinity disturbed. Surprised and possibly disappointed.

"There is an air about it," he said, in the manner of a man satisfied with his world.

"One could say that," she murmured.

He glanced at her with obvious amusement. "I take it you don't like the lingering scent of well-worn, comfortable leather chairs coupled with the hint of musty books?"

"You failed to mention the vague suggestion of tobacco and brandy. It's a very . . . masculine atmosphere."

"I hadn't thought of it that way, but I daresay you're right." He raised a curious brow. "Does it bother you? Being in yet another male domain?"

"Not in the least." She waved off his question. "We have already established that I have no qualms whatsoever about invading certain male territory, although I will confess there are limits to my boldness. For example, I would never set foot in a gentleman's club. It wouldn't be at all proper."

He choked back a laugh.

She continued as if she hadn't heard. "However, I quite agree with you: There is a comforting feel here of tradition and affection, too, I think."

He cast her an approving look, then returned to his perusal of the room. "I admit, though, that, while I do love the very smell of this place, the air I speak of isn't scent. Rather it's memory. My father and I spent hours together here."

"How long has he been gone?" she asked softly.

"Nearly a dozen years now, but in this room I feel very close to him. I liked him, a great deal really, and as a man, not merely a father, and I think he liked me as well. I think he was pleased with me." He paused for a long moment, and Cassie wondered if he was recalling those long-ago days. At last, he glanced at her with a sheepish expression. "Forgive me, Miss Effington, I am not normally so sentimental."

"Take care, my lord, that you don't damage your reputation." The light note in her voice belied how touched she was at his obvious affection for his father. "I don't think you can be infamous and sentimental at the same time."

He laughed. "I shall have to watch myself then."

His gaze met hers, and she had the oddest sense that they had just reached an understanding. Perhaps they could indeed be friends. Perhaps they could be more.

Perhaps . . .

Absolutely not.

She firmly pulled her gaze from his and returned her attention to the sketches on the table, ignoring an odd fluttering sensation somewhere in the vicinity of her stomach.

"I've added paint here and there to indicate what I would suggest in terms of color, but as I employed watercolors, do keep in mind the shades are far paler than I ultimately intend. They are simply to indicate a family of color more than a specific hue. For example," she indicated the drawing of the dining room, "the color on paper here is more approximating a pink than a deeper shade. Something akin to a pomegranate seed, I should think, would be perfect in that room."

"Pomegranate seed?"

"Red?"

"Of course, yes, red," he murmured. "Excellent color."

She resisted the urge to grin. Whatever else Lord Berkley might be, he was very much a typical male, and in that respect, most amusing. "Thank you, my lord. And in this drawing room, I thought—"

"Forgive me for interrupting, Miss Effington," he said abruptly. "But this talk of fathers has brought to mind a question that has puzzled me. Is the rest of your family, your parents in particular, as disapproving as your brothers about your work?"

"To be honest, I'm not entirely sure." She thought

for a moment. "My father will tell you that Effington women, whether born into the family or married into it, are for the most part unique and even headstrong. They have a history of doing precisely as they wish." She flashed him a smile. "Father says it's in the blood."

"I believe I may have heard something of the sort." A teasing note sounded in his voice.

"He will further tell you that as long as a certain amount of scandal is avoided, he is content to let his daughters find their own way in life." At once she realized she had never quite understood before how unique that was. "In that I think I am exceedingly lucky."

"He is a most unusual man."

"Indeed he is."

"And what of your mother?"

"My mother is not overly pleased, although she is rather," she grinned, "*eccentric* in her own right. My mother is dedicated to the belief that our futures and our fortunes and our very fates are written in the stars. She believes as well in all manner of oddities like reincarnation and the reading of palms and tea leaves and cards."

"I see. She is superstitious then."

"Not at all." Cassie shook her head. "She considers it a science and will go on and on for hours in a detailed explanation of how such things were widely accepted by the ancients and have been employed for as long as man has been on the earth. Her vast knowledge of the subject, as well as her fervor, can be most fascinating." She laughed. "As well as most annoying."

"Perhaps she will do me the honor of espousing her convictions to me one day."

"Perhaps."

"After all, you and I have promised to be friends. I have already met two of your brothers, and I should very much like to meet your well-versed mother and your long-suffering father." His amused gaze met hers.

The thought flashed through her mind that, were it not for his reputation, he would be very much the kind of man she would not mind meeting her parents. It struck her as well that he would not see her mother as eccentric, or the rest of the Effingtons as odd, but rather he would find them interesting and even delightful. Much as she thought of them herself.

What a pity he was the kind of man he was and not the kind of man she wanted.

"I'm certain you will meet them at one function or another."

What kind of woman did he want?

She turned back to the drawings and forced a casual note to her voice. "Now then, while I am pleased that you like my proposals thus far, I confess to being at something of a disadvantage in not knowing what the lady who will occupy this house would like. She might not be the least bit fond of red."

"Pomegranate," he said with a grin.

"Or lemon yellow for that matter."

"I wish I could be of assistance but, as we have already established, there is not as yet either wife or fiancée. Of course, I'm certain there will be any number of prospects at whatever social function I am to attend tomorrow night."

"Lady Puget's ball?"

"I believe so. I should be happy to acquire a future viscountess at that very event if it would help your efforts." His lips didn't so much as twitch, but there was a definite laugh in his eyes.

"Would you, my lord?" She widened her eyes in a show of mock delight. "That would indeed make my work ever so much easier, and I would be eternally grateful as, I'm sure, will any woman you choose to honor with your attentions." She fluttered her lashes and gazed up at him.

He laughed. "Well said, Miss Effington."

"Better still, we can refurbish your house and then you can select a future wife on the basis of whether or not she matches the bed hangings," she said brightly.

"Indeed we could. I'd hate to have a wife who didn't match the bed hangings." A wicked look gleamed in his eye.

She ignored it. "It seems as good a quality as many I've heard."

"Ah yes, and you should know, as you have very definite requirements regarding the man you propose to marry. That being the mythical Lord Perfect, of course."

"I must say, I do rather resent the use of the name Lord Perfect." She pulled her brows together in annoyance. "It sounds ridiculous."

"Ridiculous or not, it is accurate. Or have your sentiments softened since we last spoke of this matter? Are you now willing to settle for a man who might be less than perfect? Lord Almost Perfect or Lord Nearly Perfect or even the Honorable Mr. Not Quite Perfect?"

"Lord Perfect is sounding better and better," she snapped. "Although I don't know why what I wish for in a spouse matters to you."

"In truth, it doesn't. I don't care at all. Or at least no

more so than I would care about anyone to whom I have offered my friendship. You have, however, piqued my curiosity. There is nothing more to it than that."

He shrugged. "I simply do not understand how an intelligent woman with the courage of her convictions and any number of other admirable qualities would want perfection in a man rather than excitement or adventure or the passion inherent in such a life."

"Then it's to your advantage that you do not need to understand, as this entire subject has nothing to do with you whatsoever."

She smiled firmly, turned on her heel, and crossed the room, stopping to give the appearance of examining an ancestral painting. In truth, however, her retreat was to hide her confusion, as well as to escape from the conversation.

The blasted man had gotten right to the heart of it with no effort at all. How could she possibly tell him, when she had only recently realized it herself, that such a man of excitement and adventure, a man with a wicked look in his eye and a confident smile on his lips, a man one might call *infamous,* would doubtless prove her downfall? That once she stepped on the path to ruin she would probably like it and there could be no turning back? No, a man who was perfect, or perfect by her definition at any rate, would provide a life without danger or difficulties. A life that was . . . perfect.

And if the price for perfection was the sacrificing of a bit of adventure or excitement or *passion*, it was well worth it.

She turned toward him. "Lord Berkley, I have seen what happens to women who lose their hearts and their virtue to men of questionable reputations."

"Infamous men?" He smirked.

"Yes." She rolled her gaze toward the ceiling. The annoying man obviously delighted in his infamous status. "As you have credited me with intelligence, you must admit it would be the height of stupidity to become involved with men of that sort, and most irresponsible as well. Why, anything could happen."

"Indeed it could." He narrowed his eyes in confusion. "What could happen?"

"Well, anything. Anything at all. And probably quite dire." She folded her arms over her chest. "I can't imagine that you, of all people, don't understand exactly what could happen to a woman in that situation."

"You are jumping to yet another conclusion, Miss Effington. In spite of my reputation, I cannot recall ever putting a woman in *that situation*, nor is it in my plans for the future."

The look on his face told her more than his mere words, and she hadn't a doubt as to his sincerity. Her opinion of him notched upward.

"I do apologize, my lord. I didn't mean—"

He waved away her words. "Tell me what could happen."

"Very well." She drew a deep breath. "I could be embroiled in scandal. My reputation could be ruined, along with the rest of my life. I could—"

"You could fall passionately in love."

She stared. "Why on earth would you mention love?"

He snorted. "Because you haven't, which begs the question as to why not."

"What do you mean?"

"My dear Miss Effington, not once in our discussions of what you want, or, more to the point, what you do not want in a match have you mentioned the word love." He studied her curiously. "Aren't you at all interested in love?"

"Well, certainly I—"

He stepped toward her. "Have you ever been in love?"

She debated whether or not to tell him the truth, then wrinkled her nose. "No."

His eyes widened in surprise. "Never?"

"Never."

"Not even once?"

"No, not once, not ever." She glared. "Have you?"

"Good God, yes."

She raised a brow. "More than once, I gather?"

"Definitely more than once."

"How many times?"

He thought for a moment. "After I reached my majority or before?"

"After, I should think," she said slowly.

"Oh, after, well then." His brow furrowed in thought. "I have no idea. Dozens?"

"Dozens!"

"Well, I shouldn't think it was hundreds." He shook his head. "It could be, I suppose, close to—no, no, it's definitely dozens."

She stared in disbelief. "Perhaps we are not talking about the same thing. There is a distinct difference between," she searched for the right word, "amorous liaisons, lust if you will, and love. Precisely how do you define love, my lord?"

"The same way everyone else does, I presume. Love is . . . well it's . . . that is to say . . ." He met her gaze directly, his voice level and unwavering. "Love, Miss Effington, is the process of standing at the edge of a precipice and allowing yourself to tumble forward, freely, with the sure and certain knowledge that you can fly."

"What if you can't?" she said without thinking. "What if you . . . you . . . plummet? What if, God forbid, you hit the bottom? What then?"

"Then you are bruised and battered and your heart is more than likely broken, but you pick yourself up. You mend. You heal, and when that precipice beckons once more, you do it again." He smiled ruefully. "The sheer joy of flying, Miss Effington, is well worth the risk."

"Good Lord, you're a poet!"

"Don't be absurd. I'm not in the least—" He looked inordinately pleased with himself. "Do you really think so?"

"I didn't say you were a good poet, but yes, I do. In truth, my lord, I think you are a romantic." She shook her head. "I can't imagine such a thing."

"And I cannot imagine a moment when you will not judge me based on who you think I am rather than who I really am." He huffed in obvious annoyance.

At once Cassie realized that perhaps she had pushed him too far. She inched toward the door. "I should take my leave."

"Not quite yet, Miss Effington." His tone was firm, and there was a resolute look in his eye.

Before she could protest, he grabbed her hand and pulled her to the bookshelves at one end of the room.

"My lord, what are you—"

"I know it goes against everything you believe in and your very nature but, for once, just once, do try to hold your tongue."

She opened her mouth, caught the all too threatening look in his eye, and pressed her lips tight together.

"Excellent. Now, then," he said, nodding at the opposite side of the room, "the shelves on that side of the library are filled with books of a factual or analytical nature. History, astronomy, geography, philosophy, and so forth. On this end, however, are works of literature and poetry and the creative genius of mankind."

His hungry gaze wandered over the book-lined shelves that reached upward endlessly toward the heavens. She wondered if he remembered that he still held her hand.

"While I have read many of the books on the far wall of the library, they were read primarily as part of my school studies rather than choice, although admittedly, the knowledge I gained has served me well. But these books, Miss Effington"—intensity and, yes, *passion* colored his voice—"waited for me until I could appreciate them, I think. I did not read a great deal in my youth, but in recent years I have read them all, some more than once."

"That's quite admirable, my lord," she murmured. Was he going to release her hand?

"Here are the works of Chaucer and Donne, Spenser and De Vere." He scanned the shelves. "Malory and Defoe. Defoe was one of the few authors I was fond of as a boy." He glanced at her. "Do you like Defoe, Miss Effington?"

"Most certainly," she said lightly, searching her mind for any detail on Defoe. "Who on earth could possibly not like Defoe. All that . . . um . . ."

"Adventure?" he suggested.

"Exactly." She nodded eagerly. The name Defoe was vaguely familiar, but she could not for the life of her place the author with his work, and she was not about to admit to Lord Berkley that while her sister was extremely well read, Cassie's own literary preferences were limited to the occasional frivolous novel and magazines filled with the latest in fashion and furnishings. "It's so . . . so . . . so adventurous."

"Indeed." He studied her curiously. "Then you enjoyed *Robinson Crusoe*?"

"I could not put it down." Relief coursed through her. How could her mind have been so muddled as to not remember Defoe wrote *Robinson Crusoe*? Certainly, she hadn't actually read it, but she was fairly certain Delia had and had probably mentioned the plot at some point. Not that Cassie could remember. "It was most enjoyable."

"Because of the adventurous nature of . . . the adventure?"

His gray eyes bored into hers as if challenging her to admit she hadn't read this particular book or any others. Perhaps if the man let go of her hand her mind would be clearer. It was highly improper and terribly forward of him even if he didn't seem to pay it the least bit of attention. What could one expect from a man of his reputation, anyway? Still, it was remarkably pleasant to have her hand enfolded in the warmth of his. And as it obviously didn't mean anything to him, why should it mean anything to her?

"Perhaps you like adventure far more than you're willing to admit?"

"Adventure in literature is an entirely different matter than adventure in reality," she said primly and made a halfhearted effort to pull her hand from his.

"Forgive me, Miss Effington." He pulled her hand to his lips and kissed it lightly, his gaze intent upon her own. He released her hand, and she pushed away a twinge of annoyance at the odd sensation of loss. "It was most improper of me to continue to hold your hand, but I fear I was carried away. No doubt it's probably no more than you expected from a man of my reputation."

She started to protest but decided against it. The man was arrogant enough without her confessing anything he might interpret as her enjoyment of his touch.

He clasped his hands behind his back and continued to search the shelves. "Do you have a favorite book, Miss Effington? Or a writer you're especially fond of?"

"A favorite?"

She did like the gentleman who wrote those fascinating bits of gossip in *Cadwallender's Weekly World Messenger*. And she did enjoy *Ackermann's Repository*, although admittedly that was mostly to keep up on the latest in fashion. And she had thoroughly read Mr. Hope's *Household Furniture and Interior Decoration*, even if *read* was an inaccurate term, as the bulk of the book consisted of drawings and depictions of furnishings and room arrangements. But favorite?

"It's so hard to choose just one," she said weakly.

"Indeed it is. Often I find that who I wish to read depends very much on the state of my mind or, occasionally, my heart, as difficult as that might be for you to believe." He slanted her a quick glance. "When in the throes of *flying*, I find I often turn to Christopher Marlowe's sentiments. Are you familiar with Marlowe?"

Who? She scoffed. "Aren't we all?"

"Indeed. I myself am exceedingly fond of *The Passionate Shepherd to His Love.*"

"As are we all." She nodded sagely and wished she had spent as much time studying literature in her youth as she had avoiding it. And wished as well she could have avoided this particular conversation. No matter what she thought of Lord Berkley, she certainly didn't want him to think poorly of her—that she was ill read or had no taste for literature, even if that was perilously close to the truth.

"I know it by heart." He thought for a moment. *"Come live with me and be my love and we will all the pleasures prove that hills and valleys, dales and fields, woods or steepy mountain yields."*

"Oh, my." She gazed up at him, her words little more than a sigh. "That was . . . well . . . perfect."

He laughed. "Even when recited by someone with my obvious imperfections?"

"The perfection is in the words, my lord," she murmured. It was indeed perfect, and she would allow her tongue to be cut out before she would admit to him that it was made all the more so by the man reciting it.

She could well see how Lord Berkley had achieved his reputation with women. With his mastery of poetry and the timbre of his voice he gave a lady the overwhelming impression that these words had never before been said, that they were for her and her alone. Coupled with his mesmerizing eyes and contagious laugh, why, even she was very nearly willing to throw caution to the winds and fling herself into his arms at this very minute.

"But he wasn't, you know."

"Wasn't what?"

What would he do if she did? No doubt, he would take advantage of her at once. Exploit her weakness. Sweep her into his arms. Kiss her over and over again. Carry her off to his bed. Ravish her. Steal her virtue. Ruin her life. Destroy her—

"Perfect," Lord Berkley said matter-of-factly, his attention returning to the wall of books. "Not your sort of man at all. He was killed in a drunken brawl at a fairly young age.

"Come now, Miss Effington, you still haven't answered my question. Who among these is your favorite?" He gestured broadly at the shelves.

She pulled a calming breath, as much to restore her cool demeanor as to vanquish a distinct and most disquieting sense of disappointment that she was not currently on the path to ruin.

"Let me think. It's a difficult choice." Her gaze skimmed the shelves.

If she was forced to select a favorite, it should be an author she was at least mildly aware of. She didn't want to seem a complete idiot. Her gaze caught on a matching set of red leather volumes with *Shakespeare* gilded on the spine.

She favored him with her brightest smile. "Shakespeare, of course."

"Of course." He returned her smile, and she had the irresistible urge to reach out and touch the corner of his mouth where it quirked upward. "Which of his works do you prefer?"

She said the first thing that popped into her mind. "*Twelfth Night.*"

He laughed. "I should have known that a woman pretending to be a man would intrigue you. Or is it the idea of one twin masquerading as another that you like?"

"Both, I should think." She grinned with relief.

She honestly did like *Twelfth Night,* the performance of it much more than the reading of it. Delia had forced her to attend a production years ago, and there had been something about the story of disguise and misunderstanding that had appealed to her.

"I fear I am not as familiar with that particular play, but . . ." His brow furrowed in thought. " 'If music be the food of love, play on.' "

" 'Some are born great, some achieve greatness and some have greatness thrust upon them,' " she said without thinking. Where on earth had that come from? Apparently she was somewhat better versed in Shakespeare than she had imagined. It was an extremely satisfying thought.

"Excellent." He studied her curiously. "I must confess, Miss Effington, with every minute spent in your presence, you both amaze and confuse me."

"Do I?"

"I don't know what to make of you." He shook his head. "You are at once fascinating and annoying, intriguing and infuriating."

"Am I?" She laughed lightly as if she didn't care. As if this wasn't the most delightful compliment she'd ever had.

His gaze searched her face. "You are a dichotomy, Miss Effington, a contradiction in terms. You are at once concerned with propriety and *perfection*, yet I suspect your definition of both are very much your own. You do precisely as you wish."

"Nonsense, my lord." She stared up at him and realized how very close to him she stood. Propriety, by anyone's definition, would best be served by putting a modicum of distance between them. She should at the very least step back. She didn't move. "Not precisely."

"Precisely. You follow the rules society lays down only when they suit you. You said you would never invade the sanctity of a gentleman's club, and I would wager that's due more to lack of interest than anything else."

"Don't be absurd."

He was right, of course; if she had any desire whatsoever to venture into White's or Brooks or any of the other sacred masculine retreats that lined St. James Street she would certainly find a reason to do exactly as she wanted.

"Regardless of my own wishes, I would never—"

"Miss Effington." He stepped closer. Close enough to touch. Intensity showed in his gray eyes, but his voice was cool. "What would you do if I were to take you in my arms and kiss you at this very moment?"

"I would slap your face, my lord," she said without hesitation, the firm note in her voice belying the way she seemed to strain ever so slightly toward him, and the immediate realization that she very much wanted him to do just that.

"I see." He narrowed his eyes and considered her for a moment. "Well, that's that, then." He turned to his study of the book-lined shelves, his hands again clasped behind his back.

"What's what, then?" She stared in annoyance and more than a little frustration. "Aren't you going to kiss me?"

"I think not," he said coolly.

"Why not?" Not that she wanted him to kiss her, but it would have been most satisfying to crack her hand across his face.

"It would be highly improper."

"I realize that, but—"

"Furthermore, I have never kissed a friend before. I'm not sure I'm entirely certain how to do that or," he shook his head somberly, "whether I would enjoy it. I should hate to be slapped for something that wasn't especially worth it."

She straightened her shoulders. "I can assure you, Lord Berkley, it would most certainly be worth it."

"That remains to be seen. You said yourself people expect you to stumble into scandal because you refuse to keep your opinions to yourself, yet you've never actually behaved in a truly scandalous manner. Therefore I'm afraid, Miss Effington," he shrugged, "you have no references."

"References?" She could scarcely choke out the word. "References?"

"References," he said firmly. "My mother has heard excellent things about your abilities when it comes to redecorating houses, yet I have heard nothing about your ability to kiss. You are sadly lacking in references. And if I am going to risk your wrath, and I suspect it could well be impressive, I should at least know precisely what to expect."

She glared. "I'll have you know I have been kissed before. And quite thoroughly, too."

"Really?" He raised a brow. "Then there are men willing to provide references?"

"I should certainly hope not!" Indignation rang in her voice.

Indeed she had been kissed before. Any number of times. Admittedly, she had rarely been kissed by the same man more than once, as whatever man had been so daring in the first place had either been a rake she'd had no particular use for or deadly dull, in which case he had used up all his courage on the initial overture and had not hazarded a second attempt.

"A gentleman would never speak of such a thing in regards to a lady," she said in a haughty manner.

"No, of course not," he murmured. "And how many brothers do you have, Miss Effington?"

"More than enough."

"All considered gentlemen, I gather?"

"Point taken, my lord," she snapped.

"I thought it might be." He smiled pleasantly. "Even disregarding your lack of references, while you are small as opponents go, I have no doubt your ire would add additional strength. A slap from you might well be fatal."

Her eyes widened in disbelief. "Fatal?"

"Or do I give you too much credit? Very well. Not fatal then, but," he thought for a moment, "most definitely painful."

"Oh, you can be certain of that," she ground out the words.

"Therefore, Miss Effington, you can rest assured

you are safe from any untoward advances from me." He favored her with a brilliant smile.

"Excellent. I am most relieved."

"Besides, we have already determined I am not, nor shall I ever be, your Lord Perfect, and it follows therefore that you are not my"—his brow furrowed, then he brightened—"Miss Wonderful."

"Miss Wonderful? Miss?" She stared. "Why not Lady Wonderful? Or Princess Wonderful?"

"Alas, I am not as much of a snob as you are."

She gasped. "I'm not a snob!"

He raised a brow. "*Lord* Perfect."

"Might I remind you, you were the one who bestowed the title on him, but now that I think about it, why not? A woman's position in life is tied to that of her husband. Why shouldn't I prefer to marry Lord Perfect rather than Mr. Perfect?"

"Why indeed?" Lord Berkley nodded sagely. "And I imagine Lord Perfect should have a tidy fortune. A nice home in London, an estate in the country, that sort of thing?"

"Well, yes." She frowned. "You needn't make it sound so mercenary."

"Did I?" His eyes widened in feigned innocence. Whether he kissed her or not, she might have to slap him anyway. He was certainly begging for it. "My apologies."

She ignored him. "And what of Miss Wonderful? Surely you have standards for her?"

"I'm not sure if *standards* is the appropriate word. Far and away too harsh, but certainly there are qualities I would wish for in a wife."

"I thought as much." She smirked. "I suspect your Miss Wonderful is as perfect as my Lord Perfect is."

"Not in the least. The last thing I would want to be shackled with for the rest of my life is perfection. I can't imagine anything more boring. No, I want a woman with a few delightful flaws." He thought for a moment. "She should be biddable but not too docile, I should like a bit of a spark in her. Intelligent but not overly bookish. A touch of independence would be nice. She should be confident without being obstinate and—"

"And she should be pretty, no doubt."

"Pretty is always preferable to hideous. And as much as this will surprise you, it is not the most important thing on my list of qualities for," he cleared his throat, "*Miss Wonderful*. But beyond all else, she should love me."

"Well, I wish Lord Perfect to love me as well," Cassie said quickly. "I know I haven't mentioned it before, but I do consider love to be important. I have always wished to marry for love."

"Yet you have never been in love, and I suspect it is because you have never allowed yourself to be." He leaned toward her in a confidential manner. "You, Miss Effington, have never dared to plunge into the precipice."

"I shall dare when the time is right. When . . . when . . ." She huffed in annoyance. "When I meet Lord Perfect and not until then. Whereas you, my lord, apparently plunge whenever you meet a pretty face."

He laughed. "Plunge and plummet. Far too many times, and I confess, I am done with it. Although you have been too cautious in the past and I have not been cautious at all, at this moment, Miss Effington, it strikes me that we are more alike than different. I shall not plunge again until I can do so with Miss Wonderful by my side."

Cassie couldn't help but think what a shame it all was. The two of them were both looking for the right match and everything that meant, including love. It was almost a pity that she had decided they would not suit for one another.

At moments like this, she could completely ignore his reputation and believe wholeheartedly in reform. Why, if anyone could reform a rake like Lord Berkley, she could. Still, it seemed he had put any possibility of a match between the two of them aside when he had offered his friendship. And he certainly hadn't pressed his attentions on her and kissed her when he'd had the opportunity to do so, which, for some odd reason, was still rather annoying.

"Perhaps we could help one another, Miss Effington," he said slowly.

"Oh?"

"I know any number of gentlemen who are interested in the pursuit of marriage. One might well prove to be your Lord Perfect."

She shook her head. "I scarcely think—"

"No, Miss Effington, it's an excellent idea. I'll find you Lord Perfect and you can find me," he grinned, "Miss Wonderful."

"That's absurd. I . . ." Why was it absurd? When it came to matters of this nature, matters of the heart, neither of them had done especially well on their own thus far. Perhaps it was time to join forces. Besides, what were friends for, if not to help each other?

She did know a great many young ladies that might well fit his criteria. Regardless of his reputation, a viscount with a respectable title and fortune was still considered something of a catch. In addition, he'd have a nicely refurbished house.

"Surely you're not reluctant to take on such a challenge? Or better yet," he grinned, "a wager. For oh, say—"

"Forty pounds," she said before she could stop herself. "I have a spare forty pounds." She nodded thoughtfully. "I shall bet forty pounds that I can find you your Miss Wonderful."

"And I'll wager forty pounds that I can find you Lord Perfect."

She studied him carefully. "How do we determine a winner?"

"Obviously you would have to agree that the gentleman I name is indeed Lord Perfect, just as I would have to agree on your choice of a Miss Wonderful."

"Of course."

"Therefore, I should think if we're both successful, there is no winner of the wager—it would be a draw, although I daresay in that case we would in truth both be victorious. No, the money should not change hands unless one of us concedes defeat and gives up the quest for Miss Wonderful or Lord Perfect." He held out his hand. "Is it agreed, then?"

"Agreed." She nodded and took his hand.

He grinned down at her. "I can't remember when I've looked forward to a competition as much as I am looking forward to this one."

She grinned back. "I warn you, I shall not be as easily defeated as my brother was."

"When it comes to you, Miss Effington, I am confident nothing is ever easy. I propose we begin our quest tomorrow night at Lady Puget's ball."

"An excellent place to begin. I daresay there should be any number of potential Miss Wonderfuls present."

"And a possible Lord Perfect or two as well." He laughed, then studied her in a considering manner. "I have always enjoyed playing for high stakes, although I cannot recall ever playing for stakes quite this high."

She raised a brow. "Forty pounds?"

"Not at all. We're playing for our futures, Miss Effington, and more than likely, our hearts."

Six

I shouldn't say a woman's face and figure are of paramount importance. Indeed, a clever mind and easy manner are far more desirable. Still, I should hate to shackle myself for life to a lady I can only abide in the dark of night.

L. Effington

"I've got her right where I want her, Marcus." Reggie watched Miss Effington and her current partner over the rim of his champagne glass and tried to keep a too satisfied smile from his face.

"Does she know you have her exactly where you want her?" Marcus said idly, his gaze following his friend's.

Miss Effington laughed and flirted with her partner for the quadrille in the midst of the other dancers at Lady Puget's annual ball. Her blonde hair glowed in the candlelight, and there was a blush on her cheeks from the dance and unrestrained enjoyment. Her gown was a lovely greenish-blue color that suited her eyes and reminded him of seawater. Indeed, she could well be a nymph from the sea or a mermaid come to land to enchant mere mortals.

"Reggie?"

"She has no idea," he murmured, his gaze still focused on Miss Effington. *Cassandra*. He did so love how her name sounded on his tongue.

She was nothing sort of magnificent, and he was annoyed with himself that he had never especially noticed her before and annoyed on her behalf with every other man in existence who hadn't snapped her up long before now.

"Nor would she be overly pleased to hear such a thing. Besides," Reggie watched her execute a difficult step flawlessly, "she'd deny it."

"And where, precisely, is it that you have her?" Marcus's words were measured.

"She's confused, off balance, uncertain. And even better," Reggie grinned at his friend, "she likes me. I can tell. She doesn't want to like me, but she does. And she likes me quite a bit more than she expected."

"How very interesting," Marcus said thoughtfully. "A scant few days ago, you said you and she had agreed to be friends."

"We did. We are. I've never been friends with a woman before, not really, but it seems an excellent place to start."

The dance ended and Cassandra's partner escorted her off the floor. Reggie pushed aside a twinge of jealousy at the way she gazed up at him. He knew full well that her flirtatious manner was little more than a game she and everyone else played at functions such as this. Nor was the gentleman any particular threat. He was certainly no Lord Perfect.

Although it would take something far different than mere perfection to engage the affections of Miss Cassandra Effington. She simply did not yet realize it. Yet. It would take the fifth Viscount Berkley, although she did not realize that yet, either.

"Dare I ask what has changed between our last conversation and tonight?" Marcus chose his words with care. "You swore to me you were not falling back into old habits. You said you would not permit it. You said this time would be different."

"This time is different." Reggie drained the last of his wine.

"You said that too. In fact, you've said that many times before."

"This time—"

Marcus raised a cynical brow.

"This time," Reggie said firmly, "it *is* different. *She* is different from any woman I've ever met before. And I, old friend, am different."

Marcus snorted in disbelief, signaled a passing waiter, and exchanged their empty glasses for full ones. "And exactly how are you different? *This time?*"

"I know you're skeptical, and you, of all people, have every right to be, but I have given this a great deal of consideration." Reggie searched for the right words. "In the past, I have always offered my affections without thinking and far too soon. I have never taken the time to truly know a lady before declaring myself. In doing so, I have made one mistake after another."

"So you are being cautious with Miss Effington?" Marcus studied him carefully. "You are not rushing in without due deliberation? You are cultivating patience rather than surrendering to impulse? You are thinking before you act?"

"It sounds rather daunting when you put it like that, but yes, that's exactly what I'm doing."

"Good God, I stand corrected." Marcus shook his head. "This *is* different."

Reggie sipped his champagne. "And it's bloody well difficult to do, too, I tell you. It goes against my very nature."

He turned his attention back to Cassandra. Yet another partner was leading her onto the dance floor.

"I've never known a woman who annoys me quite as much as she does."

"Oh, that's an auspicious beginning," Marcus said wryly.

Reggie ignored him. "Sparks, Marcus, there are sparks between us, and not merely of irritation. They're glimmers of recognition or acknowledgment or something. I don't know what exactly, but there's definitely something between us. I knew it the moment we met. As if we were fated to be together. It's quite remarkable." He shook his head. "She is the woman I have been waiting for."

"You have not exactly been waiting."

"That's why it's fate." Reggie glanced at the earl. "Don't you think it's odd, given my eminently eligible status, my title, my wealth, all of those things women allegedly want in a match, that by this point in time one of the women I fancied myself in love with—"

Marcus raised a brow. "Fancied yourself in love?"

"Come now, Marcus. One can perhaps fall in love as quickly as I have on occasion—"

"On occasion?"

Reggie shrugged off the question. "But I have always recovered with remarkable speed."

"It has been damned impressive," Marcus murmured.

"Therefore I was obviously not truly in love."

Marcus's brow furrowed. "And this is fate?"

"No." Reggie shook his head. "Fate is the reason why none of the numerous ladies I have turned my attention to in the past has returned my interest. Fate was saving me for the right woman." He raised his glass in triumph. "Miss Cassandra Effington."

"I see." Marcus paused to consider Reggie's words. At last he shook his head. "You do appear to have given this a great deal of thought and, as much as I hate to admit it, it makes a certain amount of sense. Very well." Marcus blew a resigned breath. "What now? And what is my part in it?"

Reggie laughed.

"I assume you have some sort of plan in mind to win her affections? If indeed you are serious about pursuing her."

"I have never been more serious."

Reggie watched Cassandra move through the steps of the dance. He resisted the urge to stride out onto the dance floor and take her in his arms. It was exactly what she would expect from the infamous Viscount Berkley, but it would not serve his purposes at the moment. It was hardly the first rash impulse he had to quash since meeting her, and he suspected it would not be the last. But he would not play this game with her as he had with others in the past. He would not lead with his heart instead of his head. The stakes were far too high.

Cassandra laughed at something her partner said and Reggie's stomach clenched. He ignored it. He could not show so much as a hint of jealousy. As far as she was concerned, they were nothing more than friends. For now.

Reggie knew Marcus was hard-pressed to believe his claim that his feelings for Cassandra were different from any he had known before. It was difficult to explain how, precisely, but there was an intensity, a sense, as it were, of permanence and importance and, yes, destiny. It sounded absurd, of course, and how could he possibly expect his closest friend to comprehend his feelings when Reggie himself didn't quite understand?

It struck him that regardless of how many times he had thought himself in love up to now, this was the first time he had actively planned any sort of concerted campaign. He would win Miss Effington's heart, and the difficulties that entailed would simply make the prize all the more worthwhile.

"The plan is already in motion," Reggie said coolly. "She and I have placed a wager that we can each find the perfect match for the other. She is looking for the perfect man."

"As are most women, I assume."

"Oh, but Miss Effington is quite adamant. I am to find her Lord Perfect—"

Marcus choked back a laugh. "Lord Perfect?"

"Her requirements are quite specific, as are mine."

Reggie grinned. "She is to find me Miss Wonderful."

"Lord Perfect and Miss Wonderful?" Marcus laughed. "I suppose they are as good a match as the infamous Lord Berkley and the eccentric Miss Effington. So how does this plan of yours work?"

"It's brilliant in its very simplicity." Reggie slanted the earl a smug smile. "I shall give Miss Effington exactly what she wants."

"You will give her Lord Perfect?" Marcus shook his head. "I don't understand. If you're not Lord Perfect, and indeed you couldn't possibly be, as she does not want a man of your reputation—"

"Not yet."

Marcus's brows pulled together. "Now I am confused."

"She doesn't want me now, but once she meets Lord Perfect, she will discover perfection is not for her and she will realize she cannot spend the rest of her days living with a man with no imperfections." He leaned toward Marcus confidentially. "Miss Effington is most creative and quite enjoys the improvement of things. Houses in particular, but I am betting such impulses will extend to a spouse as well. She strikes me as a woman who would derive a great deal of satisfaction from reforming a man." He straightened and smiled smugly. "She simply doesn't know it yet."

"And you do need a great deal of improvement."

"That goes without saying." Reggie shrugged modestly. "With my infamous reputation, I am ripe for reform."

"Not to mention all your other flaws."

"I am perfect for her." Reggie grinned. "I am the

proverbial house waiting to be refurbished."

"I can certainly see that, but," Marcus shook his head, "where are you going to get a Lord Perfect?"

"I don't actually need to come up with a real Lord Perfect, at least not immediately."

"You don't?"

"I'm not sure that endless discussions about Lord Perfect as I conduct my search won't be enough to convince Miss Effington that this is not the kind of man she really wants. And, during the course of our conversations, and the redecoration of my house, our friendship will grow until she will realize that the one man she can't live without isn't Lord Perfect but me." Reggie pulled a long swallow of his champagne, the wine a perfect accompaniment to his sense of satisfaction.

Marcus stared, dumbfounded.

"Well?"

The earl shook his head slowly. "That's either the most ridiculous idea I have ever heard or it's brilliant." He thought for a moment. "What happens if she insists that you produce a Lord Perfect? Or worse yet, finds a Miss Wonderful?"

"Ah, but Miss Wonderful is in the eye of the beholder. I shall simply not accept whomever Miss Effington offers. As for producing a Lord Perfect, I have no idea."

Reggie drew his brows together and pondered the question. "But you're right. There could indeed come a time when I might actually need to come up with a Lord Perfect. She might well become suspicious otherwise. It could be most awkward."

Marcus snorted. "Awkward?"

"Possibly more than awkward." Reggie thought for a moment. "I could hire one, I suppose. An actor, perhaps?"

"I think not." Marcus shook his head. "Should this plan of yours collapse around your head, and I think the odds on that are fairly even, you do not want Miss Effington to know you hired an actor to be her perfect match. Women do not take that sort of thing at all well."

"Perhaps not." Reggie glanced around the room, then nodded at several gentlemen engaged in an animated discussion. "What about Lord Chapman? He could be Lord Perfect."

"Chapman is entirely too, well, pretty for a man. I daresay most women don't like men who are prettier than they are. In addition, he thinks he's perfect, which in and of itself is most irritating."

Reggie scanned the crowd. "Lord Warren is a possibility."

"Warren too believes he's perfect, and his reputation is no better than the one we created for you. No, he won't do." Marcus shook his head. "Besides, you need an unknown Lord Perfect. Someone she couldn't possibly have met. Someone from the country, perhaps, yet with a certain amount of sophistication. Honest, humble, handsome—"

Reggie scoffed. "Such a man could not possibly exist."

"Of course not, but should such a paragon exist," Marcus grinned, "I can't imagine he wouldn't drive a woman like Miss Effington stark raving mad."

"That's the idea." Reggie smiled wickedly.

"This plan of yours might actually work." Marcus

heaved a resigned sigh. "I know I shall regret this, but do allow me to do my part. You may concentrate your efforts completely on your pursuit of Miss Effington, and I shall find a Lord Perfect for you."

Reggie chuckled. "I knew I could count on you."

"I have always been something of an idiot when it comes to partaking in one of your schemes, but they do always sound so plausible. I am drawn irresistibly to them like a moth to its fiery doom." Marcus grinned, then sobered. "You do understand you are treading a dangerous course here. There is always the possibility Miss Effington will find Lord Perfect is indeed what she's always wanted."

"It's a risk, but I'm confident it's slim." Reggie's gaze slipped back to Cassandra. "The eccentric Miss Effington could never be satisfied with Lord Perfect."

"If you're wrong—"

"I'm not," Reggie said simply.

"Very well."

Reggie handed Marcus his glass. "If you don't mind, I think it's past time I joined in the dance."

Marcus smiled. "Will this be the first time you've danced with Miss Effington?"

"Oh, I have no intention of dancing with Miss Effington at the moment." Reggie adjusted the cuff of his coat and cast his friend a wicked smile. "That too will drive her mad."

"Must he dance every dance?" Cassie fluttered her fan and fixed a pleasant smile firmly on her face.

"He does seem to be somewhat in demand at the moment," Delia murmured. "Although I don't think he has danced every dance. In fact, it was no more than twenty minutes ago that you commented on the fact that he wasn't dancing at all."

"Did I?" Cassie forced a lighthearted laugh. "I can't believe I even noticed what Lord Berkley was or wasn't doing."

Certainly, she had noticed Lord Berkley and his friend Lord Pennington standing near the doors to the terrace, deep in conversation. She had noticed the moment Lord Berkley arrived, exactly whom he had spoken to since his arrival, precisely how many glasses of champagne he'd had thus far, and now, each and every lady he danced with. She noticed as well his overly flirtatious manner and the irritating way in which he looked at every woman as though there was something uniquely special about her that only he was discerning enough to note. And she noticed he didn't seem to be the tiniest bit aware of her. It was most annoying.

Delia snorted in disbelief. "You have been unable to tear your eyes from the man since he first stepped into the room."

"That's absurd. I have no interest at all in the comings and goings of Lord Berkley," Cassie said out of the corner of her mouth while returning the smile cast at her by a Mr. Wexley, her manner at once friendly but not overly encouraging. Flirtation was an art that required a certain level of balancing between being too encouraging to an interested gentleman and not encouraging enough. One hated to burn one's bridges, after all.

"Lord Berkley and I are friends. Any notice I might possibly pay him is no different than what one friend might have for another. There is nothing more to it than that."

"That's exactly what I thought." Delia nodded slowly. "I didn't for a moment think that there was anything more—"

"While he is apparently making his way around the entire room, he has not requested a dance from *me,*" Cassie said, the pleasant note in her voice belying her irritation with the man. "We are friends, and one would think a friend would at least acknowledge another friend's presence. Why, he has practically ignored me."

"And you have never taken that well."

Cassie acknowledged the speculative smile Lord Hawking directed at her with a pleasant but not too welcoming nod. "Never."

"Although you are scarcely one to complain. You have not spoken two words to him," Delia said pointedly.

"I have not had the opportunity. Besides, it would be terribly improper for me to approach him." Cassie's manner was lofty, as if she would never consider such a thing.

"What on earth has gotten into you?" Delia studied her sister carefully. "I can't recall you ever being quite this concerned about propriety before."

"It is unusual, isn't it?" Cassie sighed. "It's nothing at all, or perhaps it's everything. I've had the oddest sense of, well, dissatisfaction of late. Look at it, Delia." Cassie gestured at the scene spread out before them.

Lady Puget's ball was the height of elegance, but then it always was. Ladies and gentlemen were dressed in their finest, but then they always were. Flirtation and anticipation hung in the air, but then it always did. It was very much the same as last year or the year before and would probably remain unchanged next year and the year after that.

"Do you realize we've been out in society since our eighteenth year? This is my seventh season, my second without you. It's not nearly as much fun without you, you know."

"I am sorry."

Cassie shrugged. "It can't be helped, I suppose. Well, it could have been helped, but it's far too late for that now."

Delia's eyes narrowed. "You do realize I do not intend to spend the rest of my life apologizing to you for my indiscretions, don't you?"

"Yes of course, I don't intend for you to, and I am sorry that I brought it up." Cassie waved away her twin's comment. "It's just that I have been thinking quite a lot about the future recently and wondering if indeed the entire world considers me eccentric—"

"I, for one, am quite proud of you," Delia said staunchly.

"Your loyalty is unquestioned, dear sister, therefore you scarcely count, but I do appreciate the sentiment. And now, that . . . that man"—she nodded toward the dance floor, where Lord Berkley was at this very moment no doubt being utterly charming and beguiling some unsuspecting innocent with his irresistible laugh—"has invaded my life—"

"One could say you are the one who has invaded his life or, at the very least, his home," Delia said mildly.

Cassie paid her no heed. "—and made me consider

things I thought I had long ago decided." She waved her fan with a bit more emphasis than necessary. "It's most annoying."

"Annoying seems to be the one word you use quite a bit in connection with Lord Berkley."

"Because it's appropriate. He is infuriating, maddening, exasperating and I'm not quite sure why, which in and of itself is annoying. He can also be exceedingly charming, which I also find irritating." She pulled her brows together. "And because this is entirely his fault. For the very first time in my life, I'm not entirely certain what I'm doing is right."

"Refurbishing houses?"

"No, no, not that. I find that quite enjoyable and challenging and I shall never give it up, no matter what anyone thinks."

"Then you're talking about your avoidance of men in need of reform?" Delia paused for emphasis. "Men like Lord Berkley, perhaps?"

"No," Cassie said firmly. "I still believe that's the best course for me, but I am willing to admit that my concept of Lord Perfect might be somewhat ill conceived. I hate the thought of lowering my standards, but it may well be time to at least reexamine them. Why, there couldn't possibly be anyone who could meet the standards of a Lord Perfect—or a Miss Wonderful, for that matter."

"I see."

"What?"

Delia nodded in an all-knowing manner almost as annoying as anything Lord Berkley might do. "That's what this is all about."

"What do you mean?" Cassie said innocently and wished for once that she had held her tongue.

"Your absurd wager with Lord Berkley. I should have known." Delia studied her sister curiously. "You're regretting it, aren't you?"

"Not in the least." Cassie blew a resigned breath. "Perhaps a bit. It simply doesn't seem fair, that's all. Lord Berkley might as well hand over his forty pounds right now."

"To add to my forty pounds," Delia murmured.

"The point is he can't possibly find a Lord Perfect. You said it yourself that men aren't perfect."

"No, of course not," Delia said slowly. "What of Miss Wonderful?"

"That's scarcely a challenge. I shouldn't have any problem at all finding a suitable match for his lordship." Cassie shrugged disdainfully. "This ballroom alone is full of Miss Wonderfuls. You can scarcely take two steps without tripping over one of them.

"Look at them, Delia, this year's crop of sweet, young things all ready to be sacrificed on the altar of matrimony. They are perfect from the tips of their perfect fingers to the tops of their perfect toes. It's revolting."

"Might I point out that you are very much among their number."

"Hardly. There isn't a person here who would think of me as anything near perfect, what with the mistaken belief that I tread a mere step away from scandal and now members of my own family are describing my doing something I enjoy as an eccentricity, which admittedly in this day and age is not entirely inaccurate. In truth, I am a mere heartbeat away from being firmly on the shelf." Cassie sighed theatrically. "The eccentric Miss Effington."

Delia laughed. "Come now, Cassie—"

"You think I'm being dramatic, but I'm not. I'm simply facing the facts of my life." She wrinkled her nose. "And they're not especially pretty."

Delia stared at her twin. "I think you have a few good years left. Need I point out you have danced every dance tonight yourself. You have not lacked for partners nor for attention."

"Yes, but as always those partners fall into two categories: eminently respectable, deadly boring, and interested in nothing but marriage, or far too rakish, prone to scandal, and interested in anything but marriage. Not one gentleman here tonight, and in truth, I don't know anyone at all who is even remotely like—"

"Lord Berkley?"

"Yes." Cassie started and stared at her sister. "No. I didn't mean to say that at all. I meant to say Lord Perfect."

Delia raised a brow.

"I did." Cassie glared at her sister. "It was simply a slip of the tongue and has no more significance than that."

"Of course not." Delia's smug smile belied her words.

"It was probably only that we've been talking about him and our wager, and he was the first man that came to mind when speaking of the kind of match I want." Cassie hesitated. "That's not what I meant, either. It does sound rather incriminating, though, doesn't it?"

"Yes, it does."

"I do like him, Delia, when he's not being annoying,

that is. However, we share nothing more than friendship, and I'm certain he has no interest in me beyond that. Why, the man isn't even interested in kissing me."

"Really?" Amusement twinkled in Delia's eye. "And how would you know that?"

"It came up yesterday," Cassie said in an offhand manner.

"Somewhere between the window hangings and furniture placement, no doubt?"

"Something like that," Cassie muttered. It still rankled, that nonsense he had spouted about references. And whether or not kissing her would be worth the price.

His qualifications for Miss Wonderful were bothersome as well. Not that they weren't entirely reasonable, but they so blatantly did not describe, well, *her*.

"I should call it off," Cassie said, deciding to do so the moment she said the words.

"The wager?" Delia's brow furrowed with suspicion. "Why?"

"As you said, it's absurd. And it really isn't fair. There's a plethora of Miss Wonderfuls and scarcely a Lord Perfect in sight." Cassie shook her head. "No, winning this wager would be little more than stealing."

"Yes, of course," Delia murmured. "That sounds plausible."

Cassie narrowed her eyes. "I know that look, Delia. What are you really thinking?"

"It's silly of me, I know, but I thought your reluctance to continue with your wager was because you didn't want to find Lord Berkley's Miss Wonderful for him."

"Not at all." Cassie adopted a lofty tone. "I just don't think this contest is fair."

"You should tell him then."

"Indeed I should."

"When?"

"When next I see him." Cassie thought for a moment. "We have an appointment tomorrow."

"Why not tonight? Now?" Delia pressed her point. "This very minute."

"I don't think—"

Delia leaned closer. "Meet him on the terrace. Terraces are excellent places to work out problems or come to arrangements or anything else. And the two of you are friends, after all."

"That would be most inappropriate. What if someone saw us? My reputation—"

Delia laughed. "You are already the eccentric Miss Effington. Anything of a scandalous nature would be an improvement."

"Delia!"

"Oh come now, Cassie. You are simply no fun anymore." Delia huffed. "However, if you insist on being so annoyingly proper, and yes, I do mean annoyingly . . ." Delia glanced around quickly until her gaze met her husband's, and she nodded. A moment later, St. Stephens joined them.

He glanced from one sister to the next and frowned. "Should I leave again?"

"No dearest, you shouldn't." Delia cast her husband a loving smile. "I need you to dance the next set with Cassie."

He winced. "The entire set?"

Cassie huffed. "It's not necessary—"

"It's absolutely necessary," Delia said firmly and turned to her husband. "Half the set and then I shall meet you both on the terrace."

"Both?" His gaze slid from his wife to her sister and back. His eyes narrowed suspiciously. "Why?"

"Because Cassie needs to speak privately with Lord Berkley, and the terrace is the best place to do that." Delia's eyes widened innocently. "Surely you remember what lovely places terraces are to . . . talk."

Cassie groaned to herself.

"Oh." His expression cleared. "Oh, yes, of course. Excellent idea."

It was an idea fraught with danger and Cassie well knew it, even if she couldn't bring herself to tell her sister. All she'd thought about from the moment Lord Berkley hadn't kissed her was what it would be like if he did.

Cassie leaned close to her sister and lowered her voice. "I am going along with this, but reluctantly, and I shall hold you responsible if anything dreadful happens."

"And you shall give me all the credit if something delightful happens." Delia grinned. "And I have every hope that it will."

"Shall we?" St. Stephens said with a decent measure of good grace and offered his arm.

"I do appreciate this, Tony, even if I don't entirely agree with the reasons behind it." Cassie kept her voice soft in a confidential manner and allowed him to lead her to their positions for the next dance, all the while meeting the eye of this lord or that gentleman in a constant stream of meaningless flirtation.

One of the nicest things about dancing with a relative, particularly a brother-in-law who has been coerced into dancing in the first place, was that one didn't feel it necessary to keep up a steady stream of pleasant, if usually inane, conversation. One could think about other matters if one wished.

One could even dwell on what it might be like to share a highly improper kiss on a terrace under the stars with a very annoying man.

"Could I have a moment, my lord?" A vaguely familiar voice sounded behind him.

Reggie stifled an entirely too smug smile and turned.

"Lord Berkley?" Miss Effington beamed up at him, and he was hard-pressed not to grin back like an idiot.

"Miss Ef—" He paused and narrowed his gaze. "No, it's Lady St. Stephens, isn't it?"

Lady St. Stephens laughed, a laugh far too much like her sister's for comfort. "I should have been quite disappointed in you if you had not noticed." She studied him curiously. "How did you know? Most people don't, you know."

"The resemblance is quite remarkable, but you have a dimple in your right cheek. Miss Effington's is in her left. She also favors her left hand, and I would guess you favor your right. And even more obvious," he grinned, "you're wearing a different dress than she is."

Lady St. Stephens raised an approving brow. "You noticed what she's wearing?"

"It complements her eyes," he said levelly, knowing he was being entirely too personal. And knowing as well this meeting with Cassandra's sister was probably something of a test. "Your eyes as well, obviously."

"Obviously." She smiled and hesitated. "I'm not entirely sure how to say this. It's not really my place."

"Are you wondering if my intentions toward your sister go beyond the state of friendship? If my intentions are honorable?" He chuckled. "I must advise you, your brother has already asked me that question."

"And what did you say?"

He chose his words with care. "At that time, I said I had no intentions other than making her acquaintance."

"And now?"

He paused and thought for a moment. Just how forthcoming could he be with Cassandra's sister? "Might I ask you a question before I answer?"

"Please do."

He drew a deep breath. "If I said my intention was to make your sister my wife, would your loyalty toward her compel you to tell her?"

"Most certainly not." Lady St. Stephens shook her head emphatically. "My sister would not take such an admission well. She is convinced you will not suit, or at least that's what she says. Whereas I," she flashed him a blinding smile, "am convinced you will."

He stared. "Why?"

"You needn't look so surprised. I've noted the way you've watched her all evening when she was not aware of it."

"I thought I was being discreet," he murmured.

"You were, unless someone was watching both you and her as I was." She shook her head. "I've seen many men watch my sister through the years. Those gentlemen interested in her as nothing more than a good match always look a bit apprehensive, a touch frightened. She has that effect on occasion."

"I can certainly understand that," he said under his breath.

"Those attracted because they mistakenly believe she is prone to scandal have a smug, predatory air about them. You, my lord, look at once intrigued, confident, and quite determined."

"Do I?" He grinned. "Imagine that."

"Beyond the way you look at her, there is the way she looks at you."

"Really?" His grin widened, if possible. "And how does she look at me?"

"I think it would be wise not to reveal all of my sister's secrets, even if I believe it's in her best interests." Lady St. Stephens laughed her sister's laugh. "This is far and away too private a discussion to be held in public, and I feel the need of a breath of fresh air. Will you escort me to the terrace?"

"I should be delighted."

He offered his arm and steered her through the French doors to Lady Puget's terrace. This was an unexpected and quite delightful turn of events. Cassandra's sister was obviously in his corner. He wasn't sure why, and he didn't know that it mattered. With her sister behind him, he couldn't possibly fail. Why, who would know Cassandra better than her twin, and who better to advise him on the way to win her heart?

They stopped at the stone baluster on the edge of the terrace, overlooking the lantern-lit gardens.

"It's a lovely night, isn't it?" Lady St. Stephens murmured. "Practically perfect."

It was indeed a beautiful night, just warm enough to be comfortable, with a promise of the summer to come in the air. The scent of spring blossoms lingered on the breeze. It was a perfect evening to be out of doors, under the stars. Pity the woman by his side was the wrong sister.

Lady St. Stephens gazed out over the gardens for a long, silent moment, and Reggie resisted the urge toward idle chatter. Whatever it was she wished to say was no doubt important, and he could wait, regardless of how difficult the waiting was.

"My husband has an unnerving ability to find out all sorts of things other people seem to overlook. He knows people who know people." Lady St. Stephens directed her words to him, but her gaze remained fixed on the gardens. "For example, until approximately six months ago, the infamous Lord Berkley wasn't the least bit infamous. In fact, your reputation was not especially worse than most men of your age. Certainly, there have been some youthful misdeeds, but nothing any reasonable person would regard as true scandal."

"You seem to know a great deal," he said cautiously.

"Oh, I do. For example, aside from the race with my brother, most of the incidents that have fed the flames of gossip might well have been extremely exaggerated or indeed fabricated altogether."

"They appear so, do they?" he said weakly.

"So one could conclude for whatever reason that you, my lord," she turned to face him, "are something of a fraud."

"I can explain."

Although in truth he had no idea how to explain

what had seemed like such a splendid plan such a long time ago. He wondered if perhaps there had been too much brandy involved when he'd first conceived his absurd project—otherwise how could he have thought that something so ridiculous was a good idea? And obviously Marcus's judgment had been seriously impaired that night as well.

"Indeed, I should like to explain." He raised his shoulders in a helpless shrug. "I'm simply not sure exactly how to do that at the moment. It will come to me, I—"

She held out a hand to stop him. "Oh, I'm certain you can explain plausibly with a bit of reflection, but I'm equally certain I do not need an explanation. Your family, your finances, even your friends are more than respectable. Suffice it to say whatever your reasons for this farce, I am confident they are neither nefarious nor illegal."

"It was really rather foolish," he murmured.

"I have no doubt of that."

"And perhaps not well thought out."

"I have no doubt of that either." She blew a long-suffering breath. "My lord, I have three brothers, a host of male relations, Effington relations at that, and a husband who was at one time rather well versed in masquerading as something he was not. I am well aware of the foibles of men."

"Excellent." He breathed a sigh of relief. "I cannot tell you how difficult it would be to explain something quite as stupid as—" A thought struck him, and he stopped. "Are you going to tell your sister that I am not infamous?"

"I think not." Lady St. Stephens paused to choose

her words. "My sister might not find it as . . . *amusing* as I do. For the time being I think it best to allow her to continue to believe as she does. Right now, she is not averse to having a man of your," she bit back a smile, "*infamous* reputation as a friend. And friendship is an excellent way to start."

"I am more than willing to be reformed, my lady," he said staunchly.

"Oh, I'm confident you are." She turned back toward the gardens, her voice casual. "Have you found her Lord Perfect yet?"

"No." He shook his head. "Frankly, I don't think he could possibly exist."

"So what are you going to do?"

"I don't really know yet."

"Are all your plans this well thought out, my lord?"

He chuckled. "It might not appear so, but on occasion they have worked out rather well." A serious note sounded in his voice. "Regardless of the wager between Miss Effington and myself, I am quite determined to win her heart and her hand."

"And I, my lord, am prepared to do everything in my power to help you achieve that goal."

He studied her profile curiously. "Why?"

"Because my sister has always been completely sure of herself and her decisions and her opinions. She has never felt the tiniest need to keep them to herself." She slanted him a sharp glance. "You're aware of her penchant for outspokenness, I assume?"

"Good God, yes."

"You would have to be dead not to be." She laughed, then shook her head. "You have made Cassie question herself. Doubt that she is right. I have never seen that before. It's quite significant."

His spirits rose. "Then I have a chance?"

"A very good one, I should think." She turned to face him and smiled in a conspiratorial manner. "I have no idea what the end result will be of this game between the two of you, but it should be most entertaining."

"For you, perhaps," he said wryly.

"She doesn't know it yet—and I'm not at all certain you realize it yet either—but you, my lord, are very much my sister's Lord Perfect." She grinned. "And God help you both."

Seven

The biggest advantage men have over women is that we are not always as stupid as they think we are. It is, however, best not to let them know this.

Thomas, Marquess of Helmsley

"You seem exceedingly on edge this evening, Miss Effington," Lord Berkley said idly. "Is there anything amiss?"

"Not at all, my lord." The calm note in Cassie's voice belied the very real fluttering in her stomach. "If anything, I am not used to walking alone with a gentleman along a darkened garden path."

"It's an excellent, well-maintained path. There are any number of lanterns placed along the walk to light the way. We are scarcely out of sight of the terrace and the ballroom windows. In addition, your sister and her husband are but a few yards behind us." He glanced over his shoulder. "Around that bend, I believe. Out of view for the moment but close enough to come to your assistance should you feel the need to scream for help." A distinct note of amusement sounded in his voice.

"I doubt that will be necessary," she said coolly.

"No, of course not. We have already determined that you are probably far stronger than you appear. Why, if anything, I should be the one grateful to have rescue so near by."

She resisted the impulse to smile. "I should hate to have to hurt you."

"I shall do everything possible to avoid that." He grinned. "Probably."

She laughed in spite of herself, noting in the back of her mind how quickly he had put her at ease.

"It's a lovely night for a stroll, under the stars, with a friend by your side." He glanced at her. "Don't you think so, Miss Effington?"

"I do indeed, my lord, but," she drew a deep breath, "I should like to discuss our wager if you don't mind."

"Ready to concede defeat so soon?"

"Not at all." They rounded another bend in the path, and she wondered how far back Delia and St. Stephens were; she wasn't sure if she wanted them to appear at any moment or not at all. It was an extremely dangerous thought. "I simply think it's not entirely fair."

"I see. Having a difficult time finding Miss Wonderful for me, are you?"

"Don't be absurd." The path split around a circular plot complete with a garden bench, small fountain, and a tall yew pruned into a spiral topiary.

"Now that's absurd." Lord Berkley stared at the tree.

"I rather like it." Cassie's gaze traveled upward

along the line of the yew reaching toward the stars. "It has symmetry and order."

"Perfect, would you say?"

"In its way," she nodded, "yes, I think so."

"Some would say perfection is already found in nature and the shaping of a tree like this into a confined form is an aberration."

"Would you?" She cast him a curious glance.

"Possibly." He nodded thoughtfully. "It seems to me forcing something, be it a tree or whatever else, into a shape it's not meant to be is rather a pity. Goes against its true nature, its purpose in life, if you will. One should be true to one's nature I should think."

"Unless one's true nature is unacceptable," she said under her breath.

"Did you say something?"

She started. Had she actually said that aloud? She forced a lighthearted laugh. "I was thinking aloud I fear, but nothing of significance, I assure you."

"I doubt that." He clasped his hands behind his back and studied the yew that now oddly seemed considerably less than perfect. "As your purpose here is to discuss our wager, I can only assume your thoughts were directed toward the problems encountered in finding a Miss Wonderful and furthermore how you can gracefully escape our bargain." He cast her a solemn look, but his eyes twinkled. "However, I assure you, Miss Effington, I shall still expect my forty pounds."

"You what?" She stared in disbelief. "If we both agreed to call off—"

"Oh, but I have no intention of agreeing."

"Very well, then, do be sure to set aside *my* forty

pounds, as I have no doubt as to the winner of this contest. You are far and away too sure of yourself, my lord." Without thinking, she stepped closer and stared up at him. "I'll have you know, Miss Wonderfuls are remarkably plentiful. There are a dozen or so who would suit more than adequately in the ballroom at this very moment." She shook her head mournfully. "I fear your standards are not overly high."

He laughed. "And yours are too high."

"I agree."

"You do?" He narrowed his eyes suspiciously. "Why?"

"Because you're right." She shrugged in a nonchalant manner. "I am more than willing to admit when I am wrong."

He studied her for a moment, then shook his head. "You are not."

"I am not what?"

"We have not known one another very long, but you do not strike me as the kind of person who admits when she's wrong or even admits the possibility that she could be wrong. Ever."

"What I am willing to admit right now, my lord, is that I am usually correct, and I do detest having to acknowledge those rare moments when I'm not right. This, unfortunately, is one of them."

"What, precisely, are you wrong about?" he said slowly.

"Lord Perfect. I'm not at all sure such a man could possibly exist." She sighed in resignation. "Men, by their very nature, are not perfect."

"We aren't?" He raised a brow. "Are you sure?"

"I have it on good authority."

"Do you?" He stared down at her, and at once she realized how very near to him she stood. "What of women?" His words were light, but an odd intensity underlay them, as if he too now realized how close they were. "Are women perfect?"

"Of course not." She should step away, put distance between them, but she couldn't seem to move. Or didn't want to. "Well, not all of us."

His gaze slipped from her eyes to her lips and back. "Are you perfect, Miss Effington?"

She swallowed hard. "I fear I have a great many flaws."

"What are they?" His voice was mellow and seductive.

"My flaws? I . . ." *I want you. You are entirely wrong for me and will lead me irrevocably into scandal and I don't care. I want you and all wanting you means.* "I . . ."

"Yes, Miss Effington?" His voice was a caress and shivered through her blood.

She drew a deep breath. "You do realize this is highly improper, don't you?"

"What is highly improper?" His eyes reflected the light from a nearby lantern.

"You are standing entirely too close to me."

"And I thought it was you who were standing entirely too close to me."

"One of us should certainly step away." She couldn't move.

"Indeed, one of us should." He didn't move.

"You are not employing your rakish ways on me, are you, my lord?" It was oddly difficult to breathe, as if they stood in a confined enclosure instead of under the stars. "I assure you they will not work."

"You offend me greatly, Miss Effington. We have agreed to be no more than friends."

"Do you always stand so close to your friends?" She resisted the urge, the need, to reach out and lay her hand on his chest to feel the rise and fall of his breathing.

"Whenever possible, Miss Effington," he murmured, his voice low and altogether too intimate for mere friendship, "whenever possible."

Brush her fingers along the side of his face to feel the warmth of his skin. "You have me at a disadvantage, my lord."

"I can't imagine any man ever having you at a disadvantage."

Press her lips to his to feel his breath mingle with hers. "Nonetheless, you do."

"Good."

"Good?" Fling her arms around him and revel in the heat of his embrace.

"I like having you at a disadvantage. It's second only to having you quiet."

She drew a ragged breath. "That's one of my flaws. I talk entirely—"

"Yes, yes, I know. You are also stubborn and opinionated and no doubt have a host of other faults but," determination snapped in his eyes, "damn it all, Miss Effington, *Cassandra,* there is something about you and I cannot endure this charade another minute."

Without warning, he grabbed her, pulled her into his arms, and kissed her hard. His lips pressed firmly against hers in a manner hungry and demanding and altogether proprietary. As if he were claiming her for his own, marking her as his. He tightened his arms around her, slanted his mouth over hers, and deepened his kiss. He tasted of champagne and all things delightful and forbidden. Her knees weakened and her toes curled inside her slippers and she wanted to stay in his arms forever and plunge with him into scandal and ruin.

He pulled his lips from hers and stared into her eyes. "Do forgive me." He held her a moment longer as if debating with himself, then nodded firmly, released her, and stepped back. "That was most improper."

She swayed slightly on her feet and struggled to maintain her balance and catch her breath. "I don't . . . well certainly . . . that is I'm not . . ."

"My apologies, Miss Effington." He adjusted the cuffs of his coat. "Now, slap me."

"Slap you?" She could barely stand, scarcely breathe properly, and all she could think about was whether he would kiss her again or, better yet, when—and he wanted her to slap him? The man wasn't just infamous but insane.

"Yes, at once. That's what you said you would do if I kissed you."

"I know, but—"

"I insist," he said firmly.

"No." She hid her hands behind her back. "I won't."

"You must."

She shook her head slowly. "I do appreciate the offer, but I would prefer not to."

"Nonetheless, you declared you would slap me, and I think you should."

"I have changed my mind."

"Miss Effington, there is a principle involved here." An unyielding note rang in his voice. "I would not want to be the cause of you going back on your word."

"It wasn't a solemn vow," she scoffed. "I did not take a blood oath, after all."

"Nor did you spit on your finger, but it did seem like a promise to me."

"Nonetheless, I did not mean it to be."

"But you did say it."

"Well, yes, I suppose—"

"And you did mean it, did you not?"

"Certainly at the time I may—"

"Then you should. Indeed, I would be doing you a disservice if I allowed you to—"

Without thinking she cracked her gloved hand across his face, the dull smack echoing in the night air.

He sucked in a sharp breath.

She clapped her hand over her mouth.

"I see I was right," he said slowly. "I suspected it would be painful."

"I am so, so sorry." She stared in horror. How could she? "I can't believe I just did that. I don't know what came over me. I have never hit a man before. I have never hit *anyone* before."

"Really?" He rubbed his cheek gingerly. "I can scarce imagine what you might accomplish with a bit of practice."

She winced in sympathy. "Does it hurt a great deal?"

He huffed. "Yes."

"It's your own fault, you know." She pulled off her gloves, laid one over the back of the bench, and dipped the other in the fountain. "You made me do it."

"I didn't know you would do it with quite so much enthusiasm." He eyed the wet glove. "What are you going to do with that?"

"Sit down." She nodded at the bench and wrung the water out of the glove.

"Why?" Suspicion sounded in his voice, but he sat. "Will you be hitting me with a wet glove now as well?"

"Don't be absurd." She settled beside him and carefully patted his cheek with her glove. "Does that help?"

"Somewhat."

"I didn't want to hit you in the first place."

"I didn't really think you would," he muttered.

"Neither did I." She sighed. It was difficult to see in the dim light cast by the lanterns, but there was a faint red mark on his cheek that would no doubt fade momentarily even without her ministrations. Still, she rather liked patting his face and sitting this close to him. "I feel quite badly about this."

"As well you should." His brows pulled together. "I've never been slapped before."

"Never?" she said mildly. "I would think a man of your reputation had been slapped on more than one occasion."

"You would be wrong." The corners of his mouth quirked upward in a reluctant smile. "Again."

"I never used to be the kind of woman who would slap a man over a mere kiss."

He raised a brow. "Mere?"

Heat rushed up her cheeks and she ignored him. "I

used to be rather more, well, fun, than I am now. In truth, I was the twin everyone expected would become embroiled in scandal."

"I know. Because you speak your mind."

She nodded. "Yes, but beyond that I've always been more impulsive and adventurous than Delia. She's always been the quiet sister."

"The quiet ones are usually the ones who surprise you," he murmured.

"Probably because no one watches them as closely and therefore they have a greater opportunity," she said wryly. "Do you know about my sister?"

"No more than the usual gossip. If I remember correctly, she unexpectedly and hastily married a rather scandalous—"

"Infamous." Cassie smiled.

"*Infamous* baron who died shortly thereafter, and I believe she married St. Stephens far sooner than propriety dictated. Is that right?"

"For the most part." She should probably stop patting his face with her glove, now merely damp more than wet, but it did seem like the very least she could do. "I have been rather more concerned with my own behavior ever since."

"Do you think the scandal surrounding your sister ruined her life and resulted in her spending the rest of her days in dire distress? She certainly does not seem especially unhappy to me."

"She's not." Cassie laughed. "Delia is blissfully happy."

"So, she did everything she wasn't supposed to do, everything considered quite improper and highly scandalous, yet her life has turned out well?"

"I know what you're trying to say." She pulled her hand away, but he caught it in his.

"Don't stop," he said softly.

"I can't imagine it still hurts. In truth, as I was wearing a glove, I don't imagine it hurt all that much to begin with."

"It didn't, Miss Effington." He smiled. "But it will if you stop." He plucked the damp glove from her hand, tossed it beside the dry one, and took both her hands in his.

"My lord, I don't think—"

"Miss Effington, I—" His gaze searched hers.

"Yes?" She had the distinct impression he was about to say something very important. Even perhaps a declaration of . . . what? Feelings? Intent? She certainly didn't want such a declaration.

He leaned closer. "I don't believe I've ever . . ."

"Yes?" She strained forward. Or perhaps she did.

"That is to say I . . ." His lips were a bare breath from hers. If she moved the tiniest bit. . . .

"Yes?" The word was little more than a sigh.

The moment between them lengthened, stretched. She held her breath and waited for him to say something or, better yet, kiss her again. And realized she wanted him to kiss her again. More than she'd ever wanted anything. She didn't care what kind of man he was reputed to be—only what kind of man he was with her. "Yes?"

"I . . ." A myriad of unreadable emotions flashed through his eyes. At last he drew a deep breath. "I think we should set a deadline for our wager."

"Yes, of—" She straightened and stared at him. "What?"

"I said, I think we should set a deadline for our wager." He smiled politely, and she wondered how much more it would hurt if she slapped him with an ungloved hand.

"You still want to go through with our wager," she said slowly. "Even after . . ."

"You said yourself it was only a mere kiss." He stood and extended a hand to help her up.

She ignored it, got to her feet, and forced a smile every bit as polite as his. "It was exceedingly mere, my lord. Scarcely worth mentioning again."

"My sentiments exactly. Now then, Miss Effington, about that deadline."

"I, for one, have no need of a deadline. I can single out your Miss Wonderful the very moment we return to the ballroom." She snatched up her gloves, turned on her heel, and started down the path. "But you're right. I cannot allow our wager to go on forever." She turned abruptly. "A fortnight. That should be long enough. If you can't find Lord Perfect in two weeks' time, you shall owe me forty pounds." She swiveled again and started off.

"What of Miss Wonderful?" he called after her.

"I told you. I shall point her out to you this very night."

"But what if I don't think she's wonderful?"

"Oh, you will. I'm certain of that," she muttered.

She hadn't the vaguest idea who exactly she would present as Miss Wonderful, but it shouldn't be all that difficult. She'd simply pick one. Any one would surely do. Any insipid, simpering, lovely young thing. Regardless of what he said he wanted, he no doubt wanted what every man wanted: a pretty creature who would look good on his arm and obey his every whim and keep her mouth shut.

"But what if you don't think the Lord Perfect I select is actually perfect?"

"Then you owe me forty pounds!" she called over her shoulder.

She rounded a bend in the path and came face-to-face with Delia and St. Stephens.

"Cassie! What . . ." Delia's gaze skipped from her sister to Berkley and back.

"Come along, Delia." Cassie hooked her arm through her sister's and practically dragged her toward the house at a brisk pace.

Delia cast a helpless glance at her husband, who turned a questioning gaze toward Lord Berkley, who continued to smile pleasantly as if nothing whatsoever had happened. As if he hadn't kissed her as she'd never been kissed before. A mere kiss indeed! Why, the man deserved to be smacked again, and very hard, for that smile if nothing else.

"Why are we running?" Delia said in a low voice.

"We aren't running," Cassie said but slowed her pace slightly anyway. "We are simply anxious to return to the ballroom, where I will point out Miss Wonderful to Lord Berkley, thus fulfilling my end of the wager."

"I see," Delia's voice was thoughtful. "Then the wager is still on?"

"Absolutely." Cassie nodded with a bit more vehemence than was perhaps necessary. "Regardless of the fairness of our bet, he agreed to it, and I fully intend to end this absurdity with either forty pounds or Lord Perfect."

"I see," Delia said again.

"What, exactly, do you see?"

"He's done something even more annoying than usual, hasn't he?"

"Yes," Cassie hissed.

"What has he done now?"

They climbed the terrace steps and reached the French doors leading into the ballroom foyer. Cassie clenched her teeth and turned toward her sister. "He didn't kiss me. Again."

Delia choked back a laugh. "He is making quite a habit of not kissing you."

"Well, he did kiss me once, then—"

Delia raised a curious brow. "Oh?"

"Yes, but it was insignificant. A mere kiss. But he didn't kiss me *again*. Oh certainly, he might have hesitated because I slapped him, but I—"

"You hit him?"

"He insisted," Cassie said staunchly. "I didn't want to, but he kept going on and on about how I had given my word and—"

Delia laughed.

"You think all this is amusing?"

"Yes. It's perhaps one of the most entertaining things I've seen in a long time." Delia grinned. "I can hardly wait to see what happens next."

"Neither can I," Lord Berkley came up behind them. "Neither can I."

A few moments later, Cassie and her sister, St. Stephens and Lord Berkley stood in a large circular alcove just off the ballroom. Tall palms and other tropical plants were clustered in the center of the alcove, and floor-to-ceiling windows overlooked the gardens below. It was the perfect spot from which to survey the room.

Cassie's gaze skimmed the crowd.

"So which one is she?" Lord Berkley asked coolly.

"One moment, my lord," she said under her breath.

She'd been entirely right when she'd told Delia the room was thick with Miss Wonderfuls. The problem was simply which one to cull from the herd.

"Well?" Delia said low in her ear. "Who's it to be?"

"I haven't decided," Cassie muttered. "I was considering Miss Carmichael." She nodded at a group of smiling young ladies, chatting and giggling and casting flirtatious looks at every eligible man who unknowingly wandered within range.

Delia shook her head. "She has a tendency toward silliness, I believe."

"What about Miss Bennet?" Cassie's gaze settled on a slight blonde laughing with a touch too much fervor.

"She's a bit too high strung to be wonderful, I think," Delia said. "Besides, she talks a great deal."

Cassie stifled a sharp reply.

Delia glanced around the ballroom, then nudged her sister. "There's your Miss Wonderful. Miss Bellingham."

Cassie followed her sister's gaze. Felicity Bellingham was the daughter of the widowed Lady Bellingham. This was her second season, and while no one had paid her much notice last year, she'd apparently blossomed since then and was now considered one of this season's beauties. There were already any number of wagers about town as to how soon she would make a match. She was of a medium height with very dark hair and eyes that were reported to be a rather startling shade of violet. Cassie had heard her described as charming and witty as well.

And she didn't like her one bit.

"I should think Miss Frey over there would be a better choice," Cassie murmured.

"Miss Frey is quite nice." Delia's words were measured. "And how fortunate her hair is thick enough to cover the impressive expanse of her ears."

"Beauty is not one of Lord Berkley's requirements." Cassie waved off her sister's comments and ignored as well a stab of what might possibly be conscience. "Besides, you just said she's very nice."

"She has to be," Delia murmured.

"Well, Miss Effington." Lord Berkley stepped to her side. "Who is it to be?"

"Yes, Cassie, do tell us," Delia smiled sweetly.

Cassie rolled her gaze toward the ceiling and sighed in surrender. "Miss Bellingham, I should think."

"Miss Bellingham?" Berkley's eyes widened in surprise and, possibly, delight. "Miss Felicity Bellingham?"

"There is only one Miss Bellingham," St. Stephens said firmly.

Cassie's heart sank. "You've met her, then?"

"No." Berkley's gaze settled on the girl. "But I have heard of her."

"You'd have to have been dead not to have heard of Miss Felicity Bellingham," St. Stephens said under his breath.

"And I am quite looking forward to meeting her." A distinctly wicked gleam sparked in Berkley's eye, and he adjusted his cuffs. It was a most annoying habit and something someone should do something about.

"I'm certain we can find someone to introduce you." Cassie wasn't entirely sure why she wasn't feeling anything that felt remotely satisfying, when she should be feeling nothing but triumph.

"Oh, I've met her. We chatted on several occasions. Indeed, Cassie, I believe our mother is quite well acquainted with her mother." Delia cast her sister an innocent look, then turned to Lord Berkley. "If you'd like, I'd be happy to introduce you."

"I should like that very much." Berkley offered Delia his arm and they turned to go. Berkley glanced back over his shoulder and grinned. "Well done, Miss Effington, well done indeed."

Cassie smiled weakly.

Delia and Berkley started off, and St. Stephens leaned close. "I should start thinking about how I planned on spending my forty pounds if I were you."

"Splendid," she snapped.

She would obviously win this ridiculous wager of theirs. Berkley didn't stand a chance. Victory was almost within her grasp.

Then why did she feel as if she were about to lose? And lose something far more important than forty pounds?

"Were you aware that Effingtons do not like to lose?" Lady St. Stephens said under her breath as she and Reggie made their way around the ballroom.

"It had apparently slipped my mind," Reggie said wryly. "Do you have any suggestions as to what I should do now?"

"Yes. No. Perhaps." Lady St. Stephens paused for a moment to exchange greetings with an overly inquisitive matron who directed her words to Cassie's sister but fixed him with a speculative eye. Reggie could almost see the clockwork gears of her mind turning. He smiled in a noncommittal manner and firmly steered Lady St. Stephens back on course.

"Well, that should trigger no end of gossip," she murmured.

Reggie stifled a grin. "Lady St. Stephens in the company of the infamous Lord Berkley, you mean?"

"You needn't sound so pleased." She glanced at him and smiled. "Although, in truth, I came to terms with gossip and scandal some time ago, and I pay it little heed. Now then, as for your dilemma," her brows pulled together thoughtfully. "It seems to me, as Cassie has presented you with a Miss Wonderful, I think it's imperative that you do now produce a Lord Perfect."

"Why?" He shook his head. "Won't that just compound the problem?"

"It's a risk, I suppose, but you have little choice at the moment. You want her to realize she wouldn't be at all happy with a Lord Perfect, which I suspect may already be happening. That growing awareness, coupled with just a bit of the jealousy she'll feel with you paying any attention whatsoever to Miss Bellingham—"

"I wouldn't want to lead Miss Bellingham on," he said quickly. "I should hate for her to think I had a serious interest in her."

"My dear Lord Berkley, Miss Bellingham is one of the belles of the season and is certain to make an excellent match. I daresay a bit of attention from you will be insignificant among her other suitors."

He raised a brow.

"Oh dear, I didn't mean that quite the way it sounded. And I do think your concern for her is admirable. I suspect Miss Bellingham is the kind of young lady who would appreciate the scheme we have in mind. I shall have a word with her and secure her understanding."

"Thank you."

"Now then, as I was saying, Cassie's realization that Lord Perfect will not suit her at all, together with the jealousy I'm confident she will feel at your attention toward Miss Wonderful, should produce a great deal of amusement."

"Amusement?"

"Did I say amusement?" Lady St. Stephens stopped short and stared at him with the precise look of innocent surprise he already recognized as Cassandra's. "I meant results. The results that you want. Yes, that's what I meant."

"Of course," he murmured and considered her for a moment. "Lady St. Stephens, you are on my side, aren't you?"

"Don't be absurd, my lord. The only side I am on is that of my sister. Fortunately for you, I am confident your side and hers," she grinned, "are one and the same."

Eight

There is nothing more frightening in life than discovering one's beloved sister has turned into a completely foreign and terrifying creature. A woman.

Reginald, Viscount Berkley

"I haven't seen her for three full days, Marcus. Not since Lady Puget's ball. We don't even seem to be frequenting the same social events." Reggie paced the width of the library. "She's avoiding me, I'm certain of it."

"I thought she was decorating your house?" Marcus sat in one of the oversized leather wing chairs that had been comfortable fixtures in the Berkley House library since Reggie's father was a boy. He watched his friend with unconcealed amusement. "As long as you stay firmly planted within said house, she can't possibly avoid you."

"She hasn't been here since the day we made our

wager." Reggie heaved a heartfelt sigh. Overly dramatic perhaps, but he was feeling rather dramatic at the moment. "I have had no communication with her at all save a note telling me she would need some time to complete her drawings and would meet with me next week." He stopped and glared at his friend. "Next week? How am I supposed to wait until next week to see her again?"

"You could fill your time pursuing Miss Bellingham."

"Don't be absurd." Reggie brushed aside the suggestion. "I have no interest in Miss Bellingham, nor does she have any interest in me." He brightened. "Although she is a good sort. Lady St. Stephens wrote to say Miss Bellingham thinks our plan is quite amusing and she'd be delighted to do her part." He drew his brows together. "Am I the only one who doesn't see the amusement in this situation?"

"Yes." Marcus grinned.

"Actually, I can understand the possibility of humor." Reggie blew a long breath. "Or perhaps I will someday." He resumed his pacing. "For the immediate future, I must determine a way to spend more time with Miss Effington. I could insist she finish her drawings here in the house I suppose, or request that she hurry this process along. Say my mother has taken a turn for the worse or something like that. I would think once there are painters and craftsmen and whatever else working here in the house, Miss Effington will certainly wish to—"

"You could pay a call on her," Marcus said casually. "That's what men in your position usually do."

"Absolutely not." Reggie shook his head firmly. "I

will not go to her with my heart in my hand until I am confident my feelings are returned, and I can't believe you, of all people, would encourage me to do so."

"I wouldn't exactly say—"

"Regardless of my feelings I will practice restraint and patience and all those other blasted qualities I've never been especially gifted with." Reggie met his friend's gaze. "You have no idea how difficult it was to hold her in my arms, to look into her eyes and not tell her how I feel."

"And you have so little experience with curbing such impulses." Marcus studied him thoughtfully. "The fact that you were able to do so now is extremely significant."

"That's what I thought." Reggie paused for a moment to find the right words. "It's the oddest thing, Marcus. God knows, I've fallen in love before—"

"I have certainly lost count," Marcus murmured.

Reggie ignored him. "But this is entirely different. Miss Effington is the woman I will marry. I know it as I have known nothing else in my life."

"You simply need to convince her."

"And she's a stubborn creature. Besides, at this point she no doubt believes that everything she's heard about me is true. That I am the kind of man who would take liberties, who would steal kisses in a darkened garden, without a second thought." Reggie blew an exasperated breath. "I daresay by the time I manage to convince her I am well worth reforming and far more perfect for her than any Lord Perfect could ever be, we will both be in our dotage."

"At least by then her punch won't be quite so wicked."

"That's something, at any rate."

A firm knock sounded at the open library door. Higgins stood in the entry bearing a tray with a decanter of brandy and three glasses.

"Do hurry in, Higgins," Marcus said with a grin. "Lord Berkley and I are discussing matters of great importance, and his good brandy is a necessary ingredient for such talks."

"As always, my lord." Higgins's tone was level but nonetheless carried a world of comment.

Reggie bit back a grin. Higgins knew, as well as Marcus or Reggie himself, what impractical plans and plots had been launched in this very room through the years—assisted by brandy or, on those rare occasions when as boys they'd chanced to be in London at the same time, by sweets and pastries.

Higgins placed the tray on the desk and poured two glasses.

"Higgins." Reggie nodded at the third glass. "While we are planning strategy of a highly complicated nature, I doubt that either of us needs more than one glass."

"My mistake, sir," Higgins said smoothly.

Marcus got to his feet and crossed the room to take a glass. "Well, I'll have you know I am doing my part."

"Your part?" Reggie accepted a brandy from Higgins, who then promptly took his leave. Reggie noted he had forgotten the third glass and wondered if the old boy was at last succumbing to age, although in truth the butler wasn't substantially older than Reggie's mother. Of course, she still claimed to be on her deathbed. "And what precisely is your part?"

"You said you needed to spend more time with her." Marcus raised his glass in a triumphant salute. "I have arranged it."

"Have you indeed?" Reggie grinned. "I'd hoped you wouldn't allow me to flounder on my own."

"I never have."

Reggie knew Marcus far too well to doubt that he had come up with something clever. Through their long friendship, Reggie might well have been the instigator of any number of questionable schemes, but as often as not Marcus had found a way to smooth over the ruts in whatever road Reggie had been barreling along.

"Dare I ask what exactly have you arranged?"

"My wife wants to have a country party at Holcroft Hall. One of those things that goes on for several days with all manner of out-of-doors activities during the day and convivial gatherings at night. The kind of thing that's either great fun or deadly."

"Ah yes." Reggie sipped his brandy. "Like last year's debacle at Gifford Court."

Marcus shuddered. "We shall endeavor to avoid anything of that nature. Gwen is handling all the details, of course, but I am envisioning a few days of country life, a respite from the city, for some of our closest friends. A dozen or so, I think. Invitations are already being delivered. It will be the perfect opportunity for you to get closer to Miss Effington. She is invited, of course, as are Lord and Lady St. Stephens, as well as Miss Bellingham and her mother." Marcus smiled smugly. "You can thank me now, or later, if you'd prefer."

"I think it's rather amazing Gwen could arrange all this on such short notice. Perhaps I should thank her."

"You can if you wish." Marcus shrugged. "However, she was already planning it for next month. It was my idea to move it to four days hence."

Reggie's brow raised. "And she agreed?"

"Agreed is perhaps too mild a term." Marcus grimaced. "Let's just say, when I explained my reasons, and she is as eager to see you wed as you are yourself, you know, she was amenable to the idea."

"Amenable?"

"Admittedly with a few promises on my part." Marcus grinned. "Most of them quite pleasant."

"Four days to wait to see Miss Effington is not substantially shorter than a full week. Still, the surroundings will be much more conducive to . . ."

"Working your way into her affections?"

"Exactly." Reggie laughed. "Well done, Marcus."

At once his spirits lifted. A moment ago he wasn't sure what he would do next in his effort to win Cassandra's heart. He couldn't simply drag her from her house and force her into his company, as tempting as that might be. Now he had the opportunity to spend a great deal of time with her in the very near future. And at Marcus's estate, no less, which marched beside Reggie's own. There might even be the possibility of showing her Berkley Park.

"You do indeed have my thanks, as does your wife." Reggie sipped his brandy and thought for a moment. "The only thing left is to arrange for a Lord Perfect. I have given it a great deal of thought, and more and more I think an actor would serve the purpose. Of course, should Miss Effington ever find out—"

"She would shoot you," Marcus said firmly. "She is an Effington after all, and an independent female member of that family as well. She wouldn't hesitate to shoot you for something like this. And, given the reputation we have managed to wrap around you, she'd no doubt get away with it."

Reggie winced. "That could be awkward."

"Awkward?" Marcus snorted. "That's not the worst of it. She could shoot me too."

"Oh, yes, that would be worse," Reggie said wryly.

"Are you absolutely certain about this?" Marcus eyed him with a great deal of skepticism. "Pursuing the eccentric Miss Effington, that is? Certainly, the woman is lovely, but given her outspoken, obstinate, independent nature and the fact that she has already declared you will not suit—"

"She's wrong."

"And don't you think the vehemence with which her brother tried to peddle her to you is, well, a bad sign? The man seemed somewhat desperate."

"I wouldn't call him desperate."

"I would."

"Admittedly, I would certainly not want a female with Miss Effington's unique charms as a sister, and I imagine I, too, would be a bit desperate to get her wed. But as a wife, Marcus." The very idea brought a grin to his face. "The spirit one would prefer not to have in a sister is exactly what one wants in a wife."

"If you're certain."

"Never more so than now."

"Very well then." Marcus glanced at the clock positioned on the fireplace mantel. "Once again I have arranged to come to your assistance, even if the method of doing so is late."

"Oh?"

"Yes, well, I had invited—"

A discreet cough sounded from the doorway.

Reggie glanced at the butler. "Yes, Higgins?"

"I beg your pardon, sir, but there is a gentleman who wishes to see you." Higgins paused. "Both of you."

"Both of us?" Reggie frowned. "Who is it?"

"A Mr. Effington, sir."

"Show him in, Higgins," Marcus said and nodded at Reggie. "I asked him to come."

"You did?" Reggie pulled his brows together in confusion. "Why?"

"Because I have an idea," Marcus smirked. "And a brilliant one at that."

"Dare I ask—"

"Good day, Lord Berkley." Christian Effington strolled into the room. "Lord Pennington."

"Effington." Berkley greeted the man. What was Marcus up to? "I must say, I'm surprised to see you here."

Effington chuckled. "No more so than I am to be here. But I received a note from Pennington requesting my presence, and I know my sister is decorating your house." He sobered. "There isn't a problem with that, is there? Not much I could do anyway, I suppose, she certainly doesn't listen to anything I say. Still, as much as I think this business of hers is absurd, I understand she does a bang-up job."

"No, there's no problem at all." Reggie shook his head. "She's quite gifted."

"Excellent." Effington breathed a sigh of relief and looked around the library curiously. "I must say, she's done a good job in here."

"She's not doing this particular room."

"Oh." Effington's brow furrowed, then his expression cleared. "Good thing, too. You wouldn't want a female dabbling about in a room like this. This is a place for gentlemen and cigars and," his gaze dropped to the glass in Reggie's hand, "brandy."

"Would you care for a glass?" Reggie gestured at the tray on the desk.

"If it's good." Effington grinned.

"It is." Marcus filled the remaining glass and handed it to Effington, who promptly took a deep swallow.

"That is good," Effington said. "My compliments." He took another drink, then met Reggie's gaze. "I've been meaning to call on you. Regarding the money I owe you. I'm afraid I'm still a bit short. If you could see your way clear—"

"Actually, Effington," Marcus said, "Berkley here is ready to forgive the debt entirely."

Effington brightened. "He is?"

Reggie frowned. "I am?"

"Indeed you are," Marcus nodded.

Effington grinned. "Damned decent of you, old man."

"Think nothing of it," Reggie muttered and hoped whatever Marcus's brilliant idea was, it was worth one hundred and fifty pounds. He settled into a chair and waved the others to a seat.

Effington swirled the brandy in his glass and glanced from one man to the next. "So, gentlemen, what's the condition? There must be something."

"Indeed there is." Marcus leaned forward in his chair. "Berkley needs a favor in return."

"Very well." Effington nodded. "I am completely at your service."

"Good to know," Reggie murmured.

"What exactly is this favor?" Effington's gaze again shifted from one man to the other. "And why do I suspect I might be better off remaining in Berkley's debt?"

"This particular favor is in your best interest as well. Berkley and your sister are engaged in a wager of their own." Marcus quickly explained the terms of the bet. "And we want you to find us a Lord Perfect."

Effington shook his head. "It can't be done. Quite frankly, we've been trying for years to find Cassandra a Lord Perfect, although we haven't referred to him as such, as appropriate as the title is. Her standards are entirely too high."

"I'm well aware of that." Reggie sighed. "But we don't need a real Lord Perfect. Just someone to pass as Lord Perfect. An actor, perhaps."

Effington frowned in confusion. "If the object is simply to win your wager, why can't *you* find someone to pass as Lord Perfect?"

"Because if she were ever to find out the truth," Reggie grimaced, "she might well shoot me."

Effington snorted. "If you're lucky."

"But you are her brother, and therefore she'd have to forgive you," Marcus added. "Eventually."

"If I'm lucky." Effington took another drink and thought for a moment. "I still don't understand."

"You see, Effington, the idea is that once your sister is presented with a Lord Perfect, preferably a fraudulent one, she'll realize that's not what she wants at all. What she really wants," Marcus gestured at Reggie with a grand flourish, "is Berkley. Or Lord As-Far-From-Perfect-As-One-Can-Get."

"Thank you," Reggie muttered.

Effington's eyes narrowed. "Why?"

"Because," Reggie rolled his gaze toward the ceiling, "I wish to marry her."

"Cassandra?" Effington stared in disbelief. "Why?"

"Why?" Reggie downed the rest of his glass. "For all the usual reasons, I suppose. As much as she is certain we do not suit, I am certain that we do."

"She drives him mad." Marcus grinned.

Reggie shrugged. "And I can't imagine living the rest of my days without her, nor do I wish to."

"I see." Effington studied him for a long moment. "Does she care for you?"

"I don't know." Reggie blew a long breath. "I'm not sure she'd admit it if she did. I think she likes me a bit. We've agreed to be friends at any rate. The truth of the matter is, if she doesn't harbor some measure of affection for me, this scheme will fail. While I am certain that the kind of man she professes to want will not suit her at all, there is no guarantee she will then see me as anything but a friend. Ever. It's a risk, I suppose."

"And one you're willing to take?" Effington said evenly.

Reggie nodded. "She's not the kind of woman one can court by the usual methods."

"No indeed she's not," Effington said slowly. "I would like to help, but I'm not—"

"Reggie!" Lucy burst into the library. "I hate to interrupt you but—" She pulled up short and stared at Effington.

The men leapt to their feet, Effington a bit slower than the others, his gaze firmly fixed on Reggie's sister.

"I do apologize," she said in a voice decidedly lower and distinctly more, well, seductive than her usual tone. Her words were directed at Reggie, but her gaze didn't so much as waver from Effington. "I didn't realize you had guests."

Marcus snorted. "I scarcely count as a guest."

"I wasn't talking about you," she said under her breath and stepped toward Effington. "I don't believe we've met."

"Lucy, this is Mr. Effington," Reggie said slowly. "Mr. Effington, allow me to present my sister, Miss Berkley."

"How delightful." Lucy held out her hand.

"It is completely my honor, Miss Berkley." Effington took her hand and raised it to his lips, his gaze never leaving hers.

At once Reggie saw what the younger man did, and a cold chill gripped his stomach.

Lucy cocked her head prettily to one side and gazed up at Effington as if he were the only man in existence. Gone was the sweet, infuriating little sister, replaced by some vision of blossoming womanhood. Her dark hair billowed around her fair face, her eyes were wide and luminous, her lips were entirely too full and red, and a becoming blush tinted her cheeks. Her dress was demure yet still showed a figure far and away too inviting and positively lush. Who was this delectable creature? And where in the hell was his sister?

Reggie caught Marcus's gaze; he looked every bit as shocked as Reggie. Of course, Marcus had known Lucy all her life and considered her as much a sister as if they were blood.

Lucy and Effington continued to stare at each other as if they were alone in the room. Or in the world. It was most upsetting.

Marcus cleared his throat.

"Lucy," Reggie said, a shade sharper than was necessary. "Did you want something?"

"Not really," she said in that siren voice that came from God knew where. She drew her hand from Effington's with obvious reluctance.

"Then why are you here?" Reggie's voice was firm.

"Why?" She heaved a delicate sigh and pulled her gaze from Effington's. "Why?"

Reggie grit his teeth. "That was the question."

"Oh." She shook her head as if to clear it. "Mother wanted you to know she's feeling much better. Quite her old self, actually."

"She's no longer dying then?" Marcus asked in an innocent manner.

"Apparently not." Lucy's brows drew together. "She claims it's a miracle. She's getting dressed even now. And she insists on traveling to Berkley Park tomorrow, to get her strength back she says, in advance of attending your house party." She glanced at Marcus. "Your mother and another lady came by earlier today with an invitation for us all."

Reggie raised a brow. "All of us?"

"All of us." Lucy's smile carried a hint of triumph. "Lady Pennington and Mother both agreed that even though I am not out yet, I should be allowed to come."

"We'll see," Reggie said under his breath.

"Will you be there, Mr. Effington?" Lucy cast him a look far too flirtatious for a sixteen-year-old girl. And, good God, did she flutter her lashes?

Effington swallowed hard. "I don't—"

"No," Reggie snapped.

"Yes, of course," Marcus said smoothly, slanting Reggie a quieting glance. "I suspect his invitation and those for his parents and his brothers are already waiting for him at his residence."

"Oh, you have brothers?" Lucy's eyes widened with interest.

"Two." Effington nodded slowly, as if he had no idea as to the answer to this question—or indeed, no idea as to his very name. "But Drew is not in town at the moment."

"What a pity. Well, I do look forward to meeting your other brother, and I shall quite count every minute until you and I meet again." She beamed at Effington, nodded smugly at her brother, tossed Marcus a wicked grin, and sailed out of the room.

All three men stared after her.

"Who was that?" Marcus said under his breath.

"I have no idea." Reggie's voice was grim. "But that was the most terrifying thing I have ever witnessed."

"Did she say she was not out yet?" Effington stared at the doorway as if frozen.

Reggie and Marcus traded glances.

"She's not yet seventeen, Effington," Reggie growled.

"And she has a very protective family," Marcus added. "As well as friends of her family who would not take—"

"I'll do it," Effington said abruptly and turned toward them. "I'll help you win my sister. I'll find your Lord Perfect or anything else you need."

Reggie narrowed his eyes. "Why?"

"For one thing, I am still unable to pay my debt to you. I am not fond of being in debt, no one in the family is, even if we do find ourselves in dire straits on occasion, and unfortunately, I don't know when the state of my finances will improve. For another," he met Reggie's gaze directly, "just as you obviously care for your sister, I have a great deal of affection for Cassandra. I want nothing more than to see her happy, and I fear the path she is on will not lead to that.

"She is exceeding stubborn and rarely admits to the possibility that she could be in error. I agree with you: I don't believe the kind of man she claims to want will suit her. You may not be the right match for her, but no one will ever make her do what she doesn't want to do. If your plan works, it will work only because you've won her heart. Furthermore," Effington grinned, "I think this farce of yours sounds like great fun. It should be most amusing."

"Everyone seems to think so," Reggie muttered.

"Excellent." Marcus beamed. "Now, for the details."

"But first." Effington got to his feet, stepped to the desk, and grabbed the brandy decanter. "I think a bit of a celebration is in order." He filled the other men's glasses and raised his glass. "Welcome to the family, my lord."

"A bit premature, don't you think?" Reggie asked.

"Not in the least," Effington said firmly. "I think my sister may well have finally met her match. She is possibly the most stubborn and determined person I have ever known." He grinned. "Until now."

Marcus laughed.

Reggie grinned and raised his glass. "Now that, Effington, does indeed call for a celebration."

A few hours and several glasses of brandy later, Effington took his leave.

"I daresay, that was a productive meeting." Marcus stared at his empty glass.

"Most productive." Reggie lounged in a wing chair and savored the feeling of accomplishment.

A pleasant sense of satisfaction hovered in the air, aided by the brandy, no doubt, but more by the confidence induced by Reggie's firm and fervent belief that the three men had considered every flaw in their plan, every potential disaster, every possibility for failure. And indeed there were any number of things that could go horribly wrong. Still, knowing what the pitfalls in this enterprise were at least took away the possibility of surprise.

They'd agreed that Effington would bring the counterfeit Lord Perfect with him to Holcroft Hall the day after Cassandra's arrival, to allow Reggie time to cultivate seeds of doubt as to the paragon's suitability for her. And, if necessary, to cultivate a bit of jealousy over Miss Bellingham as well.

Reggie caught his friend's gaze. "Do you think he can really find a Lord Perfect? In three days?"

"I have no idea." Marcus's brow furrowed. "But he seemed most determined."

"Marcus." Reggie stared at his now empty glass. "Did you hear what he said about his finances?"

"His finances?" Marcus thought for a moment. "You mean that business about dire straits?"

"Yes. He said his family was in dire straits."

Marcus frowned. "I don't think that's exactly what he said."

"Not specifically. He didn't come right out and say it. Indeed, I wouldn't if I were in his position. But it was definitely implied."

"I think, once again, you're jumping to conclusions on the basis of nothing more significant than an off-hand comment." Marcus heaved a long-suffering sigh. "You have always done exactly that, and I do think the next step in your ongoing effort to control the vagaries of your life is to work on that particular problem."

"Perhaps, but his comment, coupled with his lack of funds and Miss Effington's business endeavor, cannot be mere coincidence." Reggie shook his head. "No, Marcus, I'm certain I was right all along. Miss Effington is doing what she does as much out of financial want as anything else. It's quite noble of her."

Marcus groaned. "Reggie, you can't—"

"I can and I shall."

"So once again, it's Viscount Berkley to the rescue of a damsel in distress?"

"Indeed it is." Reggie's voice was resolute. "Cassandra needs me. And I will not fail her."

"You can't avoid him forever, you know." Delia lounged on the settee in her parlor and watched her sister's restless pacing with barely concealed amusement. "You have taken on the redecoration of his house, and unless you propose to do it without again stepping foot in the building, you will see him. He does live there, you know."

"I know," Cassie said a bit more sharply than she intended. "And I'm not avoiding him."

"Oh?" Delia raised a brow.

"Well, perhaps I am a bit." Cassie blew a frustrated breath. "But I certainly can't if I accept this invitation." She waved the note from Lady Pennington, which had prompted Cassie's visit to her sister. "He's certain to be at this country house party."

"I have no doubt of it. I understand he and Lord Pennington are quite good friends." Delia paused. "Tony and I are going. In fact, I've already sent our acceptance. You may drive out with us."

"I have a great deal of work to do," Cassie said firmly. "I need to complete my drawings before I can return to Berkley House. And then there will be all sorts of measurements to take and selections of—"

"Nonsense. That's nothing more than an excuse and not a particularly good one at that. You can take your drawings with you and finish them there. A few days in the country will be good for you."

"I suspect being in close proximity to Lord Berkley will be anything but good for me," Cassie said under her breath.

If truth were told, with every passing day, she more and more wanted to be in close proximity to him. Wanted him to take her in his arms and kiss her again and again until she melted at his feet. Wanted all sorts of things she shouldn't want. All sorts of things that would ultimately lead to her ruin. It was terrifying and made all the more so by the fact that every time her thoughts turned to Viscount Berkley—as they did constantly—ruin did not seem quite so dreadful. In point of fact, ruin and scandal and everything else she'd feared being part of her very nature were becoming almost irresistible.

"I can't remember the last time I attended a party in the country that wasn't at Effington Hall," Delia said thoughtfully. "We shall be there next month for the Roxborough Ride, of course, and while it will be wonderful to see all the varied Effington relations gathered in one place, I must admit I'm quite looking forward to this party at Holcroft Hall, where I am not related to virtually everyone in sight."

"Do you know who else is attending?"

"Not everyone. Mother and Father were invited, but they've begged off. However, Mother says Leo and Christian will definitely attend. I understand Cousin Thomas and Marianne have also been invited. Lord Berkley, of course, his mother and younger sister—"

"His mother is feeling better then?" Cassie drew her brows together. "I should probably pay her a call as soon as possible."

"That will have to wait. She is leaving for the country in the morning. Berkley Park, Lord Berkley's estate, borders on Lord Pennington's."

"Which explains why they are such good friends, I suppose." Cassie narrowed her gaze. "But how do you know all this?"

"Mother told me. She's apparently been quite busy today." Delia cast her a wry smile. "Lady Pennington, Lord Pennington's mother, that is, delivered your invitations in person this morning. She and Mother then paid a call on Lady Berkley."

"I had no idea they were such bosom bows. Until recently, I don't know that I'd ever heard Mother mention either lady. Doesn't this sudden companionship strike you as odd?"

"Not really." Delia shrugged. "They are of a similar age and experience. I wouldn't be at all surprised if they hadn't shared secrets together during their first seasons in society and are simply continuing an old friendship.

"At any rate, Mother had a great deal of information that she was more than willing to impart, but her real purpose was to convince me to encourage you to attend the house party."

"Encourage?"

"Encourage is perhaps inaccurate. Her exact words were something to the effect of tie her up and toss her in a carriage if need be." Delia grinned.

Cassie laughed. "That sounds like Mother, although I can't imagine why she's so insistent on my attendance."

"She said she had her stars charted and read again and yours as well, I gather, and it would be a grave mistake for you to miss this party. Something about the confluence of this and influence of that means this foray in the country falls in a period of great possibility for you. A critical moment that could well change your life."

"Really?" Cassie sighed and collapsed into a damask-covered chair. "How . . . exciting."

As much as she and her sister scoffed at her mother's passion for astrology and all things mystical, even the strongest skeptic had to admit that her mother's predictions and forecasts, guided by the stars, her cards, and a very sweet, apple-cheeked woman named Mrs. Prusha, were accurate an amazing percentage of the time. Her children, as well as her husband, had long ago realized it was far better to abide by Georgina Effington's words than to risk the consequences. Her mother's claim that this particular gathering was of such significance could not easily be dismissed. Cassie's stomach twisted.

"She also noted that you have begged off all social events since Lady Puget's ball, and she's quite concerned. She fears you will never find a husband if you stay at home."

"Yes, well, you scarcely need the stars to determine that." Cassie traced the pattern on the fabric on the arm of the chair with her finger, noting with satisfaction in the back of her mind how perfectly suited it was for this room. She drew a deep breath and forced a casual note to her voice. "I could always reform Lord Berkley and marry him, I suppose."

"That is indeed a possibility," Delia said evenly.

Cassie's gaze snapped to her sister's. "Do you think so? I mean, do you think a man with an infamous reputation can truly be reformed?"

Delia chose her words with care. "By the right woman, I think most certainly."

"I don't know." Restlessness pulled Cassie to her feet once again, and she meandered around the edges of the room. "I've never had the tiniest desire to reform a man. It's the last thing I ever wanted." She paused by the mantel and moved the French bronze clock to the right a bare quarter of an inch. "It's never made any sense to me that you would marry someone all the while planning to change him. Indeed, change the very things that you probably found attractive in the first place. Beyond that, marriage is forever, and if attempts at reform fail . . . it's simply always seemed a very great risk."

She wandered to the window, adjusted the fall of the drapes slightly, crossed her arms over her chest, and gazed out at the street below. Still, for the right man, the risk might well be worth it.

"Delia," she said slowly, "I think I may have been wrong."

Delia gasped with feigned dismay. "You? Wrong? How could such a thing have happened?"

"I don't know." Cassie cast her sister a wry glance. "It has never happened before."

"Not that you'd admit anyway. What precisely are you wrong about?"

Cassie searched for the right words. "I am beginning to think the mere fact that a man has a questionable reputation does not mean he is not a decent sort. Beneath it all, I mean."

"I gather we're talking about Lord Berkley."

Cassie nodded. "He's not anything like I thought he would be."

"Not infamous, then?"

"Oh no, he most certainly is infamous, at least his reputation is. As for the man himself . . ." She returned to the sofa and plopped down beside her sister. "I get the most ridiculous impression that he's somehow not the kind of man to do the sorts of things that could be considered, well, infamous."

"How very interesting," Delia murmured.

"I don't understand it." Cassie shook her head. "I am usually such a good judge of character."

"You're a good judge of the obvious."

Cassie's eyes widened in disbelief. "Are you saying I'm shallow?"

"Not precisely, but you've never been good about looking below the surface. My dear Cassie, you have an excellent eye for color, and your taste is impeccable, and you can see a great deal of potential in things that I cannot, but you've never been able to extend that same skill to people."

The import of her sister's words sank in. "You are saying I'm shallow."

"No. I'm saying you have never had to look beyond face value when it comes to people. Therefore, you never have."

"That sounds suspiciously like shallow to me."

Cassie was well aware that she had any number of faults, but she had never thought of herself as shallow.

"It seems to me," Delia's words were measured, "that Lord Berkley is an excellent example. Were it not for the fact that you and he were thrown together, you would never have given him any consideration at all. Based on nothing more than gossip, you had decided he was not the right match for you. You never gave the man a chance."

"Good Lord." Cassie slumped deeper in the sofa, closed her eyes, and pressed the back of her hand to her forehead. "I am shallow."

"Furthermore, your insistence as to the kind of man you claim you want, this ridiculous Lord Perfect—"

"That's quite enough, thank you. You've made your point. I needn't hear any more." Cassie groaned. "I'm a dreadful, dreadful person. A dreadful, dreadful *shallow* person."

Delia laughed. "Don't be absurd. You're not at all dreadful. You're really very nice and terribly clever and quite generous and, I know it's very immodest of me to say, extremely pretty."

"And shallow." Cassie heaved a heartfelt sigh.

"Not shallow exactly. For goodness' sakes, Cassie, I never said shallow." Delia huffed. "You simply make up your mind about something—in this case Lord Berkley—and refuse to let anything dissuade you. You always have, you know. And you refuse to consider the possibility that you could be wrong."

"But I did admit I was wrong." Cassie opened her eyes and bolted upright. "That should count for something. I admitted it right here not more than a minute or so ago. I said I was wrong about Lord Berkley."

"And isn't that something to consider," Delia snapped.

"What on earth do you mean?"

"Come now, Cassie. Surely you can see what's right in front of you?" Delia leaned toward her sister and pinned her with an unyielding gaze. "For the first time in your life, you're admitting you're wrong. Acknowledging that you were mistaken. And the impetus for your revelation is—"

"Lord Berkley," Cassie said, a note of inevitable surrender in her voice.

It made perfect sense. No man had ever confused or annoyed her as Berkley did. And no man had ever kissed her as he had. And no man had ever made her want to kiss him back.

"Oh dear." Cassie sank back once again and met her sister's gaze. "Could I possibly be in love?"

"I think that's a possibility to be considered." Delia nodded in a somber manner, but her eyes twinkled. "You did tell me he was quite nice and you find his laugh irresistible. He's charming and kind to small children."

"And don't forget his eyes." Cassie sighed. "They're gray, you know, and quite, quite wonderful."

"If I recall, you said something about wanting to fall headfirst into them?"

Cassie grimaced. "It doesn't sound at all good, does it?"

"It sounds wonderful."

"I've never been in love before, you know."

"I do indeed, and it's past time." Delia nodded firmly. "In some manner, probably known only to the stars, Lord Berkley has penetrated your resistance. I think it's grand."

"I'm not sure it's grand at all." Cassie wrinkled her nose. "I think it may well be a bit of a problem."

"How on earth is this a problem?"

"I've presented him with Miss Wonderful. The very woman he's always wanted. Felicity Bellingham. Judging simply by the looks cast in her direction by any man in her presence, she is the woman every man has always wanted."

"Yes, well, she might not have any interest in him." Delia shrugged. "She is extremely sought after."

"How could she not be interested in him?" Indignation rang in Cassie's voice. "Why, with the possible exception of his reputation, he is an excellent match.

In truth, I'm rather surprised no one has snapped him up before now."

"One could say the very same thing about you. Obviously fate was saving you for one another." Delia cast her a smug smile.

"You needn't look at me like that." Cassie huffed. "Very well, I admit it. I want him. I've never wanted a man before, and I want this one. He's not Lord Perfect, but for whatever reason, I want him. So what am I to do about it?"

Delia laughed. "Obviously love has addled your mind." She leaned closer to her sister. "My dear Cassandra, you have always been the belle of every ball. I have seen you attract and discard any number of men through the years. You have perfected flirting to a fine art."

"I fear, my lord, you have me at a disadvantage," Cassie murmured.

"Now, you simply have to focus all your efforts on one particular man with the express purpose of keeping this one." Delia settled back and smiled. "Miss Bellingham is of no significance, and Lord Berkley doesn't stand a chance."

"It would be something of a challenge."

"And you've never backed away from a challenge."

"The stakes are exceedingly high."

"Nothing less than your heart."

"The risk is enormous."

"But well worth it. And isn't risk part and parcel of any," Delia paused to emphasize her words, "adventure."

"I simply do not understand how an intelligent

woman with the courage of her convictions and any number of other admirable qualities would want perfection in a man rather than excitement or adventure or the passion inherent in such a life."

Berkley's words rang in her ear.

"Adventure and excitement and passion," Cassie said under her breath. Was it possible, right from the start, the man knew her better than she knew herself?

Was Delia right? Was this fate?

"I really don't have a choice, do I? I think about him night and day. And when I think about never seeing him again when I've finished with his house or worse, living the rest of my days without him . . ." She drew a deep breath. "I'll do it. I'll pursue Lord Berkley. And then, if I must, I'll reform him if indeed he needs reforming at all, because admittedly, I like him precisely as he is." She met her sister's gaze. "Good Lord, Delia. I do love him."

"Now you just have to catch him."

"What if I can't?" Panic widened Cassie's eyes. "What if I can't pry him away from Miss Bellingham? What if she's already grasped on to him? Sunk her claws into him? What if I've lost him?"

"You haven't lost him, you've never had him, and you've only just realized you want him. As for Miss Bellingham, you, my dear, are Cassandra Effington. You are confident and assured and I can't recall you ever failing to get precisely what you want." Delia patted her sister's hand. "If indeed you set your sights on Lord Berkley, he's as good as yours."

Cassie stared at her sister for a long moment. "You may be right. I have never failed to get whatever I have set my mind on, and I have always been the mistress of my own fate. A simple thing like love doesn't change any of that."

"Once again, dear Cassie, you're wrong." Delia grinned. "Love changes absolutely everything."

"That," Cassie grimaced, "is exactly what I'm afraid of."

Nine

When a woman has a particular look in her eye, a gentleman has two options. He can succumb to the inevitable and be leg shackled for life. Or he can flee. Thus far I have been remarkably swift.

C. Effington

"I can't tell you how pleased I am to finally meet you." Lady Pennington, Gwendolyn, hooked her arm through Cassie's and led her along the gravel path through the Holcroft Hall rose gardens. "I am delighted you could join us."

"I'm delighted to be here," Cassie said with a genuine smile.

Indeed, in the four days since she'd received Lady Pennington's invitation, she had scarce thought of anything but her stay at Holcroft Hall and the possibilities it presented for sharing the company of Lord Berkley. She'd filled the endless hours by working on her designs, and had paid several visits to Berkley House, meeting with painters and plasterers and seamstresses. She'd found that much of the furniture, while worn, was of excellent quality and could be reused with new fabric and some repair. She'd also discovered it was far easier to concentrate on the house with Lord Berkley and his family already in the country in spite of her impatience to begin on a far more important project than his house. His heart.

The only disturbing aspect was a brief note she'd received from Berkley informing her, as time was growing short, he would produce a Lord Perfect for her during their stay in the country. Her curiosity on that subject only increased her impatience.

Cassie and Lady Pennington strolled along the path, Delia, Lord Pennington's mother, and a Miss Hilliard following some distance back. Lord Pennington's mother was apparently explaining to Delia and the other woman all the nuances of her prized gardens, and Cassie was relieved she had escaped that lecture. She'd always been far more interested in the interior of houses than their grounds.

"Are we the first to arrive then?" Cassie asked.

She, Delia, and Tony had arrived a scant hour ago, and aside from Miss Hilliard and Lord Pennington's mother, they had not yet seen any other guests. One guest in particular.

"My cousins, Lord Townsend and his sister Miss Hilliard, arrived early this morning." Lady Pennington cast a quick glance over her shoulder, obviously to ascertain how close the other ladies were, then lowered her voice confidentially. "I must tell you, Miss Effington, my cousins and I are not especially close, although I have made an effort recently toward improving our relationship. Aside from my nieces, whom I don't see nearly as often as I should like, Townsend—Adrian—and Miss Hilliard—or rather Constance—are my only living relations.

"You are exceedingly lucky, Miss Effington, to have such a large family and one that apparently, well," she smiled wryly, "likes one another."

"Most of the time." Cassie laughed. "However, the problem with a family like mine, probably because we do share a fair amount of affection, is that everyone considers everyone else's business fair game. No one hesitates for a moment to intrude in your decisions or your life. And everyone thinks they know what is best for you regardless of what you think or want."

"Still, they act as they do because they care."

"It's quite the proverbial double-edged sword." Cassie grinned.

Lady Pennington laughed and squeezed Cassie's arm. "I must confess I had an ulterior motive for my invitation to your family, most specifically to you and your sister."

"Oh?" Cassie raised a brow.

"This is rather awkward to admit." Lady Pennington's brow furrowed. "I married my husband just over a year ago, shortly after I returned to England. I had spent several years in America, after my father died, in a misguided effort to make my own way in the world as a governess. I was a dreadful governess." She shuddered. "At any rate, while I have met any number of people, I have yet to develop friendships with ladies near to my own age and station in life. Oh, Marcus's mother has been wonderful, and there is a woman who was once my teacher and her sister that I am very close to, but still I find myself longing for the type of comradeship I shared with the girls at school in my youth."

Lady Pennington drew a deep breath. "I was rather hoping you and I and your sister and your cousin Lady Helmsley, too, of course, as her husband and mine are quite good friends, could perhaps become, well, friends ourselves." A hopeful note rang in the lady's voice.

"My closest friend has always been my sister. My cousins and I have always been friends as well." Cassie thought for a moment. "Good Lord, although I have a great number of acquaintances, I'm not sure I can name any woman I'm not related to that I consider a true friend.

"Lady Pennington, I should be more than honored to be considered your friend." Cassie grinned wryly. "Apparently I need them."

"As do I." Lady Pennington laughed with relief. "But you must call me Gwen. I quite like being Lady Pennington, but it's far and away too formal between friends."

"And my friends, few though they may be, call me Cassie." The very idea of having Lady Pennington—Gwen—as a friend was not merely lovely in and of itself, but didn't one's friends lend a helping hand when necessary?

"Lord Berkley and I have agreed to be friends," Cassie said casually.

"Have you indeed? How very interesting." Gwen slanted her a speculative glance. "Lord Berkley is most charming and quite amusing. He and Marcus are extremely close and have been since their youth. Reggie's estate is a scant half hour's ride from Holcroft Hall and is quite lovely."

"You call him Reggie?"

Gwen winced. "I know it's terribly improper, but he spends a great deal of time with Marcus and I've grown very fond of him myself. Indeed, I think of him as a brother that I never had."

"I'd be more than willing to give you one of my brothers if you'd like." Cassie grinned. "In the spirit of friendship, of course."

Gwen laughed. "I shall pass, but thank you."

They continued on past all manner of roses just beginning to bud, planted artfully around assorted topiaries and urns and edgings of low boxwood hedges.

"You like him, then," Gwen said casually. "Reggie, that is."

"Yes." Cassie braced herself. "Rather a lot, really."

"But he's not . . . perfect."

Cassie stopped and stared at the other woman. "You know about the wager?"

Gwen nodded.

"It's really rather absurd, isn't it?"

"Yes, well, I suspect it may shortly get more absurd. I expect most of the rest of the guests to arrive before dinner. Among them"—reluctance sounded in Gwen's voice—"Miss Bellingham and her family."

"Really? How nice." Cassie forced a pleasant smile.

Cassie should have guessed Miss Bellingham would be invited. However, Delia was right when she'd said the young woman might not be at all interested in Berkley—or, rather, Reggie. Cassie rather liked thinking of him as Reggie and didn't think it sounded at all like the name of a hound.

And more and more, Cassie wondered, or perhaps hoped, that Miss Wonderful was just as wrong for Reggie as Lord Perfect was for her. Miss Bellingham's presence might well prove rather beneficial in that respect.

Cassie straightened her shoulders and cast Gwen a confident smile. "I'm certain we shall all get on famously."

"There's more. I believe Reggie has arranged for yet another guest. I suspect that to be . . . well . . ." Gwen held her breath. "Lord Perfect."

"Really? He's actually found a Lord Perfect? He sent me a note, but I never imagined . . . that is . . ." Cassie shook her head in disbelief. "So we shall indeed have both a Lord Perfect and a Miss Wonderful? Not to mention the eccentric Miss Effington and the infamous Lord Berkley?"

"It does appear that way," Gwen murmured.

"Good Lord, Gwen." Cassie met her gaze directly, a note of undisguised awe in her voice. "You certainly do know how to put together a party."

The women stared at each other for a long moment, then burst into laughter.

"Oh, this is going to be nothing short of a disaster, isn't it?" Gwen sniffed back a tear and smiled ruefully. "This is my first attempt at any kind of party, you know."

"I would never have guessed." Cassie grinned. "The entertainment alone should be unforgettable."

Gwen groaned. "Oh dear. I should probably send everyone away right now."

"Don't be absurd. Nothing enlivens a party, especially one where all are trapped in the same house in the country, like an interesting mix of guests, and I daresay you have surpassed any conceivable expectations in that regard."

Panic glinted in Gwen's eyes. "What do I do now?"

"My dear friend." Cassie linked her arm through the other woman's and they continued along the walk. "You do precisely what any good hostess does. You make certain your guests are comfortable. You oversee your servants. You provide excellent meals." She inclined her head confidentially. "Nothing destroys a good party as thoroughly as poorly prepared food. People will forgive anything as long as they are well fed."

"I shall remember that," Gwen murmured.

"In addition, you should provide a fair number of activities. Out-of-doors preferably, as long as the weather is pleasant."

"I had planned a picnic for tomorrow." Gwen brightened. "And we have very good stables. I quite enjoy riding."

"Excellent," Cassie nodded. "It seems to me that everything is well in hand. And should you run into any problems whatsoever, do feel free to call on myself or my sister."

Gwen stared at her. "How on earth do you know all this?"

"I've been training for functions precisely like this one since the day I was born. You see, while I discovered a gift for the decoration of houses, my life up until that point prepared me for one thing and one thing only: to be a proper wife, preferably to a man with a good title and better fortune, and an accomplished hostess. I daresay my sister and I could put together a grand ball on a moment's notice." She laughed. "Of course, it would require a great deal of money, but then we've always had a great deal of money."

"I haven't. Or at least I didn't until I received my inheritance and married Marcus. It's quite awful not having money." Gwen frowned as if remembering past times.

"I can't imagine being poor." Cassie studied the other woman. "I don't think I would do at all well at it."

"Well, it does . . ." Gwen searched for the right word, then grinned. "Reek. However, those days are well behind me, and I have everything I could ever want, far beyond money."

"And now you have friends as well." Cassie returned the other woman's smile.

The ladies continued their walk in a companionable silence. Cassie had never particularly thought about her own lack of female friends. She'd always had Delia and the endless Effington relations. It was really quite pleasant to think that she had a new friend now.

"So," Gwen said after a few moments. "You like Reggie rather a lot, do you?"

Cassie bit back a smile. "So it appears."

"And what of Lord Perfect?" Gwen shook her head. "Do you think there could possibly be a perfect man?"

"No, but I am most curious as to who Lord Berkley will present as perfect. Of course, per the terms of our bargain, I have to agree that he is indeed perfect." Cassie chuckled. "It may well be that our wager is a draw."

"I wish I had known of your feelings. I never would have invited Miss Bellingham, and I never would have allowed Reggie to invite whoever this Lord Perfect turns out to be. I am sorry."

"Don't be. I didn't know how I felt about Lord Berkley until recently. Miss Bellingham's presence will simply make the next few days far more interesting, and perhaps even something of a challenge. I have always enjoyed a challenge."

"This party is becoming more of a challenge than I anticipated," Gwen murmured.

"Just feed your guests well and often, and all will be fine. As for the rest of it, it shall play itself out." Cassie smiled wickedly. "In one way or another."

"I must say you're looking exceptionally lovely this afternoon, Lady Pennington." A familiar voice sounded behind them.

Cassie's breath caught. This would be the first time she'd seen Lord Berkley—Reggie—since she'd realized how she truly felt about him. She adopted her brightest smile and turned toward him.

"Flattery, Reggie, as always, will get you whatever you want." Gwen laughed and extended her hand.

Berkley took her hand and brushed his lips across it. "With you, Gwen, it's not merely flattery but the truth."

Gwen withdrew her hand and cast Cassie a knowing smile. "He's far and away too charming for his own good. Or for ours."

"So I have heard." Cassie held out her hand.

He took her hand and raised it to his lips. "The rumors of my charm are greatly exaggerated." His gaze locked with hers. "I'm delighted to see you again, Miss Effington."

"Thank you, my lord," Cassie said and pulled her hand from his, at a loss for words for the first time in her life.

"I met your sister on the path, and she told me where to find the two of you." He turned to Gwen. "You didn't tell me your cousins would be here."

"I was probably hoping they could not attend," Gwen said under her breath.

Reggie grinned and leaned toward Cassie. "Gwen's family is not especially close."

"One cannot choose one's relations as one can one's friends." She flashed Cassie a resigned smile. "Still, I am determined to improve our relationship. Adrian is not a bad sort, really, and I'm sure Constance has any number of good qualities. I've simply yet to find them."

Reggie laughed. "The ladies were returning to the house, and Marcus's mother asked that I request your return as well, to greet my mother and any other new arrivals."

"Of course." Gwen frowned. "I do apologize, Cassie. I had hoped to finish showing you the gardens myself."

"I should be happy to take over for you, Gwen," Reggie said quickly. "I grew up playing games with Marcus on these very paths. I daresay I know the intricacies of the Holcroft gardens as well as anyone."

"No doubt." Gwen smiled at Cassie in a confidential manner. "What he knows is the best spots to play games involving armies and military campaigns. I understand great portions of the gardens had to be replanted every year when he and Marcus were boys, a direct result of the enthusiasm of their sport."

Reggie shrugged. "Losses are bound to occur when

one re-creates the conquests of Alexander the Great or the legions of Rome amid the rosebushes. It's the nature of battle. Even the sturdiest blossom cannot stand up to the forces of boyhood military might."

Cassie laughed. "I recall the very same casualties among my own family's gardens in my youth. My brothers and cousins were always destroying some planting that a poor, put-upon gardener had slaved over. I must confess, my sister and I did a fair amount of damage ourselves." She favored Reggie with a brilliant smile. "I should quite like to see where you played as a child."

"Excellent." Gwen's gaze slipped from Cassie to Reggie and back. "Then I shall see you both back at the hall later." Gwen smiled, turned, and hurried back down the path.

"She's very nice, isn't she?" Cassie watched the other woman's retreat.

"You can't tell by looking at her, but she has a great deal of strength." Admiration sounded in his voice.

"She said something about being poor and working as a governess."

"When her father died, she was told she was penniless. Her father's title and estate went to her cousin."

"Lord Townsend?"

Reggie nodded. "She did not wish to be a poor relation in her own home so she made the rather disastrous decision to make her own way in life and took a position as a governess in America. Apparently, it did not suit her. It was a good five years, I believe, until she learned she had an inheritance after all, returned to England, and shortly thereafter married Marcus."

"I see," Cassie murmured.

"Gwen literally grew up in a school for girls. Her teachers were more family to her than her true relations. Her efforts to forge some kind of relationship now with her cousins strike me as most telling. A sign, I think, of just how far Gwen has come in her life." He smiled and gestured at the walkway. "Shall we?"

They strolled along in an amicable silence for a few minutes, but Cassie's mind churned. "She's been very lucky, hasn't she?"

"In that all has ultimately turned out well," he nodded, "yes, she has."

"It must be dreadful to have everything, family, position, and wealth, and have it all taken away because of the laws of heredity."

He cast her a sharp glance. "I would think so."

She stopped and drew her brows together. "What happens to women like that, Lord Berkley? Women who were raised to take a particular place in the world but then, through no fault of their own, have everything they've always counted on, always expected, taken away because of the death of a father?"

"I don't know." He studied her curiously. "I confess I've never given the question much consideration."

"You should," she said firmly. "We all should. It's neither fair nor right that we bring up young women like Gwen, or myself for that matter, with certain expectations in life, which can be brutally yanked away because the laws of inheritance do not provide for them. What are their options in life, my lord?"

"Well," he said slowly, "they could marry."

She snorted in disdain. "It's not as easy as that and you well know it. This whole pursuit of marriage cannot be accomplished with a simple decision to wed.

From what I've seen, a bad marriage to the wrong spouse is worse than no marriage at all. And quite frankly, when a young woman is left penniless, in dire straits, unless she is an exceptional beauty with enough funding remaining to present herself properly, making a good match is impossible. So what else could she possibly do?"

"Become a governess as Gwen did?" A hopeful note sounded in his voice.

"Some of us are not suited to dealing with children." She shook her head and started back down the path, talking more to herself than to him. "It seems to me we do a grave disservice to the young ladies of the English aristocracy. They grow up knowing how to make a perfect curtsey and be a perfect wife, but should their very survival be at stake, they, we, are helpless." She squared her shoulders. "Someone should do something."

"You have gone into business of a sort," he said casually. "And judging by the amount you charge, you are succeeding admirably."

"Yes, but I am not in need of a place to live or food for sustenance or anything of that nature. And quite frankly, my clientele hires me as much for who I am as what I do. If I were not an Effington, I daresay my work would not be as in demand as it is."

"But you are very talented."

"Nonetheless, I am under few illusions as to why I have had the success I have. No, as well as I have done, I do not have the skills necessary to survive on my own. Without my family and my name."

"I suspect, Miss Effington, you could do nearly anything you set your mind to."

She cast him a reluctant smile. "Gwen was right. You are exceptionally charming."

He shrugged in a modest manner. "I do my best."

She tucked her hand in the crook of his arm, ignored his vague look of surprise, and they continued to wind their way amid the rosebushes and boxwoods. It never failed to amaze her how quickly he put her at ease, regardless of how on edge she might be at first. The mere fact that she was nervous at all was amazing as well. No man had ever made her the least bit unsure of herself. Until now.

"I imagine you practice a great deal, Lord Berkley."

"Not at all." He wagged his brows wickedly. "It's a gift."

She laughed.

"And I think it's past time you called me Reggie, or Reginald, if you'd rather, but as much as I am not overly fond of Reggie, I do prefer it to Reginald. When I am called Reginald it is inevitably by someone who is about to chastise me for some matter, usually deserved. And, alas, I am a Reggie sort of man, don't you think?"

She nodded in a sober manner. "Most definitely."

"Excellent. But only if, of course, we are truly friends."

"Oh, we are most certainly friends, my lord—Reggie." She adopted a lighthearted tone. "And as my friend, you should call me Cassandra or Cassie." She flashed him a fast grin. "I am routinely chastised by both names."

"I like Cassandra. It suits you." He gazed down at her. "If I recall, Cassandra was a Greek prophetess. And wasn't she cursed by Apollo never to be believed?"

Cassie nodded. "She rejected his advances." She gazed up at him innocently. "I've been told it means 'the confuser of men' in Greek."

"Then I was right, it does suit you."

"Are you confused, Reggie?"

"My dear Cassandra, I have been confused since the moment I met you."

"Why?"

"I'm not entirely sure." His gaze searched hers. "Which is the very definition of confused."

She rested her hand on his cheek. "Did I hurt you terribly when I slapped you?"

He placed his hand over hers. His tone was solemn, but amusement twinkled in his eye. "Yes."

She laughed. "I did not."

"You did wound me deeply, but not here." He moved her hand to his chest. She could feel the beat of his heart through the fabric of his clothes. "Here."

"This is most improper." She rested her other hand on his chest. Her own heart sped up.

"Indeed it is." His gaze narrowed. "What are you up to, Cassandra, confuser of men?"

"Are you confused now, Reggie?" Her voice was low and sultry, and she wasn't entirely sure it was her own.

"Indeed I am."

She wet her lips in a manner she knew was most inviting. "Good."

His arms slipped around her. "Are you like your namesake? Would you resist the advances of Apollo?"

"Certainly of Apollo. I believe he was most—"

"Infamous?" He raised a brow.

She swallowed hard. "One can never trust a god with an infamous reputation."

"And what of a mere mortal?"

"I don't . . . I must admit I too am a bit confused." Her gaze met his. "And I have a confession to make. Once again I fear I am wrong."

"You?" He chuckled. "About what?"

She drew a deep breath and stared into his gray eyes. "About my conviction that we do not suit."

"Oh?" He pulled her closer and brushed his lips against hers. "And what makes you think that you were wrong?"

"You," her lips whispered against his.

He hesitated as if deciding whether to continue or set her aside. She held her breath.

He groaned slightly, the very essence of surrender, then crushed his lips to hers. She slid her arms around his neck and reveled in the feel of his mouth on hers. Her body molded against his in a most improper and remarkably exciting way. His kiss was ravenous and insistent, and she was as famished as he. She opened her mouth to his and greeted him with a yearning she had never known before. Their breaths, their very souls met and mingled and mated. She tightened her grip around his neck, and he held her close and kissed her again and again until she could feel the blood pulsing against her veins and his own pounding against her. His name echoed in her head over and over like a refrain caught in her mind or her heart. Her toes curled in her slippers and she wanted to cling to him like this forever. Wanted him to make her his, here and now, regardless of the consequences. Wanted him to lead her down the intriguing path to scandal, whatever that might entail. Wanted . . . everything.

Abruptly he pulled away. "Cassandra."

"Reggie," she sighed and pulled his lips back to hers.

"Cassandra," he said firmly and unwrapped himself from her embrace.

She stared in disbelief and a fair amount of frustration. "What?"

A discreet cough sounded behind her. Chagrin showed on Reggie's face, and his gaze slipped past her. Cassie's heart dropped to her stomach, and she cringed.

She gazed up at Reggie. "Do please tell me we are still alone."

"I should very much like to." He cast her a look of regret that eased her dismay somewhat, then glanced past her. "It's a beautiful day for a walk in the garden, don't you think, Marcus?"

"Oh, indeed I do." Amusement rang in Lord Pennington's voice. "I like nothing better than a walk in the garden myself. On a beautiful day like today. With a beautiful companion."

She drew a calming breath and turned, resisting the urge to straighten her probably disheveled hair or gown or appearance or possibly just state of mind.

Cassie plastered a pleasant smile on her face and adopted a far too casual tone. Just right for a chance encounter in a garden, as if she had not been caught in anything the least bit improper, the least bit scandalous.

"Lord Pennington, how pleasant to see you again," she said brightly, thinking it best not to offer the earl her hand. It, along with her entire insides, was distinctly unsteady.

"The pleasure is mine, Miss Effington." Pennington's gaze moved to Berkley, and he was obviously hard-pressed not to smirk. "I've been calling for you, but apparently you"—he cleared his throat—"didn't hear?"

"Yes, that's good, we'll stick with that," Reggie murmured.

"I must return to the hall." Cassie nodded firmly and stepped away from Reggie. "I promised . . . that is I offered . . . Lady Pennington—Gwen—" She laughed an odd sort of uncomfortable, high-pitched laugh. She met Reggie's gaze. "Thank you for showing me the gardens. It was most . . . enlightening." She glanced at Pennington. "I'm certain I shall see you both at dinner."

She turned to go, took a few steps, then stopped. She was not one to run from awkward situations, and even love or lust or scandal would not make her do so now.

She squared her shoulders and swiveled back to meet Pennington's gaze directly. "I trust you will not say anything about . . . this, my lord."

"I am the soul of discretion, Miss Effington." There was a distinct glimmer of laughter in his eye, but his voice was solemn. "Besides, two friends enjoying a walk in the garden on a lovely spring day is scarcely worth mentioning. To anyone."

She smiled in spite of herself. "It is a lovely day."

"Indeed it is, Miss Effington."

"Lovely," Reggie murmured.

She nodded good day and took her leave, her step and her spirits considerably lighter than a moment ago. Through no fault of her own she had avoided scandal. She refused to think what might have happened had someone else come upon them in the garden. Lord Pennington obviously had his friend's best interests at heart. Unless, of course, he was so used to encountering Reggie in such situations that he no longer considered them significant. She brushed the disturbing idea from her mind.

Still, a certain amount of scandal with Reggie might dissuade Miss Bellingham from any intentions she might have toward him—if indeed the young woman had any thoughts in that particular direction.

But what of Reggie? Cassie hadn't considered the possibility that now that she had fulfilled her end of their bargain and produced a Miss Wonderful, Reggie might seriously pursue her. What if, in spite of the way he'd kissed her, he had as little interest in her as she had claimed to have in him? What if, in spite of her growing belief that he wasn't at all the kind of man he was reputed to be, he was?

Her step slowed. What if a kiss in a garden, even a rather outstanding, magnificent, kiss, was of little significance to him? What if he always kissed women in a manner that made their senses flee and their toes curl? Why, certainly such kisses would only add to a man's infamy.

Cassie had been kissed before, but never like Reggie had kissed her. Twice. And a man who made her feel like this one did, when she was in his arms and when she wasn't, a man who annoyed her this much, could not be allowed to slip out of her life. If she was going to ride down the road to scandal, she wanted to do it with Viscount Berkley. Reginald Berkley. Reggie. And if her heart was broken in the process, well, she absolutely would not allow that to happen.

Reggie was the man for her whether he knew it or not. She simply had to make him want her the way she wanted him. Even now, she couldn't believe a man who kissed her like that, a man who gazed into her eyes the way he did, a man in whose arms she fit like they were made for one another, didn't already harbor some affection for her. All she had to do now was make him realize it.

At once the answer occurred to her. Apparently, Reggie was about to provide the very means for her to do just that. Whoever Lord Perfect was, he would indeed be perfect for her plans. In truth, wasn't it in part her realization that she might be a bit jealous of Miss Bellingham that had led Cassie to acknowledge her own feelings?

Cassie grinned and picked up her pace. Not only did she now have something of a plan in mind in regards to the pursuit of the infamous viscount but she had a glimmer of an idea regarding what to do with the money she had earned as well.

Lord Pennington was entirely right.

It was indeed, a lovely, lovely day.

Ten

There is no woman who does not possess at least one attribute to commend her.

G. Drummond

"Did you see that?" Reggie stared after Cassie's retreating figure, not entirely certain what to think and rather befuddled as to what had just transpired.

"I could scarce miss it," Marcus said wryly.

"She kissed me."

"I did try to miss it, though. It seemed only polite not to see—"

"She kissed me," Reggie said again. "And with a great deal of enthusiasm."

"Ah, well, then I was mistaken at any rate. I thought I saw you kiss her, although she did seem somewhat reluctant to desist."

"It might well have been mutual." Reggie grinned. "Yes, it was definitely mutual."

Marcus chuckled. "I would think a woman who

kisses a man with a great deal of enthusiasm is either a tart—"

Reggie raised a brow.

"Or has a certain amount of affection for the gentleman in question."

Reggie's grin widened. "Precisely what I think."

"Well done, old man." Marcus slapped his friend on the back. "It seems your plans have succeeded after all."

"Indeed they have and without . . ." Realization struck him, and he stared at the earl. "Good God, Marcus, we have to call it off."

"Call off what, exactly?" Marcus said slowly.

"This entire Lord Perfect nonsense." At once Reggie started back to the hall. "It's not necessary at this point and, in truth, might well muck up everything."

"That could be rather—"

"Damnation." Reggie turned on his heel and stared at his friend. "I sent her a note saying I would have a Lord Perfect here for her. How could I have been so stupid?" He smacked his palm against his forehead. "I don't . . ." He brightened. "I could tell her I failed? Yes, that will work. I'll concede defeat, she'll like that. I'll admit it's impossible to find such a man. At the moment, I daresay she won't mind." He breathed a sigh of relief. "We'll send a message to inform Effington he's off the hook. I'll pay her my forty pounds, and that will be the end of it." Again, he turned to go.

"I'm afraid it's a bit too late for that," Marcus murmured behind him.

A heavy weight settled in the pit of Reggie's stomach, and he turned back. "What do you mean—too late?"

"Effington and his brother and, um," Marcus winced, "*Lord Perfect* have just arrived."

"What? He and Effington weren't supposed to arrive until tomorrow. I distinctly remember that was part of the plan. Why is he here now?"

"Enthusiasm on Effington's part, I believe."

"God help us all from enthusiasm on the part of Effingtons." Reggie glared. "Whatever will we do with Lord Perfect now?"

"I expect we're rather stuck with him."

"But he's an actor, after all." Reggie paced, his mind working in tandem with his step. "I should think we can send him packing at once. Yes, that's it. He can be introduced as precisely what he is, an actor. Certainly explaining his presence might be a bit awkward."

"I don't think—"

"We can say he's here because . . . He's paying a visit to Holcroft Hall because . . ." Reggie's brow furrowed, then his gaze snapped to Marcus's. "He's a distant relative. Of . . . of mine. Yes! No." He shook his head. "That makes no sense. If he were my relative, why would he be at your estate? He's obviously a relative of yours. Yes, that's good. He's a distant relative."

"That will certainly surprise my mother," Marcus said dryly.

"He's so distant she's never heard of him. Beyond that, he's something of a black sheep. Most disreputable sort of fellow, actors and all that." Reggie grinned. "This is good, Marcus, this is very good."

"It is nothing short of amazing, but then you've always been good at this sort of thing." Marcus studied his friend with a familiar expression, a mix of complete disbelief and sheer fascination. "Why did he arrive with Effington?"

"Coincidence!" Reggie spread out his arms in a grand gesture. "Nothing more than chance. It's not at all unusual, happens all the time. Wars, even kingdoms, have been won and lost on instances of coincidence. Chance. Fate, as it were. Why, the meeting of two men on the same road with the same destination in mind may be more than mere coincidence. Such a meeting might well be inevitable." He crossed his arms over his chest and beamed at his longtime cohort in activities of this nature. "We, or rather you, shall graciously allow him to stay the night as he is, after all, a relation—"

"Distant though he may be."

Reggie nodded. "And then send him on his way tomorrow."

"Once again, old man, you astound me. That's really rather brilliant."

"Thank you," Reggie said modestly. "It's nothing, really."

"Not at all. It's extremely clever." Marcus shrugged. "Pity it won't work."

Reggie snorted. "Of course it will work. You just said it was brilliant."

"It is. And it would work if indeed Lord Perfect were an actor."

Reggie narrowed his gaze. "What do you mean?"

"It seems Effington went a bit above and beyond in his quest for a Lord Perfect." Marcus blew a long breath. "The gentleman he's brought with him is a Mr. Drummond and he's quite legitimate."

"Legitimate? How is he legitimate?" Reggie said, a familiar, sick feeling of doom returning to lodge firmly in the bottom of his stomach.

"As Effington explained it to me, Mr. Drummond is the grandson of the Earl of Longworth. His father was the earl's youngest son and made his fortune in the West Indies. Drummond is his only heir."

"Well, then, surely Cassandra has already met him and—"

"Effington says Drummond has lived much of his life on his family's plantations and has only recently arrived in England. Unfortunately for your plans, he's been here just long enough to lose a wager to Effington. And Effington, following your example, I might add—"

"Forgave his debt if he would agree to play the part of Lord Perfect," Reggie said grimly.

"Oh, it's much worse than that." Marcus grimaced. "He didn't mention anything at all about Lord Perfect. He simply requested Drummond accompany him to Holcroft Hall as a favor to my wife, who apparently needs more male guests to balance the number of females present."

Reggie raised a brow. "Does she?"

"I have no idea, but it seems Effington is as good at concocting reasonable-sounding tales as you are."

"Even so . . ." Reggie drew his brows together. "Cassandra's standards for Lord Perfect are exceedingly high. She might refuse to acknowledge that I have fulfilled my end of the wager out of stubbornness alone and insist that she has won." He brightened. "Yes, of course. I don't know why I was concerned. A

Lord Perfect, any Lord Perfect, could not possibly exist, and I daresay she would rather win than admit I have met the terms of our wager. I'll pay her—"

"I would not count out the forty pounds just yet."

Reggie studied his friend. "There's more, isn't there?"

"Drummond is . . . well . . ." Marcus drew a deep breath. "He may indeed be perfect."

Reggie scoffed. "Don't be absurd. No man is perfect."

"Perhaps not, but this one certainly appears to be."

"Nonsense, he can't possibly—"

"He can possibly." Reluctance sounded in Marcus's voice. "While I am not given to appreciating the appearance of men, this one is admittedly handsome. Indeed, judging by the way Gwen's eyes widened when he arrived, as well as the reaction of Miss Hilliard and my very own mother, extraordinarily attractive. And—again my observations being based a great deal on the reaction of these three fairly sensible women—he is extremely charming as well."

Marcus shook his head. "I tell you I wasn't the least bit pleased by the way he looked at Gwen and even less so by the manner in which she looked back. However, Drummond directed the very same attention to each of the other women. All three gazed at the man as if he were some sort of rare sweet and they were famished. The blasted man seemed genuinely cordial to me as well."

"No man is perfect," Reggie said staunchly.

"Probably not." Marcus cast his friend a sympathetic look. "But Drummond may come bloody well close."

Reggie thought for a moment. "This changes nothing, really. Cassandra definitely has feelings for me. I'm certain of it."

"When did you start calling her Cassandra?" Marcus asked with a smile.

"Always in my mind, aloud just today." Reggie clasped his hands behind his back and paced. "Producing a real Lord Perfect should do nothing more than decide the wager."

"You do realize that once she meets this gentleman, who may well embody everything she professes to want"—Marcus's words were measured—"that instead of finding perfection is not at all what she wishes, she might discover just the opposite."

"Yes, yes, of course, but it did not seem even a remote possibility until this very moment," Reggie snapped. "I never truly thought I could find a genuine Lord Perfect." He pulled up short and stared. "What am I going to do?"

"I have no idea."

"Neither have I." Reggie resumed pacing. "The best thing about an actor was that he was never a real threat. There was no possibility of true involvement with Cassandra, as he would only be playing a role." He glanced at Marcus. "I could fail to present Drummond as Lord Perfect and concede defeat."

"If, of course, you hadn't already told her he would be here. And since the only unmarried gentlemen here include two of her brothers, Lord Bellingham, who is not yet twenty, Colonel Fargate, who is entirely too old for her, my solicitor, Mr. Whiting, who continues to be *involved* with my mother." Marcus rolled his gaze toward the heavens. "Lord Townsend—"

"Why couldn't I say Townsend is Lord Perfect?"

"She'd never believe it. Townsend is adequate, I suppose, but next to Drummond," Marcus shook his head, "he definitely pales in comparison. In truth, I can't think of any man who doesn't pale in comparison."

"Surely he has some faults?"

"No doubt, but they may not surface as quickly as you might wish."

"Perhaps I can keep her from meeting Drummond?" Reggie's mind raced. "I could, I don't know, abduct her? Yes, that's good. I like that."

"Reggie." A warning sounded in Marcus's voice.

Reggie ignored him. "I could take her far from here. Just the two of us. Together. She'd be horribly compromised and would have no choice but to marry me."

"Reggie!"

"What?" Reggie met his friend's disapproving gaze and sighed. "Granted, it's not how I wanted it. And perhaps it's not particularly honorable, but I would ultimately do the honorable thing and marry her. Indeed, I would insist on it."

"Reggie," Marcus said firmly.

"Very well then, I won't abduct her. But I reserve the right to do so should it become necessary." Reggie heaved a resigned sigh. "Marcus, I'm certain she cares for me, or at least there is the very distinct possibility she could care for me given a few more moments in gardens like this one and the absence of any conceivable Lord Perfect." He shook his head. "I don't want to lose her."

"You don't have her," Marcus said pointedly. "You never have had her. Besides, there is always Miss

Wonderful—or rather, Miss Bellingham—as another option. You could do far worse."

"I don't want Miss Bellingham, she's too . . . too . . ." Reggie searched for the right word. "Easy, I think. To deal with, that is. I can't imagine life with her would be any sort of challenge at all."

"No, I daresay she'd never give a man a bit of real trouble. Indeed, she's all every man could ever want. She's an excellent match."

"I don't want an excellent match. I don't want Miss Wonderful. I want Cassandra."

"You do realize you're quite mad?"

"I've known that for some time." Reggie turned and started back toward the hall. "At the very least, I can certainly make sure Cassandra is never in Drummond's presence unaccompanied. Who knows what vile plans the man may have in mind."

"No vile plans at all, I should think. Remember, he's perfect."

"Hah," Reggie tossed back over his shoulder. "No man is perfect."

"There is a bright side to this, you know," Marcus called after him. "Your wager will be a draw. You won't lose forty pounds."

"No," Reggie muttered. "I could lose a great deal more."

The Pennington guests assembled in an unhurried manner in the hall's gallery in advance of dinner. Cassie divided her attention between watching the entry and amicable chatter with Delia, Gwen, her cousin Thomas's wife—Lady Helmsley, or rather Marianne, among friends and family—and the somewhat prune-faced, firmly-on-the-shelf Miss Hilliard. On the other side of the room, her cousin Thomas was engaged with Lord Pennington, a Colonel Fargate, Lord Townsend, and a Mr. Whiting in what appeared to be an animated discussion about politics or something equally as boring. In yet another group, Miss Bellingham chatted with her mother, her brother, Lady Pennington, and the colonel's daughter.

As much as Cassie hated to admit it, Miss Bellingham was indeed extremely pleasant even if, upon their introduction by Delia, the young woman had studied her with a frankly assessing eye. As if taking measure of her worth. Or appraising an adversary. There had been nothing untoward about it; still, it had been rather disturbing.

Cassie hadn't seen any of Reggie's family yet, nor had she seen her own brothers, although she had heard they had arrived. Indeed, Delia said they had arrived in tandem with a Mr. Drummond, and although she had yet to see the gentleman herself, Delia was fairly confident, based on Gwen's enthusiastic description, that he was Lord Perfect.

Not that Cassie had more than a passing curiosity in whomever Reggie might present. Oh, she would certainly flirt with the gentleman, but only in an effort to win Reggie's attention.

"Good Lord." Delia nudged her sister with her elbow, her gaze fixed firmly on the doorway.

"I told you I did not exaggerate." Gwen too stared at the new arrival.

"He's really rather magnificent." Miss Hilliard sighed

in the manner of a girl not yet out of the schoolroom, and for a moment she seemed far younger than her years.

"I'm not sure magnificent is the right word," Marianne said thoughtfully, "but I cannot think of one more appropriate."

"Come now." Cassie laughed. "He can't possibly . . ." She turned and stared in stunned silence.

Lord Perfect stood framed in the doorway.

Or at least the embodiment of Lord Perfect. And given the expressions on the faces of the other women, he was not merely Cassie's Lord Perfect but any woman's Lord Perfect. While Cassie was certain she had never detailed standards for Lord Perfect's appearance, the gentleman now surveying the room with a relaxed, confident air more than surpassed anything even her fertile imagination could conceive of.

He was tall, but not too tall, with fair hair that glowed around his head like the halo of an angel, made all the more golden next to the tan of his skin. In his stance alone, he had the manner of a man as used to a ballroom as to the out-of-doors. The smile on his face was genuine, as if he had no idea of the effect of his appearance on the female members of the assembly.

All in all, while it remained to be seen if his character did indeed fit the requirements of Lord Perfect, Cassie could not think of a single complaint thus far. It would not be a particular hardship to flirt with him, simply in an effort to draw out Reggie's feelings, of course. Why, what man on earth wouldn't be jealous of a man who looked like this one?

Cassie smiled in anticipation.

"I must admit, words fail me," Delia said under her breath.

Gwen nodded. "He may well be the handsomest man I have ever seen."

Miss Hilliard sighed again. "He may well be the handsomest man anyone has ever seen."

"Surely he has some flaws." Marianne peered at him over her spectacles. "He can't possibly be as perfect as he looks."

Cassie shook her head. "No man can be as perfect as he looks."

"I should think it would be rather exciting to find out," Miss Hilliard murmured.

Gwen's mouth dropped open. The other women stared. Miss Hilliard's eyes widened, and a blush swept up her face. With color in her cheeks and her dour expression replaced by a charming embarrassment, she looked almost attractive. At once, Cassie realized the woman was not nearly as old as Cassie had first thought, probably barely past thirty. And wondered as well if the severe facade Miss Hilliard presented to the world didn't hide yet another woman forced to live off the charity of her family because she had no particular skills and no other choice.

Marianne raised a brow. "My goodness, Miss Hilliard."

"My apologies, Lady Helmsley." Miss Hilliard's blush deepened, if possible. "I should never . . . Indeed, I have never . . . I don't know what came over me."

"My dear, you simply said what the rest of us were thinking." Marianne smiled in a conspiratorial manner. "As I didn't have the courage to say it myself, I am quite impressed."

"As am I," Gwen said, still staring at her cousin.

Miss Hilliard smiled weakly.

"He's coming over," Delia said under her breath.

As if of one mind, the women turned toward him.

Lord Perfect strode across the room and took Gwen's hand, raising it to his lips in a polished manner that bespoke of a natural grace—or a great deal of practice.

"Lady Pennington, I must tell you again how pleased I am to have been included in your party." He favored Gwen with a smile that was at once intimate yet not the least bit offensive. "Aside from a handful of relations, I know few people in England."

"I am delighted you could join us, Mr. Drummond." Gwen pulled her hand, and her gaze, from his and gestured at the other ladies. "I believe you have already met my cousin, Miss Hilliard."

Miss Hilliard nodded acknowledgment and cast him a startlingly brilliant smile. He returned one just as bright, as if he were genuinely pleased to see her.

"May I present Lady Helmsley."

"It is my pleasure, my lady." Drummond took Marianne's hand and favored her with the same personal yet polite attention he had given to Gwen. It remained to be seen if the man was indeed perfect, but he was most definitely good.

"Indeed," Marianne murmured.

"And this is Lady St. Stephens and her sister, Miss Effington."

"My lady." He brushed a kiss across Delia's hand, then turned to Cassie and took her hand. His rather perfect blue eyes met her gaze. "Miss Effington, your brother did not do you or your sister justice."

Cassie laughed. "I'm not sure I wish to hear precisely what he did say."

"He said," a perfect smile quirked his perfect lips, "you were lovely."

He was very good indeed, and Cassie wondered just how perfect he really was. And wondered as well why, when there was not the least bit wrong with him in either manner or appearance that she could note thus far, aside from a basic sense of curiosity, she wasn't the least bit intrigued by him.

He raised her hand to his lips and her gaze slipped past him to note her brothers and Reggie entering the room. Reggie's gaze met hers and she smiled, then redirected her attention to Mr. Drummond and laughed with true delight.

"Mr. Drummond, you shall have me blushing down to my very toes." She favored him with her most flirtatious smile.

"One can only wish, Miss Effington," he said smoothly.

Delia choked back a laugh. Marianne and Gwen exchanged amused glances, and Miss Hilliard sighed. Again.

Drummond released her hand in a flatteringly regretful manner and turned to Gwen. "Lady Pennington, could I prevail upon you to introduce me to your other guests?"

"I was just about to suggest that." Gwen cast him a perfect smile of her own. "If you will excuse us?"

The women murmured their acquiescence and watched Drummond escort Gwen to another group of guests.

"He certainly appears perfect," Cassie said thoughtfully.

"He does, doesn't he?" Marianne grinned. "What an interesting mix of guests Gwen has amassed. It should be a most intriguing next few days." She nodded to the other ladies and crossed the room to join her husband.

"Miss Hilliard." A curious light shone in Delia's eyes. "Have you met my brothers yet?"

Miss Hilliard tore her gaze from Drummond and shook her head. "I don't believe so."

"Then you simply must allow me to introduce you." Delia hooked her arm through the other woman's and escorted her to an unsuspecting Leo and Christian.

Cassie turned to find Reggie bearing down on her with an older woman and a young lady.

"Miss Effington," Reggie said, his manner polite and distinctly noncommittal, as if nothing whatsoever had ever happened between them. As if they weren't even friends. It was most annoying. "Allow me to present my mother, Lady Berkley, and my sister, Miss Lucy Berkley."

"Miss Effington." Lady Berkley took Cassie's hands. "I am delighted to meet you at last."

"The pleasure is mine, my lady. I must say I am pleased to see you looking so well." Cassie smiled down at Reggie's mother. She stood several inches shorter than Cassie, with pale blonde hair, a figure that was full but not excessively so, and a charming air of mild confusion about her. And her eyes were a distinct shade of gray. "I understand you have been quite ill."

"It was a miracle, a genuine miracle. Lord knows I don't deserve it, but I am most grateful for it. Why, one day I was at death's door, and the next, I was completely fit." The older woman sighed in a heartfelt manner. "I don't mind telling you, I quite thought I would breathe my last at any moment."

Cassie glanced at Reggie, who pressed his lips together in an obvious effort to hold his tongue. How very odd. His mother was a bit overly dramatic perhaps, but there was no need for him to adopt that long-suffering expression.

"Now that you have recovered your health, I should like to show you the final drawings for the rooms at Berkley House for your approval. I intend to complete them during my stay here in the country, and we can begin arranging the necessary work upon our return to town."

"Oh no, my dear, my opinion is of no consequence whatsoever." Lady Berkley's eyes widened, as if Cassie had suggested something truly shocking, and shook her head firmly. "No, no, I have left this entirely in Reginald's hands—and yours, of course. After all, the express purpose of doing it at all is for the benefit of his future, not mine. I never interfere in my son's life."

Reggie snorted.

His mother ignored him. "Besides, he tells me you have wonderful ideas and a great deal of talent. Beyond that, I have seen other houses that have benefited from your touch, and I am most impressed." She patted Cassie's hand and leaned forward in a confidential manner. "I have no doubt as to the outcome of this endeavor. No doubt at all." Lady Berkley released Cassie's hand and beamed.

Reggie rolled his gaze toward the ceiling.

"Miss Effington." Lucy's eyes were bright with interest. "Do tell me about your brother."

"My brother?" Cassie studied the girl cautiously. She was quite lovely, with dark hair and a hint of great beauty yet to come, and a youthful but overly lush, indeed, *ripe* figure. And gray eyes that obviously ran in the family. "Which brother?"

"Why, I'm not entirely sure." Lucy's pretty brow furrowed. "Whichever brother it was that Reggie in—"

"That I bested in the race," Reggie cut in. "That would be the younger Mr. Effington."

"Christian." Cassie nodded.

"Christian," Lucy said slowly, as if savoring the sound of the name, a distinctly calculating look in her eye.

Cassie glanced at Reggie and raised a brow. Precisely how old was this sister?

Reggie glared at the girl. "I knew allowing you to attend this party was a mistake."

"Nonsense, Reginald." Lady Berkley waved off his comment. "Aside from the fact that it was not your decision, she is nearly seventeen and will be out in society before you know it. I, for one, would much prefer she get a sample of what's ahead of her in a situation in which she can't possibly get into any real trouble." Lady Berkley gave her daughter an affectionate smile. "As I have the assurance of nearly everyone in attendance that her every move will be watched every moment."

Lucy's eyes widened with horror. "Mother! How could you even think of doing such a thing? How humiliating. My very life will be ruined before it's barely begun!"

"Yes, I know, dear. My mother ruined my life in just such a manner, and I am confident you will do the exact same thing when you have a daughter. However, I did manage to have a very good time nonetheless, in spite of my mother's best efforts, when and only when," Lady Berkley paused for effect, "I was old enough to do so."

"Mother." Lucy groaned.

"Now, darling . . ." She nodded at the other side of the room. "Do go flutter your lashes at Mr. Effington and practice all those flirtatious looks on him that I have seen you practice in the mirror, and remember it is only practice, because absolutely no one here, and I am confident, knowing his mother, that that includes Mr. Effington himself, will allow you to do more than merely practice."

Lady Berkley flashed Cassie a knowing smile, and at once Cassie understood there was far more to this woman than appeared at first glance. And understood as well why it was more than likely Lady Berkley and her own mother were indeed old friends. They had a great deal in common.

"If you will excuse me, Lady Pennington, Helena—Lord Pennington's mother, that is—is waving at me to join her in a most insistent manner." Lady Berkley met Cassie's gaze directly. "I'm certain we shall have some time together to talk during our stay here. I am quite looking forward to it."

"As am I," Cassie murmured. As much as this

woman reminded her of her own mother, she liked her. Not in spite of the similarities but because of them.

Lucy crossed her arms over her chest and pouted. "Well, I shan't so much as smile at him now. She's taken all the fun out of it."

"Excellent," Reggie snapped.

"As you wish. Still"—Cassie adopted a casual tone—"my brothers are not the only unmarried gentlemen here. Lord Bellingham is not unattractive and fairly close to your own age."

"Miss Effington." Reggie narrowed his eyes. "What do you think you're doing?"

She paid him no heed. "And of course, there is Mr. Drummond. If there was ever a gentleman one could practice the art of flirtation upon, it would be Mr. Drummond."

Lucy's gaze shifted to the gentleman in question. "He is rather handsome."

"Miss Effington," Reggie growled.

"Oh, I'd say he's more than merely handsome," Cassie said lightly. "I'd say he's . . . oh, what's the word, my lord?"

Reggie stared at her for a moment, then smiled in the grudging manner of a man who just realizes he's lost. "Perfect?"

"Yes, indeed, that's it." Cassie bit back a grin. "Perfect, or so he appears at the moment."

"I'm not sure I want perfect. I'm not sure there's anything at all fun about perfect. There is something so much more interesting about," Lucy's gaze slid from Drummond to Christian, "imperfect."

"Lucy." An odd note of panic sounded in Reggie's voice.

"You needn't worry, dear brother." Lucy directed her words at Reggie, but her gaze fixed firmly on Christian. She lifted her chin and squared her shoulders and looked far older than a mere sixteen years. "This is nothing more than . . . practice." She grinned at Cassie and sailed across the room, leaving her brother to stare after her.

"It may not be readily apparent," Cassie said in a low voice, "but Christian is an honorable man not given to dallying with young girls no matter how charming they may be. She is probably safer with him than she would be with a youth of her own age."

Reggie set his jaw in a stubborn line. "His reputation does not provoke much confidence on that score."

"Nor does yours."

"It's an entirely different thing," he said loftily.

"I see." She resisted the urge to grin. "You cannot trust your younger sister with a man of my brother's reputation, yet you see no difficulty with his trusting his younger sister with you."

The corners of his lips quirked upwards reluctantly. "You are far too clever for your own good or mine. You do know that, don't you?"

She laughed.

"Still and all, as I was saying, it is an entirely different thing, because Lucy is still a child, whereas you—"

She raised a brow. "Yes?"

"You are a woman. Intelligent and confident and," his eyes gazed down into hers, "most desirable."

She swallowed hard. "That is a most improper thing to say."

"Indeed it is. It is also accurate."

Her gaze locked with his, his gray eyes searching and mesmerizing. Her breath caught at the look she saw there, or perhaps the look she wanted to see, or maybe it was no more than a simple reflection. Nonetheless, she stared into his eyes and the rest of the room faded away, lost in an all-consuming fog that left only the two of them. Alone. Together.

"So," his gaze dropped to her lips and back to her eyes. "Will Drummond do, then? For Lord Perfect, I mean."

Her voice was oddly breathless. "That remains to be seen, but he does indeed appear perfect. And Miss Bellingham? Does she meet your qualifications?"

"I daresay Miss Bellingham meets any man's qualifications." His voice was low, his gaze intense, and he could have been saying anything at all.

"We should declare it a draw, then, I should think. The wager, that is."

"What do we do now?" He stared down at her.

A dozen answers came to mind. None of which were proper. All of which were terribly scandalous and most exciting.

Adventure, excitement, and passion.

"If indeed we have found Miss Wonderful and Lord Perfect, I would think we should now turn our attentions toward them."

"It would seem the sensible thing to do." He nodded slowly.

"If we wished to, that is." She held her breath.

"Why wouldn't we wish to?"

"No reason really, although I can't help but wonder . . ." She searched for the right words. She'd never told a man she wanted him or cared for him or even probably loved him. And once again words failed her.

"Go on, Cassandra. Wonder what?"

"If your sister might not be right." Cassie drew a deep breath. "If there might well be something much more interesting about . . . imperfect."

"There might well be something," his gaze searched hers, "wonderful."

"Lord Berkley?" a female voice said lightly.

Cassie started, as if they had just been caught in a compromising situation. They hadn't, of course. They hadn't moved. They were still here in the middle of the room, surrounded by any number of people. Very much in public view.

Still, it had felt so very private.

Reggie shook his head as if to clear it. Had he too been as caught up in the intimacy of the moment as she'd been? He cast her a regretful smile and turned toward the intruder. "Miss Bellingham, you look lovely this evening."

"You are too kind, my lord." Miss Bellingham turned wide, innocent, *violet* eyes toward Cassie. "I do hope I wasn't interrupting."

"Not at all." Cassie forced a pleasant smile. "We were simply discussing the . . . appeal of perfection."

"Really? How very fascinating." Miss Bellingham turned to gaze up at Reggie. "You must tell me more."

"I should be delighted," he said with entirely too much enthusiasm. Oh, it was subtle enough—probably only Cassie had noted it—but it was definitely there.

"Wasn't it Saint Augustine who said the very perfection of a man was to find out his own imperfection?" Miss Bellingham said with a flutter of her lashes.

"Why yes, I think so." Reggie smiled with delight. "Very good, Miss Bellingham."

"How charmingly well read of you," Cassie said under her breath.

"And, let me think, another quote comes to mind. How did that go?" Reggie paused for a moment. "Ah yes: 'Man is his own star, and the soul that can render an honest and perfect man commands all light, all influence—' "

" 'All fate.' " Miss Bellingham smiled smugly. "John Fletcher, I believe."

"Excellent, Miss Bellingham, really most impressive." Reggie stared with obvious admiration.

Cassie wanted to smack him.

Miss Bellingham turned toward Cassie with an expectant air. "Miss Effington?"

"Yes?"

"Surely you have some pertinent quote to add to the discussion?" Miss Bellingham gazed at her innocently.

Cassie shrugged in a lighthearted manner. "I must confess, nothing comes to mind at the moment."

"Miss Effington is quite well versed in Shakespeare," Reggie said staunchly.

Well versed?

Cassie forced a modest laugh. "I'm not sure I would say well versed; I am no scholar, but I am fond of Shakespeare."

"As are we all." Miss Bellingham cast her an overly sweet smile. "No doubt, he had something to say about perfection?"

"He had something to say about nearly everything."

Cassie's smile was just as sweet, belying her desperate search for something, anything that didn't sound completely stupid. Why didn't she have some of Delia's interest in literature? "Let me think . . ."

"I believe he said, 'Silence is the perfectest herald of joy,'" a voice said behind her.

Cassie turned with a fair amount of relief.

"'I were but little happy if I could say how much.'" Mr. Drummond smiled down at her. "From *Much Ado about Nothing*. It's the only quote I can think of from Shakespeare having anything to do with perfection and is really somewhat obscure. I daresay that's why it was difficult to remember."

"Exactly." Cassie beamed up at him.

"Of course," Reggie murmured.

"Forgive me for intruding, but I too am exceptionally fond of Shakespeare," Mr. Drummond said.

"As are we all," Miss Bellingham said again, her smile a shade less sweet than before.

"I was wondering if I could escort you into dinner, Miss Effington." Mr. Drummond smiled his perfect smile. "I confess I am more than a bit curious about whether or not the rest of what your brother told me about you was true."

"Did he say she's eccentric?" Reggie blurted.

"Not at all." Mr. Drummond shook his head. "He said she was remarkably clever."

"Did he? I must say I'm rather surprised." Cassie laughed. "My brothers have a tendency to be somewhat critical."

"I can't imagine what they would be critical about," Mr. Drummond said firmly and held out his arm. "Shall we?"

"I should think Lady Pennington no doubt wishes us to proceed in a specific order," Reggie said quickly. "Precedence and all that."

"On the contrary, my lord." Miss Bellingham gazed up at Reggie. "She told me, as we are in the country, and we are all friends or we soon shall be, she would prefer to dispense with such formality."

"Still, it's not at all proper." Reggie's tone was more than a little stuffy, and Cassie stared at him in surprise.

"Nonetheless, my lord, it is her home and one should think she should be able to do as she wishes," Mr. Drummond said mildly.

"Beyond that," Miss Bellingham added, "she said we are quite inundated with viscounts—Lord Bellingham is a viscount, too—which she said made who precedes whom especially complicated, and her mother-in-law agreed with her. Although I do believe she has assigned specific places for us at the table."

"That's settled then." Mr. Drummond again offered his arm. "Miss Effington?"

Cassie glanced at Reggie. A polite smile lingered on his lips, but his eyes were slightly narrowed and gleamed silver. He looked very much like a man who had well earned his reputation. A man at once dangerous and exciting. A man tasting the distinctly bitter taste of jealousy.

It was too, too wonderful.

Cassie took Mr. Drummond's arm and beamed up at him. "I am quite looking forward to our conversation, Mr. Drummond. I should like to hear all about your plantations."

He chuckled. "And I should like to hear all about you."

They started toward the dining room, and she resisted the urge to look over her shoulder. She was certain Reggie would escort Miss Bellingham into dinner, and she did not particularly wish to see Miss Wonderful on his arm, hanging on his every word.

No, the object here was to make Reggie jealous. And Lord Perfect was just the man to do it.

As much as she hated to admit it, Mr. Drummond was indeed perfect and possibly even perfect for her. Or would be if her heart was not already engaged elsewhere. And worse, Miss Bellingham seemed extremely well suited for Reggie, and who knew where his feelings lay.

Cassie was confident Reggie had some affection for her, but he did have a reputation with women and she could not completely dismiss the possibility that he might simply have been toying with her. She never would have imagined that finding Lord Perfect and Miss Wonderful would be anything but perfect and wonderful.

It could well be the biggest mistake of her life.

Eleven

A woman who claims to know what she wants is dangerous. A woman who really does know what she wants is to be avoided at all costs.

Marcus, Earl of Pennington

Reggie would like nothing better at the moment than to throttle his hostess.

Certainly Gwen's insistence on informality should have worked to Reggie's benefit, and had he been quicker, he would have been the one escorting Cassandra in to dinner. Instead, he'd been left with Miss Bellingham, which, granted, did help in his effort to make Cassandra jealous. Or at least it would have if not for Mr. Drummond.

Reggie could cheerfully throttle Christian Effington as well for procuring a Lord Perfect who did indeed seem, well, perfect. And thus far, Cassandra did not appear to be finding perfection at all dull or uninteresting.

Even the seating arrangements were not to Reggie's

liking. He was seated between Miss Bellingham and Lady St. Stephens, directly across from Cassandra, who sat between Lord St. Stephens and Mr. Drummond. He would have much preferred to have Cassandra by his side, and as far away from Drummond as possible, with the ever present possibility of intimate conversation between and the chance to gaze into her blue eyes. There was certainly no chance of anything even remotely personal transpiring with her a table width away.

If there was a benefit to the seating arrangement at all it was that Lucy was seated across from Christian Effington, and even the constant flirtatious glances she cast at him were to no avail, given the floral arrangements and goblets between them. To Effington's credit, he appeared to be doing his best not to encourage the girl and kept up a lively conversation with Miss Bellingham on his right and Miss Hilliard on his left. Indeed, Effington seemed somewhat uncomfortable by Lucy's attention, and Reggie's opinion of the man notched upward. Better yet, the young Lord Bellingham, far closer to Lucy in age than any other of their party, seemed quite taken with her. Indeed, the poor boy could scarcely eat for gazing at her with adoring eyes. Lucy seemed well aware of his interest, and Reggie was fairly certain she encouraged it. He snorted to himself. Practice indeed. He would have to have a long talk with his mother about the dangers of allowing young women, specifically sisters, such freedoms.

Across the table, Cassandra laughed at something Drummond said, and it was all Reggie could do to restrain himself from leaping across the table, planting his fist firmly in Drummond's perfect face, sweeping Cassandra up in his arms, and stealing away with her. Abduction was sounding better and better.

"Excellent meal, is it not, my lord?" Miss Bellingham said.

He wrenched his gaze from Cassandra, adopted a pleasant smile, and turned toward Miss Bellingham. "Indeed it is, Miss Bellingham, but I must admit, for as long as I can remember, the cook here at Holcroft Hall has always been outstanding."

She cocked her head and studied him curiously. "Your own estate is near here, I understand."

Reggie nodded. "Berkley Park is a scant half-hour ride away."

"I should love to see it."

"Perhaps we can arrange an outing during your stay here." Out of the corner of his eye he noted Cassandra watching him, and he smiled at Miss Bellingham. "Berkley Park is lovely at this time of year."

"I have no doubt of that. I quite like the country."

"Do you?" He raised a brow. "I should think a young woman like yourself, considered an excellent match and indeed one of the toasts of the season, would prefer the excitement of London to the rather staid life of the country."

"Not at all." She waved away his comment with a flick of her lovely hand. "I much prefer the openness of the countryside and I miss being able to ride freely, without the restrictions placed on you when you're limited to only an occasional jaunt in Hyde Park." She smiled wryly. "When one is declared a toast of the season, one's every action is watched and scrutinized and discussed. I suspect a great many in society are waiting to see if you fall from such illustrious heights, and an even greater portion are hoping that you do so."

Reggie's brows pulled together. "That's rather a jaded view of it all, isn't it?"

"Probably, but accurate nonetheless." She shrugged. "I must confess, this has a great deal to do with why, when Lady St. Stephens told me of your wager with her sister, I was most intrigued and agreed to play along with your efforts."

She leaned closer to him and lowered her voice in a confidential manner. "It can be dreadfully wearing, you know, simply trooping from one party to another, always behaving properly, all in the overriding pursuit of marriage and a good match and, if one is lucky, affection, even perhaps love." She settled back in her chair and considered him thoughtfully. "Any sort of fun or adventure is limited to what one finds in a ballroom. Unless, of course, one has the opportunity to take part in a farce like this one."

He laughed. "And you are doing an excellent job, Miss Bellingham. I am most appreciative of your efforts."

She paused for a long moment, as if choosing her words, and met his gaze directly. "My dear Lord Berkley, I'm not entirely certain I'm still playing a role."

"What do you mean?" he said slowly.

She smiled. "Why, my lord, you're an excellent match. You have a fine title and fortune. You're exceptionally attractive and quite well read. All in all, you're very much what any woman would wish for in a husband. I could do far worse."

He stifled a stab of panic. "Oh, but certainly you could do much better."

She laughed with delight. "And you are most humble as well. No, my lord, I fear I rather like you."

"But I'm in love with Miss Effington."

"Are you? Have you declared yourself?"

"Well, no."

"Then you have not asked for her hand?"

"Not yet."

"I see. Then in truth you are not spoken for."

"I suppose you could say—"

"Indeed I do say, my lord." She leaned close, her violet eyes gazing into his. "When I agreed to this charade of yours, I did so because I found it most amusing. Now, I think there may well be a far greater benefit to it than mere amusement."

He groped for the right words. "You are extraordinarily direct, Miss Bellingham."

"I see no reason not to be and no reason not to be honest as well." A wicked light sparked in her eyes. "I find I like men with a certain reputation. Men who are not afraid to do exactly as they wish without fear of the consequences. Men who take what they want. Men precisely like you."

"Good Lord, Miss Bellingham." He stared at her with rising horror. Of all the times for his original plan to attract women to begin working, this was most definitely not it.

"And in addition to all that I find most attractive about you, I would quite relish being a viscountess. The next Lady Berkley."

"Miss Bellingham!"

"Felicity." She fairly purred the word.

"Miss Bellingham," he said firmly. "I am most flattered, but my affections are engaged elsewhere."

"For the moment."

"Forever."

"We shall see, my lord." She favored him with a determined smile that sent his heart plummeting to his toes. "We shall see." She turned away to speak to Effington.

Reggie sat stunned and glanced across the table to meet Cassandra's annoyed gaze. He managed a weak smile. Her eyes narrowed slightly and she turned pointedly away to direct her attentions back to Drummond.

Blast it all. What was he to do now? He certainly couldn't avoid Miss Bellingham and make Cassandra jealous at the same time. Although, judging by the vile look Cassandra just gave him, the jealousy part of it was coming along nicely. Still, paying any attention to Miss Bellingham at this point would only serve to increase her determination to be the next Viscountess Berkley.

He groaned to himself. How could it all have gone so terribly wrong? And how was he going to fix it?

Abduction really did seem like an excellent idea now. Of course, Cassandra might well refuse to marry him anyway. In spite of her adamant views about what was and what wasn't proper, she was just stubborn enough to allow her reputation to be shredded and declare she'd been right in the beginning: They did not suit. After all, only a man with an infamous reputation in the first place would resort to abduction. Beyond that, the scandal it would create would only make him more attractive to Miss Bellingham, and who knew how far she would go to get what she wanted? Oh no, she was a dangerous and distinctly frightening creature.

Perhaps it was time to risk telling Cassandra of his feelings. To risk offering her his heart. It was just possible, given the moments they'd shared, she felt as he did.

He hadn't wanted to fall over the precipice again until he could do so hand in hand with the woman he loved. And he did not relish dragging her over that cliff kicking and screaming. But he would if he had to. He would not lose her. He ignored the voice in his head that declared he had never in truth had her. Some sort of action had to be taken, and as soon as possible.

Before Cassandra decided Lord Perfect was indeed perfect for her.

Before Miss Wonderful was firmly ensconced as the new Lady Berkley.

Before there was yet another unforeseen twist in a more and more convoluted scheme and Reginald, Viscount Berkley, gave up women entirely to spend the rest of his days in a nice, quiet monastery. Preferably run by monks who produced a decent quality of brandy.

Which, at the moment, had a great deal of appeal.

Cassie leaned against the stone baluster of the Holcroft Hall terrace and watched the company in the drawing room through the wide French doors thrown open to catch the evening breeze. At the moment, Cassie preferred to be out of doors, under the stars, in the fresh air. Besides, this was an excellent vantage point from which to see everything that went on, and it was relatively private as well.

She'd debated between joining the tables of card

players or several of the younger members of their party lingering near the pianoforte, where Miss Bellingham and Mr. Drummond played duets in harmony. Perfect harmony.

Or perhaps she should simply grab Reggie, currently deep in conversation with Lord Pennington, Thomas, and St. Stephens, drag him into the rose garden, and allow him to live up to his reputation by seducing her amidst the hedges. Not a proper option but definitely high on her list.

Dinner had been at once endless and quite enjoyable. Mr. Drummond was a charming companion and most attentive. Cassie found she liked him a great deal, and as hard as she tried, she could find nothing at all about him that could not be considered, well, perfect.

He was amusing with an excellent sense of the absurd. Cassie had laughed nearly as much as she had eaten. He was friendly but not aggressive, flirtatious but not presumptuous, intelligent without being smug, and modest without feigned humility. All in all, he was indeed everything she'd ever thought she wanted in a man.

Except that he was the wrong man.

The man she wanted was, at this very moment, the object of attention of Miss Bellingham, although how the young woman could play as well as she did while still casting seductive glances at Reggie from across the room was really quite astonishing. Was there anything Miss Bellingham did not do well? Cassie doubted anyone would ever describe her as eccentric.

Still, Cassie had to admit, Reggie did not appear as intent on Miss Bellingham as Miss Bellingham was on him. Indeed, unless Cassie was mistaken, the smiles he directed toward the younger woman were little more than polite. Cassie's spirits rose. Perhaps, in spite of the highly intimate discussions Reggie and Miss Bellingham appeared to have had at dinner, he wasn't especially interested in her after all.

At the moment, Reggie was intent on watching his sister smile fetchingly at Lord Bellingham, cast frequent come-hither looks at Mr. Drummond, and flirt outrageously with Christian, who wore an expression not unlike that of a hunted animal. Cassie bit back a grin. It served Christian right to be pursued by a woman—or rather a girl—he couldn't pursue back, especially given the endless numbers of women he had probably dallied with. And served Reggie right as well, no doubt.

Still, the man was an enigma. She studied him thoughtfully. He was protective of his sister and obviously cared about her future. He bore a long-suffering air in regards to his mother, yet he was apparently fond of her as well. He was a loyal and lifelong friend of Lord Pennington's, a friend as well of Thomas's, and both Gwen and Marianne spoke highly of him. Nothing that Cassie had learned firsthand about Reggie meshed even slightly with his reputation.

As for that, she no longer cared what he might or might not have done in the past. Only what he might or might not do in the future.

"I see you have changed your mind about Berkley." Leo sauntered up to her.

She laughed. "What on earth would make you think such a thing?"

"Well, dear sister, I know you far better than you think I do." A smug smile lifted the corners of his mouth. "I have noted that while you have obviously caught the attention of Mr. Drummond, a gentleman, I might add, that has every woman here fanning herself in a frantic manner and gazing at him as if he were a tasty morsel, you do not look at him," Leo paused for emphasis, "the way you look at Lord Berkley."

"Nonsense, Leo." Cassie fluttered her fan absently, then caught herself and stopped. "I don't look at Lord Berkley in any way out of the ordinary."

Leo raised a skeptical brow.

"I don't."

He grinned.

She heaved a resigned sigh. "Very well. I might, just possibly, mind you, be the tiniest bit interested in him."

"I knew it." His grin widened. "I gather, therefore, you are willing to venture into the realm of reforming a rake?"

"If I must." She shook her head. "But in truth, Leo, I'm not certain he needs much reform. Beyond that," she cast him a weak smile, "I seem to like him precisely the way he is."

"Do you?"

"I'm afraid so."

"Then," Leo chose his words with care, "as you have never considered reformation before and you have never spoken of a gentleman the way you speak of this one, am I to assume that you care for him? Love him, perhaps?"

"It does appear that way."

"I see." He nodded slowly. "You are not considering anything foolish, are you?"

"Everything I am considering seems rather foolish."

She studied her brother carefully. "What exactly do you mean by foolish?"

"I mean there are any number of ways a woman may, well, force a man into marriage."

"Force? *Force!*" She stared in disbelief. "I can't believe you would say such a thing!"

"I simply—"

"First of all, as you well know, I have had any number of proposals through the years, none of which were *forced*. In addition, do you honestly think I would allow him or any man to . . . to *compromise* me in an attempt to induce marriage?"

"Shh." He glanced around and lowered his voice. "I admit the idea had crossed my mind."

"Leo!"

"Come now, Cass, it's not entirely far-fetched. You have always done precisely as you've wished to get precisely what you want."

"Within the bounds of respectable behavior."

"For the most part."

"Nonetheless"—outrage colored her words—"should I be *compromised,* I would not consider for a moment demanding marriage."

"Yes, well, you wouldn't have to." His tone was lofty. "I would insist on it."

"You would have nothing to say about it. I daresay you wouldn't even know about it." She glared at him. "And I can't believe you would think I would do such a thing."

"Well, perhaps I was a bit hasty." His tone was grudging. Leo didn't like to admit he was wrong any more than she did.

"Perhaps," she snapped, then drew a calming breath. "Leo, I have no intention of forcing anyone into marriage. If indeed it comes to marriage, it shall be because that's what he and I wish."

"My apologies. I should never have said anything, and I should indeed know better." He cast her a rueful smile. "I am simply far too used to worrying about you to stop now. I must accept that you are an intelligent woman with the ability to make her own choices in life."

She narrowed her eyes. "I don't believe you."

"As well you shouldn't." He grinned. "I have no intention of allowing you to do anything that could conceivably ruin your life."

"Your concern is touching." She studied him for a long moment. The last thing she needed or wanted was for Leo to think she had illicit plans for Reggie and therefore watch her every move. "As I said, I have no intention of trapping Lord Berkley into marriage."

"Then we have nothing to worry about." His tone softened. "Cass, I am delighted that you have finally found a man you wish to marry, and I am willing to do whatever you might need to assist this romance—to a point, of course."

"Are you?"

"I am. I would like nothing more than to see you wed and happy. And I quite hope my days of concerning myself with your activities and fearing for your future will soon be at an end."

Cassie stifled the urge to tell Leo she had every intention of continuing to refurbish houses even after she wed, especially now that she had a vague idea as to what she could do with her earnings. Indeed, if she married Reggie, it was entirely possible that the services of Viscountess Berkley would command an even higher fee than those of an Effington. She dismissed the idea that Reggie might not wish her to continue.

"Do you forgive me, then?"

"Possibly." She thought for a moment. "Leo," she forced a casual note to her voice, "what do you think of Miss Bellingham?"

"Miss Bellingham?" Leo's gaze shifted to the young lady seated at the pianoforte, and a light sparked in his eye. "I daresay I think precisely the same as any other man who has crossed her path. She is exquisite. A diamond of the first water. I can't see anything about her that is not very nearly perfect. Indeed, she is a vision of perfection. Her form, her figure . . . her eyes are violet, you know."

"Yes, I've noticed." Cassie resisted an urge toward sarcasm. "I have also noticed just how often she directs those violet eyes toward Reg—Lord Berkley."

"Does she?" He studied the young woman thoughtfully. "And you would prefer she cast them elsewhere?"

Cassie grinned. "You do know me well."

"Perhaps in my direction?"

"Why, I wish I had thought of that."

Leo heaved an exaggerated sigh. "It shall be a sacrifice, but it's the least I can do to ensure my sister's happiness."

"I'm not asking you to marry her, I'm not certain how well a vision of perfection would fare among Effingtons. Simply distract her. Occupy her attention. Flirt with her. Allow her to flirt with you. That sort of thing."

"I'm certain I can think of something," Leo murmured, his gaze fixed firmly on Miss Bellingham. "The things I do for my sister."

"I'm certain it will be most unpleasant," Cassie said wryly.

"Ghastly. I daresay, I don't know how I'll survive." He slanted her a wicked grin, then strode across the terrace and through the doors to join the guests gathered around the pianoforte.

Cassie watched him with a wicked grin of her own. As a protective older brother, Leo could be most annoying. However, he did have a way about him. Cassie had watched him charm any number of women before and had to admit he was nearly irresistible. She needn't worry about Miss Bellingham, at least for the moment. Indeed she had far more important matters to concern herself with.

She turned absently and gazed out over the darkened rose gardens. Cassie wasn't entirely certain when she had come to the momentous decision to confess her feelings to Reggie. She wasn't entirely certain when she'd truly admitted them to herself. She'd come close to telling him earlier this evening and was now glad she hadn't. There was always the possibility he didn't share her feelings, and it would be far less humiliating to find out in private than in the midst of a crowded room.

She had no intention of trapping Reggie into marriage, but, although she would never admit it to Leo or anyone else except perhaps Delia, the idea of sharing his bed had indeed taken root in her mind.

Reggie was the first and only man whose kisses had curled her toes or sapped her will. The first and only man who had filled her thoughts day and night. The first and only man she'd ever loved. If she couldn't have him as her husband, she didn't want anyone else. But the idea of sharing his bed, of lying in his arms, of experiencing the act of love . . . well, she would not dismiss it out of hand.

Good Lord, what had happened to her? She was no longer concerned with the avoidance of scandal but indeed was more than willing to embrace it. She wanted marriage, but she wanted Reggie more. Wanted to race down the path of scandal with him regardless of the consequences.

It was past time to tell him how she felt. Past time to throw caution to the winds and begin a serious pursuit of the man she loved.

"It's beginning to have all the charm of a French farce, don't you think?" Reggie said low in her ear.

She turned with a smile and gazed into the drawing room. "There do seem to be all sorts of interesting currents in the room."

"There do indeed. Most of them quite—"

"Naughty?"

He laughed. "At the very least." Reggie crossed his arms over his chest, settled back against the baluster, and nodded at the card players. "In that corner, you have Marcus's mother, who has had an ongoing relationship with the gentleman across from her, the family solicitor, Mr. Whiting, for a number of years now."

"Really?"

He nodded. "And also at that table, I have noticed my own mother fluttering her lashes at Colonel Fargate."

"There's apparently quite a bit of lash fluttering

throughout the room." Cassie laughed. "Miss Hilliard seems to have shed several years in the process, and Miss Fargate is positively animated."

"It's most impressive. One can scarcely keep track of who is casting looks at whom." Reggie grinned. "Although, happily, my mother's flirtatious activity does not prevent her from keeping a watchful eye on my sister." He blew a long-suffering breath. "Lucy is determined to flirt with every available gentleman in the room."

"Practice?"

"I hate that word," he muttered.

"She does seem to be directing her attention primarily toward Christian." Cassie observed the gathering around the pianoforte for a moment. "To the detriment of young Lord Bellingham, I might add, who appears quite taken with your sister."

"Wonderful," he said grimly.

"It's rather amusing, I think."

"All this, you mean?" Reggie gestured at the room.

"This is, of course, but I mean you."

He raised a brow. "You find me amusing? In what way?"

"In any number of ways, actually, but at the moment, I think your overly protective nature toward your sister is most entertaining." She shrugged. "Especially given your reputation. Although I suppose you, of all people, would be well aware of the devious nature of men."

"I would? Yes, of course, I would. Indeed, I am." He hesitated, as if deciding exactly what to say. "About that infamous reputation of mine."

"Yes?"

"I should probably tell you . . . It might well be time . . . Honesty and all that." He stared into her eyes for a long moment, then heaved a resigned sigh. "I am willing to consider changing my ways."

"Are you indeed?"

"Yes, I am." He paused to choose his words. "It has come to my attention, thanks in part to an offhand comment at dinner—"

"A comment by Miss Bellingham?" Cassie's voice was light, belying her surprise.

He nodded. "Most definitely."

"You are willing to reform because of something Miss Bellingham said?" she said slowly, a knot forming in her stomach.

"Good Lord, yes." Reggie shook his head. "She is a most determined young lady."

Cassie stared at him. "Determined?"

"To get what she wants." Reggie glanced at Miss Bellingham. "You may not know it to look at her, but I suspect Felicity has a will of iron."

"Felicity?" The knot tightened.

"That's her name." He shrugged. "Given our discussion, I am hard-pressed to think of her as Miss Bellingham. Oh, I know it's highly improper to refer to her by her given name, but somehow, as life in the country is especially casual, what would not pass muster in the city always has seemed rather acceptable here. Although I doubt that I would call her Felicity to her face or indeed to anyone."

And twisted. "With the possible exception of myself."

"Yes, of course, but you and I are friends. We can be honest with each other." He grinned. "Under most circumstances."

"Honesty is overrated," Cassie muttered and groped for the right words. "Am I to understand you are willing to reform for Miss Bellingham?"

"Absolutely." He thought for a moment, then his eyes widened, and he shook his head vehemently. "No, that's not what I mean at all. Not *for* Miss Bellingham but *because of* Miss Bellingham. It's an entirely different thing altogether."

"Is it?"

"It is indeed."

She grit her teeth. "Perhaps you could explain it to me?"

"Perhaps I could." He shrugged helplessly. "But I can't. Not really."

"I think, my lord," she chose her words carefully and forced them out past the growing lump in her throat, "that you owe me forty pounds after all."

"What? Why?"

"Why, she is obviously indeed your Miss Wonderful."

His brows drew together. "Yes, and I found your Lord Perfect, so it's still a draw. Besides, she is not my Miss Wonderful—she is simply a Miss Wonderful." He stared for a long moment, and his eyes widened. "Why, I do believe, Miss Effington—Cassandra—that you're jealous."

"I most certainly am not," she snapped, anger washing away the anguish that gripped her at the thought of his willingness to reform for Miss Bellingham and the realization that he must like the young woman a great deal.

He smiled in an annoyingly smug manner. "You most certainly are."

"Don't be absurd. I'm not jealous, but I do admit I'm . . . concerned. Yes, that's good. That's it exactly. I'm concerned."

"Are you?" He continued to smirk, and she resisted the impulse, no, the *need,* to smack him. Hard. Bare handed.

"As I would be concerned for any friend I see about to make a dreadful mistake."

"I suspect you are the only one who thinks Miss Bellingham—*Felicity*—would be a dreadful mistake." He glanced at Miss Bellingham. "Every other gentleman, including your own brother, I see, and I daresay most of the ladies, thinks she would make an excellent match."

"Come now, Reggie, look at the way she looks at you. She's a . . . a predator."

He choked back a laugh.

"It's not the least bit funny. I've seen women look at my brothers in precisely the same way. She looks at you like she's a hound and you're a fox. A very slow and not too bright fox."

"Your flattery shall quite turn my head," he said wryly.

"She's more interested in your title and your fortune than you."

"Once again, your opinion of my appeal is overwhelming."

"Stop it, Reggie. You can be quite charming, and

you, as well as probably hundreds of unsuspecting females, well know it."

"Certainly." He shrugged in a modest manner.

"Nonetheless, I've seen her type of female before. She is unrelenting when it comes to getting what she wants."

"In that, isn't she precisely like you?"

"Not at all. I have . . ." She thought for a moment. "Lines, as it were, that I will not cross." At once the thought of compromise came to mind. Cassie might well be willing, even eager, to share his bed, but she would never use her ruin to force him into marriage. She doubted Miss Bellingham would feel the same.

"Why do you care, Cassandra?" His gaze searched hers. "After all, Mr. Drummond is everything you say you've always wanted. And he appears quite taken with you."

"I care because you're my friend. There's nothing more to it than that. And you're right, Mr. Drummond is everything I've always wanted. And I like him as well."

"Do you really like him?"

"Why wouldn't I? The man is perfect."

"Perfect is as overrated as honesty."

"Not at all." She sniffed in a haughty manner. "Perfect is . . . perfect."

"You didn't answer my question." His gaze narrowed. "How much do you like him?"

"I haven't decided yet." She turned and started toward the drawing room. "But it's past time I found out."

"Cassandra!" He caught her arm and jerked her

back. Her fan flew out of her hand and over the baluster.

She shook off his hand and glared at him. "Now look at what you've done." She pulled away, peered over the railing, and lied. "That's my favorite fan."

"My apologies." He huffed. "But I didn't think we were finished with our discussion."

"You were wrong." She headed toward the steps leading to the garden.

"And furthermore," he said behind her, "I think it was exceptionally rude of you to cut me off."

"Well, what did you expect?" She started down the stairs. "I am not Miss Wonderful."

"I daresay no one would mistake you for that!"

"I daresay any number of men have thought I was quite, quite wonderful!"

He snorted in disbelief.

She ignored him. "But obviously, I'm not the kind of woman one would reform for."

"Obviously!"

She turned on her heel and glared up at him. "That was a vile thing to say."

"Nonetheless, it was true. No man would reform for you because you're the kind of woman who leads men astray! Who makes perfectly normal men do things they would never think of doing. Insane, irrational, foolish, even bloody stupid things!"

"What kind of things?"

"I don't know," he snapped.

"I have never in my life led a man astray!" She turned again and continued down the steps.

"You could certainly lead me astray."

"You are already astray."

"Well then, I have changed my mind. Any man who wasn't a complete idiot would reform for you. I'd reform for you. I think you're well worth changing my wicked ways for. Indeed, I think you're quite wonderful."

"Hah!" She reached the ground level and skirted along the wall of the terrace to just beneath where they'd been standing. "You're just saying that because it seems the . . . the *perfect* thing to say!"

"Hardly. Only a madman would consider you wonderful."

"Nonetheless." She glanced at him with a smug smile. "Mr. Drummond believes me to be wonderful."

"My point exactly. The man is obviously mad," Reggie muttered, his gaze scanning the ground. "Where do you think that blasted fan of yours is, anyway?"

"I have no idea." She stepped away, her gaze firmly focused on the ground before her. She drew a deep breath and forced a casual note to her voice. "Mr. Drummond asked if he could call on me when we return to town."

She sensed Reggie stiffen behind her. "What did you say?"

She raised a shoulder in a casual manner. "I could scarcely say no. It would be . . . rude."

"You have never had a particular problem with rudeness when it comes to me," he said sharply.

"Entirely due to the fact that you are the most annoying man I have ever met."

"Well, I'm certainly not perfect!"

"No, indeed you are the least perfect man I have

ever met!" She huffed with exasperation and met his gaze directly.

"Most annoying and least perfect. It sounds like I have a great deal of potential."

"Potential for what?"

"Potential for reform," he snapped. "For . . . for perfection!"

She scoffed. "You could never be perfect."

"No, I couldn't. Is perfect what you really want?" His gray eyes gleamed silver in the faint light cast by the lanterns on the terrace. "What do you want, anyway?"

The question hung in the air between them.

She stared for a long moment, and all of the anger within her vanished, replaced by need and longing and desire. Without thought she grabbed the edges of his coat and pulled his lips to hers.

For a moment, shock held him still, then he wrapped his arms around her and pulled her tight against him. Yearning and desire swelled within her. She wanted him to tear her clothes from her body and wanted to rip his away as well. Wanted to feel his naked flesh next to hers. Wanted everything wanting him meant regardless of the consequences.

She opened her mouth and her tongue met and mated with his in an intimate dance of hunger and need. Her body molded to his as if they were made one for the other. As if they were half of the same whole. As if this were fate. She felt the hard evidence of his arousal against her, and it only served to increase her own desire. She could give herself to him now, this very moment, here beneath the terrace, and welcome scandal and ruin with open arms.

She wound her fingers through his hair and pressed

harder against him, acutely aware of her breasts crushed against his chest. He held her firmly with one hand splayed against the small of her back, and the other drifted lightly down her side to her hip, then traced faintly over her derrière. His mouth broke from hers to taste the side of her neck and her throat, and lower still to the valley between her breasts. Her head dropped back and she held her breath, lost in the altogether exquisite sensation of his lips on her flesh. His hand cupped her breast, and his thumb circled her nipple through the fabric of her gown.

She clutched at his shoulders and gasped.

He pulled her harder against him and reclaimed her lips with a hunger that matched her own. And she wanted more.

He wrenched his lips from hers and buried his face in her neck, his voice little more than a moan. "Cassandra, this is not the place . . ."

"No?" She struggled for breath and a semblance of sanity. "Are you sure?"

He lifted his head and stared down at her. "Cassandra, I—"

"You should probably slap me for that," she said in a breathless manner. "For taking liberties with you, that is."

"I would never hit a woman." He studied her for a moment, then smiled in a slow and wicked manner. "Although the idea of putting you over my knee and smacking your bottom has a certain amount of appeal."

She gasped with unsuspected delight. "Reggie!"

"Cassandra." He blew a long breath. "We need to talk before—"

"Yes?" She sighed up at him and brushed her lips across his.

"Before it's too late."

"It is too late." She nibbled at his bottom lip and reveled in the way his body tensed.

"You do know this way lies scandal and ruin?" There was an odd edge to his voice, as if he struggled to keep himself under control. Excellent.

She shifted to run kisses along the line of his jaw. "I know and I don't care."

"Why?" He swallowed hard.

"Because . . ." *Because I love you.* Something, fear perhaps, kept the words from her lips. "Because I am four and twenty and considered eccentric. Because I have never met a man I would even consider leaping into scandal and ruin for. It appears I have never wanted a man before." She rested her palm on his cheek and gazed into his eyes. "And I want you."

"I see," he said slowly.

"Do you?"

"No. But then I'm not confident I will ever understand anything when it comes to you."

There was a distinct note of permanence about his statement, and her breath caught.

He took her hand, pulled it to his lips, and placed a kiss in the center of her palm. Delight shivered through her.

"We should return to the others before we are missed," he said in a resolute manner she did not believe for a moment. "And we do need to talk."

"Do we?" she murmured.

"If we are not to be embroiled in scandal we do."

"I rather like the idea of being embroiled in scandal."

"I, however, do not."

"I should think you would be well used to being embroiled in scandal." She placed her hands flat on his chest and felt his muscles tighten beneath her fingers in a most satisfying manner.

"Certainly, in the past," he said quickly, "but if I am to reform . . ."

"Perhaps reform can wait." She slid her hands up his chest.

He caught her hands and stared into her eyes. "This is neither the time nor the place for a serious discussion—or for anything else, for that matter."

"I suspect I can think of all sorts of wonderful places, wonderful private places, for serious discussions or . . . anything else." Her voice was low and inviting and rather shocking, even to herself. She had flirted with men in the past, of course, but had never set out to be quite so available, even willing, and, yes, blatantly seductive before.

"I'm certain you can." He set her firmly aside and stepped back.

She planted her fists on her hips and glared. "What on earth is the matter with you?"

"Nothing. Nothing at all," he said in a less than convincing manner.

"I don't believe you. Why, here I am, more than willing to allow you to take advantage of me, and you won't."

"I have standards regarding where and when," he said loftily.

"Certainly not with whom, given your reputation." She studied him with growing annoyance. "Or maybe it is with whom?"

"I . . . I . . ." He squared his shoulders and gazed down at her. "I do not despoil virgins."

"Even willing virgins?"

"They're the worst kind."

"But I'm a willing virgin!" The words came out of her mouth before she could stop them, and heat rushed up her face.

"I believe I just made my point." He grabbed her hand and started toward the stairs. "Come on, we have to return. At once."

"Why?"

"Because." He stopped abruptly and whirled her into his arms. "Because I do have standards, Cassandra, confuser of men, not only about young women far and away too forward for their own good but about the proper way and time and place for such things, and if we remain here I cannot vouch for your continued safety or mine."

"I don't want to be safe!"

"But I want to keep you safe." He gazed down at her with a look so intense that it stole her breath and her will and her heart. "I will not allow anyone, including myself, to hurt you. Which fairly well prevents me from taking your innocence, no matter how eagerly offered, on the hard ground beneath the rosebushes during a moment stolen from a party. You deserve better."

"Do I?"

"Yes, you do." He smiled with a mix of wry amusement and what was surely affection. "You are, after all, the eccentric Miss Effington."

Never had that title sounded so very wonderful. "And you are the infamous Lord Berkley."

He stared at her for a moment, then shook his head, grabbed her hand, and once again started back to the drawing room. "You shall be the ruined Miss Effington if we don't return immediately."

"I should rather like being the ruined Miss Effington," she murmured behind him. "If my ruin were at the hands of the infamous Lord Berkley."

"Good God." He groaned and muttered something she didn't hear, then started up the stairs, practically dragging her behind him.

Sheer joy bubbled up within her. Perhaps the man was easier to understand than she had thought.

While she was not experienced with men on a truly intimate basis, she certainly knew enough to know when one wanted her in a carnal sense. And Reggie did indeed want her just as she wanted him.

She could think of only one thing that would prevent a man with an infamous reputation from taking precisely what he wanted, indeed, what he was offered.

She laughed aloud and again he mumbled something she didn't catch. Not that it mattered. At this particular moment she was fairly certain the infamous Lord Berkley was in love with the eccentric Miss Effington.

Now she simply had to get him to admit it, and accept it, and, with any luck at all, do something about it.

Twelve

When dealing with the fairer sex one must always be cognizant of the fact that what they say is not always what they mean. And woe be it to the man who does not understand the difference.

Anthony, Viscount St. Stephens

"So what am I to do?" Impatience edged Reggie's voice.

Marcus and Thomas circled the billiards table. It had taken an eternity for the rest of their party to retire for the night. While the ladies had bid their good evenings some time ago, the gentlemen had adjourned to Holcroft Hall's billiards room to play and partake of Marcus's fine brandy and good cigars.

Drummond, of course, had won every game he'd played and had done so with such good nature that his opponents could not begrudge his victories. Even Reggie had a difficult time disliking the blasted man. He couldn't imagine how Drummond had ever lost a wager to Christian, as he couldn't imagine the man ever losing anything to anyone. Both Effington brothers and St. Stephens were excellent players as well. Townsend was fairly good but not consistent, and young Bellingham had a great deal to learn. Whiting and Colonel Fargate had observed the others briefly, then taken their leave.

At long last, only the three old friends remained.

"Well?" Reggie glared at the other men.

Marcus studied the table. "I don't see that you have any particular problems remaining at this point." He leaned over the table and took his shot. "She wants you. You want her. The question as to what you do now seems rather obvious to me."

"Do try to remember this is my cousin you're speaking of," Thomas said mildly and positioned his cue. "As the next Duke of Roxborough and eventual head of the family, I have the responsibility of keeping Cassandra's best interests in mind."

"I do want to marry her, of course." Indignation colored Reggie's voice. "I certainly wouldn't concern you with this if I were interested merely in seduction."

"And I so appreciate that," Thomas murmured, took his shot, and straightened. "I must admit, though, that I agree with Marcus. What is the difficulty now?"

"There are any number of problems." Reggie drew his brows together and stared into his brandy-filled glass. "Prime among them, that I have not been entirely honest with her. She thinks I'm something I'm not."

Thomas and Marcus traded glances.

"Beyond that," Reggie blew a long breath, "while

she is apparently willing to throw herself into my bed—"

Thomas cleared his throat.

"Sorry." Reggie grimaced. "Still, that is part and parcel of my quandary. She definitely wants me in the carnal sense, and while I don't have a particular difficulty with that—"

Thomas choked, leaned his cue against the table, grabbed his glass of brandy, and quickly downed it.

"Are you all right?" Marcus studied the marquess.

"Quite." Thomas shook his head. "It is simply rather difficult to reconcile family responsibilities with longtime friendships. However," he squared his shoulders, "for the remainder of this evening, I shall do my best to think of Cassandra as the object of your affection rather than as my cousin." He met Reggie's gaze directly. "She is the object of your affection, is she not?"

Marcus grinned. "He's in love."

Thomas raised a brow. "Again?"

"For the last time," Reggie said firmly.

"I should hope so, if indeed your aim is marriage." Thomas studied him carefully. "Why don't you just declare your intentions and be done with it?"

"He can't, or rather he won't. He has made a habit of declaring himself before whatever lady in question has made her feelings known, and it's always ended badly." Marcus placed his cue against the table with a reluctant sigh. "I gather this takes precedence over the game?"

"It does seem rather more important." Thomas shrugged. "Reggie's future and all that."

"Thank you," Reggie said wryly. "I do appreciate your concern."

Marcus grinned. "It's nothing, old man, nothing at all."

"Precisely my thinking," Reggie muttered.

"We have to go about this in a logical manner." Thomas thought for a moment. "You want her. She wants you—"

"But she hasn't mentioned love."

"Nor have you," Marcus said pointedly.

"And unfortunately, you have to take the lead in endeavors like this." Thomas shook his head. "Even the most outspoken woman is restrained on this particular subject. It's been my experience, and Marcus's as well, I believe, that women aren't typically the ones to declare their feelings first."

"Mine too." Reggie's voice was grim with memory.

"Therefore you have to charge ahead. Take the horse by the reins. Jump headfirst into the freezing waters. That sort of thing," Marcus said firmly.

"Plunge off the precipice," Reggie murmured.

"Exactly."

"And plummet to smash into a million bloody pieces on the treacherous rocks below." Reggie heaved a deep sigh. "I'd much prefer to avoid that."

"Good God, he has gone over the edge." Thomas stared in disbelief. "I've seen him in the throes of love in the past, but I've never seen him quite so stricken over any woman before."

"This time it's real," Reggie said loftily, then paused. "There is another problem, you know."

Thomas glanced at Marcus. "I suspected there would be."

"If indeed she's in love and not merely in lust," Reggie blew a long breath, "then there is every possibility the man she cares for is the infamous Lord Berkley. Not the really rather ordinary . . . well . . . me."

"I believe it's time we had a serious talk with his lordship," Marcus said to Thomas.

Thomas nodded and plucked Reggie's glass from his hand. "We should have done it years ago."

As if of a single mind, each man grabbed one of Reggie's elbows, steered him to the end of the room, and deposited him in a large, comfortable leather chair.

"What are you doing?" Reggie glared up at his friends.

"Putting your life in the proper perspective." Marcus retrieved their glasses and thrust Reggie's at him.

Thomas fetched the brandy decanter and replenished the drinks. "You need to start viewing yourself as others do."

Reggie huffed. "I don't see—"

"That's precisely the problem." Marcus paced in front of him. "You don't see, and it's past time you did."

Thomas paced in the opposite direction. "Let's start with the obvious." He stopped and considered Reggie carefully, then nodded. "You are not ugly, indeed, some might call you handsome—even dashing. I have seen ladies look at you, including my own wife and her sisters, and never once have I seen a single woman turn away in disgust."

"My appearance is acceptable, I suppose," Reggie muttered.

"Also, in terms of the obvious, your station in life is not to be scoffed at." Marcus ticked the points off on his fingers. "You have an honorable title, a respectable fortune, a fine estate, and a grand house in town—"

"Currently being refurbished by the aforementioned object of your affection," Thomas said pointedly.

"Beyond that, you are unfailingly loyal in your friendships, a good son and brother, generous to a fault, and a genuinely nice person. All things considered," Marcus paused and nodded, "I'd marry you."

Thomas raised his glass. "As would I."

"As delightful as that knowledge is, women don't seem to agree." Reggie scoffed. "Even after we *enhanced* my reputation, women were still not falling at my feet, if you recall."

"Excluding Miss Bellingham, of course," Marcus chuckled.

"The irony is irresistible. The brightest star of the season wants the infamous Lord Berkley, who really isn't infamous and wants someone entirely different, who doesn't want anyone infamous at all." Thomas nudged Marcus with his elbow. "Although I do demand some of the credit for his infamy. I believe many of the amorous exploits, most notably the mythical notorious affair with the mysterious royal, were my concoctions."

"And excellent they were, too. I fear my biggest credit is the duels," Marcus said with a sigh. "Perhaps I did not truly do my part."

Reggie rolled his gaze toward the ceiling. "Infamous or not, I have never especially attracted women."

"Nonsense," Marcus snorted. "You have attracted any number of women. They were simply never the women you wanted. Until now, you've only been attracted to women who did not return your affection.

And that, my dear Reggie, is the crux of the matter. That is the only real problem you have at the moment." Marcus finished with a flourish.

"What is the only real problem?" Reggie stared up at him.

"The fact that there is no problem!" Marcus's voice rose with exasperation. "You want her, she wants you. The only thing that stands in your way is—"

Thomas gasped dramatically and clasped his free hand over his heart. "Nothing!"

"Not a blasted thing! Not one single impediment prevents you from making Cassandra Effington your own. It's never happened before. There's no precedent. Oh, dear heavens, whatever shall you do now?" Marcus threw himself onto Thomas's shoulder in a theatrical show of profuse weeping without spilling a single drop of his brandy. "It's dreadful, all of it."

"There, there." Thomas patted Marcus's back and glared at Reggie. "Now see what you've done."

Reggie narrowed his gaze. "You're foxed. Both of you."

Thomas craned his neck to look at Marcus. "Are you soused, old man?"

Marcus lifted his head and furrowed his brow. "I don't think so. In point of fact, I think I'm remarkably clearheaded."

Thomas nodded. "Indeed, I don't know when I've been so clearheaded."

"You're not the least bit funny, you know." Reggie sipped his brandy and studied his friends. "This is my life we're talking about."

Marcus stepped away from Thomas. "Then live it. For the first time, you are in love with a woman who more than likely loves you in return. And I think . . ." Marcus's eyes widened in realization. "I think you're terrified."

Reggie snorted. "Wouldn't you be if you'd had your heart broken again and again?"

"That's not what scares you. Frankly, I'm an idiot not to have seen it before now." Marcus grinned. "You're afraid of marriage. Permanence. One woman, one love if you will. Forever and ever. What do you think, Thomas? Am I right?"

"Absolutely. It makes perfect sense." Thomas nodded firmly. "Why, there have always been women more than willing to marry him, he simply had no interest in them. Now that marriage is staring him in the face, now that there is every possibility that the object of his affections will return said affection and actually marry him, the man is a quivering mass of nervous indecision." Thomas's grin matched Marcus's and was just as annoying.

"That's absurd," Reggie snapped. "It's the most ridiculous thing I've ever heard."

Or perhaps it was simply stunning in its simplicity.

Certainly handing his heart to women who did not return his affection effectively prevented any serious overtures toward marriage. Still, Reggie had thought he wanted to be wed even if he had always rather enjoyed his unencumbered life. He had never truly been the infamous Lord Berkley, but he had had an exceptionally good time of it.

"And as for this infamous nonsense, from what I understand, Cassandra cares for you not because of your alleged reputation but in spite of it," Thomas said.

"Reggie." Marcus's tone softened. "I have seen you

risk your heart any number of times without fear. Now, I suspect you're afraid to do so because the stakes are so much higher regardless of whether you lose or whether you win."

"You are far from ordinary, old man, and I am proud to count you as my friend," Thomas said with an affectionate smile. "And I should like nothing better than to welcome you into my family."

"Very well." Reggie thought for a moment. "If you're right, and marriage is what I fear, I'd best face up to it, because I have never felt about any woman the way I do about Cassandra. And I cannot risk losing her."

Determination washed through him, and he got to his feet. "I'll do it. I'll tell her. Throw caution to the winds. Confess my feelings. Bare my soul." He started toward the door, then stopped. "While I'm telling all, I should probably mention that I'm not infamous as well."

"No!" Marcus and Thomas said with one voice.

Reggie winced. "Not a good idea?"

"She's willing to reform you," Marcus said firmly. "For God's sake, permit her to do so."

"Effington women have always loved a good challenge," Thomas added.

"Then I shall provide her with one." Reggie nodded and again headed toward the door.

"You're not going to speak to her now, are you?" Thomas called after him. "It's very late. She'll be in bed."

"Nonetheless, I shall wake her," Reggie said firmly. "I can wait no longer. Thank you both for your assistance."

"He's going to her bed in the middle of the night," Thomas muttered to Marcus. "I should probably stop him. If anything untoward happens, I should have to defend her honor. Shoot him or something like that."

"Or we could play another game," Marcus said.

Thomas's answer faded behind Reggie.

Not that it mattered. Reggie hurried down the passageway and started up the stairs. He had no intention of doing anything other than declaring his intentions to the eccentric—or rather the irresistible—Miss Effington. Of course, given her enthusiasm earlier this evening, if she had something else in mind. . . . He grinned and picked up his step. It's not as if she would be ruined for long, as he had every intention of marrying her. And as soon as possible.

Scared of marriage? Of being with the same woman for the rest of his days? Hah. At least not if that same woman was Cassandra. Life with Cassandra would never be the least bit ordinary or dull or anything but filled with adventure and excitement and passion.

He had made a point of learning exactly which room she occupied. Fifth from the stairs, north side of the hallway. He counted the doors, drew a deep breath, knocked softly, and hoped she hadn't locked her door. He grasped the handle, pushed it open, and slipped into her room.

"Cassandra," he said quietly and closed the door behind him.

A low, sleepy moan sounded from the bed.

A scant ray of starlight shone through the open curtains, and he could make out nothing more than a covered mound on the bed.

He stepped closer but not too close. He really didn't want to distract her from his words, and the very thought of her lying beneath the covers was distracting enough for him.

"For once don't say anything, just listen."

He drew a deep breath and groped for the right words. And couldn't seem to find them. Why on earth was this so blasted hard?

"I don't want you to see Drummond when we return to London," he blurted. "I don't want you to see anyone. I . . . I care for you deeply. More than I've ever cared for anyone."

He clasped his hands behind his back and paced. "I know I'm not what you say you want. Lord knows, I'm not the least bit perfect and will never be perfect, but I am willing to be reformed. And I think we suit rather well together, you and I. In all things really, but then when I kissed you—"

A choking noise sounded from the bed.

"Very well then, when you kissed me and wanted, well, *more,* it was all I could do to restrain myself. You can be quite persuasive, you know. Beyond that I have never met a woman who drives me as mad as you do, and that seems rather significant, at least to me. Indeed, it's quite overwhelming."

He blew a long breath. "That's it, I think, for the moment at any rate, although I daresay there's a great deal more, but that shall have to wait for a more appropriate time because I know this isn't at all proper and I'm going to have to leave now before I do something terribly rash and . . . well . . ." He braced himself. "You could say something now, if you wish. Or not say anything and I shall just go away and pretend I never said any of this and we can continue to be friends or whatever it is that we are . . .

"No, wait. I didn't mean that." His resolve hardened. "I won't leave, I can't leave, until I know what you're thinking."

"I'd love to see you in London, Berkley." A deep male voice sounded from the bed. "But I fear you're not exactly what I'm looking for in a match."

Reggie's stomach twisted into a tight knot. "Leo Effington, I presume?"

"Indeed." At least there was a mild hint of amusement in his voice. "And oddly enough, I don't recall ever kissing you."

"Yes, well, my mistake obviously." Reggie edged toward the door. How could he have miscounted? "If you'll excuse me."

"I won't." Effington's voice was firm. "I should like a few words with you and would appreciate it if you would stay right where you are. I am willing to force you to do so if necessary, but I sleep with very little in the way of clothing, and I would much prefer to stay exactly where I am."

"Excellent idea," Reggie said under his breath. He did not relish the idea of a confrontation with Cassandra's irate, and no doubt naked, oldest brother. Indeed, he'd rather prefer to have the man on his side, but that might well be too much to hope for at the moment.

He adopted a cool tone. "This is hardly the time and place for a serious discussion, Effington."

"Need I remind you, you crept into my room with

your declaration of"—Effington paused thoughtfully—"what were you declaring, anyway?"

Reggie huffed. "Love, of course."

"You didn't mention love."

"Of course I mentioned love." Reggie tried to remember exactly what he did say. "I distinctly remember saying I love you—er—her."

"No, you didn't. You said you cared for her. You said you cared for her more than you'd ever cared for anyone. All in all, it was really quite a nice speech—"

"Thank you," Reggie murmured.

"But you never used the word *love,*" Effington said.

"Well, I meant to say love."

"Yes, but you didn't, and I must say, Berkley, if you intend to declare yourself to my sister in the middle of the night like this, I would pay more attention to precisely what you are going to say in advance of stumbling around in the dark. A moderate bit of practice is probably called for."

Reggie grimaced. "Practice, excellent idea."

"Just a suggestion, mind you."

"And most appreciated."

"I'm assuming, overall, that your intentions are honorable? Marriage, I mean."

"Yes."

"Then I have another suggestion."

"I thought perhaps you would."

"Marry her, Berkley." A warning sounded in Effington's voice. "*Then* seduce her."

"Excellent suggestion." Of course, if she were to seduce him. . . . He pushed the thought from his mind.

"I should not like it otherwise."

"Nor should you."

"I have heard of your skill on the dueling fields—"

Reggie groaned to himself.

"I should hate to have to call you out in defense of my sister's honor, but I will do so without hesitation."

"I would expect no less."

"And I will demand marriage."

"I don't think we'll suit," Reggie said under his breath.

"What?"

"I said before or after you shoot?"

Effington paused. "I haven't decided yet."

"I shall leave you, then, to your decision and your rest and bid you good night." Reggie stepped to the door and pulled it open.

"Berkley." Effington's voice was level. "I do wish you luck. In your pursuit of marriage, that is. And I daresay it won't be nearly as difficult as you imagine."

"We shall see." Reggie stepped into the hall.

"It might well be worse," Effington chuckled softly, and Reggie closed the door firmly behind him.

It had been a foolish idea to try to speak with Cassandra tonight in the first place, and he certainly hadn't furthered his cause with her brother. He still wasn't sure how he'd mistaken her room, although there was a possibility brandy had played a part. Still, he had no intention of trying another door. Who knew where he'd end up? He would make it a point to get her alone tomorrow and confess his feelings. Hopefully, far better than he'd done so tonight.

He started toward his own quarters. A door creaked open behind him as he passed. Without warning, he was jerked into the dark room, the door snapping shut behind him.

"What?"

A hand clamped over his mouth and a supple body pressed him against the door.

"Shh," Cassie whispered. "Do be quiet." She removed her hand slowly. "I don't want Leo to know you're in my room."

"That would be something of a problem," he murmured. Even this close, she was scarcely more than a dark silhouette.

"What are you doing here?"

"I wanted to speak with you. Alone."

"Why were you in Leo's room?"

"I thought it was yours."

She stifled a laugh. "It must have been most amusing to find out you were wrong."

"Amusing is not quite the word for it."

At once he was aware of the frail nature of her nightclothes and the heat of her body pressing against his.

"What did you want to talk about?"

"Us." Almost of their own accord, his arms wrapped around her, the thin fabric of her gown barely more than a suggestion beneath his fingers. "However, I see now it was ill advised."

"Why?" Her whispered voice was decidedly sultry and definitely inviting.

"Because simply being here is dangerous. Scandalous." He could scarcely believe his own words. This was precisely what he had wanted. What he wanted still.

"And highly improper?" She slid her hands slowly up his chest.

"Most certainly." He swallowed hard and caught her hands. "You should not be doing that." Perhaps it was simply that the encounter with her brother had quenched his ardor.

"No?" She shook her hands free and wrapped them around his neck. "What should I be doing?"

"Retiring for the night," he said without thinking.

"Excellent suggestion." Her fingers toyed with the hair at the back of his neck and he shivered. She should really not be doing that.

"That's not what I meant." Or perhaps this clandestine, whispered encounter in the middle of the night was little better than a tumble beneath the rosebushes. Not right for her—or rather, not right for them. "Cassandra, this isn't—"

"Oh, I think it is." She fairly purred the words, and his stomach clenched.

"It's not a good idea." He drew a deep, calming breath.

"It's an excellent idea."

"I should leave at once. You have scarcely any clothes on."

"And you have far too many." She brushed her lips across his.

He tried again. "I am not a man given to restraint."

"Yes, I know." She flicked her tongue between his lips. "I find it wonderfully uncivilized of you."

"This is a dangerous game, Cassandra." He steeled himself against her touch even as his hands caressed the small of her back.

"I know that as well." She caught his bottom lip with her teeth.

"You have no idea what you're doing." His hands drifted lower, to the firm swell of her derrière.

"Oh, I have some idea." She deftly loosened his cravat, then pulled it free and tossed it aside. "And you can certainly assist me with anything else." She opened the collar of his shirt and pressed her lips against the hollow of his throat. "After all," she murmured against his skin, "you're the infamous Lord Berkley. You have had your way with countless numbers of women."

He shuddered at her touch and tried not to think about the way her hips pushed against his growing erection. "Perhaps not countless . . ."

"But enough." Her words were barely more than a sigh in the night.

"Cassandra, I don't think . . ." He forced his thoughts away from the manner in which her breasts pressed against his chest.

She reached up and nibbled at the lobe of his ear. "Don't you wish to have your way with me as well?"

Or how the heat of her body engulfed him and lured him and sapped any resistance he still desperately clung to.

"Yes . . . well . . ."

Her fingers drifted over his chest. "I warn you, Reggie, I am extremely weak willed." And lower to trace idle patterns on his stomach. "I doubt I can stand firm against your advances." And lower still until they hovered, teasing, near the hard bulge in his trousers. "For more than a moment or two."

He bit back a groan and surrendered. He'd never been good at self-denial. Besides, he fully intended to marry her. And, in truth, this was her idea. One could even say she was seducing him.

Up until now.

He pulled her tight against him with one hand, crushed his lips hard against hers, and reached behind him to turn the key in the lock, the faint click echoing in the still room.

She drew her head away, and he could hear the smile in her whispered voice. "Your reputation is obviously well deserved."

"One can only hope." He kissed her again and reveled in the sweet promise of her eager lips against his. "I should hate to disappoint you."

"I can't imagine such a thing." She turned and started for the bed, nothing more than the largest shadow in a room of shadows.

"Oh no, you don't," he said in a low voice and pulled her back against him. He splayed one hand across the flat of her stomach and held her, her back resting against his chest, her buttocks rubbing against his erection, straining at the fabric of his trousers. He found the ribbon at the neckline of her gown, deftly pulled it free, then pushed the gown down over her shoulder. He bent to taste the curve between her neck and her shoulder, and delighted in the way her head dropped forward and she shivered beneath his lips.

He shifted to lean his back against the door and settled her closer against him, the cheeks of her buttocks cradling his arousal, the heat of her body searing his own. His hands roamed over her stomach and wandered upward to gently brush the undersides of her breasts. She gasped and arced forward, thrusting her breasts against his hands. Her nipples were hard and tight, and he rolled them between his fingers. She moaned and shifted her hips against his.

It was all he could do to keep from taking her right now. Turning her around and taking her here, standing, against the door. He forced himself to breathe slowly, deeply. This was not how he wanted their first time together, but fate in the form of a highly enthusiastic Cassandra and his own relentless desire dictated otherwise. Even so, he wanted to give her as much pleasure as he knew she would give him.

If he could survive that long.

He ran his hand down her leg, gathered up the fabric of her gown, and drifted his fingers in a teasing manner up the long length of her leg. Over skin warm and smooth as fine silk. Between her legs to the sensitive soft skin of her inner thighs. She caught her breath and he held her tighter against him. His fingers slipped upward past already dampened curls. She was wet and slick with need, and he rocked his hips slowly against her.

He slid his fingers over the delicate folds of flesh and found the hard, hot nub that was the center of her pleasure. She gasped and caught her breath.

"Quiet," he whispered and feathered kisses along the side of her neck.

He caressed her slowly, deliberately, his fingers sliding back and forth in an easy manner, and relished the way her body stiffened against his. Her breathing was labored, short and gasping. He knew she existed only in the touch of his hands and the pleasure of his caress and knew the power of being able to do this to her. It was as heady and exciting as her body rubbing against his.

He shifted to nudge her legs open with his knee and he cupped her, sliding his fingers further to slip one gently into the tight fire of her. She shuddered and clenched around him. He slid another finger into her and rubbed the heel of his hand against her. He slid his fingers in and out and rocked his hand in an ever increasing rhythm. She whimpered, and he could feel her throb against his hand. He sensed as much as felt her body tensing like a spring tightly wound and ready to break free.

"Reggie." The word was nothing more than a faint gasp. "I . . . I . . ."

"I know." He breathed against her ear, held her firmly, and stroked her harder and faster.

She sucked in a sharp breath and arched her back, and her body exploded against him in long, shuddering tremors that swept from her body through his until she sagged against him, spent and struggling for breath.

"Good Lord, Reggie." Awe sounded in her voice. "I never . . . that is, Delia said, but . . . and this wasn't . . . even . . ." She twisted free and turned to press herself against him and fling her arms around his neck. She pulled his lips to hers and murmured against them. "Now."

She was everything he'd ever wanted, everything he'd ever needed, and he needed her. Now.

Desire, swift and unrelenting and frantic, gripped him. He struggled to shrug off his coat while keeping his mouth firmly pressed to hers, scooped her into his arms, and started toward the bed shrouded in deeper shadows on the far side of the room.

Toward heaven. Toward paradise. Toward forever.

His foot tangled in his coat. He struggled to keep his balance and stumbled doggedly forward.

Toward heaven. Toward paradise. Toward forever.

Surely a mere article of clothing would not keep him from bliss? Surely, fate would not deny him at this point?

The treacherous coat refused to release him. He lurched forward in the dark, flinging her onto the bed, from which she promptly tumbled with a rustling of covers and sheets and landed with a soft yelp and a hard thud on the floor.

"Good God." He groped for her in the dark and found a limb. "Cassandra? Are you—"

"Yes, yes, I'm fine," she said in an urgent whisper. "Do you think anyone heard that?"

He listened for a moment. "I don't think so."

"Good," she said with a sigh and pulled him to her to topple together in a tangle of sheets and blankets and arms and legs.

He pushed her gown up to her neck and cupped her breasts in his hands.

A knock sounded softly in the back of his mind.

He circled her nipple with his tongue and wondered how quickly he could tear his clothes off.

Cassandra caught her breath. "Did you hear that?"

"No," he murmured and teased her nipple with his teeth.

The knock sounded again, a shade louder and a bit more insistent.

She pushed him away and struggled to sit up. "There's someone at the door. What do we do?"

"Ignore them?" he whispered hopefully.

"Don't be absurd. They'll simply keep knocking. Just be quiet and pretend you're not here." She scrambled to her feet and adopted a muffled, sleepy voice. "Who is it?"

"Leo."

"It's Leo," she whispered.

"I know, I heard. Besides, it couldn't possibly be anyone else," he muttered.

"Cass?" Effington's tone was a bit more demanding.

"One moment," she called softly, then lowered her voice back to a whisper. "What are we going to do?"

Reggie shrugged. "I don't see that there's much we can do save confess all."

It wouldn't be all that bad really. Oh, there might be a certain amount of yelling and threatening and an awkward moment or two, but the repercussions weren't particularly dire. Cassandra's brothers would demand an immediate marriage, and nothing would suit Reggie better.

"Are you mad?" Disbelief rang in her voice. "We'll do nothing of the sort."

"Cass?" Effington's voice rose. The door handle shook. "The door is locked."

"Of course the door is locked," she snapped. "I'll be there in a moment. I have to . . . find my robe. Exceedingly difficult in the dark." She dropped her voice again. "You're going to have to hide."

"That's absurd, Cassandra, we should just face—"

"Hide!"

"Where?"

"Under here." She pushed him toward the bed.

"Absolutely not." He scrambled to his feet. "Everyone hides under the bed. It's the first place he'd look."

"Out the window then."

"To do what? Cling to the side of the building?"

"I don't know." Panic underlaid her voice. "You think of something. You're the infamous one. You've probably done this sort of thing dozens of times."

"You'd be surprised," he muttered. "Let me think."

"You have no time to think!"

"It's dark. Maybe . . . I know, behind the door."

"Hah! That's scarcely better than under the bed."

Effington pounded on the door. "Cassandra!"

"Coming!"

Reggie grabbed her hand, and they stumbled to the door. He couldn't resist a quick, foolish kiss, then flattened himself behind the door. She fumbled for the key, turned it in the lock, and yanked the door open. "Whatever do you want? You're waking the entire house."

"Why didn't you answer the door?" Effington demanded.

"Why did you wake me up?" she snapped.

"I heard a noise and thought something might have happened to you." He paused. "Are you alone?"

"Leo!" She gasped as if horrified by the very idea. "Of course I'm alone. And I'm shocked that you would ask such a thing. I can't believe, if you're truly concerned that something might have happened to me, that you'd ask if I'm alone before you'd ask if I'm all right. It's most distressing and more than a little insulting."

"Of course. My apologies." His voice brightened. "Are you all right?"

"Fine! Thank you for asking." Her tone was firm. "And what you heard was nothing more than my being unused to this particular bed. I feel quite foolish, but I, well, I rolled off it. I shall be a bit sore in the morning, but I did go back to sleep immediately—that is, until you woke me."

Reggie grinned behind the door. She was good.

"You took a long time to get to the door," Effington said suspiciously.

"Heavens, Leo. This is an unfamiliar room. I don't have a lamp lit. It's very dark, and I can't seem to find my robe." She huffed in indignation. "All in all I think I was rather prompt."

Effington was silent, as if considering her explanation. "Then you are alone."

"Leo!"

"I'm sorry, Cass, but Berkley came into my room tonight."

"Really?" Surprise colored her voice. She was very good. "Why on earth would he do that?"

"He thought it was your room."

"My room? How very shocking. And how presumptuous of him. I can assure you, Leo, if Berkley or any other gentleman were to appear in my room uninvited you would certainly hear a great deal more than a mere thump."

Reggie winced.

"What?"

"Why, I would scream of course," she said in a lofty manner.

"Of course." Effington blew a long breath. "In truth, Cass, I don't think his intentions were dishonorable even if his actions were inappropriate. He wished to talk to you about . . . well . . . it's none of my business, really."

"That's never stopped you before," she said wryly.

"You can't blame me for being concerned. Especially given our discussion on how just such a situation would force a man to marriage."

Force a man to marriage?

"And I told you I'd never do such a thing, remember?" she said quickly.

"Well, yes, I—"

"I said it was vile, reprehensible, despicable—"

"I don't remember that," Effington murmured.

"I meant it nonetheless." She heaved an impatient sigh. "If we are to continue this discussion, I suggest we adjourn to your room rather than continue in the hall."

"Do be serious, Cass." Effington yawned. "It's late and between you and Berkley, I've had quite enough for one evening, so I will bid you good night. Again." Reggie heard him start down the hall.

"Thank you for your concern," Cassandra called softly after her brother. "I do appreciate it, you know."

Effington mumbled something Reggie didn't catch.

Cassandra stood in the doorway for a few moments, then finally closed the door and breathed a sigh of relief.

Reggie pulled her into his arms. "You were very good."

"I thought so." There was a definite smile in her voice. She wrapped her arms around him. "As much as I would prefer that you stay—"

"I should go." Regret sounded in his voice. "I fear this evening was ill-fated from the start."

"There is always . . . tomorrow."

"Indeed there is." He kissed her firmly and for far longer than he'd planned, then released her and wondered if he would always feel this reluctance to let her go.

"I'll make certain there is no one about." She started to open the door, and he stopped her.

"Did you mean what you said? About not forcing a man into marriage because he had compromised you?"

"Most certainly." Her voice was firm. "I would never marry any man simply to avoid scandal. And I would never force a man to marry me who didn't wish to do so."

"I see," he said with a grin he knew she probably couldn't see and might not understand at any rate.

"Do you?" she said softly, then opened the door and checked the hall.

He murmured a farewell, slipped past her, and started toward his own room. It was a good moment or two before he realized he was grinning like a madman. A grin that matched the lightness in his step and echoed the optimism in his heart.

For a man who had just failed to accomplish a seduction, he was in remarkably good spirits. Of course, he was also a man who had just discovered the woman he loved, the woman who had always professed an interest in marriage, was not willing to go to any lengths to achieve that goal.

However, she was willing to share his bed without promise of marriage. He knew her well enough to know what standards of propriety she had had to overcome to reach that point. This was not a woman who could be swayed by mere lust, or at least not mere lust alone. And he knew, or at least hoped, exactly what that meant.

The irresistible Miss Effington was obviously in love with the not really infamous and far from perfect Lord Berkley.

Now, he just had to get her to admit it.

Thirteen

It is a man's responsibility to safeguard the people in his life who need protection from those who would take undue advantage of them or from their own nature, whether or not they are appreciative of his efforts. Sisters immediately come to mind.

L. Effington

Cassie sat upon the mount chosen for her by the Holcroft stable master and surveyed the countryside.

It was the kind of spring day poets write sonnets to praise. The skies overhead were so brilliant a blue it hurt to look at them. The meadows were rich and lush and verdant, painted with endless tints and shades of green. One could almost breathe the colors of a day like this. All in all, it was perfect.

Or it would be if one had had the opportunity for even a moment alone with the gentleman one had nearly lost one's innocence to the night before.

Fully half their party had taken carriages to the spot for Gwen's picnic today, a bucolic setting near a small lake. The rest, including Cassie, had chosen to ride. She quite liked to ride, but even if she hadn't she would have chosen horseback simply because Reggie had and Miss Bellingham had not. Cassie had planned to ride by his side in the hopes of pursuing a private conversation, but Mr. Drummond had effectively prevented that by favoring her with his undivided attention. Certainly he was a delightful companion, and it was rather nice to watch Reggie watch them, but the time to provoke jealousy was past. At least on her part.

Her gaze drifted to Reggie and her heart fluttered in a most annoying way. He had dismounted and was speaking with Miss Bellingham, her mother, and Miss Hilliard. The man was quite obviously flirting with them all, and Miss Bellingham was blatantly flirting right back. Why didn't she just fling herself on him and be done with it? She might well be an incomparable, a diamond of the first water and all that, but behind those violet eyes the woman was no doubt nothing more than a tart. A tart armed with beauty and charm who was obviously determined to be the next Viscountess Berkley. Miss Wonderful—hah!

Cassie narrowed her gaze in annoyance, aimed as much at herself as it was at Miss Bellingham. Apparently, jealousy was not confined to Reggie. Still, Cassie had to admit, if grudgingly, that Reggie appeared to pay no more attention to Miss Bellingham than he did to Miss Hilliard, and given what Cassie and Reggie had shared, or almost shared, did she, in truth, have any reason to be jealous at all?

Last night had been rather remarkable and a prelude to what she hoped was to come. Even now the memory of his touch brought shivers of delight and a tense yearning deep in the pit of her stomach. Still, his obvious pleasure at her declaration that she would never force a man into marriage simply to avoid scandal nagged at her. As much as she tried to dismiss his reaction as not important, she feared it was very important indeed. If he loved her—and up until the moment he had left last night she was confident that he did—what difference did it make what led to their marriage? And marriage was certainly where they were headed.

Unless, of course, she'd been right from the very beginning about men with infamous reputations and very, very wrong about the man she thought he was.

She was, however, definitely right about her own nature. She had taken the first steps down the path to scandal and ruin, and there could be no turning back now. Whether Reggie was an honorable man or a true scoundrel, she didn't care. She would be his; indeed, she was determined to be his, regardless of the cost she might have to pay. Either with her reputation and her future or her heart.

"Do you like my brother?" Lucy pulled her horse up beside Cassie's.

"I find him exceptionally annoying," Cassie said coolly.

"As do I, but I should think for a woman like you that would be a benefit."

Cassie raised a brow. "What do you mean a woman like me?"

"Oh, you know." Lucy shrugged. "You're so . . . so . . ."

"Eccentric?" Cassie grinned.

Lucy laughed. "Yes, of course, but I would think that was something of a badge of honor for you. I know I find it so."

Cassie stared at the young woman. "Do you?"

Lucy nodded. "Indeed I do. I quite admire you, Miss Effington. You do precisely as you please."

"Within bounds," Cassie said quickly, pushing the thought of last night firmly out of her head. She would certainly not wish to encourage Lucy in any kind of improper behavior. "One should always be cognizant of the restrictions of propriety."

"Oh, most certainly." Lucy's tone belied her words, and Cassie was fairly certain the girl didn't believe it for a moment. "But I didn't really mean eccentric, although I suppose it is somewhat accurate as you do things that are not expected and speak your mind as well. But what I meant was . . ." Lucy thought for a moment. "Confident. Yes, that's it. Assured. You are the kind of woman who knows what she wants and precisely how to get it. I quite admire that."

"I'm not sure how admirable it is, and I fear you give me far too much credit at any rate." Cassie chose her words carefully. "It's rather difficult actually, to walk the fine line between the behavior society expects and yet follow your own . . ." She thought for a moment. ". . . nature, I suppose. Being true to yourself rather than everyone else, within limits, of course."

Cassie shook her head. "In truth, while I have always been fairly determined and quite willing to speak up about what I think, lately I have found myself confused more often than not."

"Nonsense." Lucy snorted. "I can't imagine you being confused about anything, especially about what you want."

"Still, I—"

"Now then, Miss Effington, may I call you Cassandra?"

"My sister calls me Cassie."

"Then I shall too. So." Lucy met her gaze directly. "Do you want my brother or not?"

Cassie hesitated, then blew a long, resigned breath. "Yes."

"Thank goodness. I was worried for a moment." Lucy leaned toward her and lowered her voice. "I shall make a bargain with you. I shall do everything possible to distract Mr. Drummond, who is far too polite to ignore my attentions, and you can focus your efforts on Reggie. And perhaps we can do something to pry Miss Bellingham from his side as well."

Lucy wrinkled her nose. "I don't mind telling you I would much rather have you in the family than Miss Bellingham."

"Why?"

"I don't like her," Lucy said simply. "I'm not sure why, but I don't. And I don't trust her. I suspect she'll do whatever it may take to get precisely what she wants, regardless of how many people she has to trample beneath her feet to do so."

Cassie laughed. "Didn't you just say the same thing about me?"

"Yes, but I am confident that you have limits. That,

when all is said and done, you are a nice person. Besides, I think you might truly care for my brother, whereas I think she only cares for what he is and what he has. And I don't like the way she looks at him. As if she's, well, hungry."

"And how do I look at him?"

"Oh, you look as if you're hungry as well. But you look as if you want to savor him, whereas she looks like she plans to chew him up and spit him aside."

"Thank you, I think, but you said a bargain." Cassie studied her cautiously. "What do you receive in return?"

"Aside from a sister-in-law that I like?" Lucy's gaze drifted to Christian, and a determined smile turned up the corners of her pretty mouth.

"Lucy!" Cassie shook her head. "You are far and away too young for Christian. Beyond that, he has a great deal of experience and a certain reputation with women, and I daresay—"

"I know all that and I don't care." Lucy tossed her dark hair and smiled in a manner far older than her years. "I know I may be too young for him now, but someday I won't be. As I don't think he's the kind of man to succumb to marriage any time soon, I can wait. And at that point, indeed between now and then, it would be rather beneficial and most convenient to have the sister of the man I intend to marry wed to my brother." She cast Cassie a determined smile.

"That would be convenient," Cassie murmured and wondered if Christian's fate wasn't already sealed.

"Wouldn't it?" Lucy beamed, then her eyes widened. "I say, would you like to see Berkley Park? We needn't go all the way to the house. You can see it from that hill." She waved at a slight hill a short distance away, crowned with a stand of trees.

"Oh, I scarcely think . . ." Cassie glanced at Reggie, who was still overly occupied with Miss Bellingham, and shrugged. "I don't see why not."

"You'll like it, it's lovely. Very old as well, I think. I have no idea how old, although Reggie probably knows. Somewhat imposing in appearance, but really not at all . . ."

They started off at a pleasant pace, Lucy chatting all the time. Mostly about how handsome Christian was or how charming or whether or not he had ever shown a serious interest in a woman and how none of Cassie's other brothers were wed, so obviously waiting for marriage ran in the family, and when did Cassie think Christian's thoughts would turn toward marriage anyway?

They reached the top of the hill and Lucy paused for breath. Only then did they hear the unmistakable sound of a horse behind them.

"And what, might I ask, are you two doing?" Reggie said as he rode up with a smile.

Cassie smiled back and tried to ignore the way her heart leapt whenever he smiled.

"I wanted to show Cassie Berkley Park," Lucy said and turned toward Cassie. "We'll have to dismount, of course. The best view is from the other side of the trees."

There wasn't more than a handful of trees here, but they did effectively hide the scenery.

"I'll be happy to point it out to her," Reggie said. "As you have to return to the others."

Lucy's brows drew together. "Why?"

"Mother sent me to fetch you."

"Whatever for?"

"I have no idea, nor do I care." He nodded in the direction they'd come from. "Now, go."

"I daresay I shouldn't leave you here without a chaperone," Lucy said with a prim note in her voice. Cassie bit back a grin. "It's most improper."

"As we are scarcely out of sight of the others, I think we can take the risk of scandal." Reggie smiled wryly. "What do you say, Miss Effington?"

Cassie shrugged in a nonchalant manner. "As you say, we can see the rest of the party from here. I don't see the harm in it."

"Nor do I. Now," he fixed Lucy with an all too familiar brotherly glare. "Go!"

"I'm going," she snapped, wheeled her horse, and started off at a brisk clip.

"She's going too fast," he murmured.

"She most certainly is not." Cassie laughed. "Indeed, she's setting no more than a moderate pace. Besides, from what I can see, she sits a horse extremely well."

"Horses and dogs used to be the only things that concerned her." Reggie heaved a long-suffering sigh. "I'm not entirely certain when she turned her attentions elsewhere, but I can tell you I don't like it one bit."

"In that, I believe you and my brothers have a great deal in common."

He winced. "That puts things in an entirely different perspective and one I'd prefer not to consider, if you don't mind."

"Still, she is little more than a child, whereas I—"

"*You* are delightful." He met her gaze, his gray eyes

full of all sorts of wonderful promises, and smiled and she thought she might well melt off her horse and into a small puddle on the ground. "In truth, I thought we'd never get rid of her."

"If it wasn't Lucy, it would have been Leo."

Reggie laughed. "Or Drummond. He seems exceptionally fond of you."

"Or it could well have been Miss Bellingham, as she is obviously quite fond of you," Cassie said pointedly.

"Perhaps we are destined never to be alone again."

"That would be a shame, I think. I rather like being alone with you." She forced a light note to her voice, as if her comments, and her meaning, were of no more significance than an observation of the weather.

"Do you?" His gaze was intense, and she wondered if he could indeed see right through her.

"I do, and as we are alone now"—she drew a deep breath—"I think there are things we should discuss."

"I can certainly think of one or two," he murmured, then grinned. "But not at the moment."

"Why not?"

"Because any minute I expect someone, probably one of your brothers, to notice our absence, jump to all sorts of unwarranted conclusions—"

"Unwarranted conclusions?" She widened her eyes, and innocence sounded in her voice. "Do you mean like thinking that you could be in my room late at night, partially clothed?"

"Something like that." He laughed and slipped off his horse, then reached up to help her dismount.

She slid off her saddle and into his arms. He held her for far longer than he needed to, far longer than he should have and not nearly long enough. She stared up at him and wanted to say everything she felt and everything she wanted, but once again words failed her. Extraordinary, really, the way he was the only man who had ever made her even remotely speechless.

"Come on." He released her but took her hand and led her through the stand of trees. "The bottom of this hill marks the boundary between Marcus's estate and mine." He skirted around a beech, stopped, and gestured in a grand manner. "There it is, although I fear you really can't see it well from here."

She shielded her eyes against the midday sun. He was right, the house at Berkley Park was far too distant to see properly, but she guessed by what she could discern and the symmetry of its shape that it was in the Palladian style. Its pale gray stone gleamed softly in the sunlight, and even at this distance the house had a solid, beneficent presence.

"It was built about a century and a half ago by either the first or second Viscount Berkley, I forget which." He shrugged, but there was a distinct note of pride in his voice. "It has been my family's home ever since, and I hope it always will be."

"You like the country, then?" She wasn't at all sure why she was surprised. She had simply assumed he would prefer the excitement of London to the peaceful life one led in the country.

"I do indeed. Oh, I certainly enjoy London. There's always something amusing to occupy one's time, and I daresay, any man who professes boredom in town is simply too lazy to partake of what is offered. But there is a calm here that is soothing to the soul." He gazed over the countryside, and his voice was thoughtful, as if he were saying aloud things he had only thought up to now. "It's busy, of course, what with the tenants and managing the estate and any number of other responsibilities. I do have an excellent estate manager, but I've always felt it was my, well, duty, as it were, to keep abreast of his activities. Indeed, I have implemented some modern improvements through the years myself. I usually meet with him daily when I'm residing at the park. When I'm in London, he sends a report once a fortnight."

"Really?" She stared at him with surprise. "I had no idea you would be so involved."

He raised a brow. "Not what you expected from the infamous Lord Berkley, then?"

"Not at all. And you have my apologies."

"I'm not sure I'll accept them," he said mildly. "I thought, or perhaps I simply hoped, that we were past the point when you would misjudge me because of your preconceived notions based on nothing more than my reputation."

"You're right. I do know you better, or at least I think I do. And it's entirely unfair of me to continue to assume anything on the basis of your infamy, which in truth I've seen little evidence of except, of course, last night, when you were certainly, well, most inventive and quite polished—"

He grinned. "Most inventive and quite polished?"

"It did strike me that way, although I really have no basis for true comparison—"

He raised a brow. "I hate to think how I might fare."

"I wouldn't were I you," she said quickly, ignoring the heat that rushed up her face. It was exceedingly odd to be discussing such intimacies with a man, although with Reggie it seemed almost natural. "And yes, I would certainly expect no less from you given your reputation."

"It's a heavy burden to bear." He shook his head in a mournful manner. "Still, in this particular instance, am I to assume your preconceived expectations based on my reputation have worked to my benefit?"

"Only in that you did not disappoint." She cast him a flippant smile. "For the most part."

He gasped in mock dismay. "For the most part?"

"As we did not actually . . . that is to say . . . what I mean is . . ." She drew her brows together and glared at him. "You know full well what I am trying to say."

"I do indeed, but it's most delightful to watch you attempt to say it and fail." He grinned. "Given your outspoken nature, of course, and my preconceived ideas that you will not hesitate to say anything that is on your mind at any given moment regardless of how inappropriate it might be."

"Why were you so pleased when I said I would never marry a man simply to avoid scandal?" she blurted, then winced. Surely there was a better way to ask that question.

"Thank you for proving my point," he said wryly.

"I'm glad you appreciate it. Now," she held her breath, "do answer the question."

"Of course it's nice to know a woman would not force a man into marriage to avoid scandal." He shrugged. "I can't imagine there's a man alive who doesn't feel the same."

She stared in disbelief. "That's not an answer."

"I thought it was an excellent answer."

She forced a note of calm to her voice. "Perhaps I am not phrasing this correctly. Perhaps you don't really understand what I am asking. I am not trying to determine the attitude of all mankind on a general basis. I simply want to know why you, Reginald, Viscount Berkley, are so pleased that I, Cassandra Effington—"

"There you are." Leo's genial voice rang out behind them.

Reggie grimaced.

Cassie sighed and was at once grateful she was not armed.

"I knew I'd find you eventually." Leo sauntered toward them with an all too satisfied grin. "Luncheon is ready, but Lady Pennington refuses to serve until everyone is present. And as we are all famished, I took it upon myself to track you down, as a dog might track a fox."

Although it would certainly not be at all difficult to borrow a pistol and shoot her brother at a later date.

"Come now. It wasn't all that difficult, Effington," Reggie said in an overly pleasant tone. "Particularly given that we were neither trying to hide, nor were we more than a step or two out of sight."

"However, a step or two can often be most significant," Leo said lightly.

Reggie shrugged. "I would say its significance depends a great deal on the intentions of those who are out of sight."

Leo's brows pulled together. "And intentions are fluid, variable, are they not? I mean to say one moment a gentleman's intentions might be completely honorable and the next they could be quite improper, too forward, too personal and absolutely scandalous."

"Good Lord," Cassie said under her breath.

Leo ignored her. "And when the lady in question is

prone to reckless behavior and acting without due consideration, she can certainly not be counted on to protest any improprieties that might occur. Indeed, she might even encourage them."

Cassie gasped. "Leo!"

"See here, Effington." Reggie narrowed his eyes and met Leo's gaze directly. "I fear you have somehow received the wrong impression. The simple fact that last night, when I mistakenly entered your room, I did not challenge your threats regarding my intentions toward Cassandra, does not mean you can continue to cast aspersions upon my behavior or hers.

"Brother or not, your implications as to her actions and quite frankly, her intelligence, are most insulting. And while I do not relish the thought of yet another duel, and would quite regret having to do you bodily harm, I shall consider it my duty to do so should you fail to apologize to her at once."

"You'd fight a duel?" Cassie stared at him in disbelief. "With Leo? For me?"

Reggie smiled, a quite intimate and extremely personal kind of smile. A smile that promised everything that Leo feared. And everything Cassie wanted. "I would indeed."

"But Leo's very good at that sort of thing."

"It scarcely matters how good he is." Reggie shrugged. "He has insulted you, and anything else is insignificant."

"Oh my." Any remaining doubts vanished with her sigh. "That's so very . . . *perfect* of you."

His smile widened to a grin. "Do you really think so?"

"Absolutely." She nodded and cast him a brilliant

smile. And wanted nothing less than to throw herself into his arms and finish what they'd started last night right here and now, in front of Leo and God and anyone else who might be watching.

"Now then, Effington?" Reggie's firm gaze met Leo's.

"No need for anything of that sort, I should think. Duels, I mean. Nasty business for all concerned, really." Leo turned to Cassie. "I do apologize, Cass."

"For?" She crossed her arms over her chest.

"For," Leo paused for a moment, obviously deciding exactly what he was sorry for. "For thinking you would let your emotions overcome your good sense."

"Very nice, Effington," Reggie murmured.

"Thank you." Leo grinned.

"I think it's scarcely more than adequate," Cassie snapped.

"Very well then." Leo rolled his gaze toward the skies. "I am truly sorry, Cass. I am sorry that I thought you could have Berkley in your room last night. I am sorry that I fully expected to find the two of you rolling about on the ground just now—"

Cassie's eyes widened with shock. "Leo!"

Reggie coughed to cover a laugh. What on earth did he find so amusing? This wasn't the least bit funny.

"My apologies, Berkley." Leo grimaced. "I didn't mean to imply that you would take such liberties."

Reggie's expression was cool, but laughter danced in his eyes.

Cassie would have given a great deal for a pistol at the moment. "However, you have no difficulties implying I would allow such liberties? Or worse, I would take such liberties myself?" She stepped closer to her brother and poked her finger hard at his chest. "What did you think I would do, throw him down on the ground and leap on him?"

An odd choking sound emanated from Reggie. She paid it no mind. She would deal with him later.

"Well?" She poked again, harder.

"Stop it, Cass, that's both annoying and painful." Leo grabbed her hand, pulled her a few feet away, leaned close, and lowered his voice for her ears alone. "I have spent too many years watching over you to stop now."

"For goodness' sakes, Leo, you needn't—"

"It may well have been unnecessary in the past and may indeed be unnecessary now, but I see the look in his eye when he looks at you. God knows, I have worn that particular look in my own eye when there was a woman I, to be blunt, *wanted*. Worse than that, there is the very same look in your eye. You've never been interested in any man the way you are interested in him." Leo's voice hardened. "I have no intention of dropping my guard when it comes to the two of you. We allowed Delia to lull us into laxity, to my eternal regret."

Cassie snorted. "You're the only one regretting it. She's the very picture of happiness."

"Through nothing more than dumb luck." Leo's eyes narrowed. "I shall watch you day and night if I have to. One sister may well have fallen into scandal, but I shall not permit another to do the same."

"It's not your decision," Cassie hissed. "Nor your life."

"It's my duty." A sanctimonious note rang in Leo's voice.

Shooting might well be too good for him.

Reggie cleared his throat. "As much as I am not included in this discussion, although I must confess to a fair amount of curiosity regarding what the two of you are whispering about, I suggest you continue it at another time and we return to the others. If indeed they are as famished as you say, Effington."

"Yes, of course." Leo cast Reggie a relieved smile, the kind of smile that claimed kinship and common ground between men that women simply could not comprehend.

Perhaps she would simply take to carrying a pistol on her person in the future.

"We shall continue this later, Leo." She turned on her heel and stalked around the trees to the waiting horses.

She was certain she had been this angry with Leo in the past, but at the moment she couldn't remember when. Why was it so impossible for her brothers to believe she was competent enough to make her own decisions? She was four and twenty after all, and if she chose to plunge into scandal or ruin or indeed, if she chose to be eminently proper, it should be her choice, not theirs. Sometimes, it was most frustrating being a woman. And a woman without a pistol at that.

Cassie reached her mount, and both Reggie and Leo stepped forward to help her remount her horse. She cast her brother a scathing glare. He returned a weak smile and obediently stepped aside.

Reggie helped her on to the saddle in a manner so proper that even the most discerning brother could not object. Why, his hands didn't so much as stray an inch from her waist, nor did they linger a moment longer than necessary. All of which would have only strengthened her resolve to do bodily harm to her brother if not for the look in Reggie's eye. No doubt the very one that so concerned her brother. And certainly the very one that dissolved any resistance and all doubts she might have.

"Thank you, my lord," she said coolly.

"My pleasure, Miss Effington." The corners of his mouth quirked upward in a private smile that bespoke shared secrets and unstated promises.

Perfect.

The trio started back toward the rest of the party. Conversation was limited, although Reggie and Leo did exchange a few polite words. Cassie, pointedly, did not so much as glance at her brother.

While she hadn't spent nearly enough time alone with Reggie, and had neither a satisfactory answer to her question nor a declaration of his feelings, she had seen a side of him she had not expected. Furthermore, he had offered to duel Leo over a mere insult and wasn't that very much an indication of his affection? Did men truly risk their lives for women they did not love?

Regardless, she loved him and she wanted him, and she was determined to have him. Anticipation trickled through her, and she smiled to herself.

The path to scandal had never looked so inevitable.

Or so delightful.

Fourteen

Women are fragile, exquisite creatures who hold our hearts in their hands and can transport us to heaven with a single look.

Robert, Viscount Bellingham

Leo was as good as his word.

Cassie paced the width of her bedchamber and tried to convince herself shooting her brother was not a reasonable response.

During yesterday's picnic, throughout the rest of the day, into the night, and again all day today and this evening, Cassie had been constantly under the watchful eye of Leo or Christian. And on those rare moments when neither brother was within sight, she suspected they had turned their attention toward Reggie. Unfortunately, Miss Bellingham seemed to devote a great deal of her attention to Reggie as well. And while his response didn't appear to be considerably more than cordial, only a dead man would not be flattered by the flirtatious attention of Miss Wonderful. It was most annoying, but there was nothing Cassie could do about it save remind herself that she was confident of Reggie's affection. Still, Cassie was unable to spend any time with him at all, and she suspected Miss Bellingham had no such restrictions.

At least—when the men of their party had been off shooting or something equally boring, and there hadn't been a brother breathing over her shoulder—Cassie had had more than enough time to finish her sketches for Reggie's house. She'd also had the opportunity for a long and most productive chat with Gwen.

Before dinner tonight, Reggie had given his wholehearted approval to her ideas. Not that the two of them had been alone, of course. No, Reggie had given his approval along with his mother and sister and most of Gwen's other houseguests.

Miss Bellingham had shown more than a passing interest in her designs. Rather odd, Cassie had thought, and vaguely disturbing. Mr. Drummond, however, had been most complimentary, and it had been enough to make her want to run screaming into the rose gardens when she'd realized she could have dragged Mr. Drummond bodily to her bed and her brothers would scarcely have noticed. Apparently neither Leo nor Christian thought Mr. Drummond or Lord Townsend or any of the other single gentlemen present save Reggie posed much of a threat to Cassie's virtue. The thought did cross her mind, though, that, for brothers who had long wanted nothing more than to have her wed, they were being rather particular now as to the possibilities available.

Christian, though, did seem to be seeking protection as much as giving it. Lucy was most determined to be wherever he was, by his side every moment if possible, although Cassie had to give the girl her due; she was both subtle and clever. Indeed, if one wasn't already cognizant of Lucy's intentions toward Christian, one might not notice the rapt attention she paid him.

Christian, however, was all too aware of the girl and did his best to avoid any action that might either encourage her or be misconstrued by anyone else. Still, Cassie noted he looked at Lucy with an odd mix of terror and fascination and wondered if indeed someday he might cast his eye in her direction.

Certainly Reggie noticed Lucy's pursuit of Christian, and while Cassie had had no opportunity for more than a passing word with him, every now and then she'd catch him watching Lucy with narrowed eyes and muttering to himself, "*Practice.*"

Lord Bellingham, on the other hand, was too besotted with Lucy to notice her single-minded concentration on Christian. And the girl encouraged his interest by occasionally favoring the young lord with a flirtatious smile or a coy glance or by laughing at something he said in a manner that indicated he was the cleverest man in the entire world. It was obvious to Cassie that Lucy had little need of *practice*.

Pity she couldn't ask Lucy to resolve her own problem at the moment. Cassie didn't doubt the girl would have any number of ideas on how to slip out of a room practically guarded by an older brother. Although Cassie had a rather excellent plan regarding that herself.

A knock sounded at the door.

She flew to it and yanked it open. "What on earth has taken you so long?"

"You told me to wait until everyone was abed." Delia stepped into the room curiously. At this late hour, she was clad only in her nightclothes and a most discreet robe. "Do try to remember I have a husband to attend to, and I thought it prudent to wait until he was asleep."

"I thought you might not come at all."

"I could scarcely ignore your fervent plea after dinner. Whatever is the matter?"

Cassie looked down the hall and was not the least bit surprised to see Leo's door cracked open again tonight. She wrinkled her nose, snapped her own door shut, and leaned back against it. "I need your help."

Delia raised a brow. "With Mr. Drummond or Lord Berkley?"

"Reggie, of course." Cassie furrowed her brow. "I don't care a fig about Mr. Drummond, although I will say he's quite charming."

Delia grinned. "I'd say he's perfect."

"Not for me."

"I agree." Delia studied her sister cautiously. "I've scarce had a minute to talk to you since our arrival. How goes the campaign for the heart of Lord Not-at-all-Perfect?"

"It's dreadful, Delia." Cassie resumed her pacing.

"Oh? And I thought, from what I have seen, anyway, that it was going rather well. There is a way he has of looking at you."

Cassie stopped and stared at her sister. "Everyone seems to have noticed that except for me. Why is it you can see something in the way he looks at me or something in the way I look at him that I can't?"

"Because, Cassie dear, we are watching for different things." Delia crossed the room and sat down on the bed. "Now then, what is the problem with his lordship?"

"Oh, the problem really isn't with Reggie. I am convinced that he does care for me. Indeed, there is every possibility he even loves me, although he has not yet said it, which is rather annoying."

"I thought his annoying nature was one of the things you found irresistible about him?"

"It is. Well, not precisely, although I do think he wouldn't be nearly as interesting if he were—"

"Perfect," Delia smirked.

"Exactly." Cassie nodded firmly. "Mr. Drummond is apparently perfect, and while I can't find a single thing objectionable about him, I am not at all attracted to him."

"Of course not."

"I do appreciate you not being overly smug about it. Not telling me how right you were and how wrong I was about the very idea of Lord Perfect."

"As well you should. It's been extremely difficult."

"Still, it's rather odd, isn't it?" Cassie glanced at her sister. "That perfect isn't especially appealing but annoying is almost irresistible."

"Love is rather odd, dear heart." Delia watched her sister pace for a moment, then sighed in resignation. "However, there is some sort of problem, isn't there?"

"It's Leo." Cassie sank down on the bed beside her sister. "He's watching me like he was a shepherd and I was a wayward lamb."

"He has always kept a close eye on you. As have Christian and Drew."

"Yes, and I am eternally grateful Drew is not here at the moment. Leo and Christian are bad enough." Cassie plucked absently at the fabric of the coverlet. "However, that does bring me to my current dilemma."

"What kind of dilemma?"

"It's not all that complicated." Cassie slipped off the bed and crossed the room to the clothespress. "We're returning to London tomorrow and I simply must see Reggie tonight."

"You're certainly not dressed for a visit." Delia cast a disapproving eye over Cassie's nightrail and wrapper.

"Nonetheless, I must return something to him." Cassie found her bag in the bottom of the clothespress, rummaged in it, and pulled out a long, white neck cloth. "This."

Delia's eyes widened. "His cravat?"

"Yes." Cassie tossed it at her sister, then dug in the bag again. "And this." She pulled his coat free with a flourish.

"Is there anything else?" A cautious note sounded in Delia's voice. "Shirt? Trousers?"

"Don't be absurd." Cassie shook her head. "He never could have returned to his own room without his trousers at the very least."

"Of course, what was I thinking?" Delia chose her words with care. "How did you come to have Berkley's cravat and coat, or would I be better off not knowing?"

"You'd probably be better off not knowing, but if I don't tell you, and you should find out, you'll be quite annoyed that I didn't confide in you."

"It is a vicious circle." Delia drew a deep breath. "Cassie, you didn't . . . you couldn't . . ."

"I most certainly could have, but," Cassie shrugged and returned to plop back down on the bed, "I didn't. At least not entirely."

"Not entirely?" Delia's voice rose. "What do you mean, not entirely?"

Cassie snorted with disgust. "Leo has the room beside mine, you know. It's decidedly difficult to lose one's virtue with your brother in the next room alert to any unusual sounds."

"Good God." Delia groaned. "I should have suspected as much."

Cassie grinned. "Indeed you should have."

"So then it's to Leo's credit that you're not—or rather you haven't—"

"It most certainly is, and I may never forgive him for it." Cassie took her sister's hands. "Now, however, I need your help."

"To see Berkley?"

Cassie nodded. "Leo left his door open last night and again tonight, and I'm fairly certain he does so to enable him to notice if I leave my room."

"Imagine him thinking such a thing," Delia murmured.

Cassie leaned forward. "However, he *expects* you to leave."

"What?" Delia stared in confusion, then her eyes widened in realization. "Oh no." She tried to pull her hands away, but Cassie held them fast. "Absolutely not."

"It will be an adventure."

"For you!"

"We haven't traded places in a very long time. It should be great fun."

"Not for me. I shall be trapped pretending to be you. Besides, I'm not supposed to have fun anymore, I'm married." Delia drew her brows together. "Oh dear, I didn't mean that at all the way it sounded. I do have a great deal of fun—it's just not the same kind of fun. Indeed, with Tony, fun is—"

"No need to explain," Cassie said quickly. "I understand completely."

"You do?" Confusion drew Delia's brows together. "What do you understand?"

"I had a great deal of fun only the night before last." Cassie cast her sister a wicked smile.

"That's not what I—" Delia shook her head firmly. "I won't do it."

"Of course you'll do it. It's quite simple. We exchange clothes. In fact you need only give me your wrapper. Then I'll pretend to be you and slip out of this room, although I suppose I needn't slip at all and can certainly walk right out the door if I'm you." Cassie grinned triumphantly.

"What if someone sees you?"

"They'll think I'm you."

"Indeed they will." Delia narrowed her eyes. "What if someone sees you as me going into Berkley's room? They'll think he and I, well, I don't even wish to say aloud what they would think."

Cassie waved off her sister's concern. "I shall be quite circumspect. Besides, it's very late. I can't imagine anyone would still be roaming the halls."

"And yet, here I am," Delia said wryly.

"Come now, Delia, I'm simply going to return these items to him and have a bit of a chat, and then I'll be back."

Delia studied her twin, then shook her head. "No you won't."

"Well, I shall try." Cassie paused to choose her words with care. "I should think, given the number of times I allowed you to take my place while you were in pursuit of your husband . . ."

"I did not pursue him."

Cassie raised a brow.

"Well, perhaps I pursued him a little," Delia said grudgingly. "But I was a widow and experienced and . . ."

Cassie crossed her arms over her chest.

"Not vastly experienced, of course." Delia huffed. "Still and all, the situation was entirely different. Cassie . . ." She met her sister's gaze directly. "If anyone even suspected you had spent time alone with Berkley in his room, late at night, regardless of how long you were there or what you in fact did, you would be ruined. Your reputation would be shattered, and you'd be the center of scandal. Might I remind you, that is not nearly as much fun as it sounds."

"I fully understand the risk, Delia. In truth, I understand more than you know." She paused for a moment to gather her thoughts.

"Were my reputation to be destroyed, those ladies who clamor for me to decorate their houses and do so as much because of my name as because of my flair with color and fabric would no longer have anything to do with me." She blew a resigned breath. "My business or pastime or whatever anyone wishes to call it will be at an end.

"Beyond that, while I am confident that Reggie cares for me and will wish to marry me, if I am wrong

I could well spend the rest of my days as," she wrinkled her nose, "the eccentric Miss Effington or even the daft Aunt Cassandra."

Delia winced. "Could you bear that?"

Cassie shrugged. "If I must. What choice will I have?"

"If you go to Berkley's room tonight, you could lose everything," Delia said softly.

"Or I could gain the world." Cassie smiled in a rueful manner. "I have already lost my heart."

Delia stared at her sister for a long moment, then got to her feet with a fair amount of reluctance. "Come on then, help me off with this robe. The sooner you are on your way, the sooner you will return."

Cassie grinned. "I knew I could count on you."

"I want you back within an hour." Delia's voice was firm.

"Is that enough time?" Cassie cast her sister an all too innocent glance. "To chat?"

Delia's jaw clenched. "It is if you're simply returning a cravat and exchanging a few words."

Cassie bit back a grin. "But I have a coat to return as well and a fair amount to say."

"Yes, well, that might take a bit longer." Delia heaved a resigned sigh. "Two hours then, and you'd best hope my husband does not awaken and wonder what has become of me."

"Will he look for you?"

"I don't know. I've never left him in the middle of the night to trade places with my sister so that she may avoid my brother and have an assignation with an annoying, imperfect gentleman," Delia snapped.

"Yes, well, I can see that it doesn't occur very often.

Although I must say I quite like the word *assignation*. It has a terribly refined yet naughty sound on the tongue, don't you think?"

"I think it has a sound similar to the word *disaster*," Delia muttered. "I can't believe I am helping you. Mother will have my head for this. Or Leo will. Or even Tony."

"Nonsense, although I daresay your husband will understand, all things considered. As for Mother and Leo, they will never know, as I do not plan on getting caught. Now then, unless you wish to be here all night—"

"And I don't." Delia sighed once more, and Cassie resisted the urge to list all of Delia's previous indiscretions, the details of which made a simple late-night *assignation* pale in comparison.

It took the sisters only a few minutes to exchange robes.

Cassie gathered up Reggie's clothes and started toward the door. "Do wish me luck."

"Luck is the very least of what I'm wishing," Delia muttered. "Please be careful. Try not to ruin my reputation as well as yours. And while I know your mind is probably made up and nothing will dissuade you, at least give the idea of doing no more than returning his clothes a moment of consideration."

"I shall," Cassie lied. She turned to go, then turned back and gave her sister an impulsive hug. "I know you think this is a dreadful mistake."

"That's one of the things that worries me." Delia grimaced. "While it probably is, I'm not certain I do feel it's a dreadful mistake. I know you too well, and I know you have never loved before. Given that, this late-night foray of yours seems rather inevitable. It's not especially wise and could have devastating repercussions, but I would probably do the same thing myself."

"And have," Cassie said with a grin.

A moment later she made her way down the darkened hall. A lamp burned on a table at the top of the stairs that divided the wings of the house and cast a small pool of light. Reggie's room was past the stairs, in the west wing. Cassie hoped she had done a better job of marking his room than he had of marking hers.

She started to knock, then caught herself. No, if his door wasn't locked, there would be less possibility of being heard by someone else if she simply went into his room. She grasped the handle firmly, gathered her courage, and started to push open the door. An odd thought struck her, and she paused.

What if he wasn't alone? Country house parties like this were notorious for late-night visits between lovers or people who wished to be lovers. What if . . .

She drew a deep breath and firmly pushed all doubt from her mind. Every moment between them indicated that Reggie was not the man he was reputed to be, and Cassie doubted he could possibly be that good an actor. Still, if indeed he was, if everything that had passed between them was nothing more than a ploy on his part to get her into his bed, well, she had no doubt it would break her heart. One might call Cassandra Effington eccentric, but no one would ever call her stupid.

She knew exactly what she was doing. What the stakes were and what the repercussions might be. And as much as she told herself she didn't care, she did. It simply didn't matter.

She straightened her shoulders, pushed open the door, slipped inside, and closed it gently behind her. She started toward the bed, then paused to turn the key in the lock. Why, anyone could walk right in otherwise, just as she had. And regardless of what might or might not happen in this room, it did seem best that no one else wander in unexpectedly.

"Reggie?" She stepped toward the bed and ignored the quaver in her voice.

Faint light filtered in through the tall windows, and even with the curtains open wide, there was little she could make out in the room save the shape of what was surely the largest bed she'd ever seen. She wasn't even entirely sure Reggie was in it, but someone was. The sound of slow, even, deep breathing echoed in the room.

She moved closer. "Reggie?"

Still no response.

She stepped to the side of the bed and raised her voice a shade. "Reggie?"

A low "Hmm," little more than a groan, really, sounded from the dim figure that sprawled across the bed. At least it did sound like Reggie, so she apparently had the right room.

However, this was a bit annoying. Here she was ready to give him, or rather, *return* to him his clothes and talk for a while, possibly about her feelings or his . . .

Even she didn't believe that. She had come here with the express purpose of seduction. Hers or his she didn't really care, and while she suspected, especially given their encounter in her room, that he was particularly good at seduction, she was certainly enthusiastic, which could not be discounted.

She tossed his cravat and coat onto the end of the bed and leaned over him. She was able to see his form but little else, and reached a tentative hand out to rest on the spot where she hoped a shoulder would lay.

"Reggie?"

His flesh was bare and warm, and the heat of him traveled from her fingertips to wash through the rest of her. She blew a long, measured breath. If merely touching him was this exciting, how much more wonderful would it be to lie by his side? With his arms wrapped around her and her body pressed close to his.

She ran her fingers lightly over his arm. He slept on his back with one arm flung out to the side. She leaned closer and could make out his other arm folded over his head. She stared with unabashed curiosity. Either the starlight from the window was growing brighter, or her eyes were adjusting nicely to the dark. His chest was bare, the pale coverlet glowed in the faint light and hung just at his waist. She couldn't see the details of his face, but she could vaguely make out his features.

She traced a line from his arm over his shoulder and down to the center of his chest. His muscles were hard, his flesh firm, covered with a smattering of coarse hair. She rested her hand in the center of his chest.

It was a curious thing, to watch a man sleep, even in the dark. To touch him without his knowledge. To hear the depth of his breathing. To feel the rise and fall of his chest and the heat of his skin and the beat of his heart.

He slept without benefit of clothing, or at least without a nightshirt. She wondered if he was completely naked. The very idea sent a thrill up her spine. Her hand drifted slightly lower. She could easily find out, of course, but it seemed the kind of liberty even she would hesitate to take.

Although he would never know. And she would certainly never—

"What are you doing?"

Cassie jumped, and her heart lodged in her throat. Heat rushed up her face. Never in her life had she felt so . . . so . . . so *caught*. It certainly did dampen her enthusiasm. She jerked her hand away, but he caught it and held it fast.

"Cassandra?"

She forced a casual note to her voice. As if he had not just awakened to find her in his room. As if her hand had not just been lingering on his chest. "Yes?"

There was a long pause.

"Is this a dream?"

"Yes," she said with a sigh of relief. "That's it exactly, you're dreaming." She tugged at her hand, but he held tight.

His voice was a low growl. "If I am in truth dreaming, I have no intention of letting you go."

She swallowed hard. "You don't?"

"Not yet." He sat up and shifted and pulled her onto the bed. "Perhaps not ever."

Before she could so much as protest he held her face between his hands and kissed her. A long, slow kiss that sapped her will and melted her soul.

Any lingering reservations vanished.

"Why are you here?" his lips murmured against hers.

"I came to return the clothes you left in my room." Her voice was breathless.

"Is that all?"

"No." She pulled free of his embrace and slid off the bed.

"Cassandra?"

"Do you have anything on?" She untied her wrapper, ignoring the slight tremble in her hands, and flung it to the floor. "Clothing, I mean."

He laughed softly. "Why?"

"Do you or don't you?" She started to pull her nightrail up over her head and hesitated. If she joined Reggie in his bed, there would be no turning back. She would be irrevocably on the path to ruin, and her life would be forever changed.

He was silent for a long moment.

"Well?"

"Have you come to seduce me, Miss Effington?"

She drew a deep breath. "Yes."

"I see."

She heard the bedclothes rustle, and his dark form slipped out of bed to stand before her, a scant inch or two away.

"Are you certain you wish to seduce me?" His voice was low and as seductive as his words.

"Yes." She fairly sighed the word.

He was so close that if she leaned forward ever so slightly, she could press her body against his naked one.

"I see."

His hands skimmed along her sides, gathering the fabric of her nightrail and she jumped at his unexpected touch.

"Then you must allow me to assist you."

With one swift move he pulled the gown over her head and discarded it.

"And to answer your question," he pulled her into his arms, "no, I'm not wearing so much as a stitch."

"Yes, I am . . . most aware of that."

Her breasts pressed against his hard and muscled chest. Coarse hair rubbed against her nipples in a provocative manner. Her naked stomach and her hips matched to his. The hard length of his arousal nudged between her legs, rather larger than she had expected. And extremely warm and most exciting.

His lips met hers in a long, leisurely kiss that promised pleasure beyond what she'd already tasted. And promised as well something more. Something forever. And she wanted it all.

Need, intense and demanding, spiraled up within her, and she threw her arms around him and pulled him tighter against her.

At once, all restraint between them vanished. He crushed his lips to hers in a kiss of plunder and possession. She countered in kind, meeting his lips, his tongue, with a hunger she'd never known, a greed she'd never suspected.

Cassie wrenched her lips from his and pushed him backwards, falling with him onto the bed, her body sprawled half across his. She rained kisses on his neck, his throat, his chest. His hands caressed her shoulders, her back, her bottom. She wanted to explore every part of him, discover every unknown inch, make him hers. She ran her hand up the length of his leg, the muscles solid and shapely, and she shifted her body to allow access to other heretofore undiscovered places. Her fingers trailed over the flat plane of his stomach, and he sucked in a sharp breath and stilled beneath her touch. She marveled at the power of her touch and reveled in it. Her excitement rose. Her hand drifted lower, and the muscles beneath her fingers tightened. She toyed with the hair at the base of his member and ran a tentative finger up its length. He gasped, and she wrapped her hand around him and slowly stroked the long, hard length. It was stone wrapped in silk, curious yet intriguing and inviting.

"Good God, Cassandra." He groaned, pulled her hard against him, and rolled her over to lie beneath him.

He straddled her legs and his arousal pushed against her. He trailed kisses down her neck, her throat, and lower. He cupped her breasts in his hands, his thumbs teasing her nipples, and she moaned and strained upward. He took one breast in his mouth and toyed with teeth and tongue until she thought she would surely die from the pure pleasure of it. And wondered at the power he now held over her.

He shifted to kneel upright, her legs firmly trapped between him. The cool night air danced over her fevered flesh. He caressed her breasts and traced circles and flourishes over her stomach, and she shivered at the delightful feel of his touch. He slid his hand between her legs and touched her again where only he had ever touched her before. She held her breath and tried to open her legs for him, but his knees held her tight. Still, he stroked her, and the pressure of her legs pressed together seemed to increase the sensation. At once unbearable and exquisite.

She writhed under his touch and welcomed that odd, sweet force building within her.

Without warning he stopped and spread her legs, then lowered himself on to her, his member pressing between her legs.

"Cassandra." Reggie propped himself up. "This could be painful."

"I don't care." She laughed and drew his lips to hers. "I want you, Reggie. And I want you now."

"Good." A shudder sounded in his voice.

Slowly, with great care, he guided himself into her. She held her breath. It was most unusual, this feel of him inside her. He reached a point and could go no further, and she wondered if this was perhaps all there was. He slid back and then thrust forward. She felt a give and a mild sting and gasped. He filled her, stretched her, and she throbbed around him. It was odd but not unpleasant.

He lay still for a moment, then slowly withdrew and just as slowly thrust again. No, it was not the least bit unpleasant. She rocked her hips slightly in tandem with his. Indeed, it was becoming more interesting every moment.

His rhythm increased, and she matched his movements. He buried himself in her. She tightened around him. He plunged deeper, harder, faster. She met his thrusts with her own, and they moved as one.

All sense of time and place vanished. She existed only in the hot tension spiraling inside her. Only in the heat of his body locked with hers. Only in this mating, the dance, this union. Eternal and right and perfect.

The coil within her wound tighter and tighter and she welcomed it, yearned for it, demanded it. It came at last with a shuddering release that racked her body against his, and she felt him jerk against her and knew he too had reached that awesome pinnacle of sheer delight.

He collapsed against her and she clung to him. His

heart thudded next to hers, as intimate, as wonderful as everything else that had passed between them.

And she knew, with this man, she could fly.

A long hour or so later—in truth she had lost track of time, but she suspected it was nearly dawn—she lay cradled in his arms. She could lay here with him forever, but she had to return to Delia, who would probably not be happy by the lateness of the hour.

"We are returning to London tomorrow," Cassie sighed and traced meaningless patterns on his chest.

"I know." He toyed with a strand of her hair. "Unfortunately, there are matters at Berkley Park I must attend to, so I shall have to stay another week or so."

"I see." As much as she tried to hide it, there was a distinct note of disappointment in her voice.

He chuckled and pulled her closer. "Can you finish the house while I'm gone?"

"Finish? I have scarcely started."

"One room then. Can you complete, oh, the drawing room within a week?"

She'd once done a bedroom for Delia in a scant three days. "Yes, I suppose so, but the charges from merchants and workmen are always much higher when a room must be completed quickly."

"I don't care. A week, then. Thursday next." He kissed the top of her head. "I have something rather important to discuss, and it seems only fitting to do it in the drawing room, which is being decorated specifically," a grin sounded in his voice, "for the woman I shall marry."

"I'm certain she will like that," she said in a prim manner that belied the fact that she was lying here naked in the arms of the infamous rake she had just eagerly lost her virtue to.

He was obviously about to make an honest woman of her just as she knew he would. Indeed, whatever kind of man the infamous Lord Berkley had been in the past, she was more and more convinced he was no longer the same. Whether he had, in truth, reformed or simply changed and why she didn't know, but it scarcely mattered.

She'd misjudged him over and over, but she was confident now that he was not at all the type of man she'd originally thought he was. And confident as well that he loved her and wanted to spend the rest of his days with her.

Indeed, she'd just bet her future on it.

Reggie crossed his arms and leaned against the portico. On the gravel drive, Gwen and Marcus bid farewell to Cassandra and her family. Cassandra joined Lord and Lady St. Stephens in their carriage, while the Effington brothers mounted their horses for the ride to London.

Reggie watched the carriage pull away. He hated the very idea of being separated from Cassandra for any time at all. Still, it couldn't be helped. Once again, he discarded the idea of abduction as a way to keep her by his side. It was scarcely necessary at this point. They would be together soon enough. And never apart again.

Cassie's gaze met his through the carriage window, and she cast him a private smile that said without words wonderful sorts of things and made wonderful sorts of promises. It was all he could do to return a casual smile when he really wanted to grin like a lunatic.

A very satisfied, very happy, very much in love madman. The carriage rolled down the Holcroft Hall drive and started off on the road toward London.

He could scarce wait for their reunion.

Reggie was confident that the estate matters at Berkley Park could be dealt with as quickly as possible. Fortunately, they were minor, if tedious, and he was certain he could return to London in no more than a week.

Gwen passed by him on her way into the house, then paused and met his gaze firmly. "I like her, Reggie. Quite a bit, actually. You don't need my approval, of course, but you have it if you want it."

"Ah, Gwen." He caught her hand and lifted it to his lips. "Your approval means a great deal, but if I can't have you, I don't know that I want anyone at all."

Gwen rolled her gaze toward the heavens. "You are incorrigible, and I daresay any woman willing to accept you deserves what she gets." She pulled her hand away and cast him an affectionate smile. "Miss Effington is a wonderful choice, and I wish you every happiness." She leaned forward, brushed a kiss across his cheek, then turned and swept into the house.

He stared after her. Gwen was one of the few women Reggie had never fallen in love with. Probably because he'd never had the opportunity. But he realized, as the wife of his closest friend, she would always have a place in his life and, indeed, in his heart.

"I gather all went well with Miss Effington, then?" Marcus stepped to his side.

"Better than well." Reggie grinned. "She hasn't said it yet, but she loves me. I know it as surely as I know my own name."

"So she has decided against a perfect man in favor of you?"

Reggie's grin widened. "I knew she would."

Marcus raised a brow.

"Very well. I hoped she would." Reggie shook his head. "I still cannot believe it myself, that she would care for me."

"I hate to cast a shadow over your happiness, but how do you know that she does indeed care for you if she hasn't said it?"

"Ah, but she has demonstrated it." Reggie blew a long, satisfied breath. "And with a great deal of enthusiasm."

"Good God, Reggie," Marcus groaned. "You didn't."

"Actually, Marcus, *she* did. Or rather we did."

"Even so—"

"Marcus." Reggie leaned close to his friend and lowered his voice. "If you found the woman you loved in your room in the middle of the night with obviously improper intentions, what would you do?"

"Precisely what you did, no doubt."

"I thought as much."

"And then I'd marry her at once," Marcus said staunchly.

"Precisely my plan."

"I knew there would be a plan." Marcus shook his head and heaved a long-suffering sigh. "Well, what is it this time?"

Reggie straightened and gazed at the carriage in the distance. "When she began this refurbishment of my house, she was supposed to be doing it for whatever woman I eventually married. I have given her free rein and approved her designs, not at all difficult really, as she is extremely talented. Unbeknownst to her she has been decorating her future home. What could be more appropriate?"

"That is a nice touch." Admiration sounded in Marcus's voice. "I still don't see much of a plan, however."

"It gets better." Reggie smirked. "She has promised to complete the drawing room within a week, by Thursday next. I told her that's when I would return to town. However, I shall send her a message from Berkley Park later today telling her I have been delayed and will not return until Friday morning. I could even send it with one of your guests who has not yet left for town."

"Only the Bellinghams and Drummond remain."

"Miss Bellingham then, as she's been in on it all along."

Reggie brushed aside the thought that given Felicity's avowed interest in him she might not be overly willing to assist his efforts regarding Cassandra. Of course, she hadn't said anything of that nature since the first night, and while she'd certainly been flirtatious toward him, it seemed no more so than toward anyone else. He was certain Felicity had abandoned any serious intentions toward him.

"Are you sure that's wise? It appeared to me that Miss Bellingham was most taken with you. Indeed, there was scarcely a moment when she was not by your side. She was discreet, of course, but I rather got the impression she was pursuing you."

"Do you really think so? Imagine that." Reggie grinned. "The idea is flattering, of course, but absurd. Indeed, if there was a pursuit in progress, I daresay it was of Miss Bellingham by every eligible man present.

I have done absolutely nothing to encourage her." He shook his head. "Regardless, my only interest is in Cassandra, and she will be most surprised when I make my appearance on Thursday."

"I've never especially liked surprises myself. Damned dangerous things in my experience. And I still don't understand—"

"Patience, Marcus. I will offer her my heart and ask for her hand. Furthermore, I shall have a special license by then and will encourage her to marry me at once." Reggie grinned. "It's an excellent plan."

"Unless, of course, she says no."

"She won't." Reggie couldn't hide the satisfied note in his voice. "Not after last night."

"Why don't you bring a minister with you as well?" Marcus said with a shrug. "Marry her right then and there."

Reggie stared at his friend. "That's good, Marcus. Very good."

"No it's not." Marcus's eyes widened with disbelief. "It's the most ridiculous thing I've ever said. It's absurd and dangerous. What if she doesn't wish to marry you at all, or at least not right then? What if she wants her family present?"

"That could present something of a problem." Reggie thought for a moment. "Although . . ." The answer struck him, and he slapped Marcus on the back. "That's where you come in, old friend. I'll surprise Cassandra, and you can arrive with a clergyman and her family and whoever else seems appropriate oh, say, an hour or so later. It's an excellent idea." Excitement sounded in Reggie's voice. "I daresay, Gwen can speak to Higgins about refreshments and whatever else is necessary for a wedding celebration without Cassandra's knowledge. She did an excellent job on this party of yours."

"I suspect Gwen will have to lie down with a damp cloth over her forehead for at least a week after this," Marcus said under his breath.

"Don't be absurd. Gwen is an excellent hostess. And I'm certain Lady St. Stephens would be willing to lend her assistance as well."

Marcus raised a brow. "Just how many people do you want involved in this surprise wedding? Or should I say this surprise disaster?"

"You may be right, we shouldn't involve Cassandra's sister," Reggie said more to himself than Marcus. "The fewer people who know about this, the better."

"Oh, that will certainly ensure its success."

"Have faith, Marcus, this is a brilliant plan. Probably my best ever."

"Precisely my point."

"I'm not sure anyone but you and Gwen should know what's happening beforehand." Reggie thought for a moment. "Not even Higgins and the London house staff, not until the last possible moment, at any rate. Too many people might well give it away. I should like to have Cassandra's parents present, of course, and her brothers. No real choice there. You and Gwen, your mother and mine. That's probably more than enough."

"What of Miss Wonderful and Lord Perfect?"

Reggie laughed. "Miss Bellingham and Mr. Drummond should most certainly be included. After all, they had a rather significant role in all this."

"Because of the bet?"

"Somewhat. But more because . . ." Reggie searched for the right words. "For Cassandra, a real Lord Perfect showed her exactly what I'd hoped. Perfect isn't nearly as desirable as she'd thought."

"Of course, she had already expressed a serious interest in you before Drummond's arrival."

"Yes, and didn't that work out nicely."

Marcus laughed. "And what did Miss Wonderful show you?"

"Nothing really, except perhaps that wonderful is as misleading as perfect." Reggie shrugged. "But I thought Cassandra was my Miss Wonderful almost from the beginning."

Marcus snorted. "Hardly. I believe you said she was not your Miss Wonderful and she never would be."

"I was wrong. Blasted imperfect of me, I'd say."

"You do have imperfect honed to a fine art." Marcus chose his words with care. "As much as I hate to say it, it seems to me this new plan of yours is fraught with difficulties, ripe for disaster, and could well be the worst idea you've ever come up with."

"You're with me then." Reggie grinned.

Marcus studied his friend for a long moment, then shrugged, a reluctant smile on his face. "I would not miss it for anything in the world."

Fifteen

There is nothing more to be feared in this life or the next than a woman bent on revenge. God help the man who has aroused such ire.

T. Higgins

"Yes, that's it exactly." Cassie nodded with satisfaction at the color sample presented by her foreman and one of the painters. The paint was intended for the cornices and moldings and plasterworks in the drawing room. "Precisely the color I had in mind. Not too blue nor too lavender nor too gray. Excellent work."

"Thank you, miss." The painter smiled with obvious pleasure at the compliment.

If Cassie had learned nothing else about working with craftsmen, for she did indeed think of those who worked magic with paint and paper and plaster and wood as craftsmen, she had learned they had a great deal of pride in their work and responded well to sincerity and honesty, whether that took the form of praise or suggestion. Oh, she had certainly encountered those who did not take well to directions from a woman, and there was always a certain amount of strife during those projects. She had learned long ago that even gaining the respect of those working for her was not always enough, and she now had a foreman, Mr. Jacobs, whom she hired for every project.

"You do understand I want this for the flat of the ceiling cornice so that that wonderful detailing, which we shall keep white, stands out in sharp contrast."

The painter nodded. "And you want the same effect on the overmantel?"

"Exactly. Thank you." She beamed at the man. "And we shall have to play with the colors, but I think a shade just a little deeper, more intense I think, will be perfect for the offsetting stripes on the walls."

He nodded again and headed toward a ladder leaning against the far wall. The entire room was a flurry of organized activity, with painters working on various sections of wall and ceiling, and Italian-trained plasterers finishing repairs, and others measuring for furnishings and fabrics.

It had been two days since Cassie had returned to London, and she'd spent nearly every minute in Reggie's house and nearly as much time thinking about him and exactly what he had planned. Not that it was much of a challenge. The man was practically transparent.

Obviously, he wanted to declare himself right here, in the room she had decorated for the woman he would marry. And it was just as obvious that woman was her.

He simply needed to say the words. As did she. She never imagined they'd be quite so difficult.

"I don't know that we can manage to finish all this in only four more days, miss." Jacobs shook his head.

"Of course we can," Cassie said firmly, although she wasn't at all sure it mattered.

He would be here on Thursday whether the room was finished or not, and she was fairly certain that even if it was not entirely completed, he wouldn't care.

What he had to say to her, what he had to *ask* was hardly dependent on the state of a room or a house or anything other than a heart. His heart and hers.

She couldn't remember ever having been so happy.

"Miss Effington." Higgins stood in the doorway, an odd expression on his face. "There is someone here requesting to see you."

She'd seen similar looks before. "It's no doubt my sister. She said she was going to come by and see how the room is progressing." She grinned. "The resemblance is remarkable, isn't it?"

"I don't think this is your sister, miss," he said slowly.

"Really? I can't imagine who—"

"Good day, Miss Effington." Lady Bellingham sailed into the drawing room like a ship in a heady wind, followed at a more sedate pace by her daughter.

"Lady Bellingham." Cassie stared in surprise. "And Miss Bellingham, good day. What an unexpected . . . pleasure." The two ladies surveyed the room with a distinctly proprietary air. "But I must tell you Lady Berkley and the rest of her family are still in the country."

"Yes, my dear, we know." Lady Bellingham smiled in a confidential manner. "We came to see the house and your work, of course."

"It's a lovely house," Miss Bellingham murmured and meandered about the room, stopping here and there to examine something that caught her notice.

"It is, isn't it?" Cassie glanced around with a fair

amount of pride. Certainly, it didn't look like much now, but in a few days it would be transformed. "This room has a great deal of potential. It's nicely proportioned and positioned to get a fair amount of sunlight, with excellent ventilation. Note as well the plasterwork on the cornice and the carved detail around the fireplace."

"Lovely," Lady Bellingham said. "Just lovely."

"And what of the furnishings?" Miss Bellingham glanced at Cassie over her shoulder. "What do you plan in that regard?"

"I have sent the upholstered pieces out for repair and new fabrics, as well as ordered a few items. All in all, while some things always change in the process, the end result should be very much like the watercolor sketches you saw. I do try to keep . . ." At once she suspected the real reason for their visit. "Lady Bellingham, are you interested in my services?"

"Very much so, my dear." Lady Bellingham nodded.

"I would be happy to call on you when this project is completed and we could—"

"Oh, no." Lady Bellingham shook her head. "I'm not interested for my house but for this house."

"Lord Berkley's house," Miss Bellingham added.

"This house?" Cassie drew her brows together. "I'm afraid I don't understand."

"That's quite all right. There's no reason why you should." Lady Bellingham lowered her voice in a confidential manner. "It's something of a secret."

"A secret? Really?" A faint sense of apprehension trickled through Cassie. She ignored it and leaned toward Lady Bellingham as if they were bosom bows. "Oh, I do love secrets. And I'm very good at keeping them."

"I daresay it wouldn't hurt to tell you. After all, we did understand from Marian, Lord Berkley's mother that is, that you were refurbishing the house for the next Lady Berkley." Lady Bellingham glanced at her daughter. "Besides, you were at Holcroft Hall when it happened."

"When what happened?" Cassie said slowly.

"I'm not sure I like these colors, Miss Effington," Miss Bellingham said pleasantly.

"I shall pass your comments on to Lord Berkley, then, as he approved them," Cassie said just as pleasantly. "Although I will confess he told me to use my own judgment as to suitable colors and everything else."

"Ah well, the viscount and I obviously disagree on that." Miss Bellingham shrugged. "I suppose it's a relatively minor matter, though, given that there is so very much we do agree on."

"He's a very . . . agreeable gentleman." Cassie forced a polite smile. "Now then, if you ladies will excuse me, I have a great deal of work—"

"Yes, of course. However," Miss Bellingham paused and furrowed her perfect brow, "I would really like to discuss the colors, as I should hate for you to have to repaint."

"Why would it be necessary to repaint?" Cassie shook her head in confusion.

"No doubt this is all very puzzling. That's most understandable, Miss Effington. After all, there was no future Viscountess Berkley when you began your work here." Lady Bellingham beamed. "Now there is."

Unease twisted Cassie's stomach. "My apologies, Lady Bellingham, I don't mean to be obtuse, but I'm still not certain what you're trying to say."

"It's quite simple." A glint of triumph sparked in Miss Bellingham's violet eyes. "My mother is trying to tell you the future Lady Berkley is standing right before you. I plan to marry Lord Berkley. *Reginald*."

Cassie's heart caught and she stared for a long moment. "I don't believe you."

"Miss Effington!" Shock rang in Lady Bellingham's voice.

"It scarcely matters whether you believe me or not, Miss Effington." Miss Bellingham shrugged a shapely shoulder. "Although I can well imagine why you might be surprised. It happened rather suddenly, but Lord Berkley and I did get on extremely well together in the country. We had the opportunity to spend a great deal of time with one another." She sighed with obvious satisfaction, "Alone."

"Alone?" Cassie clasped her hands together to keep her from ripping the smirk off Miss Bellingham's pretty face. "That's rather improper, isn't it?"

"A few minor improprieties can certainly be forgiven when marriage is the end result, Miss Effington," Lady Bellingham said firmly.

"Yes, of course," Cassie said under her breath and addressed Lady Bellingham. "Perhaps, as you have seen my sketches, you would like to see the other rooms I am to refurbish?"

Lady Bellingham brightened. "I would indeed. Although we cannot stay long. We have a great many arrangements to make."

Cassie nodded at Higgins, still lingering in the doorway. "I'm certain Higgins can find someone willing to conduct a brief tour."

"Of course, miss." The butler's expression was

noncommittal, but Cassie was fairly certain he had heard every word.

A moment later, he showed Lady Bellingham out of the drawing room.

Miss Bellingham's gaze met Cassie's, and there was a distinct challenge in their violet depths.

Cassie narrowed her eyes. "He has asked you to marry him, then?"

"You, of all people, must admit we are extremely well suited for one another. Indeed, I am most grateful to you."

"You are? Why?"

"I know of your wager. I found it most amusing."

Cassie scoffed. "I can't imagine he would tell you such a thing."

"Come now, Miss Effington, when two people become extremely close, indeed when they decide to spend the rest of their days together, they have no secrets between them." She studied Cassie curiously. "I must say I thought he did an admirable job in the selection of Mr. Drummond. The man is very nearly perfect from what I can see."

Reggie would never tell her of their wager. Still, how else would she know?

"You didn't answer my question," Cassie said carefully.

"I know, and I shouldn't say anything at all. It would be most indiscreet of me." Miss Bellingham shrugged.

"Then he hasn't asked you?"

"I'm really not at liberty to say."

"Why not? If all has been settled between you and he, then I don't see—"

"He has not yet told his family," Miss Bellingham said smoothly. "I should hate for them to hear something of this magnitude from anyone other than him. Surely you can understand that."

Cassie stared at the other woman for a long moment. Her heart told her not to believe a word. But she couldn't ignore everything she'd ever known about men of Reggie's reputation. Certainly, he'd said he was willing to reform, but what if that too had simply been part and parcel of a well-practiced act? Beyond that, why on earth would Miss Bellingham lie? She was the toast of the season and could have any man she wanted. What reason could she possibly have to claim to be marrying Reggie if it weren't true?

"Miss Effington." Miss Bellingham heaved a reluctant sigh. "Lord Berkley asked me if I would come here and tell you he would be delayed and would not return to London until Friday. Apparently matters had become more complicated than he had initially thought. I think he hoped you would finish the room by Thursday as originally agreed and then you would be gone by the time he arrived. Frankly, he seemed rather, well, eager for you to complete your work, almost as if he were reluctant to face you."

"He said that?" Cassie said coolly, as if she didn't feel as though she'd just been hit hard in the stomach. As if she could breathe.

Miss Bellingham winced. "Words to that effect, I'm afraid. But what can one expect from a man with his reputation?"

"Infamous," Cassie said under her breath.

Miss Bellingham was right. What could one expect?

"Exactly." Miss Bellingham nodded firmly. "He's

the kind of man who would tell a woman anything, indeed promise her anything, to have his way with her. Needless to say, I was made of sterner stuff, which is no doubt why I am now looking forward to marriage."

She narrowed her gaze thoughtfully, as if trying to decide whether Cassie was the type of woman who would believe such promises. "He also said that you were not the kind of woman to force a man into marriage to avoid scandal. He found it most admirable. Not that anything untoward has occurred between you, of course," she added quickly.

"Nothing of any significance," Cassie murmured. "I am wondering though, Miss Bellingham, why you would want to wed a man of Lord Berkley's scandalous nature."

"His nature is precisely why I do want to marry him." Miss Bellingham's smile had a faint touch of wickedness. "I find men of a certain reputation fascinating. Besides, I am more than willing to reform him, and beyond that, he is an excellent catch. His title, his fortune, this house. I could scarce do better."

"I see."

In spite of everything Miss Bellingham said, everything Cassie knew, she still could not believe she could have been so wrong. And so foolish. But, in truth, wasn't this what, deep somewhere inside, she'd always feared? Or expected?

"And as for the color, Miss Effington." Miss Bellingham glanced around and smiled pleasantly. "I have changed my mind. I'm certain when the room is complete it will probably be quite charming."

She considered Cassie for a moment. "Oh dear. I

can see I've upset you. About Lord Berkley that is, not the paint."

"On the contrary." Cassie summoned every bit of self-control she had and lifted a shoulder in a casual shrug, as if she didn't care the least bit. As if she weren't struggling against a pain so intense that it threatened to overwhelm her. "I'm afraid you have the wrong impression. Lord Berkley and I are nothing more than friends. Acquaintances, really. Why, I barely know the gentleman. What he does or doesn't do and whomever he chooses to do or not do it with is really no concern of mine."

"I didn't think it was." Miss Bellingham cast her a brilliant smile. "Now, my mother and I should be on our way. We have any number of things to attend to before Lord Berkley returns to London. And I would hate to keep you, as I'm certain you will wish to be done with all this before his arrival."

"Indeed I will, Miss Bellingham." Cassie forced a polite smile. "You can count on that."

"Excellent." Miss Bellingham nodded and swept from the room as if she were already mistress of the house.

Cassie stared at the door, unseeing. Somewhere, in the back of her mind, she marveled at her composure. At the undeniable fact that she was still standing. That she continued to breathe. That her heart continued to beat. An odd sense of calm gripped her, almost as if she were somehow removed from the emotions swirling about her. Somehow keeping betrayal and anguish and any number of other devastating feelings at arm's length. As if she knew that allowing herself to accept the truth would destroy her.

Dimly, from a vast distance away, she heard the butler's voice.

She wanted to respond, but she wasn't entirely sure that acknowledgment of another person—indeed, so much as moving from this spot—wouldn't undo her altogether. Perhaps she could just stand here for the rest of her days, still and unseeing.

He cleared his throat. "Miss? Your sister is here."

"It looks wonderful thus far." Delia's voice sounded as distant as Higgins's had. "I love the colors you've chosen. The blues and greens are so fresh and subtle. It's all very grand, but classic, I think. It reminds me of . . ." Delia paused. "Cassie?"

Cassie drew a deep breath and met her sister's gaze.

They stared at each other for a long moment.

"Mr. Jacobs?" Delia said, her gaze still locked with her sister's.

Cassie heard Jacobs hurry to Delia's side. "Yes, my lady?"

"Would it be a terrible imposition if I were to ask you to take the other men from the room for a few minutes? I have something quite urgent I need to discuss with my sister, and I would be grateful for a bit of privacy."

"At once, my lady." Jacobs barked directions to the workmen, and the room emptied immediately.

"Cassie," Delia said slowly, "what on earth is the matter?"

"I . . . he . . ." Cassie drew a deep breath. "I don't know how to say it. I don't think I can say it."

"What is it?" Delia's gaze searched hers. "I saw Lady Bellingham and her daughter leaving as I arrived. Does this have anything to do with them?"

"She said he's going to marry her." Cassie could barely get the words out.

"Miss Bellingham?" Confusion drew Delia's brows together. "Who's going to marry her?" She sucked in a sharp breath. "Not Leo?"

"Reggie." The moment Cassie said the word it became real, and despair ripped into her with a vengeance. It was difficult to breathe and harder yet to speak. "Reggie. She said she's going to marry Reggie."

"Oh, but surely—"

"She said he's made his intentions clear. She said he and she . . ." Cassie struggled to catch her breath. "She said they were well suited and . . ." She fought to take a breath and could do nothing more than gasp. "Delia, what's happening to me, I can't breathe."

"Calm, Cassie, calm." Delia grabbed her sister and frantically looked around the room. "There's no place to sit in here!"

"No furniture." What was happening to her? "Not back yet." The harder she tried to breathe, the worse it got. "Help me." She clutched at her sister, and they sank down onto the floor.

"Cassie." Delia's voice was sharp. "This happened once before when we were very young. Something upset you, I can't remember what. I don't recall what Mother did. . . . Cassie," Delia snapped. "Cup your hands over your mouth and nose. Do it!"

Cassie did as directed. Delia covered her sister's hands with her own.

"Now, breathe deeply. Try to be calm." Delia's voice was soothing and reassuring. "Gently, Cassie. Everything will be fine."

Within a few moments Cassie's breathing returned to a semblance of normal.

"Are you feeling better?"

Cassie nodded, and Delia removed her hands.

"I'm fine." Cassie swallowed hard and met her sister's concerned gaze. "No, I'm very far from fine." Tears welled up in her eyes. "Reggie's going to marry Miss Bellingham!"

"I don't believe it."

"I didn't either at first." Tears tumbled down Cassie's cheeks. "But her mother certainly believes it. She's planning a wedding. One's mother doesn't plan a wedding on speculation alone."

"I suppose that's true enough." Delia's brow furrowed. "Even if, for whatever reason, Miss Bellingham is misleading you, Lady Bellingham does not strike me as the kind of woman who could effectively carry off a lie of this magnitude."

"They did spend a great deal of time together in the country, whereas I scarcely had a moment alone with him from the first day until I came to his room. All kinds of things could have passed between them. He told her things, Delia, that she wouldn't know otherwise. I don't want to believe it, but . . ."

"But he made promises to you."

"No. Not really." Cassie shook her head. "He said he'd be willing to reform, but he never said that he loved me. He never mentioned marriage. He certainly didn't turn me from his bed, but a man like that . . ." She stared at her sister with growing realization. "I've been such a fool."

"You most certainly have not. You simply fell in love with the man."

"That's what makes me a fool. I was right from the beginning that a man of his reputation could not be trusted. He lulled me into believing he was not at all what I'd heard he was. He was so blasted nice and charming and thoughtful, and he made me feel . . . wonderful." Cassie sobbed and threw herself into her sister's arms.

"He fooled me too, dear heart, and Tony as well, although I can't see how," Delia murmured. "Berkley has obviously hidden his true nature for years. The man is a far more clever beast than anyone ever imagined."

"I should have known when he was so delighted to learn I would never force a man into marriage to avoid scandal."

"That is rather incriminating. Still, I was certain he cared for you." Delia sighed. "Perhaps you should speak to him."

"No! Never!" Cassie jerked her head up. "I shall not add humiliation to everything else. I never want to see him again." She choked back a sob. "I should have realized from the . . ." A thought stuck, and she drew her brows together. "Do you think he planned this all along?"

"Surely not. Why, that would make him—"

"Infamous." A horrid suspicion took hold in Cassie's mind. "Do you think I was something of a challenge for him? The first day we met, I said I had no interest in him. I said we would not suit." Her eyes widened with realization. "And he agreed with me!"

"Yes, but that doesn't mean—"

"It means this was his intention from the very beginning. The infamous Lord Berkley couldn't possibly understand how a woman, any woman, would not be the least bit interested in him." She scrambled to her feet. "He obviously set out to do exactly what he did. And I helped him! I practically seduced him. Oh, he's clever all right, the way he manipulated me. Now, he's had his fun and he'll marry Miss Wonderful and leave me ruined!"

She reached down a hand and helped her sister to her feet.

"At least you can avoid a scandal," Delia said helpfully. "After all, no one knows what passed between the two of you."

"Oh, but I want them to know." Cassie whirled around and stalked across the room. "I want everyone to know. I want to cause the biggest scandal England has ever seen." She turned and glared at her twin. "I want the entire world to know what a fiend he is!"

"I can certainly understand that, but," Delia grimaced, "such a scandal will do you irreparable damage and only add to his reputation."

"And he'd probably love that!" Cassie huffed. "Do you know, every time I'd confront him with one of his sins he'd actually seem pleased?"

"You've mentioned that before." Delia shook her head. "This really makes no sense at all."

"You're right, though." Cassie paced the room. "A scandal of immense proportions would only destroy me and make him even more smug than he already is. No, that's not the way to achieve my revenge."

"Revenge?" Delia's eyes widened. "You plan on seeking revenge?"

"Most definitely. I would kill him with my bare hands given that opportunity, but that would be too swift. I want to make him pay for his . . . his . . . *plea-*

sure. No, I wish to make him miserable, but I'm not entirely certain how I can accomplish that." She narrowed her gaze. "He's broken my heart and I shall not let him get away with it unscathed."

"What are you going to do?"

"I don't know. Yet." Cassie clasped her hands behind her back and stalked back and forth across the floor, avoiding buckets and tools and the various and assorted debris that always littered a room at this stage. "It should be something fitting his crime. Or, rather, *crimes*, I should say, as no doubt he has done this to other women."

Delia studied her sister. "I must say, you're a tiny bit frightening at the moment."

"I want to be more than a tiny bit frightening. I want to be terrifying." It was rather amazing how anger and wicked determination had quite replaced her anguish, although Cassie suspected it would return with a vengeance the moment she stopped moving. "Now, help me think of something appropriate for the infamous Lord Berkley."

"I have no idea. I'm not at all good at this sort of thing." Delia thought for a moment. "I suppose you could cease work in here. It's scarcely halfway finished and devoid of furniture at the moment."

"Oh, I have no intention of finishing the work in here for the new Lady Berkley." Cassie wrinkled her nose and ignored the sharp stab of pain brought on by the realization of just who the new Lady Berkley would be. "And I shall send him a bill for my services to this point as well. As always, I arranged to have a line of credit provided to pay for workers and materials. Quite extensive, really, as cost was not a particular concern to the viscount. I was given a great deal of freedom, both in terms of expenditures and design. Indeed, I could have done nearly anything I wished."

"You have gained an excellent and well-deserved reputation." Pride sparked in Delia's eye. "Anyone you accept as a client knows full well you will do a brilliant job. Tasteful and classic and elegant."

"What if," Cassie caught her sister's gaze, "I didn't?"

Delia scoffed. "I can't imagine—"

"What if I did dreadful work?"

"What do you mean by *dreadful?*"

"I don't know exactly." Cassie considered the room thoughtfully. "Dreadful is relative, I should think. I mean what one person considers horrid someone else might view as outstanding."

Delia studied her sister, then smiled slowly. "Cassandra Effington, what do you have in mind?"

"Well, I originally agreed to refurbish this room ultimately for a new Lady Berkley. However Reg—Lord Berkley is in truth my client. I do try to design a room with its owner in mind, you know, from the very first room I did for you."

"And what kind of room would suit Lord Berkley?"

"A dungeon is my first thought, complete with implements of torture, but that's not nearly subtle enough."

Delia raised a brow. "I didn't think subtle was a possibility."

"It's not." At once the answer struck her, and it was indeed brilliant. "No, subtle is most definitely not in order. But I may well know what is." She started for the door. "Come along, Delia. I need to speak to Mr.

Jacobs about the change in plans for this room, and then we have a number of purchases to make. There are shops I know of, importers of exotic goods and the like, who can provide me with exactly what I want."

"I am afraid to ask, but," Delia grinned, "this does sound like great fun. Something of an adventure, even."

Adventure, excitement, and passion.

Cassie pushed aside the sound of Reggie's voice echoing in her head. From the very beginning, he obviously hadn't meant anything he had said.

"Delia." Cassie paused and gazed at her sister. "I was wrong once again, you know."

Sympathy shone in Delia's eye. "Berkley deceived you. Even I was taken in by him."

"Not about that, although I was indeed wrong about the man I thought he was. But I was wrong when I said I could bear the consequences of being with him. Of loving him." Cassie blew a long breath. "It's not the potential scandal or the fact that I am now a fallen woman. I can indeed cope with that. But it hurts, Delia, it hurts dreadfully. I never imagined how much it would hurt."

"I know, dear heart." Delia took her sister's hand. "It will get better with time, I promise. And quite frankly, keeping yourself busy should help a great deal."

"Oh, this shall keep me very busy." Cassie glanced around the room and narrowed her gaze. "I shall create the perfect setting for the infamous Lord Berkley. The man broke my heart.

"And it shall cost him a small fortune."

Sixteen

Nothing is as delightful as a woman who admits she's wrong. Nor is anything so rare.

Thomas, Marquess of Helmsley

"Good afternoon, Higgins. Grand day, isn't it? Thursday has always been a particular favorite of mine." Reggie handed the butler his hat and gloves with unconcealed enthusiasm. "Is Miss Effington here?"

"She had an errand, my lord. We expect her back any minute." Higgins paused. "We did not, however, expect you until tomorrow."

"I know." Reggie lowered his voice confidentially. "I wish to surprise Miss Effington."

"Oh, I have no doubt she will indeed be surprised," Higgins murmured. "Is Lady Berkley with you?"

"She and Lucy are arriving shortly, I believe. With the others."

"Others, my lord?"

"Ah, yes. I meant to send you a note about that. No

matter. Suffice it to say we shall have a small number of guests, about a dozen, I think, in a little under an hour. I'm running a bit late." Reggie grinned. "We're going to have a wedding, Higgins."

"My congratulations, sir," the butler said smoothly. "I'm certain you and Miss Bellingham will be most happy."

"Miss Bellingham?" Reggie drew his brows together. "I have no intentions of being happy with Miss Bellingham."

"I have heard that about marriage, sir."

"That's not what I mean." Reggie shook his head. "I mean I'm not marrying Miss Bellingham. I'm marrying Miss Effington."

"Oh dear." A faint twitch that might have passed for surprise crossed the butler's face. "That puts things in an entirely different light, my lord."

"What things? Higgins." Reggie studied the butler. "Do you know something I should know?"

"I'm certain of it, sir."

"Higgins." Reggie chose his words with care. "Why did you think I was to marry Miss Bellingham?"

"That's what Miss Bellingham said, sir. She was here a few days ago."

"What?" Reggie stared in disbelief. "Are you certain?"

"Most definitely, sir."

"Good God! Why on earth would Miss Bellingham say such a thing?"

"I believe, sir, Miss Bellingham's purpose was to eliminate Miss Effington as a potential bride for you and therefore clear the way for a marriage to you herself."

Reggie's brow furrowed. "Why?"

"I believe, my lord, she"—Higgins cleared his throat—"*wants* you."

"Really? Miss Bellingham? Me?" Reggie grinned, then shook his head. "It's quite flattering, but it doesn't matter. As lovely as she is, she isn't who I want."

He started toward the drawing room. Higgins skirted around him and threw himself in front of the doors, arms spread wide to prevent Reggie from entering. Reggie couldn't recall ever seeing the butler move so fast.

"I don't think you want to go in there, sir." Higgins shook his head. "Miss Effington's work may not be exactly what you expect."

"Don't be absurd, Higgins." Reggie laughed. "Her sketches were excellent, and even if she's deviated from the design somewhat, I can't imagine it would be anything less—" Realization struck him, and he sucked in a hard breath. "Am I to understand Miss Bellingham told *Miss Effington* we were to be married?"

Higgins winced. "I'm afraid so."

"And Miss Effington believed her?" A queasy sensation settled in the pit of Reggie's stomach.

"Miss Bellingham was quite convincing, my lord." Higgins paused. "Not that I was intentionally eavesdropping, nor was anyone on the staff who might have passed on the information, mind you, but I did learn a fair amount of what transpired. There is no doubt in my mind Miss Effington believes you are planning to marry Miss Bellingham."

"Is she very angry, Higgins?" Reggie said slowly.

Higgins chose his words with care. "On the day Miss Bellingham was here, Miss Effington was furious.

Indeed, I'm not sure I have ever seen anyone as angry."

"Bloody hell."

"The second day she was still angry, but determined as well. Her sister has been here a great deal, and I must warn you I heard words like *beast* and *fiend* and *revenge* and *kill him with my bare hands*."

Reggie groaned. "Oh, that sounds promising."

"However, yesterday and again today she has seemed pensive and, my lord," Higgins looked from side to side as if to ensure their privacy and lowered his voice, "somewhat quiet as well."

"Quiet?" Reggie raised a brow. "Miss Effington? My Miss Effington?"

Higgins nodded.

"Damnation, that's a bad sign." Reggie thought for a moment. How on earth would he undo the damage Miss Bellingham had wrought? "She is coming back today, though?"

"Any minute now, sir. She said she had a finishing touch for the drawing room. She did not think you would return until tomorrow."

"Excellent. Then she will indeed be surprised," he said grimly. "Now then, Higgins, stand aside."

Higgins paused, then lifted his chin. "No sir."

"What?"

"I have served your family faithfully for most of my entire life and protected you when it was in my power to do so." The older man met Reggie's gaze directly. "I shall not fail you now."

"I think I can handle this one myself, Higgins," Reggie said wryly. "But I do appreciate the offer. It can't possibly be that bad."

Higgins snorted, then reluctantly stepped aside.

Reggie drew a deep breath, threw open the doors, and stepped into an entirely foreign world.

He stared in shocked disbelief. "What in the name of all that's holy has she done?"

The walls had vanished, hidden by yards and yards of silk in alternating colors of reds and golds and pinks and yellows, stretching from the ceiling to the floor. The ceiling itself was completely covered in the same silken stripes, gathered in the center of the room. The overall effect was one of a large, exotic tent. Where an ornate crystal chandelier had once hung, a huge pierced brass lantern that screamed of sultry nights in places like Morocco or Algiers loomed. A multitude of Persian rugs overlapped one another and littered the floor. Tall brass candlesticks the width of a man's forearm were placed among small carved wooden tables with mosaic tops. Large brass platters a yard across leaned against walls. Brass pots and antiquated oil lamps were scattered here and there. Several potted palms reached to the ceiling and filled one corner. In the other . . .

He reached out a shaky finger and pointed. "Is that what I think it is?"

"Yes, sir." There was a touch of awe in Higgins's voice.

"It's a camel." Reggie stared at the very large, thankfully stuffed, and altogether overwhelming beast decked out in full desert regalia. "Where on earth did she find this?"

"I have no idea," Higgins murmured, "but one must admire her tenacity."

"Yes, one must certainly do that." Reggie could not pull his gaze from the room.

Overlarge pillows were piled in the center of the

floor. A foreign scent, some sort of incense, he suspected, hung in the air and added to the overall impression of a place exotic and opulent and, whether Cassie intended it or not, somewhat erotic. "It looks like a cross between the British Museum and a Moroccan brothel."

"Harem, my lord."

"What?"

"I believe the intent was one of a harem for the"—Higgins bit his lip—"infamous Lord Berkley."

"It's really quite . . . remarkable." Reggie blew a long breath. "It simply doesn't belong in my house or possibly in my country."

"She was extremely angry, my lord."

"I can certainly see that." Reggie's gaze slid around the room from the palms to the camel to the pillows. "This took a great deal of effort."

"Indeed it did, my lord."

"I find that most interesting," Reggie said thoughtfully. "One would think that in her anger, she would abandon this project altogether."

"Pardon me, sir, but I suspect Miss Effington is not one to run from difficulties."

"No, she does like a challenge." There was an answer here, but he couldn't quite put his finger on it. "Higgins, from what you've observed, it sounds like she continued to do all this even though her anger has abated."

"I wouldn't wager on that."

"I would." At once he understood what he should have seen from the beginning. "And indeed I am." Reggie laughed with a sense of utter relief.

Higgins stared at him as if the state of the room had pushed him over the edge to insanity.

"Don't you see?" Reggie waved at his surroundings. "Only a woman in love would go to this much trouble."

"I should not wish to see what a woman who hated you would do," Higgins muttered.

"She loves me, Higgins, but then I knew she did." Reggie grinned. "This is simply her way of showing it."

"I scarcely think—"

"In truth, her actions fit right in with my plan."

Higgins sucked in an involuntary breath. "There's a plan, my lord?"

"Indeed there is. And this will make it all the better." He leaned toward the butler confidentially. "I'm going to surprise her with a wedding, surrounded by her family and friends."

"Oh, that will be a surprise, sir," Higgins murmured. "Will the ceremony be in here, then?"

"Why not?" Reggie laughed. "It will certainly be memorable."

"My lord," Higgins said carefully. "Have you considered the possibility that she might not want to marry you?"

Reggie thought for a moment, then grinned. "No."

"Perhaps you should."

"I can't, Higgins." He shrugged in a helpless manner. "You see, Miss Effington has claimed my very soul. I cannot even consider the possibility that she does not return my affection."

"I see."

"I know that tone, Higgins, but this is not the same

as the others. This is different. This is," he chuckled, "forever."

"Well, you have never spoken of marriage before."

"You see. Now, go tell the staff to prepare for my wedding and our guests."

"At once, my lord." Higgins started for the door, muttering under his breath. "Perhaps Cook can roast a goat."

Reggie strode to the pile of pillows and settled down to wait for Cassandra.

As confident as he had sounded to Higgins, he couldn't ignore a tiny doubt that perhaps he was wrong about Cassandra's feelings. Still, he refused to consider it.

Cassandra Effington was the last love of his life. And he absolutely refused to lose her without a fight.

Even if it was with her.

Cassie strode into the front entry of Berkley House and started toward the drawing room.

"Can I help you with that, miss?" One of Reggie's footmen stepped forward.

"No, thank you," Cassie said over her shoulder. "I can manage it." The scimitar was exceedingly heavy, but it was the final touch for Reggie's drawing room. Once it was in place, she was finished. With the room and the viscount.

The realization brought a stab of pain, but she ignored it. Just as she had ignored nearly every anguished moment in the last few days. And just as she had ignored as well the reoccurring thought that she might just possibly have made a dreadful mistake.

Still, why would Miss Bellingham and, more to the

point, Lady Bellingham lie about something as important as marriage?

She stepped into the drawing room and smiled with satisfaction. It was perfect, evoking the feel of an enormous tent billowing in the desert wind. Delia had helped, of course, having read far more stories than Cassie set among the sands of Arabia. It was probably not at all accurate, but it was very much Cassie's vision of a proper setting for the harem of a desert chieftain. At any rate, in this case accuracy wasn't nearly as important as effect. Pity she would never know of Reggie's reaction.

"I see you deviated from your sketches somewhat," a familiar voice sounded from the pile of pillows.

Her heart leapt. She ignored it and narrowed her gaze. "I didn't see you."

"I could certainly see how you'd miss me amidst all this."

"What are you doing here?"

"I live here." Reggie got to his feet in a leisurely manner. "Or at least, I think I do. It certainly does not look like anything I recall seeing before."

She squared her shoulders. "I simply created a room more in keeping with its owner."

He raised a brow. "A harem?"

"Exactly."

He glanced at the scimitar. "Are you planning on running me through with that sword?"

"Not at the moment, but I certainly would not rule out the possibility." She hefted the weapon in her hand. "And it's a scimitar, not a sword." She crossed to the other side of the room and placed the scimitar in an artistic display among brass pots and candlesticks.

"This must have cost a great deal."

"Oh, it did. A minor fortune, actually." Defiance rang in her voice. "Although I should have liked to have spent a great deal more."

"Where did you get the camel?"

She smirked. "You made a substantial donation to a small museum. They're quite grateful. They might even name a room after you."

"They can have this one. Do you like what you've done?" He gestured at the room. "In here, I mean."

"It suits you," she snapped.

"No it doesn't." He strode to the doors and slammed them shut.

She jumped and took a step backwards. "What are you doing?"

He ignored the question and started toward her. "The room doesn't suit me at all." His steely gaze pinned hers. "You, however, do."

"Then why are you going to marry Miss Bellingham?" She noted with annoyance the pain that underlay her question, and she moved to keep the brightly colored pile of pillows between them. Scant protection, of course, but it was better than nothing.

"I have no intention of marrying Miss Bellingham." He moved around the pillows toward her.

She stepped in the opposite direction. "She seems to think you are, as does her mother."

"I gave her absolutely no reason to think that." He shrugged and continued to circle the pillows. "Why did you believe her?"

Cassie kept her distance but couldn't keep a note of doubt from creeping into her voice. "For one thing, she knew all sorts of private things that I thought were just between the two of us. She knew about our wager."

He shook his head. "I was not the one who told her about that. I believe it might have been your sister."

"Hah!" Cassie's brow furrowed. Could Delia have possibly told Miss Bellingham about the wager? Of course not, unless her sister had been helping Reggie all along. Ridiculous. Although hadn't Delia said he had fooled her as well? "It's possible, I suppose, but you told her you were pleased that I wouldn't marry a man just to avoid scandal."

"I didn't tell her that either. But as your brother knew, and spent a great deal of time with her, I would wager he told her."

That too was entirely conceivable. Leo had never been especially good about keeping his mouth closed. Particularly when a beautiful woman was involved.

"She told me you weren't coming back until tomorrow so I could finish the room and be out of here before you returned because you didn't want to face me."

"That's absurd." He scoffed. "Why wouldn't I want to face you?"

"Because . . ." Cassie shook her head. "Never mind about that. It made sense at the time."

"I doubt it." He grit his teeth. "I asked her, and I might point out I asked her because she and Drummond were the only ones still remaining in the country, to carry a message to you. I certainly didn't trust Drummond—"

"Why not?"

"Because he's perfect! He's everything you said you

ever wanted. The blasted man is so bloody perfect even other men like him. I was certainly not about to throw him deliberately into your path."

Her breath caught. "Why?"

"Because you might discover he was the one you really wanted. Damnation, Cassandra, you are an annoying female." He glared and drew a calming breath. "I asked Miss Bellingham to tell you I wouldn't return until tomorrow because I wished to surprise you."

"Well, I'm certainly surprised," Cassie murmured. This was not at all what she'd expected. He did not sound the least bit like a man who was about to throw her over to marry someone else.

"As am I." Reggie stopped, and so did she. "Is that it then? That's why you believed her?"

"Why on earth would she lie?" It was becoming very clear that Miss Bellingham had indeed lied. "It makes no sense whatsoever for her to wish me to think she is marrying you. She could have any man she wants."

He grinned. "Apparently, she wants me."

"She can have you then, because I don't want you."

"Now that, Miss Effington, is indeed a lie." His gaze hardened. "What I find difficult to believe is that, once again, in spite of everything that has passed between us, you have misjudged me based on my reputation. Once again, you have not given me so much as the benefit of the doubt."

"I didn't, did I?" She cringed with the enormity of the realization. "I admit it. That might have been a mistake."

"Might have been?"

"Yes. And if you enjoyed that, you'll enjoy this as well. I have another admission to make." She drew a deep breath. "I've been doing a great deal of thinking in the past few days—"

"Between camel purchases, no doubt."

She paid him no heed. "And I think I may have jumped to unwarranted conclusions."

"You?" He snorted in disbelief.

"Yes." She paused to pull her thoughts together. "I should have at least given you the opportunity to explain, but you have to understand I was terribly confused and there were all these dreadful emotions obviously clouding my thinking—"

"Obviously."

"I was deeply hurt." She drew her brows together and met his gaze. "You broke my heart. I've never had my heart broken before. It plays havoc with rational thinking."

"I did no such thing," he said indignantly. "You allowed your heart to be broken. I had nothing to do with it."

"How was I to know?"

"You should have trusted me. You should have had faith in me."

"Why?"

"Because—"

"You gave me no real reason to have faith in you." She planted her hands on her hips. "You made no promises to me. You did not declare your undying love, you never even declared your undying friendship." She narrowed her gaze. "In truth this is all your doing. The blame for this can be laid completely at your feet."

"My feet?" His voice rose. "What did I do?"

"Aside from being the infamous Lord Berkley, absolutely nothing." She glared. "You never asked me to marry you, nor did you ever declare your feelings. And there was Miss Bellingham, *Miss Wonderful*, the woman who was just perfect for you, telling me all these things that she shouldn't know. And you did spend an inordinate amount of time with her—"

"I did not!" He paused. "Well, perhaps I did, but only because I couldn't spend any time with you."

"What was I to think anyway?"

"You didn't think!"

"We've already established that!"

"I offered to reform for you. Doesn't that mean anything?"

"No!"

"You're no better, you know."

"What do you mean?"

He crossed his arms over his chest. "You never told me you loved me, nor did you ask me to marry you."

She gasped. "It's not my place to ask."

He scoffed. "Come now, that's never stopped you from doing anything in the past."

"Nonetheless, should you ask," she said before she could stop herself, "the answer is yes."

"Why, Cassandra?" His gaze bored into hers. "Why would you agree to marry me?"

"Because I love you, you annoying, blasted beast of a man! There, I've said it. I hope you're happy."

"Blissful."

"I've never felt about any man the way I feel about you." Her voice rose. "You're not the least bit perfect. You're, you're infamous! You're everything I've never wanted and I can't believe I want you now, but I do. In spite of my best intentions I," her voice broke, "I do love you."

Her words hung in the air between them.

"I've never said that before. I've never even thought it." She huffed. "I've wanted to tell you but I couldn't get the words out." She folded her arms over her chest and looked anywhere but at him. "It's ironic, isn't it? I will say nearly anything, indeed I pride myself on it, yet I could not say something as important as this."

He was silent for a long moment.

She held her breath and met his gaze. "Aren't you going to say anything?"

"I have been in love so many times I've lost count," he said slowly. "I have said the words so often they had lost meaning." He started circling the pillows once more. She didn't move. "I was afraid to say them again and afraid to risk my heart again." He reached her and stared down at her. "And then I met you and I couldn't say them at all because they had never truly meant so much before. You have my heart, Cassandra Effington."

"Oh my." She swallowed hard against the lump in her throat. "That was very good."

His gray eyes gazed into hers. "I love you, Cassandra. I love the way you speak your mind and follow your heart. I love your passion and your stubbornness, and I love the way you admit when you're wrong."

She lifted her chin and ignored the tremble in her voice. "Then what do you intend to do about it?"

"Marry you, I suppose." He pulled her into his arms and grinned. "After all, you've already said yes."

"I've been something of an idiot, haven't I?"

"Yes, you have."

"I don't want you to marry me unless you truly want to," she said firmly. "I don't want a husband forced to do so out of a sense of obligation. Because you ruined me."

"I ruined you?" He laughed. "I was not the one who came to your bed."

"Then perhaps I ruined you." She smiled up at him and wanted nothing more than to be ruined once again.

"Ruined, my dear Cassandra, is a relative term." He brushed his lips across hers. "Look around you."

"I do apologize about this." Pure joy surged through her and she laughed. "Still, it is rather . . . inviting, don't you think?"

"I think it's the perfect setting to begin"—he nuzzled her neck and she shivered—"a lifetime of adventure and excitement and passion."

"Definitely passion." She sighed and slid her hands around his neck. "Ruin me again."

"There really isn't time," he murmured.

"We have all the time in the world." She ran her fingers through his hair and pressed her body close to his. "I have references now, you know."

He kissed the curve of her neck. "This is a mistake."

"It will not be our first."

"It will ruin the surprise."

"Any more surprises can wait."

"We probably have time." He sighed in surrender. "I am a weak man, Cassandra." He stepped backwards and pulled her with him. They tumbled together onto the pillows in a tangle of limbs and clothing and eager bodies. "And you are my weakness."

Her lips met his with hunger sharpened by joy and

the realization that they would indeed be together for the rest of their days.

He raised his head and grinned down at her. "I like this. Perhaps we should keep the drawing room this way."

"Perhaps." She laughed.

He heaved an overly dramatic sigh. "However, I do think the camel is staring at me. It's most disconcerting."

"Ignore him," she said firmly and drew his lips to hers.

She wanted him, now and here, and suspected he would always make her feel like this. He pulled his lips from hers and trailed kisses down the side of her neck and her throat. She moaned with the pleasure of his touch. Her hands wandered over the firm curves of his shoulders and the hard muscles of his back. Once again, they had entirely too many clothes on, and they should certainly do something about that.

Voices sounded outside the door, and he jerked his head up.

She stared at him. "Who in the world . . ."

"Surprise?" he said weakly.

She widened her eyes. "What do you mean, *surprise?*"

A knock sounded at the door.

"One moment," he called. "You do truly want to marry me, don't you?" He struggled to stand but couldn't quite get his footing amidst the pillows.

"Yes, of course." She had no better luck getting to her feet than he had.

The knock sounded again, more insistent this time.

"Would you consider doing it at once?" He managed to stand unsteadily and reached out a hand to help her up. "We haven't talked about it, but there is the possibility of children, and I think—"

"Yes, yes." She laughed and flung her arms around him. "At once."

He grabbed her shoulders and held her back to look into her eyes. "Now? This very moment?"

Giddiness bubbled up inside her and she laughed again. "Yes, this very moment."

The doors flew open and Leo burst into the room.

"Ah-hah!" Leo glared with the self-righteousness of a man who had been proved right. "I knew it. I knew it all along. I knew you were the sister to watch. I knew the moment I turned my back you—"

"Do be quiet, Leo." Delia pushed past her brother and paused. "Oh dear, this does look bad."

Cassie smoothed her skirts and patted her hair. "Actually, it's very, very good."

"Perfect, I'd say." Reggie took her hand, and they scrambled off the pillows.

At once the room filled with familiar faces, each and every one staring at the obviously compromised couple. Cassie's parents were here, as were two of her brothers, Delia and her husband, Lord and Lady Pennington, Lucy and Lady Berkley, and, good Lord, Mr. Drummond and all the Bellinghams.

Cassie winced. Any hope of avoiding scandal was dashed.

Reggie leaned over and said softly, "Surprise."

"You've said that." She forced a pleasant smile. "What precisely is this?"

"This is most scandalous! I have never been so

shocked." Lady Bellingham glared in righteous indignation. "I may well swoon."

"Don't swoon, Mother," Miss Bellingham murmured.

"You!" Cassie narrowed her gaze and stepped toward Miss Bellingham. "You lied to me."

"Not precisely," Miss Bellingham said coolly. "I may have led you to believe certain things that may not have been completely true."

"Very well then," Cassie snapped. "You misled me."

"Yes?" Miss Bellingham looked at her as if wondering what her point was.

"Don't you think that is, oh, what is the word?" Cassie elbowed Reggie.

"Wrong?" he said helpfully.

"That's it exactly." Cassie fairly spit the word. "Wrong!"

"Not at all. Lord Berkley is an excellent match. I saw an opportunity and I took it." Miss Bellingham shrugged. "I don't think anything is especially wrong, indeed I think nearly everything is fair, when it comes to this game we all play."

"What game?" Lord Pennington said in an aside to his wife.

"Quiet," Gwen said.

"Has anyone noticed this room?" Mr. Drummond murmured.

Miss Bellingham studied Cassie curiously. "It is a game, Miss Effington, this pursuit of marriage. One might, of course, be hopeful of finding love and happiness along the way as well, but marriage is the primary goal and we are all engaged in the game whether we admit it or not. Goodness, you should know better than anyone, you've been playing it long enough."

Leo choked back a laugh.

Christian coughed.

Cassie's father bit back a grin.

Reggie, bless his heart, didn't so much as twitch.

"What did you say?" Cassie started toward her, but Reggie pulled her back and anchored his arm firmly about her waist.

"By my count you've been out in society at least seven seasons." Miss Bellingham's smile was deceptively pleasant. "How *old* are you?"

Cassie sputtered in indignation.

"She's certainly old enough to know better." Disapproval rang in Lady Bellingham's voice. "I can't believe a respectable young woman, a member of one of England's most highly regarded families—"

"Is she talking about us?" Christian said under his breath.

"Hush," his mother said.

Lucy leaned toward Mr. Drummond, her eyes wide with delight. "It's like a tent. I like it. It's so adventurous and romantic."

"—would allow herself to be caught in a situation like this. Indeed she would not be in a situation like this in the first place." Lady Bellingham drew herself up and glared. "Caught practically in the act. Why, when word gets out—"

"No one will hear anything of this, Mother," Miss Bellingham said firmly. "As I just said, it's a game. Besides, he's going to marry her. That's why we're here, remember? She's won and I've lost and I shan't have you making more of this than it is. Now that," she cast Cassie a brilliant smile, "would indeed be wrong."

Cassie shook her head. "Regardless, your actions were wrong."

"That's very narrow-minded of you, and I suppose some people might consider them wrong, but do take a moment to consider the stakes. Lord Berkley has a good title, a fine fortune, and is most attractive. He has everything a woman could possibly want. Beyond that, he has a look about him that makes you want to ruffle his hair and then kiss him quite thoroughly."

"Dear God, take me now," Lady Bellingham moaned. "She's a tart."

"There, there, Frances." Cassie's mother patted the other lady's hand. "She may well be a tart, but I daresay, as long as you watch her closely, she should still make an excellent match."

"Do I really?" Reggie said with obvious pleasure.

"Indeed you do." Miss Bellingham nodded. "And I do so love a man with a dangerous reputation."

"Felicity Bellingham!" Lady Bellingham's eyes widened.

"Oh come now, Mother, I daresay you felt the same way in your youth."

"Never." Lady Bellingham's staunch denial, however, belied the distinct blush on her cheeks.

Cassie stared in disbelief. Apparently Miss Bellingham had as great a penchant for speaking her mind as Cassie did.

Young Lord Bellingham's longing gaze fixed on Lucy. "If you like this room, then I like it too."

"Nice camel," St. Stephens said wryly to his wife.

Delia grinned. "That was my idea."

"I have a rather dangerous reputation," Leo said casually.

"Do you think she's going to leave it this way?" Lady Berkley's worried gaze traveled the room.

"Yes, I know." Miss Bellingham tilted her head and considered Leo. "And you have paid me a great deal of attention as of late. I assume it was to distract me from my pursuit of Lord Berkley?"

"Miss Bellingham, might I point out nearly every gentleman who has had the good fortune to cross your path has paid you a great deal of attention." Leo flashed her his infamous smile. "I am, after all, only a mere mortal."

"I daresay there is nothing mere about you," Miss Bellingham murmured. "You may call on me if you wish. You may well be precisely what I'm looking for."

Lady Bellingham moaned. "A brazen tart."

"With the exception of his finances," Reggie muttered.

Lord Pennington groaned.

At once, all eyes fixed on Reggie. He cleared his throat and turned to address Cassie's father. "Lord William, as I am to be a member of your family, I want you to know I stand ready to assist you financially in any way necessary."

"That's very generous of you, my boy." William Effington studied Reggie curiously. "But I can assure you my finances are quite sound."

Reggie's brows drew together in confusion. "But I was under the impression . . ." He stared at Christian. "I was given to believe your family was experiencing financial difficulties."

Christian gazed innocently at the ceiling.

Leo snorted. "That's absurd."

"My children are each the beneficiary of a substantial trust. For my daughters, it's in the form of a dowry. My sons receive it at the age of seven and twenty." Father's gaze shifted to Christian. "If, of course, they demonstrate they can handle it responsibly."

"I still have a few years left," Christian said under his breath.

Lucy grinned wickedly. "As do I."

"But Cassie is, well, in business." Reggie shook his head. "As she charges a great deal, I assumed it was because—"

"It's because I am worth a great deal." Cassie shrugged in a most immodest manner. "Besides, it's not as if I'm keeping the money."

"She's giving it to me," Gwen said with a smug smile.

Lord Pennington's brow rose. "You don't need money."

"No, but women like Gwen do." Cassie and Gwen traded smiles. "Or rather women who find themselves in the situation Gwen did. Women raised with certain expectations who, because of the laws of inheritance or nasty twists of fates, are suddenly left with few options in life save to live off of the generosity of their relations."

"We're going to fund, oh, an academy of sorts, to help such women." Excitement rang in Gwen's voice. "We haven't decided on all the details. It could be that the academy helps them develop skills to earn their own way."

"Or, for those who prefer, sponsors them for a season or two, perhaps even provides them with a small dowry so they can marry well," Cassie added. "After all, they were raised to do exactly that."

"Something of a . . . a school then." Delia grinned. "For the pursuit of marriage."

"Exactly." Gwen grinned. "It was Cassie's idea, and I think it's brilliant."

"As do I." Cassie's mother beamed. "I am quite proud of you, Cassandra."

"I agree, and I think it's an admirable cause." Drummond nodded. "I should be happy to donate to such an enterprise."

"My, you are perfect." Delia gazed in admiration.

"Not at all." Drummond smiled in a humble manner that was, of course, perfect. He turned to Miss Bellingham. "Miss Bellingham, I too would like permission to call on you."

"You may, of course. However," Miss Bellingham studied him for a moment, "I am not especially interested in perfection. And I fear you have no reputation at all."

Drummond smiled in a decidedly wicked and not at all perfect manner. "The day is young yet, Miss Bellingham."

"Still, while I have heard you are heir to a significant fortune, you have no title." Miss Bellingham shook her head regretfully. "Mr. Effington at least is a member of a most prestigious and noble family."

"She's extremely mercenary." Leo grinned. "But I like her."

"Would it help you to know that while my father was the second son of an earl, his brother recently died without issue." Drummond shrugged modestly. "It therefore appears I will indeed have a title one day."

"Perfect," Reggie muttered.

"An earl would be nice," Lady Bellingham murmured.

"However, should none of this prove fruitful"—Cassie's mother exchanged glances with Reggie's mother, who nodded her encouragement—"we have a group of ladies, a society, if you will, who may be helpful—"

"I hate to interrupt, as this has all been most entertaining." A gentleman Cassie hadn't noticed stood by the door and raised a hand. "But I believe I was asked to perform a wedding ceremony?"

Reggie glanced at Lord Pennington, who mouthed the word, "*Vicar.*"

"Well?" Reggie took Cassie's hands and grinned down at her. "Will you indeed marry me this very moment, Miss Effington?"

Her heart caught, and she stared up at him. "You do promise to reform, don't you?"

"Absolutely."

Stared into his wonderful gray eyes and knew she could gaze into them for the rest of her days.

"No more infamous Lord Berkley?"

"The infamous Lord Berkley is most definitely retired."

"You will give up all your wicked ways?"

"For you." He nodded firmly. "Every one."

"Although there's no need to be hasty." She cast him a wicked smile of her own. "Perhaps you could retain one or two."

He leaned toward her and lowered his voice for her ears alone. "I shall confine all my wicked ways and infamous pursuits to you and you alone."

"Then I will indeed marry you." She swallowed hard and wondered at the feeling of absolute happiness that threatened to overwhelm her. "This very moment."

The ceremony was mercifully brief—not that it mattered, for Cassie scarcely heard the words. It had the feel of a dream. A delightful, unimagined dream that she hoped—no, indeed she knew—would last forever.

Her path down the road to scandal had taken her straight to marriage and the future she had always wanted. And the man she had been convinced would not suit her at all was indeed the perfect man for her. He was not who she'd thought he was, and she would be eternally grateful that fate had thrust them together and forced her to see the man behind the reputation. The man who was, and would always be, her love. Her life. Her Lord Perfect.

The moment they were declared man and wife, Higgins and several footmen circled the room with trays of champagne.

"This is an auspicious occasion, you know." Reggie gazed down at her with a private smile that promised they would finish later what they had begun on the pillows. A thrill of anticipation raced through her.

"How can it be otherwise? It's our wedding." She stared up at him with unabashed longing and desire. "And our wedding night."

He bent to brush a kiss across her lips. "Indeed it is. Beyond that," he grinned and nodded in Higgins's direction, "Higgins is smiling."

Cassie laughed. The butler did indeed have something that closely resembled a smile on his face. And a rather satisfied one at that.

"If I could have your attention, I should like to propose a toast." Lord Pennington raised his glass. "To the eccentric Miss Effington and the infamous Lord Berkley, now Lord and Lady Berkley." He grinned at his old friend. "May they fly forever and may their feet never touch the ground."

Reggie took her hand and raised it to his lips. Her gaze met his, and Cassie knew they had tumbled forward, hand in hand, over the precipice and would fly together for the rest of their days.

"And," Leo raised his glass, "to the game Miss Bellingham so gracefully detailed, which, whether or not we admit it, we are all players in." He leveled a grin at his sister and her husband. "To the pursuit of love, and the pursuit of happiness and the pursuit of marriage.

"And God help us all."